D1639596

*EVERYMAN, I will go with thee,*

*and be thy guide,*

*In thy most need to go by thy side*

### GEORGE MOORE

Born at Moore Hall, Co. Mayo,
Ireland, on 24th February 1852.
Educated at Oscott. Studied art in
Paris. In 1901 returned to Ireland,
where he remained until 1910. Died
in London on 21st January 1933.

# GEORGE MOORE

# Esther Waters

INTRODUCTION BY
WALTER ALLEN

DENT: LONDON, MELBOURNE AND TORONTO
EVERYMAN'S LIBRARY
DUTTON: NEW YORK

© Introduction, J. M. Dent & Sons Ltd, 1962

All rights reserved
Made in Great Britain
at the
Aldine Press · Letchworth · Herts
for
J. M. DENT & SONS LTD
Aldine House · Albemarle Street · London
This edition was first published in
Everyman's Library in 1936
Last reprinted 1977

Published in the U.S.A. by arrangement
with J. M. Dent & Sons Ltd

This book if bound as a paperback is
subject to the condition that it may
not be issued on loan or otherwise
except in its original binding

No. 933   Hardback ISBN 0 460 00933 8
No. 1933  Paperback ISBN 0 460 01933 3

# INTRODUCTION

*Esther Waters* was first published in 1894. It was Moore's six-teenth book and his eighth novel. Mr Gladstone, construing it as a tract against the evils of betting, sent its author an 'approving postcard'. The *Sporting Times* also took it as a work of propaganda but failed to approve; instead, sadly it cast its mind back to the Doncaster Spring Meeting of 1851, recalling 'a handsome little Irish colt named Slieve Carne', the property of 'Mr G. H. Moore, an *Irish gentleman*, who would probably have disinherited his son could he have foreseen that he would write such a book as *Esther Waters*'. Mudie's, the famous circulating library, disapproved too, but for very different reasons: they banned it, as they had done Moore's earlier novels, for what they considered its immorality. As for Moore, he seems to have spent the rest of his life in a state of high glee that so notoriously amoral a man as he liked to portray himself could have written so moral a work. Later in life, when he was the sage of Ebury Street, he would proclaim to his friends: 'I have just read it; it has done me good, it radiates goodness.' And when a cousin, a Carmelite nun, begged him in the name of holiness to burn all his books, he riposted by reminding her of *Esther Waters*. Characteristically, he sent a copy of his letter to her to the press: *Esther Waters*, he claimed, had 'perhaps done more good than any novel in my generation'; and he took pleasure in believing that it had inspired legislation to make baby-farming illegal and had led philanthropists to endow homes for unmarried mothers.

On the face of it, *Esther Waters* may seem a strange novel for Moore to have written, at any rate if we accept the person he delighted to present to the world as the true Moore. The fact is, his work apart, Moore often appears a great silly. No doubt he was himself to blame; an indefatigable autobiographer throughout his life, he seems bent in his memoirs on making both his own and his readers' flesh creep at the revelation of his daring opinions and unorthodox behaviour. The opinions have not worn well; they were the small change of *fin-de-siècle* decadence; and he was unfortunate in that the contemporary writers for whom he expressed the greatest contempt were precisely those—Hardy, James and Yeats—who continue to command the maximum of critical esteem. As for his reputation as a great lover, it could not survive Susan Mitchell's famous dismissal of him as a man who 'didn't kiss, but told'.

*Esther Waters* proves, in fact, the truth of a remark about him made by one of his earliest biographers, the poet John Freeman, who knew him well. 'What he perversely dissembled', Freeman said, 'was not a human indifference, but a human warmth.' Freeman had in mind the contrast between the exquisite sympathy of *Esther Waters* and a passage in *Confessions of a Young Man* which is anything but exquisite. *Confessions of a Young Man* appeared in 1888. Moore was then thirty-six and had been living in London for eight years. The son of an Irish landowner of County Mayo, he had gone to Paris at the age of twenty-one, as soon as he had come into his inheritance, in order to learn to be a painter, a somewhat curious ambition for one who came of a line of soldiers, patriot-politicians and racehorse owners. In Paris he did not learn to be a painter, but he did sit at the feet of Manet, Mallarmé, Zola, Edmond Goncourt, Daudet and Turgenev. Then, in 1880, without warning, his income from his rents in County Mayo dried up, he found himself suddenly a poor man, and he returned to London. He had failed to be a painter but he could at least become the impresario in England of the French Impressionist painters; and he had other ambitions too, to be a poet and to be the first Naturalistic novelist in English.

He took rooms in the Strand, and in *Confessions of a Young Man* he describes the servant there, whom he refers to as 'Awful Emma' and 'the horrible servant', though, after the success of *Esther Waters*, he cut out the adjectives in later editions. Here is his account of 'Awful Emma':

The lodgers sometimes threw you a kind word, but never one that recognized that you were akin to us, only the pity that might be extended to a dog. And I used to ask you all sorts of cruel questions, I was curious to know the depth of animalism you had sunk to, or rather out of which you had never been raised. And you generally answered innocently or naïvely enough. But sometimes my words were too crude, and they struck through the thick hide into the quick, into the human, and you winced a little; but this was rarely, for you were very nearly, oh, very nearly an animal: your temperament and intelligence was just that of a dog who has picked up a master, not a real master, but a makeshift master who may turn it out at any moment. . . . Yes, you are a mule, there is no sense in you;

you are a beast of burden, a drudge too horrible for anything but work; and I suppose, all things considered, that the fat landlady with a dozen children did well to work you seventeen hours a day and cheat you out of your miserable wages. . . .

There is more, and none of it is exactly ingratiating. The sensibility it expresses could scarcely predispose anyone in Moore's favour. But the point is that the sensibility expressed in *Esther Waters*, a novel about a servant-girl, is entirely different. *Esther Waters* is written throughout with a grave sympathy for its heroine, a recognition of her natural goodness, heroism and dignity. Moore, in fact, was right: the novel radiates goodness. How is it that the man who could write so brutally, one might say caddishly, of 'Awful Emma', could also write *Esther Waters*?

Part of the answer is certainly that *Esther Waters* represents a triumph for aesthetic theory. Moore was not adept in self-criticism, as his two volumes of verse, *Flowers of Passion* and *Pagan Poems*, show. They are, mercifully, forgotten. And though he was as ambitious as a writer can be, he had little native originality. He was incurably literary, which meant that success—or lack of it—in what he attempted depended very largely on the excellence or otherwise of the writers he took as his models. He had come back to England as the apostle of Naturalism, the advocate and defender of Zola; and Naturalism, however wanting it may seem now as a theory of writing, was his salvation. By offering him something worth emulating, it saved him from his own silliness and vulgarity. It is this that makes it so difficult to realize that the poems and *Confessions*, on the one hand, and the novels—or most of them—on the other, are the work of the same man. The discipline of Naturalism gave him a dignity and a seriousness as a writer which otherwise he might have been quite without.

By 1885 he had already written, in his second novel, *A Mummer's Wife*, a novel that can still be read with admiration, though its interest is now mainly historical. It is an attempt, in an English setting, to fuse Flaubert's *Madame Bovary* with Zola's *L'Assommoir*, a study of the degeneration of an actor's wife through drink; and it remains impressive because of the single-mindedness with which Moore tackles the theme. In *A Mummer's Wife* he had written: 'Change the surroundings in which man lives, and in two or three generations, you will have changed his physical constitution, his habits of life, and a goodly number of his ideas.' This was sound Naturalistic doctrine.

In one of its aspects Naturalism was the literary equivalent of Impressionism in painting; as the Impressionists painted objects as seen under certain conditions of atmosphere and light, so the Naturalistic novelists depicted human beings in terms of their environment. They saw themselves as scientists of a kind; they were writing, they believed, the natural history of man; and they demanded of themselves a scrupulous fidelity to observable reality. It was for the lack of this in the novel, for what seemed to him the flagrant breaches of probability and the melodrama, that Moore attacked and made fun of *Tess of the d'Urbervilles*, which had appeared three years before *Esther Waters*. The two novels differ so greatly from each other that it comes almost as a shock to realize that they share a common situation, that of the servant-girl seduced. Their authors' intentions were utterly unlike, so that no real comparison between the novels is possible. Esther is not a tragic heroine; indeed, Naturalism has no place for the tragic. But she is heroic, though heroic, it seems, in the most ordinary, the most unsensational way. And much of the power of the novel comes from this, the feeling we are bound to have while reading it that this is truth, a sober recital of the facts at their most mundane. Never was a work of fiction written that contained less of the obviously fictitious. We are in the world of the completely ordinary. There are no villains, merely men and women caught in the grip of circumstance and environment. There are no high sentiments, nothing beyond Esther's 'No, I've not changed, Fred, but things has turned out different. A woman can't do the good that she would like to in the world; she has to do the good that comes to her to do. I've my husband and my boy to look to. Them's my good. At least, that's how I see things.'

Yet the final impression the novel makes is of beauty, and it is a complex beauty, since it is both moral and aesthetic. Here another quotation, from another early novel of Moore's, *A Drama in Muslin*, is relevant: 'Seen from afar, all things are of equal worth and the meanest things when viewed with the eye of God are raised to heights of tragic awe which conventionality would limit to the deaths of kings and patriots.' This again was Naturalist dogma. The proposition at best is dubious, and when applied to Moore's own work is obviously false: tragic awe is not the emotion we feel when contemplating Esther Waters's fate. All the same, so far as Moore was concerned, the viewpoint was its own justification. The Naturalists believed that there was no subject in itself noble or ignoble, beautiful or ugly, but that treatment was all. Inevitably, the effort to see *sub specie aeternitatis*, as God might see, raised matter formerly regarded as unworthy of art to a wholly new dignity. The first great example, no doubt, is Flaubert's *Madame Bovary*. *Esther Waters* is one of the first in English. Esther is accorded all the rights due to a human personality, and this was axiomatic from Moore's aesthetic creed. All very well to sneer at 'Awful Emma', but when a slavey became a subject for art she automatically partook of the reverence Moore felt for art. She demanded to be taken with the fullest seriousness possible.

I have said that the beauty of *Esther Waters* is both moral and aesthetic. In the end, of course, they are indistinguishable. We know of the former through the latter. Sullen, stubborn, independent, proud, Esther is the incarnation both of instinctive love—the love of a mother for her child—and of wifely duty, and everything in the novel is subordinated to her. When we look at the novel technically we realize how skilfully Moore has adjusted his means to his end. *Esther Waters* remains a masterpiece of form. 'Art as I understand it', he wrote, 'is a rhythmical sequence of events described with rhythmical sequence of phrase.' *Esther Waters* is precisely that.

Yet this is to say nothing of the content of the novel: the glimpses of the great house of Woodview dominated by its racing stables; the glimpses of London slum life, of the depressed existences of servant-girls, the horrors and rigours of hospitals and of the squalid profession of baby-farming. And it is to ignore the great set scenes of the novel, the whole wonderful panorama of the Derby. It is to ignore, too, the superb rendering of life at William Larch's pub, the King's Head, at the corner of Dean Street and Old Compton Street, Soho, so faithfully and exactly observed. The novel teems with life and characters, all faithfully and exactly observed, and summed up in imagery never sensational but always precise, as, for example, when Moore says of Larch: 'He did not mean to be unkind, but his nature was as hard and as plain as a kitchen table.' One corner of nineteenth-century English life, one feels, is caught completely, as it is caught in no other novel in our literature; and a corner that takes in the Plymouth Brethren as well as the bookies and the betting men is not so narrow a corner either. It is a splendid period piece; but to leave it at that would be to fall into an error not so very different from Mr

Gladstone's. It is a most remarkable picture of life at a certain point in history; it is also by implication, whether Moore intended it or not, a most persuasive account of the evil consequences of gambling. But of course it is much more than both of these. Its truth is untouched by the passage of time; there will always be Esthers among us.

WALTER ALLEN.

## SELECT BIBLIOGRAPHY

The following list of Moore's works gives the date of their first appearance in book form. Most of his more important writings were extensively revised in later editions.

VERSE. *Flowers of Passion*, 1878; *Martin Luther*, 1879; *Pagan Poems*, 1881; *Pure Poetry: an Anthology* (edited by George Moore), 1924.

PROSE. *A Modern Lover*, 1883; *A Mummer's Wife*, 1885; *Literature at Nurse*, 1885; *A Drama in Muslin*, 1886 (reissued under the title of *Muslin*, 1915); *A Mere Accident*, 1887; *Parnell and his Island*, 1887; *Confessions of a Young Man*, 1888; *Spring Days*, 1888; *Mike Fletcher*, 1889; *Vain Fortune*, 1890; *Impressions and Opinions*, 1891; *Modern Painting*, 1893; *Esther Waters*, 1894; *Celibates*, 1895; *The Royal Academy 1895*, 1895; *Evelyn Innes*, 1898; *Sister Theresa*, 1901; *Literature and the Irish Language*, 1901; *The Untilled Field*, 1903; *The Lake*, 1905; *Memoirs of my Dead Life*, 1905; *Reminiscences of the Impressionist Painters*, 1906; *Hail and Farewell!*, 1911–14; *The Brook Kerith*, 1916; *Lewis Seymour and some Women* (a revision and reissue of *A Modern Lover*), 1917; *A Storyteller's Holiday*, 1918; *Avowals*, 1919; *Héloïse and Abélard*, 1921; *Fragments from Héloïse and Abélard*, 1921; *In Single Strictness* (a revision and reissue of *Celibates*), 1922; *The Pastoral Loves of Daphnis and Chloë*, 1924; *Conversations in Ebury Street*, 1924; *Ulick and Soracha*, 1926; *Letters from George Moore to Edward Dujardin*, 1929; *Aphrodite in Aulis*, 1930; *Peronnik the Fool*, 1933; *A Communication to my Friends*, 1933.

PROSE DRAMAS. *Worldliness*, c. 1874; *The Strike at Arlingford*, 1893; *The Bending of the Bough*, 1900; *The Apostle*, 1911; *Elizabeth Cooper*, 1913; *Esther Waters*, 1913; *The Coming of Gabrielle*, 1920; *The Making of an Immortal*, 1927; *The Passing of the Essenes*, 1930.

COLLECTED WORKS, 1933–6. *Letters from George Moore*, ed. John Eglinton, 1942.

BIOGRAPHY AND CRITICISM. Susan L. Mitchell, *George Moore*, 1916; John Freeman, *A Portrait of George Moore in a Study of his Work*, 1922; Geraint Goodwin, *Conversations with George Moore*, 1929, 1951; Humbert Wolfe, *George Moore*, 1931; Charles Morgan, *Epitaph on George Moore*, 1935; Joseph Hone, *The Life of George Moore*, 1936.

# EPISTLE DEDICATORY

*My dear Rolleston. It is quite in accordance with the humour of the great Aristophanes above us, beneath us, within us, without us, that an Irishman should write a book as characteristically English as* Don Quixote *is Spanish, and when the author of* Esther Waters *dedicates his work to another Irishman, it must be plain to all that he is holding the mirror up to Nature. But there is another reason why I should dedicate this book to you. You are an Irish Protestant like myself, and you could always love Ireland without hating England and——. But I am past my patience trying to find logic in a dedication which is an outburst of friendly feeling for an old friend.*

*It would be pleasant to look down the last five-and-twenty years, but I will look no further than yester-year, when we were engaged in trying to wheedle the English public into accepting the only solution (yours) of the Irish difficulty— a line of railway linking a western harbour with a northern tunnel joining Ireland to Scotland. We failed, of course, in practical result (the official mind repels reason), but our adventure was not without moral gain, for two Irishmen did set out 'to strike a blow for Ireland' without coming to blows. How shall we explain it : that the great Aristophanes above us, beneath us, within us, without us, willed it so ? and that his divine humour was not content with less than that the letters that you wrote and that I signed must be better written than those you signed yourself.*

> *'It is a modest creed, and yet*
> *Pleasant if one considers it,'*

*to think that your solicitude for others compelled you to give your best to your friend.*

*Yours always : George Moore.*

# CHAPTER I

SHE stood on the platform watching the receding train. The white steam curled above the few bushes that hid the curve of the line, evaporating in the pale evening. A moment more and the last carriage would pass out of sight, the white gates at the crossing swinging slowly forward to let through the impatient passengers.

An oblong box painted reddish brown and tied with a rough rope lay on the seat beside her. The movement of her back and shoulders showed that the bundle she carried was a heavy one, and the sharp bulging of the grey linen cloth that the weight was dead. She wore a faded yellow dress and a black jacket too warm for the day. A girl of twenty, firmly built with short, strong arms and a plump neck that carried a well-turned head with dignity. Her well-formed nostrils redeemed her somewhat thick, fleshy nose, and it was a pleasure to see her grave, almost sullen, face light up with sunny humour; for when she laughed a line of almond-shaped teeth showed between red lips. She was laughing now, the porter having asked her if she were afraid to leave her bundle with her box. Both, he said, would go up together in the donkey-cart. The donkey-cart came down every evening to fetch parcels. The man lingered, and she heard from him that all the down lands she could see right up to Beading belonged to the squire.

'Beading?' she said. 'I thought the Barfields lived in Shoreham.'

'So they do,' he answered, 'near Shoreham yonder,' and he pointed to a belt of trees; 'they be too fine folk for the town. Shoreham, you see, isn't what it was in days gone by with shipyards about the harbour, and ships from all parts dropping their sails as they come within the breakwaters. Not much doing in the way of building down this way—a three-ton boat or two on the stocks, not much more.' He would have stayed longer, for the girl was to his fancy, but the station-master called him away to remove

3

some luggage. 'You 'll find the gate behind yon trees,' he cried, looking back. The girl thanked him and strolled up the platform, gazing across the low-lying fields out of which the downs rose in gradual ascents, uncertain if she should leave her bundle with her box.

At the end of the platform the station-master took her ticket and she passed over the level crossing, trying to gather her wits but unable to do so till she caught sight of some 'villas,' a row of twenty-four semi-detached houses, iron railings, laurels, and French windows. She had been in service in such houses and knew that a general servant was kept in each. But the life in Woodview was a great dream, and she could not imagine herself accomplishing all that would be required of her. There would be a butler, a footman, and a page; she would not mind the page—but the butler and footman, what would they think? There would be an upper-housemaid and an under-housemaid, and perhaps a lady's maid, and may be that these ladies had been abroad with the family, and would talk about France and Germany, about trains, hotels, and travelling all night. But she would not be able to join in; her silence would give them the tip; they would ask her what situations she had been in, and when they learned the truth she would leave disgraced. But she hadn't sufficient money to pay for a ticket to London. And what excuse could she give to Lady Elwin, who had rescued her from Mrs. Dunbar and got her the place of kitchenmaid at Woodview? No, she couldn't go back. Her father would curse her, and perhaps beat her mother and her too. Ah! he would not dare to strike her again, and the girl's face flushed with shameful remembrance. Her little brothers and sisters would cry if she came back. They had little enough to eat as it was. Of course she mustn't go back. How silly of her to think of such a thing!

All the same she would be glad when the first week was over. If she had only a dress to wear in the afternoons! The old yellow thing on her back would never do. But one of her cotton prints was pretty fresh; she must get a bit of red ribbon—that would make a difference. She had heard that the housemaids in places like Woodview always changed their dresses twice a day, and on Sundays went out in silk mantles and hats in the newest fashion. As for the lady's maid, she of course had all her mistress's clothes, and walked with the butler. What would such people think of a little girl like her? Her heart sank at the thought, and she sighed, anticipating much bitterness and disappointment. Even when her first quarter's wages came due she would hardly be able to buy herself a dress: they would want the money at home. Her quarter's wages! A month's wages most like, for she 'd never be able to keep the place. So all those fields belonged to the squire, and those great woods too. 'My word! they must be fine folk, quite as fine as Lady Elwin—finer, for she lived in a house like those near the station.'

On both sides of the straight road there were tall hedges and the nurserymaids lay in the shadows on the rich summer grass, their perambulators at a little distance, and with the hum of the town dying out of the ear, the girl continued to imagine the future she was about to enter into. She could see two houses, one in grey stone, the other in red brick with a gable covered with ivy; and between them the spire of a church, and questioning a passer-by she learnt that the first house was the Rectory, and that the second was Woodview Lodge. If that was the lodge, what must the house be?

Two hundred yards farther on the road branched, passing on either side of a triangular clump of trees; and the lungs of the jaded town girl drew in a deep breath of health. The little green wood soothed her fears and encouraged her to be brave and interrupt the gatekeeper who was playing a flageolet in a small lodge by a white-painted gate. He told her to keep straight on and to be sure to turn to the left when she got to the top; and, having never seen an avenue before, she stopped to admire the rough branches of elms, like rafters above the roadway, and to hear the monotonous dove.

Her doubts returned; she never would be able to keep the place. The avenue bent a little, and she came suddenly upon a young man leaning over the paling, smoking his pipe.

'Please, sir, is this the way to Woodview?'

'Yes, right up through the stables, round to the left.' And then, noticing the sturdily built figure, yet graceful in its sturdiness, and the bright cheeks, he said: 'You look pretty well done; that bundle is a heavy one, let me hold it for you.'

'I am a bit tired,' she said, leaning the bundle on the paling. 'They told me at the station that the donkey-cart would bring up my box later on.'

'Ah, then you are the new kitchenmaid? What's your name?'

'Esther Waters.'

'My mother's the cook here; you'll have to mind your p's and q's or else you'll be dropped on. The devil of a temper while it lasts, but not a bad sort if you don't put her out.'

'Are you in service here?'

'No, but I hope to be afore long. I could have been two years ago, but mother didn't like me to put on livery, and I don't know how I'll face her when I come running down to go out with the carriage.'

'Is the place vacant?' Esther asked, raising her eyes timidly, looking at him sideways.

'Yes, Jim Story got the sack about a week ago. When he had taken a drop he'd tell every blessed thing that was done in the stables. They'd get him down to the "Red Lion" for the purpose; of course the squire couldn't stand that.'

'And shall you take the place?'

'Yes. I'm not going to spend my life carrying parcels up and down the King's Road, Brighton, if I can squeeze in here. It isn't so much the berth that I care about, but the advantages, information fresh from the fountainhead. You won't catch me chattering over the bar at the "Red Lion" and having every blessed word I say wired up to London and printed next morning in all the papers.'

Esther wondered what he was talking about, and, looking at him, she saw a low, narrow forehead, a small, round head, a long nose, a pointed chin, and rather hollow, bloodless cheeks. Notwithstanding the shallow chest, he was powerfully built, the long arms could deal a swinging blow. The low forehead and the lustreless eyes told of a slight, unimaginative brain, but regular features and a look of natural honesty made William Latch a man that ten men and eighteen women out of twenty would like.

'I see you've got books in that bundle,' he said, at the end of a long silence. 'Fond of readin'?'

'They are mother's books,' she replied hastily. 'I was afraid to leave them at the station, for it would be easy for any one to take one out, and I shouldn't miss it until I undid the bundle.'

'Sarah Tucker—that's the upper-housemaid—will be after you to lend them to her. She's a wonderful reader. She has read every story that has come out in *Bow Bells* for the last three years, and you can't puzzle her, try as you will. She knows all the names, can tell you which lord it was that saved the girl from the carriage when the 'osses were tearing like mad towards a precipice a 'undred feet deep, and all about the baronet for whose sake the girl went out to drown herself in the moonlight. I 'aven't read the books mesel', but Sarah and me are great pals.'

Esther trembled lest he might ask her again if she were fond of reading, for she could not read; and noticing a change in the expression of her face, he thought she was disappointed to hear he liked Sarah and wished he 'd kept his mouth shut.

'Good friends, you know—no more. Sarah and me never hit it off; she will worry me with the stories she reads. I don't know what's your taste, but I likes something out of which I can make a bit. The little 'oss in there, 'e 's more in my line.'

'They told me at the station,' she said, 'that the donkey-cart would bring up my box.'

'The donkey-cart isn't going to the station to-night—you 'll want your things, to be sure. I 'll see the coachman; perhaps he 's going down with the trap. But, golly! it has gone the half-hour. I shall catch it for keeping you talking, and my mother has been expecting you for the last hour. She hasn't a soul to help her, and six people coming to dinner. You must say the train was late.'

'Let us go, then,' cried Esther. 'Will you show me the way?'

Evergreen oaks looped into an arch over the iron gate which opened into the pleasure-ground and the angles and urns of an Italian house showed between beech trees to which rooks were returning. A high brick wall separated the pleasure-ground from the stables, and as William and Esther turned to the left and walked up the roadway they passed by many doors, hearing the trampling of horses and the rattling of chains. The roadway opened into a handsome yard overlooked by the house, the back premises of which had been lately rebuilt in red brick. There were gables and ornamental porches, and through the large kitchen windows Esther caught sight of the servants passing to and fro. At the top of this yard a gate led into the park and through it a string of horses was coming. The horses wore grey clothing and hoods and Esther noticed the black round eyes looking through the eyelet holes, and the small, ugly boys, who swung their legs, and struck the horses with little ash plants when they reached their heads forward chawing at the bits. 'Look, see him, the third one; that's he—that's Silver Braid.'

An impatient knocking at the kitchen window interrupted his admiration, and William, turning quickly, said: 'Mind you say the train was late; don't say I kept you, or you'll get me into a devil of a pickle. This way.' The door led into a passage covered with coconut matting, and the handsome room she found herself in did not conform to anything that Esther had seen or heard of kitchens. For the range almost filled one end of the room, and on it a dozen saucepans were simmering; the dresser reached to the ceiling, and was covered with a multitude of plates and dishes, and Esther thought how she must strive to keep it in its present beautiful condition: the elegant white-capped servants passing round the white table made her feel her own insigificance.

'This is the new kitchenmaid, mother.'

'Ah, is it indeed?' said Mrs. Latch, looking up from the tray of tartlets which she had taken from the oven and was filling with jam, and Esther noticed Mrs. Latch's likeness to her son—the same long, narrow nose, the same temples.

'I suppose you'll tell me the train was late?'

'Yes, mother, the train was a quarter of an hour late,' William chimed in.

'I didn't ask you, you idle, lazy good-for-nothing vagabond. I suppose it was you who kept the girl all this time. Six people coming to dinner, and I've been the whole day without a kitchenmaid. If Margaret Gale hadn't come down to help me, I don't know where we should be; as it is, the dinner will be late.'

The two housemaids, both in print dresses, stood listening, and Esther's face clouded when Mrs. Latch told her to take her things off and set to and prepare the vegetables, so that she might see what she was made of. Esther did not answer at once, but turned away, saying under her breath: 'I must change my dress, and my box hasn't come up from the station yet.'

'You can tuck your dress up, and Margaret Gale will lend you her apron.'

Esther hesitated.

'What you 've got on don't look as if it could come to much damage. Come, now, set to.'

The housemaids burst into loud laughter, and then a sullen look of dogged obstinacy passed over and settled on Esther's face, even to the point of visibly darkening the white and rose complexion.

## CHAPTER II

ESTHER lay in a low, narrow iron bed, pushed close against the wall in the full glare of the sun, staring half awake, her eyes open but still dim with dreams.   One end of the room that she had awakened in was under the roof; a lean-to; and through a broad, single pane the early sunlight fell across a wall papered with blue and white flowers.   On the wall were two pictures—a girl with a basket of flowers, the coloured supplement of an illustrated newspaper, an old and dilapidated last-century print, and there were photographs of the Gale family in Sunday clothes on the chimney-piece and the green vases that Sarah had given Margaret on her birthday.

It was not yet time to get up, and Esther raised her arms as if to cross them behind her head, but a sudden remembrance of yesterday arrested the movement, and a shadow settled on her face.   She had refused to prepare the vegetables, and cook had turned her out of the kitchen. She had rushed from the house in the hope that she might succeed in walking back to London; but William had overtaken her in the avenue; he had argued with her, refusing to allow her to pass; she had tried to tear herself from him, and, failing, had burst into tears.   He was kind, and, almost against her will, led her back, saying all the while that he 'd speak up for her and make it all right with his mother.   But Mrs. Latch had closed her kitchen against her, and she had had to go to her room.   Even if they paid her fare back to London, how was she to face her mother?   What would father say?   He would drive her from the house.   But she had done nothing wrong.   Why did cook insult her?

Margaret's bed stood in the shadow of the sloping wall; and she lay, one arm thrown forward, her short, square face raised to the light, sleeping so heavily that for a moment Esther felt afraid.   But her eyes opened, and Margaret stared at her as if out of eternity.   Raising her hands to her eyes she said:

'What time is it?'

'It has just gone six.'

'Then there's plenty of time; we needn't be down before seven.  You get on with your dressing; there's no use my getting up till you are done—we'd be tumbling over each other.  This is no room to put two girls to sleep in—one glass and not much bigger than your hand.  You'll have to shove your box under your bed.  In my last place I had a beautiful room with a Brussels carpet and a marble washstand.  I wouldn't stay here three days if it weren't——'  The girl laughed and turned lazily over.

Esther did not answer.

'Now, isn't it a grubby little room to put two girls to sleep in?  What was your last place like?'

Esther answered that she had hardly been in service before, and Margaret was too much engrossed in her own thoughts to notice the curtness of the answer.

'There's only one thing to be said for Woodview, and that is the eating; we have everything we want, and we'd have more than we want if it weren't for the old cook: she must have her little bit out of everything, and she cuts us short in our bacon in the morning.  But that reminds me! You've set the cook against you, and will have to bring her over to your side if you want to remain here.'

'Why should I be asked to wash up the moment I came in the house, before even I had time to change my dress?'

'It was hard on you.  She always gets as much as she can out of her kitchenmaid.  But last night she was pressed, there was company to dinner.  I'd have lent you an apron, and the dress you had on wasn't of much account.'

'It isn't because a girl is poor——'

'Oh, I didn't mean that; I know well enough what it is to be hard up.'  Margaret clasped her stays across her plump figure and walking to the glass began to brush her hair from her forehead, remarking to Esther that she would be glad when fringes were out of fashion, 'for I should have no face at all if I was to wear one.  Well, I never!' she said, turning, for Esther did not answer her.  'Well, I never, saying her prayers.  Do you think they do any good?'

Esther looked up angrily.

'I don't want to say anything against saying prayers,
but I wouldn't before the others if I was you—they'll
chaff dreadful, and call you Creeping Jesus.'

'Oh, Margaret, I hope they won't do anything so wicked.
But I am afraid I shan't be long here, so it doesn't matter
what they think of *me*.'

On their way downstairs they opened the windows and
doors, and Margaret took Esther round, showing her where
the things were kept, and telling her for how many she must
lay the table. At that moment a number of boys and men
came clattering up the passage asking for breakfast. They
cried to Esther to hurry up, declaring that they were late.
Esther did not know who they were, but she served them as
best she might; and they had not been long gone when the
squire and his son Arthur appeared in the yard.

Mr. Barfield, nicknamed the Gaffer by the stable lads,
was in his youth a famous steeplechase rider, but he was
now portly and it was difficult to see in him the young man
who had ridden the winner at Liverpool, a feat of horsemanship that his son, Mr. Arthur, known in the stables as
Ginger on account of his yellow hair, hoped to outdo by
riding at least two winners of the steeplechase, an ambition
which he might well entertain, for there seemed no danger
of his going up in weight (he could ride a little over nine
stone); a lanky, narrow-chested, absurd-looking young
man, who, however, came into a new individuality the
moment he prepared to get into the saddle. He wore
long-necked spurs attached to his boots, and Esther
admired the beautiful chestnut horse he rode, a little too
thin, she thought; the ugly little boys were mounted on
horses equally thin; the squire rode a stout grey cob, and
turned in his saddle to better see the chestnut, or was it the
brown horse that interested him? the one that walked with
his head in the air, pulling at the smallest of all the boys, a
little freckled, red-headed fellow.

'That's Silver Braid, the brown horse, the one the Demon
is riding. Ginger is riding the chestnut Bayleaf: he won
the City and Suburban. Oh, we did have a fine time
then, for we all had a bit on. The betting was twenty to
one, and I won twelve and sixpence. Grover won thirty
shillings. They say that John—that's the butler—won a
little fortune: but he is so close no one knows what he has

on. Cook wouldn't have anything on; she says that
betting is the curse of servants—you know what is said,
that it was through betting that Mrs. Latch's husband got
into trouble. He was steward here, in the late squire's
time.'

Margaret had heard the story many times, and she reeled
off her rigmarole that 'old Latch was a confidential servant,
whose accounts were not examined properly till Marksman
failed to get in first for the Chester Cup. A great upset
that was, the squire's property having to be put into the
hands of a receiver, who very soon got on the track of
something odd, and was sending for Latch to ask him to
explain how the same sums of money had been entered
twice over. It was some trick like that he 'd been up to,
and a clever one too, for it was some days before the
accountant found it out, so I 've heard. Latch, like the
squire, believed in Marksman, so there he was up a tree,
and they 'd have clapped him into jail if Mrs. Latch hadn't
come forward with all her savings and offered to go without
wages till the money was paid up. Old Latch died soon
after, and Mrs. Latch has been taking her wages, for the
Barfields aren't a bad lot; but I think,' Margaret continued,
'that she 'd as soon they 'd let her out, as the place has
become hateful to her for the past and the present too,
seeing that William can't keep his thoughts off the racehorses. It does seem a shame that the Gaffer should have
had William taught riding in the hope of making a jockey
of him, but he 'd grown out of jockey's size before he was
sixteen, and she put him into an office in Brighton. But
he is the very spit for a footman, as he well knows himself,
and into livery he 'll go sooner or later; and it is said that
it will break his mother's heart when he comes running
down the stairs in silk stockings and powder, a cockade in
his hat. Now you know the whole of the story as much as
I 've heard of it myself, and you 've come in the nick of
time, for there 's going to be a trial this morning,' said
Margaret; 'Silver Braid was stripped—you noticed that—
and Ginger always rides in the trials.'

'I don't know what a trial is,' said Esther. 'They are
not carriage-horses, are they? They look too slight.'

'Carriage-horses, you ninny! Where have you been to
all this while—can't you see that they are racehorses?'

Esther hung down her head and murmured something which Margaret didn't catch.

'To tell the truth, I didn't know much about them when I came, but then one never hears anything else here. And that reminds me—it is as much as your place is worth to breathe one syllable about them horses; you must know nothing when you are asked. That's what Jim Story got sacked for — saying in the "Red Lion" that Valentine pulled up lame. We don't know how it came to the Gaffer's ears. I believe that it was Mr. Leopold who told; he finds out everything. But I was telling you how I learnt about the racehorses. It was from Jim Story— Jim was my pal—Sarah is after William, you know, the fellow that brought you into the kitchen last night. Jim could never talk about anything but the 'osses. We'd go every night and sit in the wood-shed, that's to say if it was wet; if it was fine we'd walk in the drove-way, and I'd have married Jim, I know I should, if he hadn't been sent away. That's the worst of being a servant. They sent Jim away just as if he was a dog. It was wrong of him to say the horse pulled up lame; I know that, but they needn't have sent him away as they did.'

Esther was not listening. She was thinking of what would happen to her. Would they send her away at the end of the week, or that very afternoon? Would they give her a week's wages, or would they turn her out to find her way back to London as best she might? What should she do if they turned her out of doors that very afternoon? Walk back to London? She didn't know how far she had come—a long distance, no doubt, for she had seen woods, hills, rivers, and towns flying past. She'd never be able to find her way back through them miles of country; besides, she couldn't carry her box on her back. What was she to do? Not a friend, not a penny in the world. Now why did such misfortune fall on a poor girl who had never harmed any one in the world! And if they did give her her fare back—what then? Should she go home? To whom? To her mother—to her poor mother, who would burst into tears, saying: 'Oh, my poor darling, I don't know what we shall do; your father will never let you stay here.'

Mrs. Latch told Esther to make haste and lay the table afresh; it seemed to Esther that she looked round with the air of one anxious to discover something that might serve as a pretext for blame. But she laid the table, saying to herself: 'So those that are gone are the stable folk, and breakfast has now to be prepared for the other servants.' A little later she discovered that the person in the dark green dress who spoke with her chin in the air, whose nose had been pinched to purple just above the nostrils, was Miss Grover, the lady's maid. She heard her address an occasional remark to Sarah Tucker, a tall girl with a thin, freckled face and dark red hair. But the butler, who was not feeling well, did not appear at breakfast, and Esther was sent to him with a cup of tea.

There were the plates to wash and the knives to clean, and when they were done there were potatoes, cabbage, onions to prepare, saucepans to fill with water, coal to fetch for the fire, and Esther worked steadily without flagging, fearful of Mrs. Barfield, who would come down, no doubt, about ten o'clock to order dinner.

'Well, do you think the Gaffer's satisfied?' said Margaret, pointing; for the racehorses were coming through the paddock gate, and John, a little man, wizened, with frequent indigestion, made no articulate reply, but went by muttering something, his manner showing that his mind was set against all female interest in racing. When Sarah and Grover came running down the passage and overwhelmed him with questions, crowding round him, asking both together if Silver Braid had won his trial, he testily pushed them aside, declaring that if he had a racehorse he wouldn't have a woman-servant in the place. 'A positive curse, this chatter, chatter. Won his trial, indeed! What business had a lot of female folk——' The rest of John's sarcasm was lost in his shirt collar as he hurried away to his pantry, closing the door after him.

'What a testy little man he is!' said Sarah; 'he might have told us which won. He has known the Gaffer so long that he can tell the moment he looks at him whether the gees are all right.'

'One can't speak to a chap in the lane that he don't know all about it next day,' said Margaret, 'and that's why Peggy hates him; you know the way she skulks about the back garden and up the 'ill so that she may meet young Johnson as he is ridin' 'ome.'

'I'll have none of this scandal-mongering going on in my kitchen,' said Mrs. Latch. 'Do you see that girl there? She can't get past to her scullery.'

It seemed to Esther that she could have managed pretty well if it hadn't been for the dining-room lunch. Miss Mary was expecting some friends to play tennis with her, and, besides the roast chicken, there were the cutlets, Soubise sauce, and a curry, a jelly, and a blancmange. She didn't know where the things were. 'Don't you move, I might as well get it myself,' said the old woman. Mr. Randal, too, lost his temper, for she had no hot plates ready, nor could she distinguish between those that were to go to the dining-room and those that were to go to the servants' hall. She understood, however, that it would not be wise to give way to her feeling, and that the only way she could hope to retain her situation was by doing nothing to attract attention. She must learn to control that temper of hers—she must and would. And it was in this frame of mind and with this determination that she entered the servants' hall.

There were not more than ten or eleven at dinner, but sitting close together they seemed more numerous, and quite half the number of faces that looked up, as she took her place next to Margaret Gale, were unknown to her. The four ugly little boys whom she had seen on the race-horses were there, but she did not recognize them at first, and nearly opposite, sitting next to the lady's maid, was a small, sandy-haired man about forty: he was beginning to show signs of stoutness, and two little round whiskers grew on his cheeks. At the end of the table Mr. Randal sat helping the pudding, addressing the sandy-haired man as Mr. Swindles, whose real name was Ward, as Esther learnt afterwards: he was Mr. Barfield's head groom. She learnt, too, that 'the Demon' was not the real name of the little carroty-haired boy, and looked at him in amazement when he whispered in her ear that he would dearly love a real go-in at that pudding, but it was so fattening that he didn't ever dare to risk more than a couple of sniffs. Seeing that the girl did not understand, he added, by way of explanation: 'You know I must keep under the six stone, and at times it becomes awful 'ard.'

Esther thought him a nice little fellow, and tried to per-

suade him to forgo his resolution not to touch pudding, until
Mr. Swindles told her to cheese it. The attention of the
table being drawn to the boy, Esther wondered at the
admiration with which everybody viewed him; it seemed
strange that he should be the centre of so much interest,
for he was but a little fellow; the bigger boys were overlooked, and as for the long-nosed lad, with weak eyes and
sloping shoulders, who sat on the other side of the table on
Mr. Swindles's left, why, he was everybody's laughing-
stock, and Mr. Swindles had just begun the story of poor
Jim's misadventures with the Gaffer.

'But why do you call him Mr. Leopold when his
name is Mr. Randal?' Esther ventured to inquire of the
Demon.

'On account of Leopold Rothschild,' said the Demon;
'he 's pretty near as rich, if the truth was known—won a
pile over the City and Sub. Pity you weren't here; might
have had a bit on.'

'I have never seen the City,' Esther replied innocently.

'Never seen the City and Sub! I was up, had a lot in
hand, so I came away from my 'orses the moment I got
into the dip. The Tinman nearly caught me on the post—
came with a terrific rush; he is just hawful, Tinman is.
I did catch it from the Gaffer—he did give it me.'

The plates of all the boys except the Demon's were now
filled with beefsteak pudding, potatoes, and greens, likewise Esther's. Mr. Leopold, Mr. Swindles, the housemaid,
and the cook dined off the leg of mutton, a small slice of
which was sent to the Demon. 'That for a dinner!' and
as he took up his knife and fork and cut a small piece of
his one slice, he said: 'I suppose you never had to reduce
yourself three pounds; girls never have. I do run to flesh
so, you wouldn't believe it. If I don't walk to Portslade
and back every second day, I go up three or four pounds.
Then there 's nothing for it but the physic, and that 's
what settles me. Can you take physic?'

'I took three Beecham's pills once.'

'Oh, that 's nothing. Can you take castor-oil?'

Esther looked in amazement at the little boy at her side,
and Swindles, who had overheard the question, burst into
laughter. Every one wanted to hear the joke, and, feeling
they were making fun of her, Esther refused to answer.

The first helpings of pudding or mutton had taken the edge off their appetites, and before sending their plates for more they leaned over the table listening and laughing open-mouthed. It was a bare room, lit with one window and the window looked on to one of the little back courts and tiled ways which had been built at the back of the house. The shadowed northern light softened the listening faces with grey tints.

'You know,' said Mr. Swindles, glancing at Jim as if to assure himself that the boy was there and unable to escape from the hooks of his sarcasm, 'how fast the Gaffer talks, and how he hates to be asked to repeat his words. Knowing this, Jim always says, "Yes, sir; yes, sir." "Now, do you quite understand?" says the Gaffer. "Yes, sir; yes, sir," replies Jim, not having understood one word of what was said; but relying on us to put him right. "Now what did he say I was to do?" says Jim, the moment the Gaffer is out of hearing. But this morning we were on ahead, and the Gaffer had Jim all to himself. As usual he says: "Now do you quite understand?" and as usual Jim says: "Yes, sir; yes, sir." As I had it in my mind that Jim hadn't understood, I said when he joined us: "Now if you ain't sure what he said you had better go back and ask him," but Jim said he had understood. "And what did he tell you to do?" said I. "He told me," says Jim, "to bring the colt along and finish up close by where he'd be standing at the end of the track." I thought it rather odd to send Firefly such a stiff gallop as all that, but Jim was certain that he had heard right. And off they went, beginning the other side of Southwick Hill. I saw the Gaffer with his arms in the air, and don't know now what he said. Jim will tell you. He did give it you, didn't he, you old Woolgatherer?' said Mr. Swindles, slapping the boy on the shoulder.

'You may laugh as much as you please, but I'm sure he did tell me to come along three-quarter speed after passing the barn,' replied Jim, and to change the conversation he asked Mr. Leopold for some more pudding, and the Demon's hungry eyes watched the last portion being placed on the Woolgatherer's plate. Noticing that Esther drank no beer, he exclaimed:

'Well, I never; to see yer eat and drink one would think

that it was you who was a-wasting to ride the crack at Goodwood.'

The remark stirred up some laughter, and, excited by his success, the Demon threw his arms round Esther, and seizing her hands, said: 'Now yer a just beginning to get through yer 'osses, and when you get on a level——' But the Demon, in his hungry merriment, had bestowed no thought of finding a temper in such a staid girl, and a sound box on the ear threw him backwards into his seat surprised and howling. 'Yer nasty thing!' he blubbered out. 'Couldn't you see it was only a joke?' But passion was hot in Esther. She hadn't understood a word that had been said since she had sat down to dinner, and, conscious of her poverty and her ignorance, she imagined that a great deal of the Demon's conversation had been directed against her; and, choking with indignation, she only heard indistinctly the reproaches with which the other little boys covered her—'nasty, dirty, ill-tempered thing, scullery-maid'—nor did she understand their whispered plans to duck her when she passed the stables. All looked a little askance, especially Grover and Mr. Leopold. Margaret said:

'That will teach these impertinent little jockey boys that the servants' hall is not the harness-room; they oughtn't to be admitted here at all.'

Mr. Leopold nodded, and told the Demon to leave off blubbering. 'You can't be so much hurt as all that. Come, wipe your eyes and have a piece of currant tart, or leave the room. I want to hear from Mr. Swindles an account of the trial. We know that Silver Braid won, but we haven't heard how he won nor yet what the weights were.'

'Well,' said Mr. Swindles, 'what I makes out is this. I was riding within a pound or two of nine stone, and The Rake is, as you know, seven pounds, no more, worse than Bayleaf. Ginger rides usually as near as possible my weight — we'll say he was riding nine two — I think he could manage that—and the Demon, we know, he is now riding over the six stone; in his ordinary clothes he rides six seven.'

'Yes, yes, but how do we know that there was any lead to speak of in the Demon's saddle-cloth?'

'The Demon says there wasn't above a stone.  Don't you, Demon?'

'I don't know nothing!  I'm not going to stand being cuffed by the kitchenmaid.'

'Oh, shut up, or leave the room,' said Mr. Leopold; 'we don't want to hear any more about that.'

'I started making the running according to orders. Ginger was within three-quarters of a length of me, being pulled out of the saddle.  The Gaffer was standing at the three-quarters of the mile, and there Ginger won fairly easily, but they went on to the mile—them were the orders— and there the Demon won by half a length, that is to say if Ginger wasn't a-kidding of him.'

'A-kidding of me!' said the Demon.  'When we was a hundred yards from 'ome I steadied without his noticing me, and then I landed in the last fifty yards by half a length. Ginger can't ride much better than any other gentleman.'

'Yer see,' said Mr. Swindles, 'he'd sooner have a box on the ear from the kitchenmaid than be told a gentleman could kid him at a finish.  He wouldn't mind if it was the Tinman, eh, Demon?'

'We know,' said Mr. Leopold, 'that Bayleaf can get the mile; there must have been a lot of weight between them.  Besides, I should think that the trial was at the three-quarters of the mile.  The mile was so much kid.'

'I should say,' replied Mr. Swindles, 'that the 'orses were tried at twenty-one pounds, and if Silver Braid can beat Bayleaf at that weight, he'll take a deal of beating at Goodwood.'

And leaning forward, their arms on the table, with large pieces of cheese at the end of their knives, the maidservants and the jockey listened while Mr. Leopold and Mr. Swindles discussed the chances the stable had of pulling off the Stewards' Cup with Silver Braid.

'But he will always keep on trying them,' said Mr. Swindles, 'and what's the use, says I, of trying 'orses that are no more than 'alf fit?  And them downs is just rotten with 'orse watchers; it has just come to this, that you can't comb out an 'orse's mane without seeing it in the papers the day after.  If I had my way with them gentry——' Mr. Swindles finished his beer at a gulp, and he put down his glass as firmly as he desired to put down the horse watchers. At the end of a long silence Mr. Leopold said:

'Come into my pantry and smoke a pipe. Mr. Arthur will be down presently. Perhaps he 'll tell us what weight he was riding this morning.'

'Cunning old bird,' said Mr. Swindles, as he rose from the table and wiped his shaven lips with the back of his hand; 'and you 'd have us believe that you didn't know, would you? You 'd have us believe, would you, that the Gaffer don't tell you everything when you bring up his hot water in the morning, would you?'

Mr. Leopold laughed under his breath, and looking mysterious and very rat-like, he led the way to his pantry. Esther watched them in strange trouble of soul.

She had heard of racecourses as shameful places where men were led to their ruin, and betting she had always understood to be sinful, but in this house no one seemed to think of anything else. It was no place for a Christian girl.

'Let 's have some more of the story,' Margaret said. 'You 've got the new number. The last piece was where he is going to ask the opera-singer to run away with him.'

Sarah took an illustrated journal out of her pocket and began to read aloud.

'I am sure it is wicked to read such tales.'

Sarah looked at Esther in astonishment, and Grover said:

'You shouldn't be here at all. Can't Mrs. Latch find nothing for you to do in the scullery?'

'Then,' said Sarah, awaking to a sense of the situation, 'I suppose that where you come from you were not so much as allowed to read a tale?'

'Esther's box is full of books,' said Margaret.

'I should like to see them books,' said Sarah. 'I 'll be bound that they are only prayer-books.'

'I don't mind what you say to me, but you shall not insult my religion.'

'Insult your religion! I said you never had read a book in your life, unless it was a prayer-book.'

'We don't use prayer-books.'

'Then what books have you read?'

Esther hesitated, and, suspecting the truth, Sarah said:

'I don't believe you can read at all. Come, I 'll bet you

twopence that you can't read the first five lines of my story.'

Esther pushed the paper from her and walked out of the room suffocated with shame, though it was not her fault if she didn't know how to read, and, her thoughts returning to Barnstaple, she went upstairs, drawn thither by her mother's books: *Peter Parley's Annual*, *Sunny Memories of Foreign Lands*, *Children of the Abbey*, *Uncle Tom's Cabin*, Lamb's *Tales of Shakespeare's Plays*, a Cooking Book, *Rhoda's Mission of Love*, the Holy Bible and the Book of Common Prayer.

And she turned them over, wondering what were the mysteries that this print held from her.

## CHAPTER III

ESTHER WATERS was brought up in the strictness of a sect,
and her earliest memories were of people who tried to live
like the early Christians.   Her life among these sectaries
lasted till she was ten years old, till her father died, a house-
painter, who in early youth had been led into intemperance
by some wild companions.   She had often been told the
story how one day the fumes of the beer he had drunk overpowered him as he sat in the sun on his derrick, and that he
had called upon God to relieve him of his suffering in the
hospital, and that a Plymouth Brother who occupied the
next bed had answered him: 'You never thought of God
before.   Be patient, your health is coming back; it is a
gift from God.   You would like to know Him and thank
Him from the bottom of your heart?'

John Waters's heart was touched by these simple words;
he became one of the Brethren, and his conversion and
subsequent grace won for him the sympathies of Mary
Thornby.   But Mary's father would not consent to the
marriage unless John abandoned his dangerous trade of
house-painter, which John Waters consented to do, and
old James Thornby, who had made a competence in the
curiosity line, offered to make over his shop to the young
couple on certain conditions; these conditions were accepted, and under his father-in-law's direction John drove
a successful trade in old glass, old jewellery, and old
furniture.

The Brethren did not like this trade, and they often came
to John to speak with him on the subject, and their words
were:

'Of course, this is between you and the Lord, but these
things' (pointing to the old glass and jewellery) 'often are
but snares for the feet, and lead weaker brethren into
temptation.   Of course, it is between you and the Lord.'
So John Waters was tormented with scruples concerning
the righteousness of his trade, but his wife's gentle voice

and eyes, and the restrictions that his accident, from which he never wholly recovered, set upon his life, overruled his scruples, and he remained until he died a dealer in artistic ware, eliminating, however, from his dealings those things to which the Brethren most objected. After his death his widow strove to carry on the business, but her father, who was now a confirmed invalid, could not help her; in the following year she lost both her parents, and about this time many changes were taking place in Barnstaple, new houses were being built, a much larger and finer shop had been opened in the more prosperous end of the town, and Mrs. Waters found herself obliged to sell her business for almost nothing, and marry again. This second marriage proved more fruitful than the first, children were born in rapid succession, the cradle was never empty, and Esther was spoken of as the little nurse. But her great care was for her poor mother, who had lost her health, whose blood was impoverished by constant childbearing, and mother and daughter were often seen in the evenings, one with a baby at her breast, the other with an eighteen months' old child in her arms. Esther did not dare leave her mother; and to protect her against her stepfather she gave up school, and this was why she had never learnt how to read.

One of the many causes of quarrel between Mrs. Saunders and her husband was her attendance at prayer-meetings, when he said she should be at home minding her children. He used to rail at her, saying she carried on with the Scripture readers, and to punish her he would say: 'This week I'll spend five bob more in the public—that'll teach you, if beating won't, that I don't want none of your hymn-and-misery lot hanging round my place.' The father's drinking left the Saunders family with little to eat; once they were nearly thirty hours without food, and it was often in Esther's thoughts how her mother called her little tribe about her, and, kneeling down amongst them, she had prayed that God might help them. Their prayers were answered, for at half-past twelve a Scripture lady came in with flowers in her hands, and asked Mrs. Saunders how her appetite was. Mrs. Saunders answered that it was more than she could afford, for there was nothing to eat in the house. And then the Scripture lady gave them eighteenpence, and they all knelt down again and thanked God together.

But although Saunders spent a great deal of his money in the public-house, he rarely got drunk, and always kept his employment. He was a painter of engines, a first-rate hand, earning good money, from twenty-five to thirty shillings a week—a proud man, but so avaricious that he stopped at nothing to get money, selling his vote to the highest bidder at elections, and when Esther was seventeen he drove her into service, without a thought of the character of the people or of what the place was like. They were then in London, living in a little street off the Vauxhall Bridge Road, near the factory where Saunders worked; and since they had been in London, Esther had been constantly in service in many different lodging-houses, many of them of immoral character, for she couldn't pick and choose—she wasn't wanted at home, not being one of his children, and he had quite enough of his own. Sometimes of an evening her mother would step round to fetch her, and mother and daughter, wrapped in the same shawl, would walk to and fro telling each other their troubles, just as in old times. But these moments were few, for to get her living she had to work from early morning till late at night, scrubbing grates, preparing bacon and eggs, cooking chops and making beds: she was one of the many London girls to whom rest, not to say pleasure, is unknown, and who, if they should sit down for a few moments, hear the mistress's voice, crying: 'Now, Eliza, have you nothing to do, that you are sitting there idle?' Two of her mistresses, one after the other, had been sold up, and now all the rooms in the neighbourhood were unlet, no one wanted a 'slavey.' Esther had to return home, and it was on the last of these occasions that her father had taken her by the shoulders, saying:

'No lodging-'ouses that want a slavey? I'll see about that. Tell me, first, did you go to 78?'

'Yes, but another girl was before me, and the place was taken when I got there.'

'I wonder what you was doing that you didn't get there sooner; dangling about after your mother, I suppose! Well, what about 27 in the Crescent?'

'I couldn't go there—that Mrs. Dunbar is a bad woman.'

'Bad woman! Who are you, I should like to know, that you can take a lady's character away? Who told you she was a bad woman? One of the Scripture readers, I suppose! I knew it was. Well, then, just get out.'

'Where shall I go?'

'Go to hell for all I care. Do you 'ear me? Get out!'

Esther did not move—words, and then blows. Her escape from her stepfather seemed a miracle, and his anger was only appeased by Mrs. Saunders promising that Esther should accept the situation.

'Only for a little while. Perhaps Mrs. Dunbar is a better woman than you think for, dearie. For my sake. If you don't, he may kill you and me too.'

Esther looked at her one moment, then she said: 'Very well, mother, to-morrow I 'll take the place.'

And seeing that she was a good girl, Mrs. Dunbar respected her scruples and was kind to Esther, who learnt to like her, and, through her affection for her, to think less of the life she led. And it was at this critical moment that Lady Elwin heard her story, and promised Mrs. Saunders to find Esther another place; and to obviate all difficulties about references and character, proposed to take Esther as her own servant for time enough to justify a recommendation.

And now, as Esther turned over her books—books which she could not read—her pure, religious mind recalled the story of her life; her poor little brothers and sisters and her dear mother, and that tyrant revenging himself upon them because of the little she might eat and drink. But her troubles seemed small compared with those she would endure were she to return home. Yet her heart strained for departure. At home there was her mother and the meeting-house, but in Woodview there was only Margaret, who had just come to beg her to return to the kitchen. Margaret was kind, and, turning aside to quench her tears, Esther answered she would follow her down.

Two or three days passed without anything happening that seemed to point to staying or going. Mrs. Barfield would like her or dislike her—that was according to her luck—and reports continued to come down of the missus's health (she was confined to her room with a cold), and with them gossip that heartened Esther, who one day, while at work in the scullery, heard the Saint's voice in the kitchen —it seemed to her to ring truth; it inspired hope in Esther till her heart began to beat faster and she held her breath; for Mrs. Barfield was telling Mrs. Latch that this was the third kitchenmaid in four months, and that she must make up her mind to bear with 'What 's-her-name?'—Esther Waters's faults and failings whatever they were. Mrs. Latch gave back some sullen answers under cover of a great rattling of saucepans; Esther heard Mrs. Barfield call her, and a moment after found herself face to face with a little red-haired woman, with a pretty, pointed face.

'I hear, Waters—that is your name, I think—that you refused to obey cook, and walked out of the kitchen the night you arrived.'

'I said, ma'am, that I would wait till my box came up from the station, so that I might change my dress. Mrs. Latch said my dress didn't matter, but when you 're poor and haven't many dresses——'

'Are you short of clothes, then?'

'I haven't many, ma'am, and the dress I had on the day I came——'

'Never mind about that. Tell me, are you short of clothes?—for if you are I dare say my daughter might find you something—you are about the same height—with a little alteration——'

'Oh, ma'am, that 's very good of you. But I think I shall be able to manage till my first quarter's wages come to me.'

Mrs. Barfield's eyes and voice awoke in Esther a sense of kinship, and all that day she moved about her work happy, singing to herself as she washed the cauliflowers and peeled the potatoes. If she could only win over Mrs. Latch! Even this wouldn't be impossible, Margaret said, if Esther gave up her beer—'a solid pint a day will soften her'; and Esther answered: 'She can have my beer and welcome.'

'You 'll be friends yet, I can see, for you 're a worker like herself. The old thing can't rest a minute. Her last kitchenmaid said to her: "I don't mind telling you, Mrs. Latch, that I 'm not like you. I don't like work, and I hope I never shall."'

'Well, she had a cheek, and no mistake,' Esther answered; and she felt she had a friend in Margaret, which she had, though Margaret seemed to make common cause sometimes with Grover and Sarah, teasing Esther about her morning and evening prayers, which she could not forgo. But there was no spite in her quizzes, and Esther felt that while seeming to make a mock of her she was defending her—warding off strokes or allowing them to fall lightly.

Sometimes Margaret helped her with her work, which Mrs. Latch seemed to make as heavy as possible; but Esther was now determined to remain in Woodview till she learned to make jellies and gravies. Mrs. Latch, however, seemed to have guessed what was in her mind, and was sure to find some saucepans that had not been sufficiently cleaned with white sand; and if these were lacking, she would send Esther upstairs to scrub out her bedroom.

'I can't think why she is so down on me,' Esther often said to Margaret.

'She 's not more down on you than she was on the others; but you can put it out of your head that she 's going to learn you cooking. She isn't going to see one of her kitchenmaids take her place, and it 's only natural. But I don't see why she should always be sending you upstairs to clean out her bedroom. If Grover wasn't so stand-offish we might tell her about it, and she would tell the Saint—that 's what we calls the missus—and the Saint would soon put a stop to all that nonsense. I 'll say this for the Saint, that she do like every one to have fair play. One of your lot, you know, Esther.'

'A Plymouth Sister!' Esther cried. All the instincts of her mind came together, and in a moment of intense collectedness she heard her mistress's story.

Mrs. Barfield was the daughter of one of the farmers on the estate—an old man, Elliot by name.

'He don't often come down 'ere, but we sees 'im when we go out on the hill-side of an evening, his long black coat buttoned tightly about him, his soft felt hat crushed down over his thin grey face. He don't come down 'ere on account of the 'orses, and it 's said that he never liked the marriage, though it was to the Manor House his daughter was going. But he couldn't help 'isself, for the Squire— the Gaffer as we calls 'im—was dead set on Miss Elliot.

You can't keep a landlord off his own land, nor you can't keep your own daughter always within doors; and so the two of them used to meet beyond the barn, and a familiar sight they were walking through the furze together, the Gaffer leading his cob and she by his side. I don't know how much truth there is in the story, but it was said that one evening old Elliot and the Squire came to words, and very nearly to something more than words. One of the shepherds tells that he seed the old fellow raise his stick. Mayhap, but the end of it was that the Squire promised to become one of the Brethren, and never to bet again or to own racehorses, and the stables was to be done away with. The Gaffer was then a farmer 'imself, holding his land from his father; and the old folk tried to break off the match, for they were anxious to be well in with the county—a thing that they never could be, for you see the Barfields were not county from the beginning. They only became county three generations ago. Before that they were in trade—livery stable-keepers, it was said. So you see it's a see-saw, up and down, and no more than that.'

'But the Gaffer didn't keep his promise,' Esther said.

'He kept his promise as long as he could. The racing came back; but how it came back I can't tell you. Nobody knows that but Mr. Leopold. Only he can tell you. I've heard him say that when the Saint heard that the Gaffer entered one of his hunters in the Hunt Steeplechase (that's how it begun), she was broken-hearted. But a woman's bound to stand by her husband. So Elliot just sends a cheque for his rent, and the Saint goes over to see her father sometimes, and the Gaffer never interferes with the prayer-meetings. What are you thinking now, Esther?'

Esther was thinking that her mistress's life was like her own in many ways, but she was not moved to confide her story to Margaret. She wished to ponder on all she had heard, and looked forward to the moment when Mrs. Barfield would ask her some question that would allow her to say, 'I'm a Plymouth Sister, ma'am.' Margaret had told her that one of the Saint's rules was to have the women-servants for half an hour every Sunday afternoon in the library for instruction in the life of Christ.

Although nearly fifty, her figure was slight as a young girl's, and Esther was attracted by the little oval face—

reddish hair growing thin at the parting and smoothed back above the ears, as in an old engraving. When their eyes met at prayers there was acknowledgment of religious kinship. A glow of happiness filled Esther's soul, for she knew she was no longer wholly among strangers; she knew they were united—she and her mistress—under the sweet dominion of Christ. She couldn't take her eyes off Mrs. Barfield, so much did she remind her of her pious childhood in the old shop, and, listening to the beautiful story, in the annunciation of which her life had grown up, she answered her mistress's questions in sweet light-heartedness of spirit, pleasing her with her knowledge of the Holy Book. Turn and turn about the servants had to read verses aloud from the New Testament, and Esther saw that her secret would be torn from her. Sarah had read a verse, and Mrs. Barfield had explained it, and now Margaret was reading. Esther listened, thinking if she might plead illness and escape from the room; but she could not summon sufficient presence of mind, and while she was still agitated and debating within herself, Mrs. Barfield called to her to continue. She hung down her head, suffocated with the shame of the exposure, and when Mrs. Barfield told her again to continue the reading, Esther shook her head.

'Can't you read, Esther?' she heard a kind voice saying; and the sound of this voice loosed the feelings long pent up, and the girl, giving way utterly, burst into passionate weeping. She was alone with her suffering, conscious of nothing else, until a kind hand led her from the room, and this hand soothed away the bitterness of the tittering which reached her ears as the door closed. It was hard to persuade her to speak, but even the first words showed that there was more on the girl's heart than could be told in a few minutes, so Mrs. Barfield dismissed the other servants and returned to the library with Esther, and in that dim room of little green sofas, bookless shelves, and bird-cages, the women—mistress and maid—sealed the bond of a friendship which was to last for life.

She told her mistress of the work that Mrs. Latch required of her, the persecution she received from the other servants, principally because of her religion. They dropped into talking of the racehorses, and Esther saw on her mistress's face a look of grief, that made clear to her the cause to which Mrs. Barfield traced the demoralization of her household.

'I will teach you how to read, Esther. Every Sunday after our Bible instruction you shall remain for half an hour when the others have left. You will soon learn.'

And from that day forth, every Sunday afternoon, Mrs. Barfield devoted half an hour to the instruction of her kitchenmaid. But Esther did not make much progress, nor did her diligence seem to help her, and Mrs. Barfield ascribed her pupil's slowness to her own inaptitude to teach and the little time for lessons.

## CHAPTER IV

ESTHER'S position in Woodview was now secure, and her
fellow-servants recognized the fact, though they liked her
none the better for it.   Mrs. Latch still did what she could
to prevent her from learning her trade, but she no longer
attempted to overburden her with work.   Of Mr. Leopold
she saw almost as little as she did of the people upstairs.
He passed along the passages or remained shut up in his
pantry.   Ginger used to go there to smoke; and when the
door stood ajar Esther saw his narrow person seated on the
edge of the table, his leg swinging.   Among the pantry
people Mr. Leopold's erudition was a constant subject of
admiration.   His reminiscences of the races of thirty years
ago were full of interest; he had seen the great horses
whose names live in the stud-book, the horses the Gaffer
had owned, had trained, had ridden, and he was full of
anecdote concerning them and the Gaffer.   Praise of his
father's horsemanship always caused a cloud to gather
on Ginger's face, and when he left the pantry Swindles
chuckled.   'Whenever I wants to get a rise out of Ginger
I says: "Ah, we shall never see another gentleman jock
who can use the whip at a finish like the Governor in his
best days."'

Every one delighted in the pantry, and to make Mr.
Leopold comfortable Mr. Swindles used to bring in the wolf-
skin rug that went out with the carriage, and wrap it round
Mr. Leopold's wooden armchair, and the sallow little man
would curl himself up, and, smoking his long clay, discuss
the weights of the next big handicap.   If Ginger contra-
dicted him he would go to the press and extract from its
obscurity a package of *Bell's Life* or a file of the *Sportsman*.

Mr. Leopold's press!   For forty years no one had looked
into that press.   Mr. Leopold guarded it from every gaze,
but it seemed to be a much-varied repository from which,
if he chose, he could produce almost any trifle that might
be required.   It seemed to combine the usefulness of a
hardware shop and a drug store.

The pantry had its etiquette and its discipline. Jockey boys were rarely admitted, unless with the intention of securing their services for the cleaning of boots or knives. William was very proud of his right of entry. For that half-hour in the pantry he would surrender willingly the pleasure of walking in the drove-way with Sarah. But when Mrs. Latch learnt that he was there her face darkened, and the noise she then made about the range with her saucepans was alarming. Mrs. Barfield shared her cook's fear of the pantry, and often spoke of Mr. Leopold as 'that little man.' Although outwardly the family butler, he had never ceased to be the Gaffer's private servant; he represented the old days of bachelorhood. Mrs. Barfield and Mrs. Latch disliked him. Mrs. Barfield felt sure her husband would not have returned to racing had it not been for Mr. Leopold, and Mrs. Latch attributed her husband's downfall to him. Legends and mystery had formed around Mr. Leopold and his pantry, and in Esther's unsophisticated mind this little room, with its tobacco-smoke and glasses on the table, became a symbol of all that was wicked and dangerous; and when she passed the door she closed her ears and instinctively lowered her eyes.

The simplest human sentiments were abiding principles in Esther—love of God, and love of God in the home. But above this Protestantism was human nature; her twentieth year thrilled within her; and no longer half starved, her eyes opened to the beauty of the world, and she sang at her work, gladdened by the sights and sounds of the yard, the young rooks cawing lustily in the ilex trees, the gardener passing to and fro with plants in his hands, the white cats licking themselves in the sun or running to meet the young ladies who brought them plates of milk. The racehorses were always going to or coming from the downs. Sometimes they came in so covered with white mud that part of their toilette was accomplished in the yard; and from her kitchen window she could see the beautiful animal haltered to the hook fixed in the high wall, and the little boy in his shirt sleeves and hitched-up trousers, not a bit afraid, but shouting and quieting him into submission with the stick when he kicked and bit, tickled by the washing brush, passing under the belly. Then the wrestling, sparring, ball-playing of the lads when their work was done, and the pale, pathetic figure of the Demon, who was about to start for Portslade and back, wrapped as he would put it, in a red-hot scorcher of an overcoat.

Esther often longed for a romp with these boys, with whom she was now prime favourite. Once they caught her in the hay yard, and fine sport it was in the warm hay throwing each other over. Sometimes her wayward temper would get the better of her, but her momentary rage vanished at the sound of laughter. And after their tussling they would walk a little while pensively, until perhaps one, with an adroit trip, would send the other rolling over on the grass, and then, with wild cries, they all run down the drove-way. And there was the day when the Woolgatherer told her he was in love; what fun they had had, and how well she had led him into belief that she was jealous. Of course it was all very wrong to take a rope as if she were going to hang herself, and having fastened it to a branch, to kneel down as if she were saying her prayers. The poor Woolgatherer could stand it no longer; he rushed to her side, swearing that if she would promise not to hang herself he would never look at another girl again. The other boys, who had been crouching in the drove-way, rose up. How they did mock the Woolgatherer till he burst into tears, and Esther felt sorry for him, and almost inclined to marry him out of pity for his forlorn condition.

Her life grew happier and happier. She was still very poor, she had not sufficient clothes, and her life was full of little troubles, but there were compensations. It was to her that Mrs. Barfield always came when she wanted anything in a hurry, and Miss Mary, too, seemed to prefer to apply to Esther when she wanted milk for her cats or bran and oats for her rabbits.

The Gaffer and his racehorses, the Saint and her greenhouse, Miss Mary entertaining her visitors in the drawing-room or on the tennis lawn—so went the stream of life at Woodview. Mrs. Barfield saw no one, preferring to remain in her old gown—an old thing that her daughter had discarded long ago—pinned up around her, and on her head an old bonnet with a faded poppy hanging from the crown. In such attire she wished to be allowed to trot about to and fro from her greenhouse to her potting-shed, watering, pruning, and syringing her plants. These plants were dearer than all things to her except her children; she seemed, indeed, to treat them as if they were children, and with the sun pouring through the glass down on her back she would sit freeing them from devouring insects all the day long. She would carry can after can of water up the long path and never complain of fatigue. She broke into complaint only when Miss Mary forgot to feed her pets, of which she had a great number—rabbits and cats and rooks—and all the work developed upon her. She could not see these poor dumb creatures hungry, and would trudge to the stables, coming back laden with oats and bran. But it was sometimes more than a pair of hands could do, and she would send Esther with scraps of meat and bread and milk to the unfortunate rooks that Mary had so unmercifully forgotten. 'I 'll have no more pets,' she 'd say; 'Miss Mary won't look after them, and all the trouble falls upon me. See these poor cats, how they come mewing round my skirts.' She loved to expatiate on her affection for dumb animals, and she continued an anecdotal discourse till, suddenly wearying of it, she would break off and speak to Esther about Barnstaple and the Brethren.

The Saint loved to hear Esther tell of her father and the little shop in Barnstaple, of the prayer-meetings and the simple earnestness and narrowness of the faith of those good Brethren. Circumstances had effaced, though they had not obliterated, the once sharply marked confines of her religious habits. Her religion was like a garden— a little less sedulously tended than of yore, but no whit less fondly loved; and while listening to Esther's story she dreamed her own early life over again, and paused, laying down her watering-can, overcome with the listlessness of happy memories. And so Esther's life grew and was fashioned amid the ceaseless round of simple daily occupations, mistress and maid learning to know and to love one another in the tender and ineffable sympathies of race and religion.

## CHAPTER V

THE summer drowsed, baking the turf on the hills, and after every gallop the Gaffer passed his fingers along the fine legs of the crack, in fear and apprehension lest he should detect any swelling. William had five shillings on, and stood to win five pounds ten—quite a little fortune. He often stopped to ask Esther if there was any news as he made his way to the pantry, and she told him that so far as she knew Silver Braid was all right, and continued shaking the rug.

'You 'll never get the dust out of that rug,' he said at last; 'here, give it to me.' She hesitated, then gave it him, and he beat it against the brick wall. 'There,' he said, handing it back to her, 'that 's how I beats a mat; you won't find much dust in it now.'

'Thank you. Sarah went by an hour and a half ago.'

'Ah, she must have gone to the Gardens. You have never been to those Gardens, have you? Dancing-hall, theatre, sorcerers—every blessed thing. But you 're that religious, I suppose you wouldn't come?'

'It is only the way you are brought up.'

'Well, will you come?'

'I don't think I should like those Gardens. But I dare say they are no worse than any other place. I 've heard so much since I was here, that really——'

'That really what?'

'That sometimes it doesn't seem much good to be particular.'

'Of course—all rot. Well, will you come next Sunday?'

'Certainly not on Sunday.'

The Gaffer had engaged him as footman: his livery would be ready by Saturday, and he would enter service on Monday week; and this reminded them that henceforth they would see each other every day, and, speaking of the pain it would give his mother when he came running downstairs to go out with the carriage, he said:

'It was always her idea that I shouldn't be a servant,

but I believe in doing what you gets most coin for doing. I should like to have been a jockey, and I could have ridden well enough—the Gaffer thought better at one time of my riding than he did of Ginger's. But I never had any luck; when I was about fifteen I began to grow. If I could have remained like the Demon——'

Esther looked at him, wondering if he were speaking seriously, and really wished away his splendid height and shoulders.

A few days later he tried to persuade her to take a ticket in a shilling sweepstakes which he was getting up among the out and the indoor servants. She pleaded poverty—her wages would not be due till the end of August. But William offered to lend her the money, and he pressed the hat containing the bits of paper on which were written the horses' names so insinuatingly upon her that a sudden impulse to oblige him came over her, and before she had time to think she had put her hand in the hat and taken a number.

'Come, none of your betting and gambling in my kitchen,' said Mrs. Latch, turning from her work. 'Just you leave the girl alone.'

'Don't be that nasty, mother; it ain't betting, it's a sweepstakes.'

'It is all the same,' muttered Mrs. Latch; 'it always begins that way, and it goes on from bad to worse. I never saw any good come from it, and heaven knows I've seen enough misfortune.'

Margaret and Sarah paused, looking at her open-mouthed, a little perplexed, holding the numbers they had drawn in both hands. Esther had not unfolded hers. She looked at Mrs. Latch, and feared jeers from Sarah, and from Grover, who had just come in, for her inability to read the name of the horse she had drawn. Seeing what was up, William took her paper from her.

'Silver Braid. By Jingo! She has got the right one.'

At that moment the sound of hoofs was heard in the yard, and the servants flew to the window.

'He'll win,' cried William, leaning over the women's backs, waving his bony hand to the Demon, who rode past on Silver Braid. 'The Gaffer will bring him to the post as fit as a fiddle.'

'I think he will,' said Mr. Leopold. 'The rain has done us a lot of good; he was beginning to go a bit short a week ago. We shall want some more rain. I should like to see it come down in buckets for the next week or more.'

Mr. Leopold's desires looked as if they were going to be fulfilled. The heavens seemed to have taken the fortunes of the stable in hand. Rain fell generally in the afternoon and night, leaving the mornings fine, and Silver Braid went the mile gaily, becoming harder and stronger. And, in the intermittent swish of showers blown up from the sea, Woodview grew joyous, and a conviction of triumph gathered and settled on every face except Mrs. Barfield's and Mrs. Latch's. And askance they looked at the triumphant little butler. He became more and more the topic of conversation. He seemed to hold the thread of their destiny in his press. Peggy was especially afraid of him.

And, continuing her confidence to the under-housemaid, the young lady said: 'I like to know things for the pleasure of talking about them, but he spies around for the pleasure of holding his tongue.' Peggy was Miss Margaret Barfield, a cousin, the daughter of a rich brewer. 'If he brings in your letters in the morning he hands them to you just as if he knew whom they are from. Ugly little beast; it irritates me when he comes into the room.'

'He hates women, miss; he never lets us near his pantry, and he keeps William there talking racing.'

'Ah, William is very different. He ought never to have been a servant. His family was once quite as good as the Barfields.'

'So I have heard, miss. But the world is that full of ups and downs, you never can tell who is who. But we all likes William, and 'ates that little man and his pantry. Mrs. Latch calls him the "evil genius."'

A furtive and clandestine little man, ashamed of his women-folk, keeping them out of sight as much as possible, and his wife a pale, dim woman, tall as he was short, pre-serving still some of the graces of the lady's maid, shy either by nature or by the severe rule of her lord, always anxious to obliterate herself against the hedges when you met her in the lane, or against the pantry door when any of the family knocked to ask for hot water, or came with a letter for the post. And by nature a bachelor, he was instinctively ashamed of his family, for when the weary-looking wife, the thin, shy girl, or the corpulent, flat-faced son were with him and he heard steps outside, he would come out like a little wasp, and, unmistakably resenting the intrusion, would ask what was wanted.

If it were Ginger, Mr. Leopold would say: 'Can I do anything for you, Mr. Arthur?'

'Oh, nothing, thank you; I only thought that——' And Ginger would invent some paltry excuse and slink away to smoke elsewhere.

Every day, a little before twelve, Mr. Leopold went out for his morning walk; every day, if it were fine, you would meet him at that hour in the lane either coming from or going to Shoreham. For thirty years he had done his little constitutional, always taking the same road, always starting within a few minutes of twelve, always returning in time to lay the cloth for lunch at half-past one. The hour between twelve and one he spent in the cottage which he rented from the squire for his wife and children, or in the 'Red Lion,' where he had a glass of beer and talked with Watkins, the bookmaker.

'There he goes, off to the "Red Lion,"' said Mrs. Latch. 'They try to get some information out of him, but he's too sharp for them, and he knows it; that's what he goes there for—just for the pleasure of seeing them swallow the lies he tells them. He has been telling them lies about the horses for the last twenty years, and still he gets them to believe what he says. It is a cruel shame! It was the lies he told poor Jackson about Blue Beard that made the poor man back the horse for all he was worth.'

'And the horse didn't win?'

'Win! The master didn't even intend to run him, and Jackson lost all he had, and more. He went down to the river and drowned himself. John Randal has that man's death on his conscience. But his conscience don't trouble him much; if it did, he'd be in his grave long ago. Lies, lies, nothing but lies! But I dare say I'm too 'ard on him; isn't lies our natural lot? What is servants for but to lie when it is in their master's interests, and to be a confidential servant is to be the prince of liars!'

'Perhaps he didn't know the 'orse was scratched.'

'I see you are falling in nicely with the lingo of the trade.'

'Oh,' replied Esther, laughing: 'you never hears anything else; you pick it up without knowing.   Mr. Leopold
is very rich, so they say.   The boys tell me that he won a
pile over the City and Suburban, and has thousands in the
bank.'

'So some says; but who knows what he 'as?   You hear
of the winnings, but they says very little about the losings.'

## CHAPTER VI

THE pony and the donkey came towards the paddock gate, and she rubbed their muzzles in turn. It was a pleasure to touch anything, especially anything alive. She even noticed that the elm trees were strangely tall and still against the calm sky, and the rich odour of some carnations, which came through the bushes from the pleasure-ground, excited her; the scent of earth and leaves tingled in her, the cawing of the rooks coming home took her soul away skyward in an exquisite longing; and she was, at the same time, full of a romantic love for the earth, and of a desire to mix herself with the innermost essence of things. The beauty of the evening and the sea breeze instilled a sensation of immortal health, setting her thinking that if a young man came to her as young men came to the great ladies in Sarah's books, it would be pleasant to talk in the dusk, seeing the bats flitting about the barns and byres vanishing into nothingness.

The family was absent from Woodview, and she was free to enjoy the beauty of every twilight and every rising moon for still another week. But she wearied for a companion. The boys were playing ball in the stables, but she did not feel as if she wanted to romp with them. Sarah and Grover were far too grand to walk out with her; and Margaret had a young man who came to fetch her, and in their room at night she related all he had said. But for Esther there was nothing to do all the long summer evenings but to sit at the kitchen window sewing. Her hands fell on her lap, and her heart heaved a sigh of weariness. In all this world there was nothing for her to do but to continue her sewing or to go for a walk up the hill. She was tired of that hill! But she could not sit in the kitchen till bedtime, and thinking that she might meet the old shepherd coming home with his sheep, she put a piece of bread in her pocket for his dogs and strolled up the hill-side. Margaret had gone down to the Gardens with her young man, and one of these days a young man would come to take her out.

Now what would he be like? She laughed the thought away, for it did not seem likely that any young man would bother about her. But at that moment, she saw a man coming through the hunting gate. His height and shoulders told her that he was William. 'Trying to find Sarah,' she thought. 'I must not let him think I am waiting for him.' And she continued her walk, wondering if he were following, afraid to look round. At last she began to hear footsteps; her heart beat faster and seemed to stand still when he called to her.

'I think Sarah has gone to the Gardens,' she said, turning round.

'You always keep rubbing it in about Sarah! There's nothing between us, or anything there ever was is all off long ago. Are you going for a walk on the downs?'

She was glad of the chance to get a mouthful of fresh air, and William held the hunting gate open, which she had never been through before, and was surprised to find herself in front of so much wild country: two great ranges of downs —the Shoreham Downs in front of them, rising up hill after hill as if the earth had once aspired to reach the sky; the Worthing range, some miles away, over against the great shallow valley of the Adur, full of green water meadows and long herds of cattle.

There was a smell of sheep in the air, and the flock trotted past them in good order, followed by the shepherd, with a huge hat on his head, a crook in his hand, and two shaggy dogs at his heels. A brace of partridges rose out of the sainfoin, and flew down the hills; and watching their curving flight Esther and William saw the sea under the sun-setting and the string of coast towns.

'A lovely evening, isn't it?'

Esther acquiesced; and tempted by the warmth of the grass they sat down.

'We shan't have any rain yet awhile.'

'How do you know!'

'I'll tell you,' William answered, eager to show his superior knowledge. 'Look due south-west, straight through that last dip in them line of hills. Do you see anything?'

'No, I can't see nothing,' said Esther, after straining her eyes for a few moments.

'I thought not. . . . Well, if it was going to rain you'd see the Isle of Wight.'

For something to say, and hoping to please, Esther asked him where the racecourse was.

'Over yonder. I can't show you the start, a long way behind that hill, Portslade way; and then they come right along by that gorse and finish up by Truly barn. You can't see Truly barn from here—that's Thunder's barrow barn; they go quite half a mile farther.'

'And do all that land belong to the Gaffer?'

'Yes, and a great deal more, too; but this downland isn't worth much—not more than about ten shillings an acre.'

'And how many acres are there?'

'Do you mean all that we can see?'

'Yes.'

'The Gaffer's property reaches to Southwick Hill, and it goes north a long way. I suppose you don't know that all this piece that lies between us and that barn yonder once belonged to my family.'

'To your family?'

'Yes, the Latches were once big swells; in the time of my great-grandfather the Barfields couldn't hold their heads as high as the Latches. My great-grandfather had a pot of money, but it all went.'

'Racing?'

'A good bit, I've no doubt. A rare 'ard liver, cock-fighting, 'unting, 'orse-racing from one year's end to the other. Then after 'im came my grandfather; he went to the law, and a sad mess he made of it—went stony-broke and left my father without a sixpence; that is why mother didn't want me to go into livery. The family 'ad been coming down for generations, and mother thought that I was born to restore it; and so I was, but not as she thought, by carrying parcels up and down the King's Road.'

Esther looked at William in silent admiration, and, feeling that he had secured an appreciative listener, he continued his monologue regarding the wealth and rank his family had formerly held, till a heavy dew forced them to their feet, and they followed the paths through the furze, stopping to listen to a nightingale in the coombe below.

'In that thorn tree over yonder—don't you see?' he said.

The coast began to light up soon after, and William pointed out Brighton, Portslade, Southwick, Shoreham, Lancing, and Worthing.

The sheep had been folded, and seeing them lying between the wattles, the greyness of this hill-side, and beyond them the massive moonlit landscape and the vague sea, Esther suddenly became aware, as she had never done before, of the exceeding beauty of the world. Looking up in William's face, she said:

'Oh, how beautiful!'

As they descended the drove-way their feet raised the chalk, and William said:

'This is bad for Silver Braid; we shall want some more rain in a day or two. Let's come for a walk round the farm,' he said suddenly. 'The farm belongs to the Gaffer, but he's let the Lodge to a young fellow called Johnson. He's the chap that Peggy used to go after—there was awful rows about that, and worse when he forestalled the Gaffer about Egmont.'

He turned from Johnson into the story of the chap who had jilted Miss Mary, and the various burlesque actresses at the Shoreham Gardens that Ginger had been after; and these stories, which she only half understood, conveyed a sense of liberation. She had never been happy before; and now it seemed that she could never be unhappy again, and while wondering how this great change had come about, she listened to William, who was showing her the pigeon-house with all the birds dozing on the tiles, a blue one here and there; they visited the workshop, the forge, and the old cottages where the bailiff and the shepherd lived; and everything was so wonderful that it seemed as if she had been asleep all the while and had only just awakened. They regained the high road soon after; the downs and sea came into sight, and Esther, her eyes fixed on the long marshlands of the foreshore, walked listening to William who had returned to his projects for his advancement in life. At last they came to a stile leading into a cornfield by a little wood in which a nightingale was singing. It took some searching to find him, for he had not chosen any of the trees for his perch but a lowly hedge, which seemed strange to Esther but not to William, who said, 'He's not singing for us but for the little mate in her nest.' He struck a match, putting the music to flight, and all along the white road William continued his monologue, interrupted only by the necessity of puffing at his pipe.

'Mother says that if I had twopence worth of pride in me I wouldn't have consented to put on the livery; but what I says to mother is, "What's the use of having pride if you haven't money?" I tells her that I am rotten with pride, but my pride is to make money. I can't see that the man what's willing to remain poor all his life has any pride at all But, Lord! I have argued with mother till I'm sick; she can see nothing farther than the livery; that's what women are—they are that short-sighted. A lot of good it would have done me to carry parcels all my life, and, when I could do four mile an hour no more, to be turned out to die in the ditch and be buried by the parish. "Not good enough," says I. "If that's your pride, mother, you may put it in your pipe and smoke it, and as you 'aven't got a pipe, perhaps behind the oven will do as well"—that's what I said to her. I saw well enough there was nothing for me but service, and I means to stop here until I can get on three or four good things and then retire into a nice comfortable public-house and do my own betting.'

'You'd give up betting, then?'

'I'd give up backing 'orses, for what I'd like to do would be to get on to a dozen good things at long prices—half a dozen like Silver Braid would do it. For a thousand or fifteen hundred pounds I could have the "Red Lion," and just inside my own bar I could do a hundred-pound book on all the big races.'

She listened just as if she understood, for it mattered to her little what he talked so long as he was talking to her. She heard references to jockeys, publicans, weights, odds, and the certainty, if he had the 'Red Lion,' of being able to get all Joe Watkins's betting business away from him. William's allusions to the police, and the care that must be taken not to bet with any one who has not been properly introduced, frightened her; but her fears died in the sensation of his arm about her waist, and the music that the striking of a match had put to flight began in her heart, and it rose to its height when his face bent over hers.

# CHAPTER VII

THE Barfield reckoning was that they had a stone in hand. Mr. Leopold said that Bayleaf at seven stone would be backed to win a million of money, and Silver Braid, who had been tried again with Bayleaf, and with the same result as before, had been let off with only six stone.

More rain had fallen, the hay crop was spoilt, and the prospects of the wheat harvest were jeopardized, but what did a few bushels of wheat matter? Another pound of muscle was worth all the corn that could be grown between here and Henfield. Let the rain come down, let every ear of wheat be destroyed, so long as those delicate fore-legs remained sound. These were the ethics at Woodview, and within the last few days they were accepted by the little town and not a few of the farmers, grown tired of seeing their crops rotting on the hill-sides. The fever of the gamble was in eruption, breaking out in unexpected places—the station-master, the porters, the flymen, all had their bit on, and notwithstanding the enormous favouritism of two other horses in the race—Prisoner and Stoke Newington—Silver Braid was creeping up in the betting, for reports of trials won had reached Brighton, and with the result that not more than five-and-twenty to one could now be obtained.

An alarming piece of news it was that the Demon had gone up several pounds in weight, and the strictest investigation was made as to when and how he had obtained the food required to produce such a mass of adipose tissue. The Gaffer had the boy upstairs and handed him a huge dose of salts, keeping his eye upon him till he had swallowed every drop; and, when the effects of the medicine had worn off, he was sent for a walk to Portslade in two large over-coats, accompanied by William to make the running. On his return a couple of feather beds were ready, Mr. Leopold and Mr. Swindles laid him between them, and when he began to cease sweating Mr. Leopold made him a cup of hot tea.

'That 's the way the Gaffer used to get the flesh off in the old days when he rode the winner at Liverpool.'

'It 's the Demon's own fault,' said Mr. Swindles; 'if he hadn't been so greedy he wouldn't have had to sweat, and we should 'ave been spared a deal of bother and anxiety.'

'Greedy!' murmured the little boy, in whom the warm tea had induced a new sweat; 'I haven't had what you might call a dinner for the last three months. I think I 'll chuck the whole thing.'

'Not until this race is over,' said Mr. Swindles. 'Supposing I was to pass the warming-pan down these 'ere sheets. What do you say, Mr. Leopold? They are beginning to feel a bit cold.'

'Cold! I 'ope you 'll never go to a 'otter place. For God's sake, Mr. Leopold, don't let him come near me with the warming-pan, or else he 'll melt the little flesh that 's left off me.'

'You 'ad better not make such a fuss,' said Mr. Leopold; 'if you don't do what you are told, you 'll have to take salts again and go for another walk with William.'

'If we don't warm up them sheets 'e 'll dry up,' said Mr. Swindles.

'No, I won't; I 'm teeming.'

'Be a good boy, and you shall have a nice cut of mutton when you get up,' said Mr. Leopold.

'How much? Two slices?'

'Well, you see, we can't promise; it all depends on how much has come off, and 'aving once got it hoff, we don't want to put it on again.'

'I never did 'ear such rot,' said Swindles. 'In my time a boy's feelings weren't considered—one did what one considered good for them,' and while Mr. Swindles raised the bedclothes, Mr. Leopold strove to engage the Demon's thoughts with compliments regarding his horsemanship in the City and Sub.

'Oh, Mr. Swindles, you are burning me.'

'For 'eaven's sake don't let him start out from under the bedclothes like that! Can't yer 'old him? Burning you! I never even touched you with it; it was the sheet that you felt.'

'Then the sheet is as 'ot as the bloody fire. Will yer leave off?'

'What! a Demon like you afraid of a little touch of 'eat; wouldn't 'ave believed it unless I 'ad 'eard it with my own ears,' said Mr. Leopold. 'Come, now, do yer want to ride the crack at Goodwood or do yer not? If you do, keep quiet, and let us finish taking off the last couple of pounds.'

'It is the last couple of pounds that takes it out of you; the first lot comes off jest like butter,' said the boy, rolling out of the way of the pan. 'I know what it will be; I shall be so weak that I shall just ride a stinking bad race.'

Mr. Leopold and Mr. Swindles exchanged glances. It was clear that they thought there was something in the last words of the fainting Demon, and the pan was withdrawn. But when the boy was put into the scale again it was found that he was not yet nearly the right weight, and the Gaffer ordered another effort to be made. The Demon pleaded sore feet, but he was sent off all the same to Portslade in charge of William.

As the last pounds came off the Demon's little carcass Mr. Leopold's face resumed a more tranquil expression, and it began to be whispered that instead of hedging any part of his money he would stand it all out, and one day a market gardener brought up word that he had seen Mr. Leopold going into Brighton.

'Old Watkins isn't good enough for him, that 's about it. If Silver Braid wins, Woodview will see very little more of Mr. Leopold. He 'll be for buying one of them big houses on the sea road and keeping his own trap.'

## CHAPTER VIII

THE great day was now fast approaching. The Gaffer had promised to drive his folk in a drag to Goodwood. No more rain was required, the colt's legs remained sound, and three days of sunshine would make all the difference in their sum of happiness. In the kitchen Mrs. Latch and Esther had been busy for some time with chickens and pies and jellies, and in the passage there were cases packed with fruit and wine. The dressmaker had come from Worthing, and for several days the young ladies had not left her; and one fine morning, very early—about eight o'clock— the wheelers were backed into the drag that had come from Brighton. The yard resounded with the blaring of the horn. It was Ginger practising under his sister's window.

'You 'll be late! You 'll be late!'

With the exception of two young gentlemen, who came at the invitation of the young ladies, it was quite a family party. Miss Mary sat beside her father on the box, and looked very charming in white and blue. Peggy's black hair seemed blacker than ever under a white silk parasol, which she waved negligently above her as she stood up calling and talking to every one until the Gaffer told her angrily to sit down, as he was going to start. Then William and the coachman let go the leaders' heads, and running alongside swung themselves into their seats. At the same moment a glimpse was caught of Mr. Leopold's sallow profile amid the boxes and the mackintoshes that filled the inside of the coach.

'Oh, William did look that handsome in those beautiful new clothes! Every one said so—Sarah and Margaret and Miss Grover. I 'm sorry you didn't come out to see him.'

Mrs. Latch made no answer, and Esther remembered how she hated her son to wear livery, and thought that she had perhaps made a mistake in saying that Mrs. Latch should have come out to see him. 'Perhaps this will make her dislike me again,' thought the girl. Mrs. Latch moved about rapidly, and she opened and closed the oven; then, raising her eyes to the window and seeing that the other women were still standing in the yard and safely out of hearing, she said:

'Do you think that he has bet much on this race?'

'Oh, how should I know, Mrs. Latch? But the horse is certain to win.'

'Certain to win! I have heard that tale before; they are always certain to win. So they have gained you round to their way of thinking, have they?' said Mrs. Latch, straightening her back.

'I know very well indeed that it is not right to bet; but what can a girl do? If it hadn't been for William I never would have taken a number in that sweepstakes.'

'Do you like him very much, then?'

'He has been very kind to me—he was kind when——'

'Yes, I know, when I wasn't. You don't know all. I was much troubled at that time, and somehow I did not—— But there is no ill feeling? . . . I'll make it up to you—I'll teach you how to be a cook.'

'Oh, Mrs. Latch, I am sure——'

'Never mind that. When you went out to walk with him the other night, did he tell you that he had many bets on the race?'

'He talked about the race, like every one else, but he didn't tell me what bets he had on.'

'No, they never do do that. But you'll not tell him that I asked you?'

'No, Mrs. Latch, I promise.'

'It would do no good, he'd only be angry; it would only set him against me. I am afraid that nothing will stop him now. Once they gets a taste for it, it is like drink. I wish he was married, that might get him out of it. Some woman who would have an influence over him, some strong-minded woman. I thought once that you were strong-minded——'

At that moment Sarah and Grover entered the kitchen talking loudly. They asked Mrs. Latch how soon they could have dinner—the sooner the better, for the Saint had told them that they were free to go out for the day. They were to try to be back before eight, that was all. Ah! the Saint was a first-rate sort. She would get herself a bit of lunch in the dining-room. She did not want any one to attend on her. Mrs. Latch allowed Esther to hurry on the dinner, and by one o'clock they had all finished. Sarah and Margaret were going into Brighton to do some shopping, Grover was going to Worthing to spend the afternoon with the wife of one of the guards of the Brighton and South Coast Railway. Mrs. Latch went upstairs to lie down. So it grew lonelier and lonelier in the kitchen. Esther's sewing fell out of her hands, and she wondered what she should do. It seemed to her that she might sit by the sea, and soon after she was putting on her hat and stood thinking that she had not seen the sea since she watched tall ships coming into the harbour at Barnstaple, sail falling over sail, and tall ships floating out of the harbour, sail rising over sail, catching the breeze as they went aloft.

But few if any ships came into Shoreham Harbour. 'None in my time, anyway,' she said, as she crossed a suspension bridge, ornamented with straight-tailed lions. It took her over the weedy river, and, having crossed some pieces of rough grass, she climbed the shingle bank, and sat looking at a blank, sailless sea, lonely as a prison it seemed to her. But her thoughts reverting to William suddenly she fell to thinking of the happy evening when she saw him coming through the hunting gate, and they walked together over the downs; and she remembered the moment when, with his arm about her, he explained that if the horse won she'd take seven shillings out of the sweepstakes, for she knew then that William did not care about Sarah, and, happy in this belief, she lay on the shingle, her day-dream becoming softer and more delicate as it rounded into summer sleep. . . . Her eyes opened, and she returned to consciousness with difficulty, unable to connect herself with the sea and the shingle beach on which she was lying. At last she remembered. Ah, yes, the others had gone to Goodwood, that's how it was. And unable to think further she lay dreamily watching flights of clouds till a footfall roused her.

'Good evening, Mrs. Randal,' said Esther, glad to find someone to speak to. 'I've been asleep.'

'Good evening, miss. You're from Woodview, I think?'

'Yes, I'm the kitchenmaid. They've gone to the races; there was nothing to do, so I came down here.'

Mrs. Randal's lips moved as if she were going to say something.

'I think that it must be getting near tea-time,' she said at last; 'I must be going. You might come in and have a cup of tea with me, if you're not in a hurry back to Woodview.'

Esther said she'd be glad of a cup of tea, and in silence the two women crossed the meadows that lay between the shingle bank and the river, seeing trains passing all the while over the spider-legged bridge.

'It is all over now,' Mrs. Randal said, as she unlocked the cottage door. 'The people in those trains know well enough which has won.'

'Yes, I suppose they know, and somehow I feel as if I knew too. I feel as if Silver Braid had won.'

'I 've heard others say that before. Won't you come in?' And Esther entered the leanest house she had ever been in. Everything looked as if it had been scraped, and the spare furniture expressed a meagre, lonely life. Mrs. Randal dropped a plate as she laid the table, and stood pathetically looking at the pieces, and when Esther asked for a teaspoon she gave way utterly.

'I haven't one to give you; I had forgotten that they were gone. I should have remembered and not asked you to tea.'

'It don't matter, Mrs. Randal; I can stir up my tea with anything—a knitting-needle will do very well.'

'I should have remembered and not asked you back to tea; but I was so miserable, and it is so lonely sitting in this house, that I could stand it no longer. And talking to you saved me from thinking, and I didn't want to think until this race was over. If Silver Braid is beaten we are ruined. Indeed, I don't know what will become of us. For fifteen years I have borne up; I have lived on little at the best of times, and very often have gone without; but that is nothing compared to the anxiety—to see him come in with a white face, to see him drop into a chair and hear him say, "Beaten a head on the post," or, "Broke down, else he would have won in a canter." I have always tried to be a good wife and tried to cheer him up, and to do the best when he said, "I have lost half a year's wages, I don't know how we shall pull through." I have stood ten thousand times more than

I can tell you. The sufferings of a gambler's wife cannot be told. Tell me what do you think my feelings must have been when one night I heard him calling me out of my sleep, when I heard him say, "I can't die, Annie, without bidding you good-bye. I can only hope that you will be able to pull through, and I know that the Gaffer will do all he can for you, but he has been hit awful hard too. You mustn't think too badly of me, Annie, but I have had such a bad time that I couldn't put up with it any longer, and I thought the best thing I could do would be to go." That's just how he talked—nice words to hear your husband speak in your ear through the darkness! There was no time to send for the doctor, so I jumped out of bed, put the kettle on, made him drink glass after glass of salt and water and at last he brought up the laudanum.'

Esther listened to the tall melancholy woman, and remembered the little man whom she saw every day so orderly, so precise, so sedate, so methodical, into whose life she thought no faintest emotion had ever entered—and this was the truth.

'So long as I only had myself to think of I didn't mind; but now there are the children growing up. He should think of them. Heaven only knows what will become of them. John is as kind a husband as ever was if it weren't for that one fault; but he can't resist having something on any more than a drunkard can resist the bar-room.'

'Winner, winner, winner of the Stewards' Cup!'

The women started to their feet, but when they got into the street the boy was far away; besides, neither had a penny to pay for the paper, and they wandered about the town hearing and seeing nothing, so nervous were they. At last Esther proposed to ask at the 'Red Lion' who had won. Mrs. Randal begged her to refrain, urging that she was unable to bear the tidings should it be evil.

'Silver Braid,' the barman answered. The girl rushed through the doors. 'It's all right, it's all right; he has won!'

Soon after the little children in the lane were calling forth 'Silver Braid won!' And overcome by the excitement Esther walked along the sea road to meet the drag. She walked on and on until the sound of the horn came through the crimson evening and she saw the leaders trotting in a cloud of dust. Ginger was driving, and he shouted to her, 'He won!' The Gaffer waved the horn and shouted, 'He won!' Peggy waved her broken parasol and shouted, 'He won!' Esther looked at William. He leaned over the back seat and shouted, 'He won!' She had forgotten all about late dinner. What would Mrs. Latch say? On such a day as this she would say nothing.

## CHAPTER IX

NEARLY everything came down untouched. The Barfields had been eating and drinking almost all day on the course, and Esther had finished washing up before nine. But if little was eaten upstairs, plenty was eaten downstairs; the mutton was finished in a trice, and Mrs. Latch had to fetch from the larder what remained of a beefsteak pudding. Even then they were not satisfied, and fine inroads were made into a new piece of cheese. Beer, according to orders, was served without limit, and four bottles of port were sent down so that the health of the horse might be adequately drunk.

While assuaging their hunger the men had exchanged many remarks regarding the Demon's bad ending, how nearly he had thrown the race away; and the meal being now over, and there being nothing to do but to sit and talk, Mr. Leopold, encouraged by William, entered on an elaborate and technical account of the race. The women listened, playing with a rind of cheese, glancing at the cheese itself, wondering if they could manage another slice, and the men sipping their port wine, puffing at their pipes, William listening most greedily, enjoying each sporting term, and reminding Mr. Leopold of some detail ingeniously whenever he seemed disposed to shorten his narrative. The criticism of the Demon's horsemanship took a long while, for by a variety of suggestive remarks William led Mr. Leopold into reminiscences of the skill of certain famous jockeys in the first half of the century. These digressions wearied Sarah and Grover, and their thoughts wandered to the dresses that had been worn that day, and the lady's maid remembered she would hear all that interested her that night in the young ladies' rooms. At last, losing all patience, Sarah declared that she didn't care what Chifney had said when he just managed to squeeze his horse's head in front in the last dozen yards, she wanted to know what the Demon had done to nearly lose the race— had he mistaken the winning-post and pulled up? William looked at her contemptuously, and would have answered rudely, but at that moment Mr. Leopold began to tell the last instructions that the Gaffer had given the Demon. The orders were that the Demon should go right up to the leaders before they reached the half-mile and remain there. Of course, if he found that he was a stone or more in hand, as the Gaffer expected, he might come away pretty well as he liked, for the greatest danger was that the horse might get shut out or might show temper and turn it up.

'Well,' said Mr. Leopold, 'there were two false starts, and Silver Braid must have galloped a couple of 'undred yards afore the Demon could stop him. There wasn't twopenny worth of strength in him—pulling off those three or four pounds pretty well finished him. He'll never be able to ride that weight again. He said afore starting that he felt weak; you took him along too smartly from Port-slade the last time you went there.'

'When he went by himself he'd stop playing marbles with the boys round the Southwick public-house.'

'If there had been another false start I think it would have been all up with us. The Gaffer was pale, and he stood there not taking his glasses from his eyes. There were over thirty of them, so you can imagine how hard it was to get them into line. However, at the third attempt they were got straight and away they came, a black line stretching right across the course. Presently the black cap and jacket came to the front, and not very long after a murmur went round, "Silver Braid wins." Never saw anything like it in all my life. He was three lengths a'ead, and the others were pulling off. "Damn the boy; he'll win by twenty lengths," said the Gaffer, without removing his glasses. But when within a few yards of the stand——'

At that moment the bell rang. Mr. Leopold said, 'There, they are wanting their tea; I must go and get it.'

'Drat their tea,' said Margaret; 'they can wait. Finish up; tell us how he won.'

Mr. Leopold looked round, and seeing every eye fixed on him he considered how much remained of the story, and with quickened speech continued, 'Well, approaching the stand, I noticed that Silver Braid was not going quite so fast, and at the very instant the Demon looked over his shoulder, and seeing he was losing ground he took up the whip. But the moment he struck him the horse swerved right across the course, right under the stand, running like a rat from underneath the whip. The Demon threw the whip across and caught him one across the nose, but seeing what was 'appening, the Tinman, who was on Bullfinch, sat down and began riding. I felt as if there was a lump of ice down my back,' and Mr. Leopold lowered his voice, and his face became grave as he recalled that perilous moment. 'I thought it was all over,' he said, 'and the Gaffer thought the same; I never saw a man go so deadly pale. It was all the work of a moment, but that moment was more than a year—at least, so it seemed to me. Well, about half-way up the rails the Tinman got level with the Demon. It was ten to one that Silver Braid would turn it up, or that the boy wouldn't 'ave the strength to ride but so close a finish as it was bound to be. I thought then of the way you used to take him along from Portslade, and I 'd have given something to 've put a pound or two of flesh into his thighs and arms. The Tinman was riding splendid, getting every ounce and something more out of Bullfinch. The Demon, too weak to do much, was sitting nearly quite still. It looked as if it was all up with us, but somehow Silver Braid took to galloping of his own accord, and 'aving such a mighty lot in 'and, he won on the post by a 'ead—a short 'ead.

'I never felt so queer in my life, and the Gaffer was no better; but I said to him, just afore the numbers went up, "It is all right, sir, he 's just done it," and when the right number went up I thought everything was on the dance, going for swim like. By golly, it was a near thing!' At the end of a long silence Mr. Leopold said, shaking himself out of his thoughts, 'Now I must go and get their tea.'

Esther sat at the end of the table; her cheek leaned on her hand. By turning her eyes she could see William; and when Sarah caught sight of these stealthy glances, a look of anger crossed her face; she called to William; she asked him when the sweepstakes money would be divided, startling him from a reverie of small bets. 'It can be divided at once,' he answered. 'There 's no reason why it shouldn't. There 's twelve of you. That 's right, isn't it?—Sarah, Margaret, Esther, Miss Grover, Mr. Leopold, myself, the four boys, and Swindles and Wall. Well, it was agreed that seven should go to the first, three to the second, and two to the third. No one got the third 'orse, so I suppose the two shillings that would have gone to him 'ad better be given to the first.'

'Given to the first! Why, that 's Esther! Why should she get it? What do you mean? No third! Wasn't Soap-bubble third?'

'Yes, Soap-bubble was third right enough, but he wasn't in the sweep.'

'And why wasn't he?'

'Because he wasn't among the eleven first favourites. We took them as they were quoted in the betting list published in the *Sportsman*.'

'How was it, then, that you put in Silver Braid?'

'Yer needn't get so angry, Sarah; no one 's cheating; it is all aboveboard. If you don't believe us, you 'd better accuse us straight out.'

'What I want to know is, why Silver Braid was included? —he wasn't among the eleven first favourites.'

'Oh, don't be so stupid, Sarah; you know that we agreed to make an exception in favour of our own 'orse—a nice sweep it would 'ave been if we 'adn't included Silver Braid.'

'And suppose,' she exclaimed, tightening her brows, 'that Soap-bubble had won, what would have become of our money?'

'It would have been returned—every one would have got his shilling back.'

'And now I am to get three shillings, and that little Methodist or Plymouth Brethren there, whatever you like to call her, is to get nine!' said Sarah, with a light of inspiration flashing through her beer-clouded mind. 'Why should the two shillings that would have gone to Soap-bubble, if any one 'ad drawn 'im, go to the first 'orse rather than to the second?'

William hesitated, unable for the moment to give a good reason why the extra two shillings should be given to Silver Braid; and Sarah, perceiving her advantage, accused him of wishing to favour Esther.

'Don't we know that you went out to walk with her, and that you stayed out till nearly eleven at night! That 's why you want all the money to go to her. You don't take us for a lot of fools, do you? Never in any place I ever was in before would such a thing be allowed—the footman going out with the kitchenmaid, and one of the Dissenting lot.'

'I am not going to have my religion insulted! How dare you?' And Esther started up from her place; but William was too quick for her. He grasped her arm.

'Never mind what Sarah says.'

'Never mind what I says! . . . A thing like that, who never was in a situation before; no doubt taken out of some 'ouse. Rescue work, I think they call it——'

'She shan't insult me—no, she shan't!' said Esther, tremulous with passion.

'A nice sort of person to insult!' said Sarah, her arms akimbo.

'Now look you here, Sarah Tucker,' said Mrs. Latch, starting from her seat, 'I 'm not going to see that girl aggravated, so that she may do what she shouldn't do, and give you an opportunity of going to the missis with tales about her. Come away, Esther, come with me. Let them go on betting if they will; I never saw no good come of it.'

'That 's all very fine, mother; but it must be settled, and we have to divide the money.'

'I don't want your money,' said Esther, sullenly; 'I wouldn't take it.'

'What blooming nonsense! You must take your money. Ah, here 's Mr. Leopold! he 'll decide it.'

Mr. Leopold said at once that the money that under other circumstances would have gone to the third horse must be divided between the first and second; but Sarah refused to accept this decision. Finally, it was proposed that the matter should be referred to the editor of the *Sportsman*; and, as Sarah still remained deaf to argument, Willia n offered her choice between the *Sportsman* and the *Sporting Life*.

'Look here,' said William, getting between the women; 'this evening isn't one for fighting; we have all won our little bit, and ought to be thankful. The only difference between you is two shillings, that were to have gone to the third horse if any one had drawn him. Mr. Leopold says it ought to be divided; you, Sarah, won't stand by his decision. We have offered to write to the *Sportsman*, and Esther has offered to give up her claim. Now, in the name of God, tell us what do you want?'

Sarah couldn't keep to the point, and the argument tangled, rattled on, and stood still. At last the speakers stared at each other, talked dry.

'Well, that 's how it is. Give me the money I 've won—them three shillings, my winnings, is all I 'm asking for.'

'Haven't I made it plain?'

'No, you haven't.'

'Oh, indeed! Well, good night, ladies. I have had enough of you for to-night; I am going to finish my smoke in the pantry. Don't scratch all your 'air out; leave enough for me to put into a locket.'

When the pantry door was shut, and the men had smoked some moments in silence, William said:

'Do you think he has any chance of winning the Chesterfield Cup?'

'He 'll win in a canter if he 'll only run straight. And if I was the Gaffer I think I 'd put up a bigger boy. He 'll 'ave to carry a seven-pound penalty, and Johnnie Scott could ride that weight.'

The likelihood that a horse will bolt with one jockey and run straight with another was illustrated with interesting reminiscences drawn from that remote past when Mr. Leopold was the Gaffer's private servant—before either of them had married—when life was composed entirely of horse-racing and prize-fighting. But cutting short his tale of how he met one day the Birmingham Chicken in a booth, and, not knowing who he was, offered to fight him, Mr. Leopold confessed he did not know how to act—he had a bet of fifty pounds to ten shillings, for the double event, and couldn't make up his mind if he should stand it out or lay some of it off. William thrilled with admiration. What a 'ead, and who 'd think it? that little 'ead hardly bigger than a coco-nut! What a brain there was inside! Fifty pounds to ten shillings; should he stand it out or hedge some of it? Who could tell better than Mr. Leopold? It would, of course, be a pity to break into the fifty. What did ten shillings matter? Mr. Leopold was a big enough man to stand the racket of it even if it didn't come back. William felt very proud of being consulted, for Mr. Leopold had never before been known to let any one know what he had on a race.

And next day they walked into Shoreham together.

The bar of the 'Red Lion' was full of people. Above the thronging crowd the voice of the barman and the customers were heard calling, 'Two glasses of Burton, glass of bitter, three of whisky cold.' There were railway porters, sailors, boatmen, shop-boys, and market gardeners. They had all won something, and had come for their winnings.

The bookmaker, an elderly man with white whiskers and a curving stomach, had just run in to wet his whistle. He walked back to his office with Mr. Leopold and William, a little corner shelved out of some outhouses into which you could walk from the street.

'Talk of favourites!' he said; 'I'd sooner pay over the three first favourites than this one—thirty, twenty to one starting price, and the whole town on to him; it's enough to break any man. Now, my men, what is it?' he said, turning to the railway porters.

'Just the trifle me and my mates 'av won over that 'ere 'orse.'

'What was it?'

'A shilling at five-and-twenty to one.'

'Look it out, Joey. Is it all right?'

'Yes, sir; yes, sir,' said the clerk.

And old Watkins slid his hand into his breeches pocket, and it came forth filled with gold and silver.

'Come, come, mates, we are bound to 'ave a bet on him for the Chesterfield—we can afford it now; what say yer, a shilling each?'

'Done for a shilling each,' said the under porter; 'finest 'orse in training. What price, Musser Watkins?'

'Ten to one.'

'Right, 'ere's my bob.'

The other porters gave their shillings; Watkins slid them back into his pocket, and called to Joey to book the bet.

'And, now, what is yours, Mr. Latch?'

William stated the various items. He had had a bet of ten shillings to one on one race and had lost; he had had half a crown on another and had lost; in a word, three-and-sixpence had to be subtracted from his winnings, which amounted to more than five pounds. A great sum for a footman, to be sure, and the world seemed to be his when he slipped four sovereigns and a handful of silver into his waistcoat pocket. Should he put a sovereign of his winnings on Silver Braid for the Chesterfield? Half a sovereign was enough! The danger of risking a sovereign —a whole sovereign—frightened him.

'Now, Mr. Latch,' said old Watkins, 'if you want to back anything, make up your mind; there are a good many besides yourself who have business with me.'

William hesitated, and then said he'd take ten half-sovereigns to one against Silver Braid.

'Ten half-sovereigns to one?' said old Watkins.

William murmured 'Yes,' and Joey booked the bet.

Mr. Leopold's business demanded more consideration. The fat betting man and the scarecrow little butler walked aside and talked, both apparently indifferent to the impatience of a number of small customers; sometimes Joey called in his shrill cracked voice if he might lay ten half-crowns to one, or five shillings to one, as the case might be. Watkins would then raise his eyes from Mr. Leopold's face and nod or shake his head, or perhaps would sign with his fingers what odds he was prepared to lay. With no one else would Watkins talk so lengthily, showing so much deference. Mr. Leopold had the knack of investing all he did with an air of mystery, and the deepest interest was evinced in this conversation. At last, as if dismissing matters of first importance, the two men approached William, and he heard Watkins pressing Mr. Leopold to lay off some of that fifty pounds.

'I'll take twelve to one—twenty-four pounds to two. Shall I book it?'

Mr. Leopold shook his head, and William, much impressed, congratulated himself on his courage in taking the ten half-sovereigns to one. For if there was a man in this world that knew a thing or two, that man was Mr. Leopold. He had been talking to the Gaffer that morning, and if it hadn't been all right he would have laid off some of the money.

Next day one of the Gaffer's two-year-olds won a race, and the day after Silver Braid won the Chesterfield Cup.

The second victory of Silver Braid nearly ruined old Watkins. He declared that he had never been so hard hit; but as he did not ask for time and continued to draw notes and gold and silver in handfuls from his capacious pockets, his lamentations only served to stimulate the happiness of the fortunate backers, and, listening to the sweet note of self, ringing in their hearts, they returned to the public-house to drink the health of the horse.

So the flood of gold continued to roll into the little town, decrepit and colourless by its high shingle beach and long reaches of muddy river. The dear gold jingled merrily in the pockets, quickening the steps, lightening the heart, curling lips with smiles, opening lips with laughter. The dear gold came falling softly, sweetly as rain, soothing the hard lives of working folk. Lives pressed with toil lifted up and began to dream again. The dear gold was like an opiate; it wiped away memories of hardship and sorrow, it showed life in a lighter and merrier guise, and the folk laughed at their fears for the morrow and wondered how they could have thought life so hard and relentless. The dear gold was pleasing as a bird on the branch, as a flower on the stem; the tune it sang was sweet, the colour it flaunted was bright.

The trade of former days had never brought the excitement and the fortune that this horse's hoofs had done. The dust they had thrown up had fallen a happy, golden shower upon Shoreham. In every corner and crevice of life the glitter appeared. That fine red dress on the builder's wife, and the feathers that the girls flaunt at their sweethearts, the loud trousers on the young man's legs, the cigar in his mouth—all is Goodwood gold. It glitters in that girl's ears and on this girl's finger.

It was said that the town of Shoreham had won two thousand pounds on the race; it was said that Mr. Leopold had won two hundred; it was said that William Latch had won fifty; it was said that Wall, the coachman, had won five-and-twenty; it was said that the Gaffer had won forty thousand pounds, and for ten miles around nothing was talked of but the wealth of the Barfields. The county came to call, and some of the best people walked up and down the lawn with the Gaffer, listening to his slightest word. A golden prosperity shone upon the yellow Italian house. At every hour carriages passed under its elm trees and swept round the evergreen oaks. Rumour said that large alterations were going to be made, so that larger and grander entertainments might be given; an Italian garden was spoken of, balustrades and terraces, stables were in course of construction; many more racehorses were bought; they arrived daily, and the slender creatures, their dark eyes glancing out of the sight holes in their cloth hoods, walked up from the station followed by an admiring and commenting crowd. Drink and expensive living, dancing and singing upstairs and downstairs, and the jollifications culminated in a servants' ball given at the Shoreham Gardens. All the Woodview servants, excepting Mrs Latch, were there; likewise all the servants from Mr. Northcote's and those from Sir George Preston's—two leading county families. A great number of servants had come from West Brighton, and Lancing, and Worthing—altogether between two and three hundred. 'Evening dress is indispensable' was printed on the cards. The butlers, footmen, cooks, ladies' maids, housemaids, and housekeepers hoped by this notification to keep the ball select. But the restriction seemed to condemn Esther to play again the part of Cinderella.

## CHAPTER X

A GROUP of men turned from the circular buffet when Esther entered. Miss Mary had given her a white muslin dress, a square-cut bodice with sleeves reaching to the elbows, and a blue sash tied round the waist. The remarks as she passed were, 'A nice, pretty girl.' William was waiting, and she went away with him on the hop of a vigorous polka.

Many of the dancers had gone to get cool in the gardens, but a few couples had begun to whirl, the women borne along by force, the men poising their legs into curious geometrical positions.

Mr. Leopold was very busy dragging men away from the circular buffet—they must dance whether they knew how or not. 'The Gaffer has told me partic'lar to see that the "gals" all had partners, and just look down that 'ere room; 'alf of that lot 'aven't been on their legs yet. 'Ere 's a partner for you,' and the butler pulled a young game-keeper towards a young girl who had just arrived. She entered slowly, her hands clasped across her bosom, her eyes fixed on the ground, and the strangeness of the spectacle caused Mr. Leopold to pause. It was whispered that she had never worn a low dress before, and Grover came to the rescue of her modesty with a pocket-handkerchief.

But it had been found impossible to restrict the ball to those who possessed or could obtain an evening suit, and plenty of check trousers and red neckties were hopping about. Among the villagers many a touch suggested costume. A young girl had borrowed her grandmother's wedding dress, and a young man wore a canary-coloured waistcoat and a blue coast-guardsman's coat of old time. These touches of fancy and personal taste divided the villagers from the household servants. The butlers seemed on the watch for side dishes, and the valets suggested hairbrushes and hot water. Cooks trailed black silk dresses adorned with wide collars, and fastened with gold brooches containing portraits of their late husbands; and the fine shirt-fronts set off with rich pearls, the lavender-gloved hands, the delicate faces, expressive of ease and leisure, made Ginger's two friends—young Mr. Preston and young Mr. Northcote — noticeable among this menial, worka-day crowd. Ginger loved the upper circles, and now he romped the polka in the most approved London fashion, his elbows advanced like a yacht's bowsprit, and, his coat-tails flying, he dashed through a group of tradespeople who were bobbing up and down, hardly advancing at all.

Esther was now being spoken of as the belle of the ball; she had danced with young Mr. Preston and his friends, and seemed to be enjoying herself, but was now sitting alone, so Grover called her and asked her why she was not dancing.

William came for the next polka, 'just to show there is no ill feeling,' he said, and repeated his request half a dozen times. At last she said:

'You 've spoilt all my pleasure in the dancing.'

'I 'm sorry if I 've done that, Esther. I was jealous, that 's all.'

'Jealous! What was you jealous for? What do it matter what people think, so long as I know I haven't done no wrong?'

But she did not refuse to walk in the garden, where the night was warm, even oppressive, and the moon hung among the trees with strange markings on its yellow disk that momentarily allured the thoughts of the revellers. 'You must see the arbours and ruins,' William said, and he showed her the theatre and explained its purpose. She listened, without troubling to understand. Could she believe that she was not dreaming when they stood on the borders of a beautiful lake full of the shadows of tall trees, and crossed by a wooden bridge at the narrowest end?

'How still the water is; and the stars, they are lovely!'

'You should see the gardens about three o'clock on Saturday afternoons, when the excursion comes in from Brighton,' he answered, and they walked on a little farther, and Esther said, 'What 's these places? Ain't they dark?'

'These are arbours, where we 'as shrimps and tea. I 'll take you next Saturday, if you 'll come.'

A noisy band of young men, followed by three or four girls, ran across the bridge, and they stopped suddenly to argue on which side the boat was to be found. Some chose the left, some the right; those who went to the right sent up a yell of triumph, and from the boat addressed remarks to their companions, and then they admired the moon and stars. A song was demanded, and at the end of the second verse William threw his arm round Esther.

'Oh, Esther, I do love you.'

She looked at him, her grey eyes fixed in a long interrogation.

'I wonder if that is true. What is there to love in me?'

He squeezed her tightly, and continued his protestations. 'I do, I do, I do love you, Esther.'

She did not answer, and they walked slowly on. A holly bush threw a black shadow on the gravel path, and a moment after the ornamental tin roof of the dancing-room appeared between the trees.

Even in their short absence a change had come upon the ball. About the circular buffet numbers of men called for drinks, and talked loudly of horse-racing. Many were away at supper, and those that remained were amusing themselves in a desultory fashion. A tall, lean woman, dressed like Sarah in white muslin, wearing amber beads round her neck, was dancing the lancers with the Demon, and every one shook with laughter when she whirled the little fellow round or took him in her arms and carried him across. William wanted to dance, but Esther was hungry, and led him away to an adjoining building where cold beef, chicken, and beer might be had by the strong and adventurous. As they struggled through the crowd Esther spied three young gentlemen at the other end of the room.

'Now tell me, if they ask me, the young gents yonder, to dance, am I to look them straight in the face and say no?'

William considered a moment, and then he said, 'I think you had better dance with them if they asks you; if you refuse, Sarah will say it was I who put you up to it.'

'Let's have another bottle,' cried Ginger. 'Come, what do you say, Mr. Thomas?'

Mr. Thomas coughed, smiled, and said that Mr. Arthur wished to see him in the hands of the police. However, he promised to drink his share. Two more bottles were sent for, and, stimulated by the wine, the weights that would probably be assigned to certain horses in the autumn handicap were discussed. William was very proud of being admitted into such company, and he listened, a cigar which he did not like between his teeth, and a glass of champagne in his hand. Suddenly the conversation was interrupted by the cornet sounding the first phrase of a favourite waltz, and the tipsy and the sober hastened away.

Neither Esther nor William knew how to waltz, but they tumbled round the room, enjoying themselves immensely. In the polka and mazurka they got on better, and there were quadrilles and lancers in which the gentlemen joined, and all were gay and pleasant; even Sarah's usually sour face glowed with cordiality when they joined hands and raced round the men standing in the middle. In the chain they lost themselves as in a labyrinth and found their partners unexpectedly. But the dance of the evening was Sir Roger de Coverley, and Esther's usually sober little brain evaporated in the folly of frolicking up the room, then turning and frolicking backwards, getting into her place as best she could, and then starting again. It always appeared to be her turn, and it was so sweet to see her dear William, and such a strange excitement to run forward to meet young Mr. Preston, to curtsy to him, and then run away; and this over and over again.

'There's the dawn.'

Esther looked, and in the whitening doorways she saw the little jockey staggering about helplessly drunk. The smile died out of her eyes; she returned to her true self, to Mrs. Barfield and the Brethren. She felt that all this dancing, drinking, and kissing in the arbours was wicked. But Miss Mary had sent for her, and had told her that she would give her one of her dresses, and she had not known how to refuse Miss Mary. Then, if she had not gone, William—— Sounds of loud voices were heard in the garden, and the lean woman in the white muslin repeated some charge. Esther ran out to see what was happening, and there she witnessed a disgraceful scene. The lean woman in the muslin dress and the amber beads accused young Mr. Preston of something which he denied, and she heard William tell someone that he was mistaken, that he and his pals didn't want no rowing at this 'ere ball, and what was more they didn't mean to have none.

So her heart filled with love for her big William. What a fine fellow he was! and how handsome were his shoulders beside that round-shouldered little man whom he so easily pulled aside! and having crushed out the quarrel, he helped her on with her jacket, and, hanging on his arm, they returned home through the little town, Margaret following them with the railway porter; Sarah came next with a faithful admirer, a man with a red beard, whom she had picked up at the ball; Grover waddled in the dim rear, embarrassed with the green silk, which she held high out of the dust of the road.

The barren downs—more tin-like than ever in the shadowless light of dawn—stretched across the sunrise from Lancing to Brighton, and Esther looked at the hills, examining the landscape intently, remembering the first time she saw it, and some vague association of colours—the likeness that the morning landscape bore to the evening landscape, or the wish to prolong the sweetness of these, the last moments of her happiness—impelled her to linger and to ask William if the woods and fields were not beautiful. The too familiar landscape awoke in William neither idea nor sensation; Esther interested him more, and, while she gazed dreamily on the hills he admired the white curve of her neck which showed beneath the unbuttoned jacket. She never looked prettier than she did that morning, standing on the dusty road, her white dress crumpled, the ends of the blue sash hanging beneath the black cloth jacket.

## CHAPTER XI

For days nothing was talked of but the ball—how this man had danced, the bad taste of this woman's dress, and the possibility of a marriage. The ball had brought amusement to all, to Esther it had brought happiness. Her happiness was now visible in her face and audible in her voice, and Sarah's ironical allusions to her inability to learn to read no longer annoyed her, no longer stirred her temper —her love seemed to induce forgiveness for all and love for everything.

In the evenings when their work was done Esther and her lover lingered about the farm buildings, listening to the rooks, seeing the lights die in the west; and in the summer darkness about nine she tripped by his side when he took the letters to post. The wheat stacks were thatching, and in the rickyard, in the carpenter's shop, and in the warm valleys, listening to the sheep bells tinkling, they often lay together talking of love and marriage, till one evening, putting his pipe aside, William threw his arm round her, whispering that she was his wife. The words were delicious in her fainting ears. She could not put him away, nor could she struggle with him, though she knew that her fate depended upon her resistance, and swooning away she awakened in pain, powerless to free herself. . . . Soon after thoughts betook themselves on their painful way, and the stars were shining when he followed her across the down, beseeching her to listen. But she fled along the grey road and up the stairs to her room. Margaret was in bed, and awakening a little asked her what had kept her out so late. She didn't answer, and hearing Margaret fall asleep she remembered the supper-table. Sarah, who had come in late, had sat down by her; William sat on the opposite side; Mrs. Latch was in her place, the jockeys were all together; Mr. Swindles, his snuff-box on the table; Margaret and Grover. Every one had drunk a great deal; and Mr. Leopold had gone to the beer cellar many times. She thought that she remembered feeling a little dizzy when William asked her to come for a stroll up the hill, and after passing through the hunting gate they had wandered into the loneliness of the hills. Over the folded sheep the rooks came home noisily through a deepening sky. So far she remembered, and she could not remember further; and all night lay staring into the darkness, and when Margaret called her in the morning she was pale and deathlike.

'Whatever is the matter? You do look ill.'

'I didn't sleep all last night. My head aches as if it would drop off. I don't feel as if I could go to work to-day.'

'That's the worst of being a servant. Well or ill, it makes no matter.' She turned from the glass, and holding her hair in her left hand, leaned her head so that she might pin it. 'You do look bad,' she remarked dryly.

Never had they been so late! Half-past seven, and the shutters still up! So Margaret said as they hurried downstairs, but Esther had no thought for anything but William. She had seen him cleaning boots in the pantry as they passed, and knew he was waiting till he heard the baize door which separated the back from the front of the house close. She heard him coming to meet her, but meeting his mother in the passage he mumbled some excuse, and retreated. As there were visitors in the house, he had a good deal to do that morning, and Esther kept close to Mrs. Latch; but at breakfast it suddenly became necessary that she should answer him, and Sarah saw that Esther and William were no longer friends.

'Well I never! Look at her! She sits there over her tea-cup as glum as a prayer-meeting.'

'What is it to you?' said William.

'What's it to me? I don't like an ugly face at the breakfast table, that's all.'

'I wouldn't be your looking-glass, then. Luckily there isn't one here.'

In the midst of an angry altercation, Esther walked out of the room. During dinner she hardly spoke at all. After dinner she went to her room, and did not come down until she thought William had gone out with the carriage. But she was too soon, he came running down the passage to meet her. He laid his hand supplicatingly on her arm.

'Don't touch me!' she said, and her eyes filled with dangerous light.

'Now, Esther! Come, don't lay it on too thick!'

'Go away. Don't speak to me!'

'Just listen one moment, that's all.'

'Go away. If you don't, I'll go straight to Mrs. Barfield.'

She passed into the kitchen and shut the door in his face. He had gone a trifle pale, and after lingering a few moments he hurried away to the stables, and Esther saw him spring on the box.

As it was frequent with Esther not to speak to any one with whom she had had a dispute for a week or fifteen days, her continued sulk excited little suspicion, and the cause of the quarrel was attributed to some trifle. Sarah said:

'Men are such fools. He is always begging of her to forgive him. Just look at him—he is still after her, following her into the wood-shed.'

She rarely answered him a yes or no, but would push past him, and if he forcibly barred the way she would say, 'Let me go by, will you? You are interfering with my work.' And if he still insisted, she spoke of appealing to Mrs. Barfield. And if her heart sometimes softened, and an insidious thought whispered that it did not matter since they were going to be married, instinct forced her to repel him; her instinct was that she could only win his respect by refusing forgiveness for a long while. The religion in which her soul moved and lived—the sternest Protestantism—strengthened and enforced the original convictions and the prejudices of her race; and the natural shame which she had first felt almost disappeared in the violence of her virtue. She even ceased to fear discovery. What did it matter who knew, since she knew? She opened her heart to God, and Christ looked down, but He seemed stern and unforgiving. Her Christ was the Christ of her forefathers; and He had not forgiven, because she could not forgive herself. Hers was the unpardonable sin, the sin which her race had elected to fight against, and she lay down weary and sullen at heart.

The days seemed to bring no change, and, wearied by her stubbornness, William said, 'Let her sulk,' and he went out with Sarah; and when Esther saw them go down the yard her heart said, 'Let him take her out, I don't want him.' For she knew it to be a trick to make her jealous, and that he should dare such a trick angered her still further against him, and when they met in the garden, where she had gone with some food for the cats, and he said, 'Forgive me, Esther, I only went out with Sarah because you drove me wild,' she closed her teeth and refused to answer. But he stood in her path, determined not to leave her. 'I am very fond of you, Esther, and I will marry you as soon as I have earned enough or won enough money to give you a comfortable 'ome.'

'You are a wicked man; I will never marry you.'

'I am very sorry, Esther. But I am not as bad as you think for. You let your temper get the better of you. So soon as I have got a bit of money together——'

'If you were a good man you would ask me to marry you now.'

'I will if you like, but the truth is that I have only three pounds in the world. I have been unlucky lately——'

'You think of nothing but that wicked betting. Come, let me pass; I'm not going to listen to a lot of lies.'

'After the Leger——'

'Let me pass. I will not speak to you.'

'But look here, Esther: marriage or no marriage, we can't go on in this way: they'll be guessing something shortly.'

'I shall leave Woodview.' She had hardly spoken the words when it seemed clear to her that she must leave, and the sooner the better. 'Come, let me pass. If Mrs. Barfield——'

An angry look passed over William's face, and he said:

'I want to act honest with you, and you won't let me. If ever there was a sulky pig! Sarah's quite right; you are just the sort that would make hell of a man's life.'

She did not answer, nor did she care what he said; her business was to make him respect her. She had vaguely felt from the beginning that this was her only hope, and now the sensation developed and defined itself into a thought, and she decided that she would not yield, but would continue to affirm her belief that he must acknowledge his sin, and then come and ask her to marry him. Above all things, Esther desired to see William repentant. Her natural piety, filling as it did her entire life, unconsciously made her deem repentance an essential condition of their happiness.   How could they be happy if he were not a God-fearing man?   And she was convinced that she could not marry him until he had asked forgiveness of the Lord.   But rays of passion pierced her stubborn nature, dissolving it, and her eyes sought William's, and her steps strayed from the kitchen when her ears told her he was in the passage.   At last her love went out freely to William, but when she longed to throw herself in his arms, saying, 'Yes, I love you; make me your wife,' she noticed, or thought she noticed, that he avoided her eyes, and she felt that thoughts of which she knew nothing had obtained a footing in his mind.

Her heart being intent on him, she was aware of much that escaped the ordinary eye, and she was the first to notice when the drawing-room bell rang, and Mr. Leopold rose, that William would say, 'My legs are the youngest, don't you stir.'   No one else, not even Sarah, thought William intended more than to keep in Mr. Leopold's good graces, but Esther, although unable to guess the truth, heard the still-tinkling bell ringing the knell of her hopes.   She noted, too, the time he remained upstairs, and asked herself anxiously what it was that detained him so long.   The weather had turned colder lately.   Could it be that a fire was wanted?   In the course of the afternoon, she heard from Margaret that Miss Mary and Mrs. Barfield had gone to Southwick to make a call, and on her way past the stables to the garden she learnt from one of the stable lads that the Gaffer and Ginger had ridden over in the morning to Fendon Fair, and had not yet returned.   So it must have been Peggy who rang the bell.   Peggy?   And she remembered something she had almost forgotten. The first Sunday, the first time she went to the library for family prayers, Peggy was sitting on the little green sofa, and as Esther passed across the room to her place she saw her cast a glance of admiration on William's tall figure, and the memory of that glance shot up like a flame, and all that night Esther saw the girl with the pale face and the coal-black hair looking at her William.

And next day she waited for the bell that was to call her lover from her.   The afternoon wore away in nervous apprehensions, and at three o'clock she began to hope she was mistaken; at ten minutes past the metal tongue tinkled and she heard the baize door close behind him. A moment after all was still in the corridor, and like one sunk to the knees in quicksands she felt the time had come for a decided effort. But what could she do? She could not follow him through the baize door and into the drawing-room. If she got there, what then? she might be mistaken. But no, there was something in it, her heart told her so, and she began to remember that he no longer sought her forgiveness; he seemed to avoid her. And now her temper and pride fell from her, and she lived conscious only of him, noting every sign, and intensely, all that related to him, divining all his thoughts, and meeting him in the passage when he least expected her.

'I'm always getting in your way,' she said, with a low, nervous laugh.

'No harm in that; we're fellow-servants; there must be give and take.'

They stood looking at each other, with an explanation on their lips; but at that moment the drawing-room bell rang above their heads, and William said, 'I must answer that bell.' And before she could say another word he had passed through the baize door.

Sarah remarked that William seemed to spend a great deal of his time in the drawing-room, and Esther started out of her moodiness, and, speaking instinctively, she said, 'I don't think much of ladies who go after their servants.'

Everybody looked up. Mrs. Latch laid her carving-knife on the meat and fixed her eyes on her son.

'Lady?' said Sarah; 'she's no lady! Her mother used to mop out the yard before she was "churched."'

'I can tell you what,' said William, 'you had better mind what you are a-saying of, for if any of your talk got wind upstairs you'd lose yer situation, and it might be some time before yer got another!'

'Lose my situation! and a good job, too. I shall always be able to suit mesel'; don't you fear about me. But if it comes to talking about situations, I can tell you that you are more likely to get the sack than I am.'

William hesitated, and, while he sought for a spiteful answer, Mr. Leopold advised that nothing more should be said, and his eyes went to the jockey-boys, who were exchanging grins; Sarah sulked; Mr. Swindles pursed up his mouth, and fell to thinking that it would be no easy matter to keep Miss Peggy out of the gossip in the 'Red Lion,' and that it was a dead cert. that in the next day or two she would be the talk of the town.

At four o'clock Esther saw Mrs. Barfield and the young ladies walk across the yard towards the garden, and as she had to go soon after to the wood-shed she got a peep of Peggy escaping through the wicket. 'Going back to the drawing-room,' Esther said, and she returned to the kitchen and stood waiting for the bell to ring. Nor had she to wait long. The bell tinkled a moment after, but so faintly that Esther said, 'She only just touched it; it is a signal; he was on the lookout for it; she didn't want any one else to hear.'

And then Esther remembered Peggy's fortune, some thousands of pounds. There was no hope for her. How could there be? Her poor little wages and her print dress! He would never look at her again! But oh! how cruel and wicked it was! How could one who had so much come to steal from one who had so little? Oh, it was very cruel and very wicked, and no good would come of it either to her or to him; of that she felt quite sure. For God always punished the wicked. She knew he did not love Peggy. It was sin and shame; and after his promises—after what had happened. Never would she have believed him to be so false. Then her thought turned to passionate hatred of the girl who was robbing her. He had gone through that baize door, and no doubt was sitting by Peggy in the new drawing-room. He had gone where she could not follow. He had gone where the grand folk lived in idleness, in the sinfulness of the world and the flesh, eating and gambling, thinking of nothing else, with servants to wait on them, obeying their orders and saving them from every trouble. She knew that these fine folk thought servants inferior beings. But they were all of the same flesh and blood. Peggy wore a fine dress, but she was no better; take off her dress and they were the same, woman to woman.

She pushed through the door and walked down the passage. A few steps brought her to the foot of a polished oak staircase, lit by a large window in coloured glass, on either side of which there were statues. The staircase sloped slowly to an imposing landing set out with columns

and blue vases and embroidered curtains. The girl saw
these things vaguely, and she was conscious of a profusion
of rugs, matting, and bright doors, and of her inability to
decide which door was the drawing-room door—the drawing-
room of which she had heard so much, and where even now,
amid gold furniture and flower-scented air, William listened
to the wicked woman who had tempted him away from her.
A door opened, William appeared, and seeing Esther he
seemed uncertain whether to draw back or come forward;
and then his face caught an expression of mixed fear and
anger, and coming rapidly towards her he said:

'What are you doing here?' Then changing his voice,
'This is against the rules of the 'ouse.'

'I want to see her.'

'Anything else? What do you want to say to her?
I won't have it, I tell you. What do you mean by spying
after me? That's your game, is it?'

'I want to speak to her.'

With averted face the young lady fled up the oak staircase, her handkerchief to her lips. Esther made a movement as if to follow, but William prevented her. She
turned and walked down the passage and entered the
kitchen. Her face was one white tint, her short, strong
arms hung tremblingly, and William saw that it would be
better to temporize.

'Now look here, Esther,' he said, 'you ought to be damned
thankful to me for having stopped you from making a
fool of yourself.'

Esther's eyelids quivered, and then her eyes dilated.

'Now, if Miss Margaret,' continued William, 'had——'

'Go away! go away! I am——' At that moment the
steel of a large, sharp-pointed knife lying on the table
caught her eye. She snatched it up, and seeing blood she
rushed at him.

William retreated from her, and Mrs. Latch, coming
suddenly in, caught her arm. Esther threw the knife; it
struck the wall, falling with a rattle on the meat screen.
She rushed to secure it, but her strength gave way, and she
fell back in a dead faint.

'What have you been doing to the girl?' said Mrs. Latch.

'Nothing, mother. We had a few words, that was all.
She said I shouldn't go out with Sarah.'

'That is not true. I can read the lie in your face; a girl doesn't take up a knife unless a man wellnigh drives her mad.'

'That's right; always side against your son! If you don't believe me, get what you can out of her yourself.'

Mrs. Latch saw him pass down the yard towards the stables, and when Esther opened her eyes she looked at Mrs. Latch questioningly, unable to understand why the old woman was standing by her.

'Are you better now, dear?'

'Yes, but—but what——' Then remembrance struggled back. 'Is he gone? Did I strike him? I remember that I——'

'You didn't hurt him.'

'I don't want to see him again. Far better not. I was mad. I didn't know what I was doing.'

'You will tell me about it another time, dear.'

'Where is he? tell me that; I must know.'

'Gone to the stables, I think; but you must not go after him—you'll see him to-morrow.'

'I do not want to go after him; but he isn't hurt? That's what I want to know.'

'No, he isn't hurt. You're getting stronger. Lean on me. You'll begin to feel better when you are in bed. I'll bring you up your tea.'

'Yes, I shall be all right presently. But how'll you manage to get the dinner?'

'Don't you worry about that; you go upstairs and lie down.'

A desolate hope floated over the surface of her brain that William might be brought back to her.

In the evening the kitchen was full of people: Margaret, Sarah, and Grover were there, and she heard that immediately after lunch Mr. Leopold had been sent for, and the Gaffer had instructed him to pay William a month's wages, and see that he left the house that very instant. Sarah, Margaret, and Grover watched Esther's face and were surprised at her indifference. She even seemed pleased. She was pleased: nothing better could have happened. William was now separated from her rival, and released from her bad influence he would return to his real love. At the first sign she would go to him, she would forgive him. But a little later, when the dishes came down from the dining-room, it was whispered that Peggy was not there.

Later in the evening, when the servants were going to bed, it became known that she had taken the six o'clock to Brighton. Esther turned from the foot of the stair with a wild look. Margaret caught her.

'It's no use, dear; you can do nothing to-night.'

'I can walk to Brighton.'

'No you can't; you don't know the way, and even if you did you don't know where they are.'

Neither Sarah nor Grover made any remark, and in silence the servants went to their rooms. Margaret closed the door, and turned to look at Esther, who had fallen on the chair, her eyes fixed in vacancy.

'I know what it is; I was the same when Jim Story got the sack. It seems as if you couldn't live through it, and yet you do somehow.'

'I wonder if they'll marry.'

'Most likely. She has a lot of money.'

Two days after a cab stood in the yard in front of the kitchen window. Peggy's luggage was piled upon it— two large, handsome basket boxes with the initials painted on them: and, kneeling on the box-seat, the coachman leaned over the roof making room for another—a small box covered with red cowhide and tied with a rope. And the little box in its poor simplicity brought William back to Esther, whelming her for a moment in so acute a sense of her loss that she had to leave the kitchen. She went into the scullery, drew the door after her, sat down, and hid her face in her apron. A stifled sob or two, and then she recovered her habitual gravity of expression, and continued her work as if nothing had happened.

## CHAPTER XII

'THEY are just crazy about it upstairs. Ginger and the Gaffer are the worst. They say they had better sell the place and build another house somewhere else. None of the county people will call on them now—and just as they were beginning to get on so well! Miss Mary, too, is terrible cut up about it; she says it will interfere with her prospects, and that Ginger has nothing to do now but to marry the kitchenmaid to complete the ruin of the Barfields.'

'Miss Mary is far too kind to say anything to wound another's feelings. It was only a nasty old deceitful thing like yourself who could think of such a thing.'

'Eh, you got it there, my lady,' said Sarah, who had had a difference with Grover, and was anxious to avenge it.

Grover looked at Sarah in astonishment, and her look clearly said, 'Is every one going to side with that little kitchenmaid?'

Then, to flatter Mrs. Latch, Sarah spoke of the position the Latches had held three generations ago; the Barfields were then nobodies; they had nothing even now but their money, and that had come out of a livery stable. 'And it shows, too; just compare Ginger with young Preston or young Northcote. Any one could tell the difference.'

Esther listened with an unmoved face and a heavy ache in her heart. She had now not an enemy nor yet an opponent; the cause of rivalry and jealousy being removed, all were sorry for her. They recognized that she had suffered and was suffering, and, seeing none but friends about her, she was led to think how happy she might have been in this beautiful house if it had not been for William. She loved her work, for she was working for those she loved. She could imagine no life happier than hers might have been. But she had sinned, and the Lord had punished her for sin, and she must bear her punishment uncomplainingly, giving Him thanks that He had imposed no heavier one upon her.

Such reflection was the substance of Esther's mind for

three months after William's departure; and in the afternoons, about three o'clock, when her work paused, Esther's
thoughts would congregate and settle on the great misfortune of her life—William's desertion.

It was one afternoon at the beginning of December;
Mrs. Latch had gone upstairs to lie down, and Esther had
drawn her chair towards the fire; a broken-down racehorse,
his legs bandaged from his knees to his fetlocks, had passed
up the yard; he was going for walking exercise on the downs,
and when the sound of his hoofs had died away Esther was
quite alone. She sat on her wooden chair facing the wide
kitchen window. She had advanced one foot on the iron
fender; her head leaned back, rested on her hand. She
did not think—her mind was lost in vague sensation of
William, and it was in this death of active memory that
something awoke within her, something that seemed to her
like a flutter of wings; her heart seemed to drop from its
socket, and she nearly fainted away, but recovering herself
she stood by the kitchen table, a deathlike pallor over her
face, with drops of sweat on her forehead. The truth was
borne in upon her; she foresaw the drama that awaited
her, from which nothing could free her, which she would
have to live through hour by hour. And it seemed so
dreadful that she thought her brain must give way. She
would have to leave Woodview. Oh, the shame of confession! Mrs. Barfield, who had been so good to her and
who thought so highly of her. Her father would not have
her at home; she would be homeless in London. No hope
of obtaining a situation. They would send her away
without a character, homeless in London, and every month
her position growing more desperate.

A sickly faintness crept through her. The flesh had
come to the relief of the spirit; and she sank upon her chair,
almost unconscious, sick, it seemed, to death, and she
rose from the chair wiping her forehead slowly with her
apron. She might be mistaken. And she hid her face in
her hands, and then, falling on her knees, her arms thrown
forward upon the table, she prayed for strength to walk
without flinching under any cross that He had thought
fit to lay upon her.

There was still the hope that she might be mistaken;
and this hope lasted for one week, for two, but at the end

of the third week it perished, and she abandoned herself
in prayer. She prayed for strength to endure with courage
what she now knew she must endure, and she prayed for
light to guide her in her present decision. Mrs. Barfield,
however much she might pity her, could not keep her once
she knew the truth, whereas none might know the truth
if she did not tell it. She might remain at Woodview
earning another quarter's wages; the first she had spent on
boots and clothes, the second she had just been paid.
If she stayed on for another quarter she would have eight
pounds, and with that money, and much less time to keep
herself, she might be able to pull through. But would she
be able to go three whole months without any one seeing
how big she was getting, till her next wages came due?
She must risk it.

She went about her work, leaving nothing undone, and
doing everything so well that no fault could be found, her
aim being to escape notice; and as she perceived no bodily
change in herself during the fifth month she began to think
she might risk another month. Another month passed,
and Esther was preparing for departure, when a whisper
went round, and before she could take steps to leave she
was told that Mrs. Barfield wished to see her in the library.
Esther turned a little pale, and the expression of her face
altered; it seemed to her impossible to go before Mrs.
Barfield and admit her shame. Margaret, who was standing near, and saw what was passing in her mind, said:

'Pull yourself together, Esther. You know the Saint—
she's not a bad sort. Like all the real good ones, she is
kind enough to the faults of others.'

'What's this? What's the matter with Esther?' said
Mrs. Latch, who had not yet heard of Esther's misfortune.

'I'll tell you presently, Mrs. Latch. Go, dear, get it
over.'

Esther hurried down the passage and passed through
the baize door without further thought. She had then but
to turn to the left and a few steps would bring her to the
library door. The room was already present in her mind.
She could see it. The dim light, the little green sofa, the
round table covered with books, the piano at the back,
the parrot in the corner, and the canaries in the window.
She knocked at the door. The well-known voice said,

'Come in.' She turned the handle, and found herself alone with her mistress. Mrs. Barfield laid down the book she was reading, and looked up. She did not look as angry as Esther had imagined, but her voice was harder than usual.

'Is this true, Esther?'

Esther hung down her head. She could not speak at first; then she said, 'Yes.'

'I thought you were a good girl, Esther.'

'So did I, ma'am.'

Mrs. Barfield looked at the girl quickly, hesitated a moment, and then said:

'And all this time—how long is it?'

'Nearly seven months, ma'am.'

'And all this time you were deceiving us.'

'I was three months gone before I knew it myself, ma'am.'

'Three months! Then for three months you have knelt every Sunday in prayer in this room, for twelve Sundays you sat by me learning to read, and you never said a word?'

A certain harshness in Mrs. Barfield's voice awakened a rebellious spirit in Esther, and a lowering expression gathered above her eyes. She said:

'Had I told you, you would have sent me away there and then. I had only a quarter's wages, and should have starved or gone and drowned myself.'

'I'm sorry to hear you speak like that, Esther.'

'It's trouble that makes me, ma'am, and I have had a great deal.'

'Why did you not confide in me? I have not shown myself cruel to you, have I?'

'No, indeed, ma'am. You are the best mistress a servant ever had, but——'

'But what?'

'Why, ma'am, it is this way. I hated being deceitful—indeed I did. But I can no longer think of myself. There is another to think for now.'

There was in Mrs. Barfield's look something akin to admiration, and she felt she had not been wholly wrong in her estimate of the girl's character. She said, and in a different intonation:

'Perhaps you were right, Esther. I couldn't have kept

you on, on account of the bad example to the younger servants. I might have helped you with money. But six months alone in London and in your condition! I am glad you didn't tell me, Esther; and as you say there is another to think of now: I hope you will never neglect your child, if God give it to you alive.'

'I hope not, ma'am; I shall try and do my best.'

'My poor girl! my poor girl! you do not know what trial is in store for you. A girl like you, and only twenty! Oh, it is a shame! May God give you courage to bear up in your adversity!'

'I know there is many a hard time before me, but I have prayed for strength, and God will give me strength, and I must not complain. My case is not so bad as many another; I have nearly eight pounds. I shall get on, ma'am—that is to say, if you will stand by me and not refuse me a character.'

'Can I give you a character? You were tempted, you were led into temptation. I ought to have watched over you better—mine is the responsibility. Tell me, it was not your fault.'

'It is always a woman's fault, ma'am. But he should not have deserted me as he did—that 's the only thing I reproach him with; the rest was my fault—I shouldn't have touched the second glass of ale. Besides, I was in love with him, and you know what that is. I thought no harm, and I let him kiss me. He used to take me out for walks on the hill and round the farm. He told me he loved me, and would make me his wife—that 's how it was. Afterwards he asked me to wait till after the Leger, and that riled me, and I knew then how wicked I had been. I would not go out with him or speak to him any more; and while our quarrel was going on Miss Peggy went after him, and that 's how I got left.'

At the mention of Peggy's name a cloud passed over Mrs. Barfield's face. 'You have been shamefully treated, my poor child. I knew nothing of all this. So he said he would marry you if he won his bet on the Leger? Oh, that betting! I know that nothing else is thought of here—upstairs and downstairs, the whole place is poisoned with it—and it is the fault of——' Mrs. Barfield walked hurriedly across the room, but when she turned the sight of Esther provoked her into speech. 'I have seen it all my life, nothing else, and I have seen nothing come of it but sin and sorrow. You are not the first victim. Ah, what ruin, what misery, what death!'

Mrs. Barfield covered her face with her hands, as if to shut out the memories that crowded upon her.

'I think, ma'am, if you will excuse my saying so, that a great deal of harm do come from this betting on racehorses. The day when you was all away at Goodwood when the horse won, I went down to see what the sea was like here; for I was brought up by the seaside, at Barnstaple. On the beach I met Mrs. Leopold—that is to say, Mrs. Randal, John's wife; she seemed to be in great trouble, she looked that melancholy, and for company's sake asked me to come home to tea with her. She was in that state of mind, ma'am, that she forgot the teaspoons were in pawn, and when she couldn't give me one she broke down, and told me what her troubles had been.'

'What did she tell you, Esther?'

'I hardly remember, ma'am, but it was all the same thing—ruin if the horse didn't win, and more betting if he did. But she said they never had been in such a fix as the day Silver Braid won. If he had been beaten they would have been thrown out on the street, and from what I have heard the best half of the town, too.'

'So that little man has suffered. I thought he was wiser than the rest. This house has been the ruin of the neighbourhood; we have dispensed vice instead of righteousness.' Walking towards the window, Mrs. Barfield continued to talk to herself. 'I have struggled against the evil all my life, and without result. How much more misery shall I see come of it?' Turning then to Esther, she said: 'Yes, the betting is an evil—one from which many have suffered; but the question is now about yourself, Esther. How much money have you?'

'I have about eight pounds, ma'am.'

'And how much do you reckon will see you through it?'

'I don't know, ma'am; I have no experience. I think father will let me stay at home if I can pay my way. I could manage easily on seven shillings a week. When my time comes I shall go to the hospital.'

While Esther spoke Mrs. Barfield reckoned that Esther

would need about ten pounds. Her train fare, two months'
board at seven shillings a week, the room she would have
to take near the hospital before her confinement, and to
which she would return with her baby—all these would
run to about four or five pounds. There would be baby's
clothes to buy. If she gave four pounds, Esther would
be able to manage. Mrs. Barfield went over to an old-
fashioned escritoire, and, pulling out some small drawers,
took from one some paper packages, which she unfolded.
'Now, my girl, look here. I'm going to give you four
pounds. Twelve should see you through your trouble.
You have been a good servant, Esther; I like you very
much, and am truly sorry to part with you. You will
write and tell me how you are getting on, and if one of these
days you want a place, and I have one to give you, I shall
be glad to take you back.'

If harshness deadened, she was easily moved by kindness,
and she longed to throw herself at her mistress's feet; but
her nature did not admit of such effusion, and she said, in
her blunt English way:

'You are far too good, ma'am. I do not deserve such
treatment—I know I don't.'

'Say no more, Esther. I hope that the Lord may give
you strength to bear your cross. Now go and pack up
your box. But, Esther, do you feel your sin? Can you
truly say honestly before God that you repent?'

'Yes, ma'am, I think I can say all that.'

'Then, Esther, come and kneel down and pray to God to
give you strength in the future to stand against temptation.'

Mrs. Barfield took Esther's hand, and they knelt down by
the round table, leaning their hands on its edge. And, in a
high, clear voice, Mrs. Barfield prayed aloud, Esther re-
peating the words after her:

'Dear Lord, Thou knowest all things—knowest how Thy
servant has strayed and has fallen into sin. But Thou hast
said there is more joy in heaven over one sinner that re-
penteth than over ninety and nine just men. Therefore,
Lord, kneeling here before Thee, we pray that this poor
girl, who repents of the evil she has done, may be
strengthened in Thy mercy to stand firm against temptation. Forgive her sin, even as Thou forgavest the woman
of Samaria. Give her strength to walk uprightly before

Thee, and give her strength to bear the pain and the suffering that lie before her.'

The women rose from their knees and stood looking at each other. Esther's eyes were full of tears. Without speaking she turned to go.

'One word more, Esther. You asked me just now for a character; I hesitated, but it seems to me now that it would be wrong to refuse. If I did you might never get a place, and then it would be impossible to say what might happen. I am not certain that I am doing right, but I know what it means to refuse to give a servant a character, and I can't take upon myself the responsibility.'

Mrs. Barfield wrote out a character for Esther, in which she described her as an honest, hard-working girl. She paused at the word 'reliable,' and wrote instead, 'I believe her to be at heart a thoroughly religious girl.'

Esther went upstairs to pack her box, and when she came down she found all the women in the kitchen; evidently they were waiting for her. Coming forward, Sarah said:

'I hope we shall part friends, Esther; any quarrels we may have had—— There's no ill feeling now, is there?'

'I bear no one any ill feeling. We have been friends these last months; indeed, every one has been very kind to me.' And Esther kissed Sarah on both cheeks.

'I'm sure we're all sorry to lose you,' said Margaret, pressing forward, 'and we hope you'll write and let us know how you are getting on.'

Margaret, who was a tender-hearted girl, began to cry, and, kissing Esther, she declared that she had never got on with a girl who slept in her room so well before. Esther shook hands with Grover, and then her eyes met Mrs. Latch's. The old woman took her in her arms.

'It breaks my heart to think that one belonging to me should have done you such a wrong—— But if you want for anything let me know, and you shall have it. You will want money; I have some here for you.'

'Thank you, thank you, but I have all I want. Mrs. Barfield has been very good to me.'

The babbling of so many voices drew Mr. Leopold from the pantry; he came with a glass of beer in his hand, and this suggested a toast to Sarah. 'Let's drink baby's health,' she said. 'Mr. Leopold won't refuse us the beer.'

The idea provoked some good-natured laughter, and Esther hid her face in her hands and tried to get away. But Margaret would not allow her. 'What nonsense!' she said. 'We don't think any the worse of you; why, that's an accident that might happen to any of us.'

'I hope not,' said Esther.

The jug of beer was finished; she was kissed and hugged again, some tears were shed, and Esther walked down the yard through the stables.

The avenue was full of wind and rain; the branches creaked dolefully overhead; and the drenched lane, and the bare fields fringed with white mist, were a landscape in keeping with the girl's soul. She had come to Woodview to escape from a home become unbearable, and was going back to it in circumstances a hundred times worse than those in which she had left it; all the grief and trouble that girls of her class have to bear gathered in her heart when she looked out of the railway-carriage window and saw for the last time the stiff plantations on the downs and the angles of the Italian house between the trees. She drew her handkerchief from her jacket to hide her tears from her fellow-travellers in the carriage.

## CHAPTER XIII

SHE had left her box in the cloak-room at Victoria, for she did not know if her father would have her at home. Her mother would tell her what she thought, but no one could say for certain what he would do. If she brought the box he might fling it after her into the street; better come without it, even if she had to go back through the wet to fetch it. At that moment another gust drove the rain violently over her, forcing it through her boots. The sky was a tint of ashen grey, and all the low brick buildings were veiled in vapour; the rough roadway was full of pools, and nothing was heard but the melancholy bell of the tramcar. She hesitated, not wishing to spend a penny unnecessarily, but remembering that a penny wise is often a pound foolish she called to the driver and climbed in. The car passed by the little brick street where the Saunders lived, and when Esther pushed the door open she could see into the kitchen and overheard the voices of the children. Mrs. Saunders was sweeping down the stairs, but at the sound of footsteps she ceased to bang the broom, and, stooping till her head looked over the banisters, she cried:

'Who is it?'

'Me, mother.'

'What! You, Esther?'

'Yes, mother.'

Mrs. Saunders hastened down, and, leaning the broom against the wall, she took her daughter in her arms and kissed her. 'Well, this is nice to see you again, after this long while. But you are looking a bit poorly, Esther.' Then her face changed expression. 'What has happened? Have you lost your situation?'

'Yes, mother.'

'Oh, I am that sorry, for we thought you was so 'appy there and liked your mistress above all those you 'ad ever met with. Did you lose your temper and answer her back? They is often trying, I know that, and your own temper— you was never very sure of it.'

'I 've no fault to find with my mistress; she is the kindest in the world — none better — and my temper — it wasn't that, mother——'

'My own darling, tell me——'

Esther paused. The children had ceased talking in the kitchen, and the front door was open. 'Come into the parlour. We can talk quietly there. When do you expect father home?'

'Not for the best part of a couple of hours yet.'

Mrs. Saunders waited until Esther had closed the front door. Then they went into the parlour and sat down side by side on the little horsehair sofa placed against the wall facing the window. The anxiety in their hearts betrayed itself on their faces.

'I had to leave, mother. I 'm seven months gone.'

'Oh, Esther, Esther, I can't believe it!'

'Yes, mother, it is quite true.'

She hurried through her story, and when her mother questioned her regarding details, she said:

'Mother, what does it matter? I don't care to talk about it more than I can help.'

Tears had begun to roll down Mrs. Saunders's cheeks, and when she wiped them away with the corner of her apron, Esther heard a sob.

'Don't cry, mother,' said Esther. 'I have been very wicked, I know, but God will be good to me. I always pray to Him, just as you taught me to do, and I dare say I shall get through my trouble somehow.'

'Your father will never let you stop 'ere; 'e 'll say, just as afore, that there be too many mouths to feed as it is.'

'I don't want him to keep me for nothing—I know well enough if I did that 'e 'd put me outside quick enough. But I can pay my way. I earned good money while I was with the Barfields, and though she did tell me I must go, Mrs. Barfield—the Saint they call her, and she is a saint if ever there was one—gave me four pounds to see me, as she said, through my trouble. I 've better than eleven pound. Don't cry, mother dear; crying won't do no good, and I want you to help me. So long as the money holds out I can get a lodging anywhere, but I 'd like to be near you; and father might be glad to let me have the parlour and my food for ten or eleven shillings a week—I could afford as much as that, and he never was the man to turn good money from his door. Do yer think he will?'

'I dunno, dearie; 'tis hard to say what 'e 'll do; he 's a 'ard man to live with. I 've 'ad a terrible time of it lately, and them babies allus coming. Ah, we poor women have more than our right to bear with!'

'Poor mother!' said Esther, and, taking her mother's hand in hers, she passed her arm round her, drew her closer, and kissed her. 'I know what he was; is he any worse now?'

'Well, I think he drinks more, and is even rougher. It was only the other day, just as I was attending to his dinner—it was a nice piece of steak, and it looked so nice that I cut off a weeny piece to taste. He sees me do it, and he cries out: "Now then, guts, what are you interfering with my dinner for?" I says: "I only cut off a tiny piece to taste." "Well, then, taste that," he says, and strikes me clean between the eyes. Ah, yes, lucky for you to be in service; you 've half forgot by now what we 've to put up with 'ere.'

'You was always too soft with him, mother; he never touched me since I dashed the hot water in his face.'

'Sometimes I thinks I can bear it no longer, Esther, and long to go and drown meself. Jenny and Julia—you remember little Julia; she 'as grown up such a big girl, and is getting on so well—they are both at work now in the kitchen. Johnnie gives us a deal of trouble; he can't tell a word of truth; father took off his strap the other day and beat him dreadful, but it ain't no use. If it wasn't for Jenny and Julia I don't think we should ever make both ends meet; but they works all day at the dogs, and at the warehouse their dogs is said to be neater and more lifelike than any other. Their poor fingers is worn away cramming the paper into the moulds; but they never complains, no more shouldn't I if he was a bit gentler and didn't take more than half of what he earns to the public-'ouse. I was glad you was away, Esther, for you allus was of an 'asty temper and couldn't 'ave borne it. I don't want to make my troubles seem worse than they be, but sometimes I think I will break up, 'special when I get to thinking what will become of us and all them children, money growing less and expenses increasing. I haven't told yer, but I dare say you have noticed that another one is coming. It is the children that breaks us poor women down altogether. Ah, well, yours be the hardest trouble, but you must put a brave face on it; we 'll do the best we can; none of us can say no more.'

Mrs. Saunders wiped her eyes with the corner of her apron; and without further words mother and daughter went into the kitchen—a long, low room, with one window looking on a small backyard, at the back of which was the coal-hole, the dust-bin, and a small outhouse. And at the long kitchen table, seated on a bench fastened to the wall, Jenny and Julia were at work making toy dogs, some no larger than your hand, others almost as big as a small poodle, finishing the last few that remained of the order they had received from their shop. · They were helped by three small children seated on the floor, who handed them the brown paper which was speedily pressed into iron moulds, pasted down and tucked in with strong dexterous fingers.

'Why, it is Esther!' said Jenny, the elder girl. 'And, lorks, ain't she grand!—quite the lady. Why, we hardly knowed yer.' And having kissed their sister circumspectly, they stood lost in contemplation till Esther took Harry, a fine little boy of four, up in her arms, and asked him if he remembered her.

'Naw, I don't think I do. Will oo put me down?'

'But you do, Lizzie?' she said, addressing a girl of seven, whose bright red hair shone like a lamp in the gathering twilight.

'Yes, you 're my big sister; you 've been away this year or more in service.'

'And you, Maggie, do you remember me too?'

Maggie at first seemed doubtful, but after a moment's reflection she nodded her head vigorously.

'Come, Esther, see how Julia is getting on,' said Mrs. Saunders; 'she makes her dogs nearly as fast as Jenny. She is still a bit careless in drawing the paper into the moulds. Well, just as I was speaking of it: 'ere 's a dog with one shoulder just 'arf the size of the other.'

'Oh, mother, I 'm sure nobody 'd never know the difference.'

'Wouldn't know the difference! Just look at the hanimal! Is it natural? Sich carelessness I never seed.'

'Esther, just look at Julia's dog,' cried Jenny, ''e 'asn't got no more than 'arf a shoulder. It's lucky mother saw it, for if the manager 'd seen it he 'd have found something wrong with I don't know 'ow many more, and docked us maybe a shilling or more on the week's work.'

Julia began to cry.

'Jenny is always down on me. She is jealous just because mother said I worked as fast as she did. If her work was overhauled——'

'There are all my dogs there on the right-hand side of the dresser—I always 'as the right for my dogs—and if you find one there with an uneven shoulder I 'll——'

'Jenny is so fat that she likes everything like 'erself; that's why she stuffs so much paper into her dogs.'

It was little Ethel speaking from her corner, and her explanation of the excellence of Jenny's dogs, given with stolid childish gravity in the interval of tearing a large sheet of brown paper, made them laugh. But in the midst of the laughter thought of her great trouble came upon Esther. Mrs. Saunders noticed this, and, to make an end of the merriment, she took Julia's dog and told her that it must be put into the mould again. She cut the skin away, and helped to force the stiff paper over the edge of the mould.

'Now,' she said, 'it is a dog; both shoulders is equal, and if it was a real dog he could walk.'

'Oh, bother!' cried Jenny, 'I shan't be able to finish my last dozen this evening. I 'ave no more buttons for the eyes, and the black pins that Julia is a-using of for her little one won't do for this size.'

'Won't they give yer any at the shop? I was counting on the money they would bring to finish the week with.'

'No, we can't get no buttons in the shop: that's 'ome work, they says; and even if they 'ad them they wouldn't let us put them in there. That's 'ome work, they says to everything; they 're a disagreeable lot.'

'But 'aven't you got sixpence, mother? and I 'll run and get them.'

'No, I 've run short.'

'But,' said Esther, 'I 'll give you sixpence to get your buttons with.'

'Yes, that's it; give us sixpence, and yer shall have it

back to-morrow if you are 'ere.   How long are yer up for?
If not, we 'll send it.'

'I 'm not going back just yet.'

'What, 'ave yer lost yer situation?'

'No, no,' said Mrs. Saunders, 'Esther ain't well—she
'as come up for 'er 'ealth; take the sixpence and run along.'

'May I go too?' said Julia.   'I 've been at work since
eight, and I 've only a few more dogs to do.'

'Yes, you may go with your sister.   Run along; don't
bother me any more, I 've got to get your father's supper.'

When Jenny and Julia had left, Esther and Mrs. Saunders
could talk freely, the other children being too young to
understand.

'There is times when 'e is well enough,' said Mrs.
Saunders, 'and others when 'e is that awful.   It is 'ard to
know 'ow to get 'im, but 'e is to be got if we only knew 'ow.
Sometimes 'tis most surprising how easy 'e do take things,
and at others—well, as about that piece of steak that I was
a-telling you of.   Should you catch him in that humour 'e 's
as like as not to take ye by the shoulder and put you out;
but if he be in a good humour 'e 's as like as not to say:
"Well, my gal, make yerself at 'ome."'

'He can but turn me out.   I 'll leave yer to speak to
'im, mother.'

'I 'll do my best, but I don't answer for nothing.   A nice
bit of supper do make a difference in 'im, and as ill luck will
'ave it, I 've nothing but a rasher, whereas if I only 'ad a
bit of steak 'e 'd brighten up the moment he clapt eyes on
it and become more cheerful.'

'But, mother, if you think it will make a difference I can
easily slip round to the butcher's and——'

'Yes; get half a pound, and when it 's nicely cooked and
inside him it 'll make all the difference.   That will please
him.   But I don't like to see you spending your money—
money that you 'll want badly.'

'It can't be helped, mother.   I shan't be above a minute
or two away, and I 'll bring back a pint of porter with the
steak.'

Coming back she met Jenny and Julia, and when she
told them her purchases they remarked significantly that
they were now quite sure of a pleasant evening.

'When he 's done eating 'e 'll go out to smoke his pipe

with some of his chaps,' said Jenny, 'and we shall have the
'ouse to ourselves, and yer can tell us all about your
situation. They keeps a butler and a footman, don't they?
They must be grand folk. And what was the footman
like? Was he very handsome? I 've 'eard that they
all is.'

'And you 'll show us yer dresses, won't you?' said Julia.
'How many 'ave you got, and 'ow did yer manage to save
up enough money to buy such beauties, if they 're all like
that?'

'This dress was given to me by Miss Mary.'

'Was it? She must be a real good 'un. I should like
to go to service; I 'm tired of making dogs; we have to work
that 'ard, and it nearly all goes to the public; father drinks
worse than ever.'

Mrs. Saunders approved of Esther's purchase; it was a
beautiful bit of steak, and a few minutes after the meat was
roasting on the gridiron. The clock continued its coarse
ticking on the dresser, amid the rough plates. Jenny and
Julia hastened with their work, pressing the paper with
nervous fingers into the moulds, calling sharply to the little
group for what sized paper they required. Esther and Mrs.
Saunders waited, full of apprehension, for the sound of a
heavy tread in the passage. At last it came. Mrs. Saunders
turned the meat, hoping that its savoury odour would
greet his nostrils from afar, and that he would come to
them mollified and amiable.

'Hullo, Jim; yer are 'ome a bit earlier to-day. I 'm
not quite ready with yer supper.'

'I dunno that I am. Hullo, Esther! Up for the day?
Smells damned nice, what you 're cooking for me, missus.
What is it?

'Bit of steak, Jim. It seems a beautiful piece. Hope
it will eat tender.'

'That it will. I was afeared you would have nothing
more than a rasher, and I 'm that 'ungry.'

Jim Saunders, a stout, dark man about forty, who had
not shaved for some days, wore a ragged comforter around
his short, bull neck. He threw his basket into a corner,
and then himself on to the rough bench nailed against the
wall, and there, without speaking another word, he lay
sniffing the odour of the meat like an animal going to be

fed. Suddenly a whiff from the beer jug came into his nostrils, and reaching out his rough hand he looked into the jug to assure himself he was not mistaken.

'What's this?' he exclaimed; 'a pint of porter! Yer are doing me pretty well this evening, I reckon. What's up?'

'Nothing, Jim; nothing, dear, but just as Esther has come up we thought we'd try to make yer comfortable. It was Esther who fetched it; she 'as been doing pretty well, and can afford it.'

Jim looked at Esther in a sort of vague and brutal astonishment, and feeling he must say something, and not knowing well what, he said:

'Well, 'ere 's to your good health!' and he took a long pull at the jug. 'Where did you get this?'

'In Durham Street, at the "Angel."'

'I thought as much; they don't sell stuff like this at the "Rose and Crown." Well, much obliged to yer. I shall enjoy my bit of steak now; and I see a tater in the cinders. How are you getting on, old woman—is it nearly done? Yer know I don't like all the goodness burnt out of it.'

'It isn't quite done yet, Jim; a few minutes more——'

Jim sniffed in eager anticipation, and then addressed himself to Esther.

'Well, they seem to do yer pretty well down there. My word, what a toff yer are! Quite a lady. There 's nothing like service for a girl; I 've always said so. Eh, Jenny, wouldn't yer like to go into service, like yer sister? Looks better, don't it, than making toy dogs at three and sixpence the gross?'

'I should just think it was. I wish I could. As soon as Maggie can take my place, I mean to try.'

'It was the young lady of the 'ouse that gave 'er that nice dress,' said Julia. 'My eye! she must have been a favourite.'

At that moment Mrs. Saunders picked the steak from the gridiron, and putting it on a nice hot plate she carried it in her apron to Jim, saying, 'Mind yer 'ands, it is burning 'ot.'

Jim fed in hungry silence, the children watching, regretting that none of them ever had suppers like that. He didn't speak until he had put away the better part of the steak; then, after taking a long pull at the jug of porter, he said:

'I 'aven't enjoyed a bit of food like that this many a day; I was that beat when I came in, and it does you good to put a piece of honest meat into your stomach after a 'ard day's work!'

Then, prompted by a sudden thought, he complimented Esther on her looks, and then, with increasing interest, inquired what kind of people she was staying with. But Esther was in no humour for conversation, and answered his questions briefly without entering into details. Her reserve only increased his curiosity, which fired up at the first mention of the racehorses.

'I don't know much about them. I only used to see them passing through the yard as they went to exercise on the downs. There was always a lot of talk about them in the servants' hall, but I didn't notice it. They were a great trouble to Mrs. Barfield—I told you, mother, that she was one of ourselves, didn't I?'

A look of contempt passed over Jim's face, and he said:

'We 've quite enough talk 'ere about the Brethren; give them a rest. What about the 'orses? Did they win any races? Yer can't 'ave missed 'earing that.'

'Yes, Silver Braid won the Stewards' Cup.'

'Silver Braid was one of your 'orses?'

'Yes; Mr. Barfield won thousands and thousands, every one in Shoreham won something, and a ball for the servants was given in the Gardens.'

'And you never thought of writing to me about it! I could have 'ad thirty to one off Bill Short. One pound ten to a bob! And yer never thought it worth while to send me the tip. I 'm blowed! Girls aren't worth a damn. Thirty to one off Bill Short—he 'd have laid it. I remember seeing the price quoted in all the papers. Thirty to one taken and hoffered. If you had told me all yer knowed I might 'ave gone 'arf a quid—fifteen pun to 'alf a quid! as much as I 'd earn in three months slaving eight and ten hours a day, paint-pot on 'and about them blooming engines. Well, there 's no use crying over what 's done— sich a chance won't come again, but something else may. What are they going to do with the 'orse this autumn— did yer 'ear that?'

'I think I 'eard that he was entered for the Cambridge-shire, but if I remember rightly, Mr. Leopold—that 's the butler, not his real name, but what we call him——'

'Ah, yes; I know; after the Baron. Now what do 'e say? I reckon 'e knows. I should like to 'ave 'alf an hour's talk with your Mr. Leopold. What do 'e say? For what 'e says, unless I 'm pretty well mistaken, is worth listening to. A man wouldn't be a-wasting 'is time in listening to 'im. What do 'e say?'

'Mr. Leopold never says much. He 's the only one that 's the Gaffer's confidential. They are as thick as thieves—so they say. Mr. Leopold was the Gaffer's valet when he was a bachelor.'

Jim chuckled. 'Yes, I think I know what kind of man your Mr. Leopold is like. But what did 'e say about the Cambridgeshire?'

'He only laughed a little once, and said he didn't think the 'orse would do much good in the autumn races—no, not races, that isn't the word.'

'Handicaps?'

'Yes, that 's it. But there 's no relying on what Mr. Leopold says—he never says what he really means. But I 'eard William, that 's the footman——'

'What are you stopping for? What did yer 'ear 'im say?'

'That he intends to have something on next spring.'

'Did he say any race? Did he say the City and Sub?'

'Yes, that was the race he mentioned.'

'I thought that would be about the length and the breadth of it,' Jim said, as he took up his knife and fork. There was only a small portion of the beefsteak left, and this he ate gluttonously, and, finishing what remained of the porter, he leaned back, and in the happiness of repletion crammed tobacco into a dirty clay, with a dirtier finger-nail, and said:

'I 'd be uncommon glad to 'ear how he is getting on. When are you going back? Up for the day only?'

Esther did not answer, and Jim looked inquiringly as he reached across the table for the matches. The decisive moment had arrived, and Mrs. Saunders:

'Esther ain't a-going back; leastways——'

'Not going back! You don't mean that she ain't con-tented in her situation—that she 'as——'

'Esther ain't going back no more,' Mrs. Saunders answered, incautiously. 'Look 'ee 'ere, Jim——'

'Out with it, old woman—no 'umbug! What is it all about? Ain't going back to 'er sitooation, and where she 'as been treated like that—just look at the duds she 'as got on.'

The evening was darkening rapidly, and the firelight flickered over the back of the toy dogs piled up on the dresser. Jim had lit his pipe, and the acrid and warm odour of quickly burning tobacco overpowered the smell of grease and the burnt skin of the baked potato, a fragment of which remained on the plate; only the sickly flavour of drying paste was distinguishable in the reek of the short black clay which the man held firmly between his teeth. Esther sat by the fire, her hands crossed over her knees, no signs of emotion on her sullen, plump face. Mrs. Saunders stood on the other side of Esther, between her and the younger children, now quarrelling among themselves, and her face was full of fear as she watched her husband anxiously.

'Now then, old woman, blurt it out!' he said. 'What is it? Can it be the girl 'as lost her sitooation—got the sack? Yes, I see that 's about the cut of it. Her beastly temper! So they couldn't put up with it in the country any more than I could mesel'. Well, it 's 'er own lookout! If she can afford to chuck up a place like that, so much the better for 'er. Pity, though; she might 'ave put me up to many a good thing.'

'It ain't that, Jim. The girl is in trouble.'

'Wot do yer say? Esther in trouble? Well, that 's the best bit I 've heard this long while. I always told ye that the religious ones were just the same as the others—a bit more hypocritical, that 's all. So she that wouldn't 'ave nothing to do with such as was Mrs. Dunbar 'as got 'erself into trouble! Well, I never! But 'tis just what I always said. The goody-goody sort are the worst. So she 'as got 'erself into trouble! Well, she 'll 'ave to get 'erself out of it.'

'Now, Jim, dear, yer mustn't be 'ard on 'er; she could tell a very different story if she wished it, but yer know what she is. There she sits like a block of marble, and won't as much as say a word in 'er own defence.'

'But I don't want 'er to speak. I don't care, it's nothing to me; I only laughed because——'

'Jim, dear, it is something to all of us. What we thought was that you might let her stop 'ere till her time was come to go to the 'orspital.'

'Ah, that's it, is it? That was the meaning of the 'alf-pound of steak and the pint of porter, was it? I thought there was something hup. So she wants to stop 'ere, do she? As if there wasn't enough already! Well, I be blowed if she do! A nice thing, too; a girl can't go away to service without coming back to her respectable 'ome in trouble—in trouble, she calls it. Now, I won't 'ave it; there's enough 'ere as it is, and another coming, worse luck. We wants no bastards 'ere. And a nice example, too, for the other children! No, I won't 'ave it!'

Jenny and Julia looked curiously at Esther, who sat quite still, her face showing no sign of emotion. Mrs. Saunders turned towards her, a pitying look on her face, saying clearly, 'You see, my poor girl, how matters stand; I can do nothing.'

The girl, although she did not raise her eyes, understood what was passing in her mother's mind, for there was a grave deliberativeness in the manner in which she rose from the chair.

But just as the daughter had guessed what was passing in the mother's mind, so did the mother guess what was passing in the daughter's. Mrs. Saunders threw herself before Esther, saying, 'Oh, no, Esther, wait a moment; 'e won't be so 'ard on 'ee.' Then turning to her husband, 'Yer don't understand, Jim. It is only for a little time.'

'No, I tell yer. No, I won't 'ave it! There be too many 'ere as it is.'

'Only a little while, Jim.'

'No. And those who ain't wanted 'ad better go at once —that's my advice to them. The place is as full of us that we can 'ardly turn round as it is. No, I won't 'ear of it!'

'But, Jim, Esther is quite willing to pay her way; she's saved a good little sum of money, and could afford to pay us ten shillings a week for board and the parlour.'

A perplexed look came on Jim's face.

'Why didn't yer tell me that afore? Of course I don't wish to be 'ard on the girl, as yer 'ave just heard me say.

Ten shillings a week for her board and the parlour—that seems fair enough; and if it 's any convenience to 'er to stop 'ere, I 'm sure we 'll be glad to 'ave 'er. I 'll say right glad, too. We was always good friends, Esther, wasn't we, though ye wasn't one of my own?' So saying, Jim held out his hand.

Esther tried to pass by her mother. 'I don't want to stop where I 'm not wanted; I wants no one's charity. Let me go, mother.'

'No, no, Esther. 'Aven't yer 'eard what 'e says? Ye are my child if you ain't 'is, and it would break my 'eart, that it would, to see you go away among strangers. Yer place is among yer own people, who 'll look after you.'

'Now, then, Esther, why should there be ill feeling? I didn't mean any 'arm. There 's a lot of us 'ere, and I 've to think of the interests of my own. But for all that I should be main sorry to see yer take yer money among strangers, where you wouldn't get no value for it. You 'd better stop. I 'm sorry for what I said. Ain't that enough for yer?'

'Jim, Jim, dear, don't say no more; leave 'er to me. Esther, for my sake stop with us. You are in trouble, and it is right for you to stop with me. Jim 'as said no more than the truth. With all the best will in the world we couldn't afford to keep yer for nothing, but since yer can pay yer way, it is yer duty to stop. Think, Esther, dear, think. Go and shake 'ands with 'im, and I 'll go and make yer up a bed on the sofa.'

'There 's no bloody need for 'er to shake my 'and if she don't like,' Jim replied, and he pulled doggedly at his pipe.

Esther tried, but her fierce and heavy temper held her back. She couldn't go to her father for reconciliation, and the matter might have ended quite differently, but suddenly, without another word, Jim put on his hat and went out to join 'his chaps' who were waiting for him about the public-house, close to the cab rank in the Vauxhall Bridge Road. The door was hardly closed behind him when the young children laughed and ran about joyously, and Jenny and Julia went over to Esther and begged her to stop.

'Of course she 'll stop,' said Mrs. Saunders. 'And now, Esther, come along and help me to make you up a bed in the parlour.'

## CHAPTER XIV

MRS. SAUNDERS stood looking at her, and Esther turned suddenly on the sofa and said:

'What time is it, mother?'

'It's gone six; but don't you get up. You're your own mistress whilst you're here; you pays for what you 'as.'

'I can't afford them lazy habits. There's plenty of work here, and I must help you with some of it.'

'Plenty of work here, that's right enough. But why should you bother, and you nearly seven months gone? I dare say you feels that 'eavy that you never care to get out of your chair. But they says that them who works up to the last 'as the easiest time in the end. Not that I've found it so.'

The conversation paused. Esther threw her legs over the side of the sofa, and, still wrapped in the blanket, sat looking at her mother.

'You can't be over-comfortable on that bit of sofa,' said Mrs. Saunders.

'Lor, I can manage right enough, if that was all.'

'You're cast down, Esther; you mustn't give way. Things sometimes turn out better than you'd expect for.'

'You never found they did, mother.'

'Perhaps I didn't, but that says nothing for others. We must bear up as best we can.'

One word led to another, and very soon Esther was telling her mother the whole tale of her misfortune—all about William, the sweepstakes, the ball at the Shoreham Gardens, the walks about the farm and hill-side.

'Service is no place for a girl who wants to live as we used to live when father was alive—no service that I've seen. I see that plain enough. Mistress was one of the Brethren like ourselves, and she had to put up with betting and drinking and dancing, and never a thought of the Lord. There was no standing out against it. They call you Creeping Jesus if you say your prayers, and you can't say them with a girl laughing or singing behind your back, so you think you 'll say them to yourself in bed, but sleep comes sooner than you expect, and so you slips out of the habit. Then the drinking. We was brought up teetotal, but they 're always pressing it upon you, and to please him I said I would drink the 'orse's 'ealth. That 's how it began. You don't know what it is, mother; you only knew God-fearing men until you married him. We aren't all good like you, mother. But I thought no harm, indeed I didn't.'

'A girl can't know what a man is thinking of, and we takes the worst for the best.'

'I don't say that I was altogether blameless, but——'

'You didn't know he was that bad.'

Esther hesitated.

'I knew he was like other men. But he told me—he promised me he 'd marry me.'

Mrs. Saunders did not answer, and Esther said, 'You don't believe I 'm speaking the truth.'

'Yes, I do, dearie. I was only thinking. You 're my daughter; no mother had a better daughter. There never was a better girl in this world.'

'I was telling you, mother——'

'But I don't want no telling that my Esther ain't a bad girl.'

Mrs. Saunders sat nodding her head, a sweet, uncritical mother; and Esther understood how unselfishly her mother loved her, and how simply she thought of how she might help her in her trouble. Neither spoke, and Esther continued dressing.

'You 'aven't told me what you think of your room. It looks pretty, don't you think? I keeps it as nice as I can. Jenny hung up them pictures. They livens it up a bit,' she said, pointing to the coloured supplements, from the illustrated papers, on the wall. 'The china shepherd and shepherdess, you know; they was at Barnstaple.'

When Esther was dressed, she and Mrs. Saunders knelt down and said a prayer together. Then Esther said she would make up her room, and when that was done she insisted on helping her mother with the housework.

In the afternoon she sat with her sisters, helping them with their dogs, folding the paper into the moulds, pasting it down, or cutting the skins into the requisite sizes. About five, when the children had had their tea, she and her mother went for a short walk. Very often they strolled through Victoria Station, amused by the bustle of the traffic, or maybe they wandered down the Buckingham Palace Road, attracted by the shops. And there was a sad pleasure in these walks. The elder woman had borne years of exceeding trouble, and felt her strength failing under her burdens, which instead of lightening were increasing; the younger woman was full of nervous apprehension for the future and grief for the past. But they loved each other deeply. Esther threw herself in the way to protect her mother, whether at a dangerous crossing or from the heedlessness of the crowd at a corner, and often a passer-by turned his head and looked after them, attracted by the solicitude which the younger woman showed for the elder. And in those walks very little was said. The two walked in silence, slipping now and then into occasional speech, and here and there a casual allusion or a broken sentence would indicate what was passing in their minds.

One day some flannel and shirts in a window caught Mrs. Saunders's eye, and she said:

'It is time, Esther, you thought about your baby clothes. You must be prepared; you never knows if you'll go your full time.'

The words came upon Esther with something of a shock, helping her to realize the imminence of her trouble.

'You must have something by you, dear; you never knows how it is going to turn out; even I who have been through it do feel that nervous. I looks round the kitchen when I'm taken with the pains, and I says, "I may never see this room again."'

The words were said in an undertone to Esther, and the shopwoman turned to get down the ready-made things which Mrs. Saunders had asked to see.

'Here,' said the shopwoman, 'is the gown, longcloth, one and sixpence; here is the flannel, one and sixpence; and here is the little shirt, sixpence.'

'You must have these to go on with, dear, and if the baby lives you'll want another set.'

'Oh, mother, of course he'll live; why shouldn't he?'

Even the shopwoman smiled, and Mrs. Saunders, addressing the shopwoman, said:

'Them that knows nothing about it is allus full of 'ope.'

The shopwoman raised her eyes, sighed, and inquired sympathetically if this was the young lady's first confinement.

Mrs. Saunders nodded and sighed, and then the shopwoman asked Mrs. Saunders if she required any baby clothes. Mrs. Saunders said she had all she required. The parcel was made up, and they were preparing to leave, when Esther said:

'I may as well buy the stuff and make another set—it will give me something to do in the afternoons. I think I should like to make them.'

'We have some first-rate longcloth at sixpence halfpenny a yard.'

'You might take three yards, Esther; if anything should happen to the baby it will always come in useful. And you had better take three yards of flannel. How much is yer flannel?'

'We have some excellent flannel,' said the woman, lifting down a long, heavy package in dull yellow paper; 'this is tenpence a yard. You'll want a finer longcloth for the little shirts.'

And every afternoon Esther sat in the parlour by the window, seeing, when she raised her eyes from the sewing, the low brick street full of children, and hearing the working women calling from the open doors or windows; and as she worked at the baby clothes, never perhaps to be worn, her heart sank at the long prospect that awaited her, the end of which she could not see, for it seemed to reach to the very end of her life. In these hours she realized in some measure the duties that life held in store, and it seemed to her that they exceeded her strength. Never would she be able to bring him up—he would have no one to look to but her. She never imagined other than that her child would be a boy. The task was clearly more than she could perform, and in despair she thought it would be better for it to die. What would happen if she remained out of a situation? Her father would not have her at home, that she knew well enough. What should she do, and the life of another depending on her? She would never see William again— that was certain. He had married a lady, and, were they to meet, he wouldn't look at her. Her temper grew hot, and the memory of the injustice of which she had been a victim pressed upon her. But when vain anger passed away she thought of her baby, anticipating the joy she would experience when he held out tiny hands to her, and that, too, which she would feel when he laid an innocent cheek to hers; and, her dream persisting, she saw him learning a trade, going to work in the morning and coming back to her in the evening, proud in the accomplishment of something done, of good money honestly earned.

She thought a great deal, too, of her poor mother, who was looking strangely weak and poorly, and whose condition was rendered worse by her nervous fears that she would not get through this confinement. For the doctor had told Mrs. Saunders that the next time it might go hard with her; and in this house, her husband growing more reckless and drunken, it was altogether a bad lookout, and she might die for want of a little nourishment or a little care. Unfortunately they would both be down at the same time, and it was almost impossible that Esther should be well in time to look after her mother. That brute! It was wrong to think of her father so, but he seemed to be without mercy for any of them. He had come in yesterday half boozed, having kept back part of his money—he had come in tramping and hiccuping.

'Now, then, old girl, cough up! I must have a few half-pence; my chaps is waiting for me, and I can't be looking down their mouths with nothing in my pockets.'

'I only have a few halfpence to get the children a bit of dinner; if I give them to you they 'll have nothing to eat.'

'Oh, the children can eat anything; I want beer. If yer 'aven't money, make it.'

Mrs. Saunders said that if he had any spare clothes she would take them round the corner. He only answered:

'Well, if I 'aven't a spare waistcoat left just take some of yer own things. I tell yer I want beer, and I mean to have some.'

Then, with his fist raised, he came at his poor wife, ordering her to take one of the sheets from the bed and 'make money,' and would have struck her if Esther had not come between them and, with her hand in her pocket, said, 'Be quiet, father; I 'll give you the money you want.'

She had done the same before, and, if needs be, she would

do so again.   She could not see her mother struck, perhaps killed by that brute; her first duty was to save her mother, but these constant demands on her little savings frightened her.   She would want every penny of her savings; the ten shillings he had already had from her might be the very sum required to put her on her feet again, and send her in search of a situation where she would be able to earn money for the boy.   But if this extortion continued she didn't know what she would do, and that night she prayed that God might not delay the birth of her child.

## CHAPTER XV

'I wish, mother, you was going to the hospital with me; it would save a lot of expense and you 'd be better cared for.'

'I 'd like to be with you, dearie, but I can't leave my 'ome, all these young children about and no one to see to them. I must stop where I am.　But I 've been meaning to tell you —it is time that you was thinking about yer letter.'

'What letter, mother?'

'They don't take you without a letter from one of the subscribers.　If I was you, now that the weather is fine and you have strength for the walk, I 'd go up to Queen Charlotte's.　It is up the Edgware Road way, I think. What do you think about to-morrow?'

'To-morrow 's Sunday.'

'That makes no matter, them horspitals is open.'

'I 'll go to-morrow when we have washed up.'

On Friday Esther had had to give her father more money for drink.　She gave him two shillings, and that made a sovereign that he had had from her.　On Saturday night he had been brought home helplessly drunk long after midnight, and next morning one of the girls had to fetch him a drop of something to pull him together.　He had lain in bed until dinner-time, swearing he would brain any one who made the least noise.　Even the Sunday dinner, a nice beefsteak pudding, hardly tempted him, and he left the table saying that if he could find Tom Carter they would take a penny boat and go for a blow on the river. The whole family waited for his departure.　But he lingered, talked inconsequently, and several times Mrs. Saunders and the children gave up hope.　Esther sat without a word. He called her a sulky brute, and, snatching up his hat, left the house.　The moment he was gone the children began to chatter like birds.　Esther put on her hat and jacket.

'I 'm going, mother.'

'Well, take care of yourself.　Good luck to you.'

Esther smiled sadly.　But the beautiful weather melted on her lips, her lungs swelled with the warm air, and she noticed the sparrow that flew across the cab rank, and saw the black dot pass down a mews and disappear under the eaves. It was a warm day in the middle of April; a mist of green had begun in the branches of the elms of the Green Park; and in Park Lane, in all the balconies and gardens, wherever nature could find roothold, a spray of green met the eye. There was music, too, in the air, the sound of fifes and drums, and all along the roadway as far as she could see the rapid movement of assembling crowds. A procession with banners was turning the corner of the Edgware Road, and the policeman had stopped the traffic to allow it to pass. The principal banner blew out blue and gold in the wind, and the men that bore the poles walked with strained backs under the weight; the music changed, opinions about the objects of the demonstration were exchanged, and it was some time before Esther could gain the policeman's attention. At last the conductor rang his bell, the omnibus started, and gathering courage she asked the way. It seemed to her that every one was noticing her, and fearing to be overheard she spoke so low that the policeman understood her to say Charlotte Street. At that moment an omnibus drew up close beside them.

'Charlotte Street, Charlotte Street,' said the policeman, 'there's Charlotte Street, Bloomsbury.' Before Esther could answer he had turned to the conductor. 'You don't know any Charlotte Street about here, do you?'

'No, I don't. But can't yer see that it ain't no Charlotte Street she wants, but Queen Charlotte's Hospital! And ye'd better lose no time in directing her.'

A roar of coarse laughter greeted this pleasantry, and burning with shame she hurried down the Edgware Road. But she hadn't gone far before she had to ask again, and she scanned the passers-by seeking some respectable woman, or in default an innocent child.

She came at last to an ugly desert place. There was the hospital, square, forbidding, opposite—a tall, lean building with long grey columns. Esther rang, and the great door, some fifteen feet high, was opened by a small boy.

'I want to see the secretary.'

'Will you come this way?'

She was shown into a waiting-room, and while waiting

she looked at the religious prints on the walls. A lad of fifteen or sixteen came in. He said:

'You want to see the secretary?'

'Yes.'

'But I'm afraid you can't see him; he's out.'

'I have come a long way; is there no one else I can see?'

'Yes, you can see me—I'm his clerk. Have you come to be confined?'

Esther answered that she had.

'But,' said the boy, 'you are not in labour; we never take any one in before.'

'I do not expect to be confined for another month. I came to make arrangements.'

'You've got a letter?'

'No.'

'Then you must get a letter from one of the subscribers.'

'But I don't know any.'

'You can have a book of their names and addresses.'

'But I know no one.'

'You needn't know them. You can go and call. Take those that live nearest—that's the way it is done.'

'Will you give me the book?'

'I'll go and get one.'

The boy returned a moment after with a small book, for which he demanded a shilling. Since she had come to London her hand had never been out of her pocket. She had her money with her, for she didn't dare leave it at home on account of her father. The clerk looked out the addresses for her and she tried to remember them—two were in Cumberland Place, another was in Bryanstone Square. In Cumberland Place she was received by an elderly lady who said she did not wish to judge any one, but it was her invariable practice to give letters only to married women. There was a delicate smell of perfume in the room; the lady stirred the fire and lay back in her arm-chair. Once or twice Esther tried to withdraw, but the lady, although unswervingly faithful to her principles, seemed not indifferent to Esther's story, and asked her many questions.

'I don't see what interest all that can be to you, as you ain't going to give me a letter,' Esther answered.

The next house she called at the lady was not at home, but she was expected back presently, and the maidservant asked her to take a seat in the hall. But when Esther refused information about her troubles she was called a stuck-up thing who deserved all she got, and was told there was no use her waiting. At the next place she was received by a footman who insisted on her communicating her business to him. Then he said he would see if his master was in. He wasn't in; he must have just gone out. The best time to find him was before half-past ten in the morning.

'He'll be sure to do all he can for you—he always do for the good-looking ones. How did it all happen?'

'What business is that of yours? I don't ask your business.'

'Well, you needn't turn so rusty.'

At that moment the master entered. He asked Esther to come into his study. He was a tall, youngish-looking man of three- or four-and-thirty, with bright eyes and hair, and there was in his voice and manner a kindness that impressed Esther. She wished, however, that she had seen his mother instead of him, for she was more than ever ashamed of her condition. He seemed genuinely sorry for her, and regretted that he had given all his tickets away. Then a thought struck him, and he wrote a letter to one of his friends, a banker in Lincoln's Inn Fields. This gentleman, he said, was a large subscriber to the hospital, and would certainly give her the letter she required.

The visit brought a little comfort, and thinking of his kind eyes she walked slowly, inquiring out her way until she got back to the Marble Arch, and stood looking down the long Bayswater Road where the tall houses towered above the sunset; and some sensation of the poetry of the hour must have stolen into her heart, for she turned into the Park, choosing to walk among the crowds scattered like strips of black tape. Here and there by the railings the tape had been wound up in a black ball, and the peg was some democratic orator, promising poor human nature unconditional deliverance from evil. Farther on were heard sounds from a harmonium, and hymns were being sung, and in each doubting face there was something of the perplexing, haunting look which the city wore.

A chill wind was blowing.   Winter had returned with the night, but the instinct of spring continued in the branches. The deep, sweet scent of the hyacinth floated along the railings, and the lovers that sat with their arms about each other on every seat were of Esther's own class.   She would have liked to have called them round her and told them her miserable story, so that they might profit by her experience.

## CHAPTER XVI

ONLY three weeks remained, and she had hoped to spend them with her mother, who was timorous and desponding, and stood in need of consolation. But this was not to be; her father's drunkenness continued, and daily he became more extortionate in his demands for money. Esther had not six pounds left, and she felt that she must leave. It had come to this, that she doubted if she were to stay on that the clothes on her back might not be taken from her. Mrs. Saunders was of the same opinion, and she urged Esther to go. But scruples restrained her.

'I can't bring myself to leave you, mother; something tells me I should stay with you. It is dreadful to be parted from you. I wish you was coming to the hospital; you'd be far safer there than at home.'

'I know that, dearie; but where's the good in talking about it? It only makes it harder to bear. You know I can't leave. It is terrible hard, as you says.' Mrs. Saunders held her apron to her eyes and cried. 'You have always been a good girl, never a better—my one consolation since your poor father died.'

'Don't cry, mother,' said Esther; 'the Lord will watch over us, and we shall both pray for each other. In about a month, dear, we shall be both quite well, and you'll bless my baby, and I shall think of the time when I shall put him into your arms.'

'I hope so, Esther; I hope so, but I am full of fears. I'm sore afraid that we shall never see one another again—leastways on this earth.'

'Oh, mother dear, yer mustn't talk like that; you'll break my heart, that you will.'

The cab that took Esther to her lodging cost half a crown, and this waste of money frightened her thrifty nature, inherited through centuries of working folk. The waste, however, had ceased at last, and it was none too soon, she thought, as she sat in the room she had taken near the hospital, in a little eight-roomed house, kept by an old woman whose son was a bricklayer.

It was at the end of the week, one afternoon, as Esther was sitting alone, there came within her a great and sudden shock—life seemed to be slipping from her, and she sat for some minutes quite unable to move, and when the pain ceased she went downstairs to consult Mrs. Jones.

'Hadn't I better go to the hospital now, Mrs. Jones?'

'Not just yet, my dear: them is but the first labour pains; plenty of time to think of the hospital; we shall see how you are in a couple of hours.'

'Will it last so long as that?'

'You'll be lucky if you get it over before midnight. I have been down for longer than that.'

'Do you mind my stopping in the kitchen with you? I feel frightened when I'm alone.'

'No, I'll be glad of your company. I'll get you some tea at once.'

'I couldn't touch anything. Oh, this is dreadful!' she exclaimed, as she walked to and fro holding her sides, balancing herself dolefully. Often Mrs. Jones stopped in her work about the range and said, looking at her, 'I know what it is, I have been through it many a time; we all must; it is our earthly lot.' At seven o'clock Esther was clinging to the table, and with pain so vivid on her face that Mrs. Jones laid aside the sausages she was cooking and approached the suffering girl.

'What! is it so bad as all that?'

'Oh,' she said, 'I think I'm dying, I cannot stand up; give me a chair, give me a chair!' and she sank upon it, leaning across the table, her face and neck bathed in a cold sweat.

'John will have to get his supper himself; I'll leave these sausages on the hob, and run upstairs and put on my bonnet. The things you intend to bring with you, the baby clothes, are made up in a bundle, aren't they?'

'Yes, yes.'

Little Mrs. Jones came running down; she threw a shawl over Esther, and it was astonishing what support she lent to the suffering girl, calling on her the whole time to lean on her and not be afraid. 'Now then, dear, you must keep your heart up, we have only a few yards farther to go.'

'You are so good, you are so kind,' Esther said, and she leaned against the wall, and Mrs. Jones rang the bell.

'Keep up your spirits; to-morrow it will be all over. I will come round and see how you are.'

The door opened. The porter rang the bell, and a sister came running down.

'Come, come, take my arm,' she said, 'and breathe hard as you are ascending the stairs. Come along, you mustn't loiter.'

On the second landing a door was thrown open, and she found herself in a room full of people, eight or nine young men and women.

'What! in there? and all those people?' said Esther.

'Of course; those are the midwives and the students.'

The screams she had heard in the passage came from a bed on the left-hand side. A woman lay there huddled up, and Esther was taken behind a screen by the sister who brought her upstairs, undressed, and clothed in a chemise a great deal too big for her, she heard the sister say so at the time; and as she walked across the room to her bed she noticed the steel instruments on the round table and the basins on the floor.

The students and the nurses were behind her. She knew they were eating sweets, for she heard a young man ask the young women if they would have any more fondants. A moment after her pains began again, and she saw the young man whom she had seen handing the sweets approaching her beside.

'Oh, no, not him, not him!' she cried to the nurse. 'Not him, not him! he is too young! Don't let him come near me!'

They laughed loudly, and she buried her head in the pillow, overcome with pain and shame; and when she felt him by her she tried to rise from the bed.

'Let me go! take me away! Oh, you are all beasts!'

'Come, come, no nonsense!' said the nurse; 'you can't have what you like; they are here to learn;' and when he had tried the pains she heard the midwife say that it wasn't necessary to send for the doctor. Another said that it would be all over in about three hours' time. 'An easy confinement, I should say. The other will be more interesting.' And then they talked of the plays they had seen, and those they wished to see. She was soon listening to a discussion regarding the merits of a shilling novel which every one was reading, and then Esther heard a stampede of nurses, midwives, and students in the direction of the window. A German band had come into the street.

'Is that the way to leave your patient, sister?' said the student who sat by Esther's bed, and Esther looked into his clear blue, girl-like eyes, wondered, and turned away for shame.

The sister stopped her imitation of a popular comedian, and said, 'Oh, she's all right; if they were all like her there'd be very little use our coming here.'

'Unfortunately, that's just what they are,' said another student, a stout fellow with a pointed red beard, the ends of which caught the light. Her eyes often went to those stubble ends, and she hated him for his loud voice and jocularity. One of the midwives, a woman with a long nose and small grey eyes, seemed to mock her, and she hoped that this woman would not come near her, for there was something sinister in her face, and Esther was glad when her favourite, a little blonde woman with wavy flaxen hair, came by and asked her if she felt better. She looked a little like the young student who still sat by her bedside, and Esther wondered if they were brother and sister, and then she thought that they were sweethearts.

Soon after a bell rang, and the students went down to supper, the nurse in charge promising to warn them if any change should take place. The last pains had so thoroughly exhausted her that she had fallen into a doze. But she could hear the chatter of the nurses so clearly that she did not believe herself asleep. And in this film of sleep reality was distorted, and the unsuccessful operation which the nurses were discussing Esther understood to be a conspiracy against her life. She awoke, listened, and gradually sense of the truth returned to her. She was in the hospital, and the nurses were talking of someone who had died last week. The woman in the other bed seemed to suffer dreadfully. Would she live through it? Would she herself live to see the morning? How long the time, how fearful the place! If the nurses would only stop talking. It did not matter. The pains would soon begin again. It was awful to lie listening, waiting.

The windows were open, and the mocking gaiety of the street was borne in on the night wind. Then there came

a trampling of feet and sound of voices in the passage—
the students and nurses were coming up from supper; and
at the same moment the pains began to creep up from her
knees. One of the young men said that her time had not
come. The woman, with the sinister look that Esther
dreaded, held a contrary opinion. The point was argued,
and, interested in the question, the crowd came from the
window and collected round the disputants. The young
man expounded much medical and anatomical knowledge;
the nurses listened with the usual deference of women.

Suddenly, the discussion was interrupted by a scream
from Esther; it seemed to her that she was being torn
asunder, that life was going from her. The nurse ran to
her side, a look of triumph came upon her face, and she
said, 'Now we shall see who 's right,' and forthwith went
for the doctor. He came running up the stairs; silence and
scientific collectedness gathered round Esther, and after
a brief examination he said, in a low whisper:

'I 'm afraid this will not be as easy a case as one might
have imagined. I shall administer chloroform.'

He placed a small wire case over her mouth and nose.
The sickly odour which she breathed from the cotton-wool
filled her brain with nausea; it seemed to choke her; life
faded a little, and at every inhalation she expected to lose
sight of the circle of faces.

And then the darkness began to lighten; night passed
into dawn; she could hear voices, and when her eyes opened
the doctors and the nurses were still standing round her,
but there was no longer any expression of eager interest
on their faces. She wondered at this change, and then
out of the silence there came a tiny cry.

'What 's that?' Esther asked.

'That 's your baby.'

'My baby! Let me see it: is it a boy or a girl?'

'It is a boy; and he will be given to you when we get you
out of the labour ward.'

'I knew it would be a boy.' A scream carried her
thoughts back to the woman whom she saw in labour
when she entered the room. 'Hasn't she been confined yet?'

'No, and I don't think she will be till midday; she 's
very bad.'

The door was thrown open, and Esther was wheeled into the passage. 'Where is my boy?' she said; 'give him to me.'

The nurse entered, and answered, 'Here.' A pulp of red flesh rolled up in flannel was laid alongside of her. Its eyes were open; it looked at her, and her flesh filled with a sense of happiness so deep and so intense that she was like one enchanted. And when she took the child in her arms she thought she must die of happiness. She did not hear the nurse speak, nor did she understand her when she took the babe from her arms and laid it alongside on the pillow, saying, 'You must let the little thing sleep; you must try to sleep yourself.'

Her personal self seemed entirely withdrawn; she existed like an atmosphere about the babe and lay absorbed in this life of her life, this flesh of her flesh, unconscious of herself as a sponge in warm sea-water. She touched this pulp of life, and was thrilled, and once more her senses swooned with love; it was still there. She remembered that the nurse had said it was a boy. She must see her boy, and her hands, working as in a dream, unwound him, and she gazed until he awoke and cried. She tried to hush him and to enfold him, but her strength failed; she could not help him, and fear came lest he should die; she strove to reach her hands to him, but all strength had gone from her, and his cries sounded hollow in her weak brain. Then the nurse came and said:

'See what you have done, the poor child is all uncovered; no wonder he is crying. I will wrap him up, and you must not interfere with him again.' But as soon as the nurse turned away Esther had her child back in her arms. She could not sleep. She could not sleep for thinking of him, and the night passed in long adoration.

## CHAPTER XVII

ALL her joints were loosened; the long hospital days passed in gentle weariness; lady visitors came and asked questions, and Esther said her father and mother lived in the Vauxhall Bridge Road, and that she had saved four pounds. But the woman in the bed next to Esther (there were two beds in this ward) was wiser, and by declaring herself to be without home, or money, or friends, she secured all the sympathy and many promises of help. They received visits from a clergyman, who spoke to Esther of God's goodness and wisdom, but his exhortations seemed a little remote. If it had been her own people who came and knelt about her bed, lifting their voices in the plain prayers she was accustomed to, it would have been different; but this well-to-do clergyman, with his sophisticated speech, seemed foreign to her, and failed to draw her thoughts from the sleeping child.

The ninth day passed; Esther recovered but slowly, and it was decided she should not leave the hospital before the end of the third week. But as soon as she crossed the threshold of the hospital there would be no more peace, and, listening to the never-ending rumble of the street, she thought of her dear mother. At last her sister came to see her.

'Jenny, what has happened; is mother very bad?'

'Mother is dead, that's what I've come to tell you; I'd have come before, but——'

'Mother dead! Oh, no, Jenny! Oh, Jenny, not my poor mother!'

'Yes, Esther. I knew it would cut you up dreadful; we was all very sorry, but she's dead. She's dead a long time now, I was just a-going to tell you——'

'Jenny, what do you mean? Dead a long time?'

'Well, she was buried more than a week ago. We were so sorry you couldn't be at the funeral. We was all there, and had crape on our dresses and father had crape on his 'at. We all cried, especially in church and about the grave, and when the sexton threw in the soil it sounded that hollow it made me sob. Julia, she lost her 'ead and asked to be buried with mother, and I had to lead her away; and then we went 'ome to dinner.'

'Oh, Jenny, our poor mother gone from us for ever! How did she die? Tell me, was it a peaceful death? Did she suffer?'

'There ain't much to tell. Mother was taken bad almost the minute after you was with us the last time. Mother was that bad all the day long and all night too, we could 'ardly stop in the 'ouse; it just gave you the creeps to listen to her crying and moaning.'

'And then?'

'Why, then the baby was born. It was dead, and mother died of weakness; prostration the doctor called it.'

Esther hid her face in the pillow, and an anxious look of self began to appear on Jenny's vulgar London street face.

'Look 'ere, Esther, you can cry when I 've gone; I 've a lot to say to yer and time is short.'

'Oh, Jenny, don't speak like that! Father, was he kind to mother?'

'I dunno that he thought much about it; he spent 'alf 'is time in the public, 'e did. He said he couldn't abide the 'ouse with a woman a-screaming like that. One of the neighbours came in to look after mother, and at last she had the doctor.'

Esther looked at her sister through streaming tears, and the woman in the other bed spoke of the folly of poor women being confined 'in their own 'omes—in a 'ome where there is a drunken 'usband, and most 'omes is like that nowadays.'

At that moment Esther's baby awoke, crying for the breast, and in a moment Esther's face took on an expression of holy solicitude as she watched the little lips catching at the nipple, and the wee hand pressing the white curve, like a lamb with a ewe, for all nature is akin; and Jenny watched the gluttonous lips, interested in the spectacle, yet absorbed in what she had come to say to her sister.

'Your baby do look 'ealthy.'

'Yes, and he is too, not an ache or a pain. He 's as beautiful a boy as ever lived. But think of poor mother, Jenny, think of poor mother.'

'I do think of her, Esther. But I can't help seeing your baby. He's like you, Esther. I can see a look of you in 'is eyes. But I don't know that I should care to 'ave a baby meself—the expense comes very 'eavy on a girl.'

'Please God, my baby shall never want for anything as long as I can work for him. But, Jenny, my trouble will be a lesson to you. I hope you will always be a good girl, and never allow yourself to be led away; you promise me?'

'Yes, I promise.'

'A 'ome like ours, a drunken father, and now that poor mother is gone it will be worse than ever. Jenny, you are the eldest and must do your best to look after the younger ones, and as much as possible to keep father from the public-house. I shall be away; the moment I'm well enough I must look out for a place.'

'That's just what I came to speak to you about. Father is going to Australia. He is tired of England, and as he lost his situation on the railway he has made up his mind to emigrate. It is pretty well all fixed up; he has been to an agency and they say he'll 'ave to pay two pounds a 'ead, and that runs to a lot of money in a big family like ours. So I'm likely to get left, for father says that I'm old enough to look after myself. He's willing to take me if I gets the money, not without. That's what I came to tell yer about.'

Esther understood that Jenny had come to ask for money. She could not give it, and lapsed into thinking of this sudden loss of all her family. She did not know where Australia was; she fancied that she had once heard that it took months to get there. But she knew that they were all going from her, they were going out on the sea in a great ship that would sail and sail farther and farther away. She could see the ship from her bedside, at first strangely distinct, alive with hands and handkerchiefs; she could distinguish all the children — Jenny, Julia, and little Ethel. She lost sight of their faces as the ship cleared the harbour. Soon after the ship was far away on the great round of waters, again a little while and all the streaming canvas not larger than a gull's wing, again a little while and the last speck on the horizon hesitated and disappeared.

'What are you crying about, Esther? I never saw yer cry before. You ain't one to grizzle.'

'I 'm so weak. Mother's death has broken my heart, and now to know that I shall never see any one of you again.'

'It do seem 'ard. We shall miss you sadly. But I was going to say that father can't take me unless I finds two pounds. You won't see me stranded, will you, Esther?'

'I cannot give you the money, Jenny. Father has had too much of my money already; there 's 'ardly enough to see me through. I 've only four pounds left. I cannot give you my child's money; God knows how we shall live until I can get to work again.'

'You 're nearly well now. But if yer can't help me, yer can't. I don't know what 's to be done. Father can't take me if I don't find the money.'

'You say the agency wants two pounds for each person?'

'Yes, that 's it.'

'And I 've four. We might both go if it weren't for the baby, but I don't suppose they 'd make any charge for a child on the breast.'

'I dunno. There 's father; yer know what he is.'

'That 's true. He don't want me; I 'm not one of his. But, Jenny dear, it is terrible to be left all alone. Poor mother dead, and all of you going to Australia. I shall never see one of you again.'

The conversation paused. Esther changed the baby from the left to the right breast, and Jenny tried to think what she had best say to induce her sister to give her the money she wanted.

'If you don't give me the money I shall be left; it is hard luck, that 's all, for there 's fine chances for a girl, they says, out in Australia. If I remain 'ere I dunno what will become of me.'

'You had better look out for a situation. We shall see each other from time to time. It 's a pity you don't know a bit of cooking, enough to take the place of kitchenmaid.'

'I only know that dog-making, and I 've 'ad enough of that.'

'You can always get a situation as general servant in a lodging-'ouse.'

'Service in a lodging-'ouse! Not me. You know what that is. I 'm surprised that you 'd ask me.'

'Well, what are yer thinking of doing?'

'I was thinking of going on in the pantomime as one of the hextra ladies, if they 'll 'ave me.'

'Oh, Jenny, you won't do that, will you? A theatre is only sinfulness, as we 'ave always knowed.'

'You know that I don't 'old with all them preachy-preachy Brethren says about the theatre.'

'I can't argue—I 'aven't the strength, and it stops the flow of the milk.' And again Esther said, 'I hope, Jenny, that you 'll take example by me and will do nothing foolish; you 'll always be a good girl.'

'Yes, if I gets the chance.'

'I 'm sorry to 'ear you speak like that, and poor mother only just dead.'

The words that rose to Jenny's lips were: 'A nice one you are, with a baby at your breast, to come a-lecturing me,' but, fearing Esther's temper, she checked the dangerous words and said instead:

'I didn't mean that I was a-going on the streets right away this very evening, only that a girl left alone in London may go wrong, if luck 's against her.'

'A girl never need go wrong; if she does it is always 'er own fault.' Esther spoke mechanically, but suddenly remembering her own circumstances she said: 'I 'd give you the money if I dared, but for the child's sake I mustn't.'

'You can afford it well enough—I wouldn't ask you if you couldn't. You 'll be earning a pound a week presently.'

'A pound a week! What do you mean, Jenny?'

'Yer can get that as wet-nurse, and yer food too.'

'How do yer know that, Jenny?'

'A friend of mine who was 'ere last year told me she got it, and you can get it too if yer likes. Fancy a pound for the next six months, and all found. Yer might spare me the money and let me go to Australia with the others.'

'I 'd give yer the money if what you said was true.'

'Yer can easily find out what I say is the truth by sending for the matron. Shall I go and fetch her? I won't be a minute; you 'll see what she says.'

A few moments after Jenny returned with a good-look-ing, middle-aged woman. On her face there was that testy and perplexed look that comes of much business and many interruptions. Before she opened her lips her face had said: 'Come, what is it? Be quick about it.'

'Father and the others is going to Australia. Mother's dead and was buried last week, so father says there's nothing to keep 'im 'ere, for there is better prospects out there. But he says he can't take me, for the agency wants two pounds a 'ead, and it was all he could do to find the money for the others. He is just short of two pounds, and as I'm the eldest barring Esther, who is 'is step-daughter, 'e says that I had better stop be'ind, that I'm old enough to get my own living, which is very 'ard on a girl, for I'm only just turned sixteen. So I thought that I would come up 'ere and tell my sister——'

'But, my good girl, what has all this got to do with me? I can't give you two pounds to go to Australia. You are only wasting my time for nothing.'

''Ear me out, missis. I want you to explain to my sister that you can get her a situation as a wet-nurse at a pound a week—that's the usual money they gets, so I told her but she won't believe me; but if you tells her, she'll give me two pounds and I shall be able to go with father to Australia, where they says there is fine chances for a girl.'

The matron examined disdainfully the vague skirt, the broken boots, and the misshapen hat, coming all the while to quick conclusions regarding the moral value of this unabashed child of the gutter.

'I think your sister will be very foolish if she gives you her money.'

'Oh, don't say that, missis, don't.'

'How does she know that your story is true? Perhaps you are not going to Australia at all.'

'Perhaps I'm not—that's just what I'm afraid of; but father is, and I can prove it to you. I've brought a letter from father—'ere it is; now, is that good enough for yer?'

'Come, no impertinence, or I'll order you out of the hospital in double quick time,' said the matron.

'I didn't mean no impertinence,' said Jenny humbly, 'only I didn't like to be told I was telling lies when I was speaking the truth.'

'Well, I see that your father is going to Australia,' the matron replied, returning the letter to Jenny; 'you want your sister to give you her money to take you there too.'

'What I wants is for you to tell my sister that you can

get her a situation as wet-nurse; then perhaps she 'll give me the money.'

'If your sister wants to go out as wet-nurse, I dare say I could get her a pound a week.'

'But,' said Esther, 'I should have to put baby out to nurse.'

'You 'll have to do that in any case,' Jenny interposed; 'you can't live for nine months on your savings and have all the nourishing food that you 'll want to keep your milk going.'

'If I was yer sister I 'd see yer further before I 'd give yer my money. You must 'ave a cheek to come a-asking for it, to go off to Australia where a girl 'as chances, and yer sister with a child at the breast left behind. Well I never!'

Jenny and the matron turned suddenly and looked at the woman in the opposite bed who had so unexpectedly expressed her views.

'What odds is it to you?' Jenny screamed; 'what business is it of yours, coming poking your nose in my affairs?'

'Come now, I can't have any rowing,' exclaimed the matron.

'Rowing! I should like to know what business it is of 'ers.'

'Hush, hush, I can't have you interfering with my patients; another word and I 'll order you out of the hospital.'

'Horder me out of the horspital! and what for? Who began it? No, missis, be fair; wait until my sister gives her answer.'

'Well, then, she must be quick about it—I can't wait about here all day.'

'I 'll give my sister the money to take her to Australia if you say you can get me a situation as wet-nurse.'

'Yes, I think I can do that. It was four pounds five that you gave me to keep. I remember the amount, for since I 've been here no one has come with quarter that. If they have five shillings they think they can buy half London.'

'My sister is very careful,' said Jenny, sententiously.

The matron looked sharply at her and said:

'Now come along with me—I 'm going to fetch your

sister's money. I can't leave you here — you 'd get quarrelling with my patients.'

'No, missis, indeed I won't say nothing to her

'Do as I tell you. Come along with me.'

So with a passing scowl Jenny expressed her contempt for the woman who had come 'poking 'er nose in 'er business,' and went after the matron, watching her every movement, and when they came back Jenny's eyes were fixed on the matron's fat hand as if she could see the yellow metal through the fingers.

'Here is your money,' said the matron; 'four pounds five. You can give your sister what you like.'

Esther held the four sovereigns and the two half-crowns in her hand for a moment, then she said:

'Here, Jenny, are the two pounds you want to take you to Australia. I 'ope they 'll bring you good luck, and that you 'll think of me sometimes.'

'Indeed I will, Esther. You 've been a good sister to me, that you 'ave; I shall never forget you, and will write to you. It is very 'ard parting.'

'Come, come, never mind those tears. You have got your money; say good-bye to your sister and run along.'

'Don't be so 'eartless,' cried Jenny, whose susceptibilities were now on the move. ''Ave yer no feeling? Don't yer know what it is to bid good-bye to yer sister, and perhaps for ever?' Jenny flung herself into Esther's arms crying bitterly. 'Oh, Esther, I do love you; yer 'ave been so kind to me I shall never forget it. I shall be very lonely without you. Write to me sometimes; it will be a comfort to hear how you are getting on. If I marry I 'll send for you, and you 'll bring the baby.'

'Do you think I 'd leave him behind? Kiss 'im before you go.'

'Good-bye, Esther; take care of yourself.'

She was now alone in the world, and she remembered the night in her mind when she walked home from the hospital. She lay dreaming of those who were going away for ever. She was now alone in a great wilderness with her child, for whom she would have to work for many, many years, and did not know how it would all end. Would she be able to live through it? Had she done right in letting Jenny have the money? She should not have given it; but she hardly knew what she was doing, she was so weak, and the news of her mother's death overcame her. She should not have given Jenny her boy's money. But perhaps it might turn out all right after all. If the matron got her a situation as wet-nurse she 'd be able to pull through. 'So they would part us,' she whispered, bending over the sleeping child. 'There is no help for it, my poor darling. There 's no help for it, no help for it.'

Next day Esther was taken out of bed. She spent part of the afternoon sitting in an easy-chair, and Mrs. Jones came to see her. The little old woman seemed like one whom she had known always, and Esther told her about her mother's death and the departure of her family for Australia. Mrs. Jones bade her cheer up, saying that things were never as bad as they seemed, and she fell to thinking that no more than a week lay between her and the beginning of the struggle which she dreaded. She had been told that they did not usually keep any one in the hospital more than a fortnight. But the matron would do all she could, which was not, however, very much, for three days after Mrs. Jones's visit she came into the room hurriedly.

'I 'm very sorry,' she said, 'but a number of new patients are expected; there 's nothing for it but to get rid of you. It is a pity, for I can see you are both very weak.'

'What, me too?' said the woman in the other bed. 'I can hardly stand; I tried just now to get across the room.'

'I 'm very sorry, but we 've new patients coming, and there 's all our spring cleaning. Have you any place to go to?'

'No place except a lodging,' said Esther; 'and I have only two pounds five now.'

'What 's the use in taking us at all if you fling us out on the street when we can hardly walk?' said the other woman. 'I wish I had gone and drowned myself. I was very near doing it. If I had it would be all over now for me and the poor baby.'

'I 'm used to all this ingratitude,' said the matron. 'You have got through your confinement very comfortably, and your baby is quite healthy; I hope you 'll try and keep it so. Have you any money?'

'Only four and sixpence.'

'Have you got any friends to whom you can go?'

'No.'

'Then you 'll have to apply for admission to the work-house.'

The woman made no answer, and at that moment two sisters came and forcibly began to dress her. She fell back from time to time in their arms, almost fainting.

'Lord, what a job!' said one sister; 'she 's just like so much lead in one's arms. But if we listened to them we should have them loafing here over a month more,' and, as Esther did not require so much assistance, the sister said, 'Oh, you are as strong as they make 'em; you might have gone two days ago.'

'You 're no better than brutes,' Esther muttered. Then turning to the matron, she said, 'You promised to get me a situation as wet-nurse.'

'Yes, so I did, but the lady to whom I intended to re-commend you wrote this morning to say that she had suited herself.'

'But do you think you could get me a situation as wet-nurse?' said the other woman; 'it would save me from going to the workhouse.'

'I really don't know what to do with you all; you all want to stop in the hospital at least a month, eating and drinking the best of everything, and then you want situa-tions as wet-nurses at a pound a week.'

'But,' said Esther, indignantly, 'I never should have given my sister two pounds if you hadn't told me you could get me the situation.'

'I 'm sorry,' said the matron, 'to have to send you away. I should like to have kept you, but really there is no help for it. As for the situation, I 'll do the best I can. It is true that the place I intended for you is filled up, but there will be another shortly, and you shall have the first. Give me your address. I shall not keep you long waiting, you can depend upon me. You are still very weak, I can see that. Would you like to have one of the nurses to walk round with you? You had better—you might fall and hurt the baby. My word, he is a fine boy.'

'Yes, he is a beautiful boy; it will break my heart to part with him.'

Some eight or nine poor girls stood outside, dressed alike in dingy garments, like half-dead flies trying to crawl through an October afternoon; and with their babies and a keen wind blowing, they found it difficult to hold on their hats.

'It do catch you a bit rough, coming out of them 'ot rooms,' said a woman standing by her. 'I 'm that weak I can 'ardly carry my baby. I dunno 'ow I shall get as far as the Edgware Road. I take my bus there. Are you going that way?'

'No, I 'm going close by, round the corner.'

## CHAPTER XVIII

HER hair hung about her, her hands and wrists were shrunken, her flesh was soft and flabby, for suckling her child seemed to draw all strength from her, and her nervous depression increased from day to day, she being too weary and ill to think of the future; and for a whole week her physical condition held her to the exclusion of every other thought. Mrs. Jones was very kind, charging her only ten shillings a week for her board and lodging; but this was a great deal when no more than two pounds five shillings remained between her and the workhouse, and this fact was brought home to her sternly when Mrs. Jones came to her for the first week's money. Ten shillings gone; only one pound fifteen shillings left, and still she was so weak that she could hardly get up and down stairs. But if she were twice as weak, if she had to crawl along the street on her hands and knees, she must go to the hospital and implore the matron to find her a situation as wet-nurse. Well, it was raining heavily, and Mrs. Jones said it was madness for her to go out in such weather, but go she must; and, though it was but a few hundred yards, she often thought she'd like to lie down and die. At the hospital disappointment awaited her. Why hadn't she called yesterday? Yesterday two ladies of title had come and taken two girls away. Such a chance might not occur for some time. 'For some time,' thought Esther. 'Very soon I shall have to apply for admission at the workhouse.' She reminded the matron of her promise, and returned home more dead than alive. Mrs. Jones helped her to change her clothes, and bade her be of good heart. Esther looked at her hopelessly, and sitting down on the edge of her bed she put the baby to her breast.

Another week passed. She had been to the hospital every day, but no one had been to inquire for a wet-nurse. Her money was reduced to a few shillings, and she tried to reconcile herself to the idea that she might do worse than accept the harsh shelter of the workhouse. Her nature revolted against it; but she must do what was best for the child, and often asked herself how it would all end. And the more she thought, the more terrible did the future seem. Her miserable thoughts were interrupted by a footstep on the stairs. It was Mrs. Jones, coming to tell her that a lady who wanted a wet-nurse had come from the hospital; and a lady dressed in a beautiful brown silk came in, and looked around the humble room, clearly shocked at its poverty. Esther, who was sitting on the bed, rose to meet the fine lady—a thin woman, with narrow temples, aquiline features, bright eyes, and a disagreeable voice.

'You are the young person who wants a situation as wet-nurse?'

'Yes, ma'am.'

'Are you married?'

'No, ma'am.'

'Is that your first child?'

'Yes, ma'am.'

'Ah! that's a pity. But it doesn't matter much, so long as you and your baby are healthy. Will you show it to me?'

'He is asleep now, ma'am,' Esther said, raising the bed-clothes. 'There never was a healthier child.'

'Yes, he seems healthy enough. You have a good supply of milk?'

'Yes, ma'am.'

'Fifteen shillings, and all found. Does that suit you?'

'I had expected a pound a week.'

'It is only your first baby. Fifteen shillings is quite enough. Of course, I only engage you subject to the doctor's approval. I'll ask him to call.'

'Very well, ma'am; I shall be glad of the place.'

'Then it is settled. You can come at once?'

'I must arrange to put my baby out to nurse, ma'am.'

The lady's face clouded. But following up another train of thought, she said:

'Of course, you must arrange about your baby, and I hope you'll make proper arrangements. Tell the woman in whose charge you leave it that I shall want to see it every three weeks. It will be better so,' she added, under her breath, 'for two have died already.'

'This is my card,' said the lady—'Mrs. Rivers, Curzon Street, Mayfair—and I shall expect you to-morrow afternoon—that is to say, if the doctor approves of you. Here is one and sixpence for your cab fare.'

'Thank you, ma'am.'

'I shall expect you not later than four o'clock. I hope you won't disappoint me. Remember, my child is waiting.'

And when Mrs. Rivers left, Esther asked Mrs. Jones what she was to do. She 'd have to find somebody to look after her child. It was now just after two o'clock. Baby was asleep, and would want nothing for three or four hours, and Mrs. Jones gave her the address of a respectable woman. But this woman was looking after twins, and could not undertake the charge of another baby. Esther visited many streets, always failing for one reason or another, till at last she found herself in Wandsworth, in a battered, tumbledown little street, no thoroughfare, only four houses, a coal-shed, and some broken wooden palings. In the area of No. 3 three mites were playing, and at Esther's call a short, fat woman came out of the kitchen, her dirty apron sloping over her big stomach, and her pale brown hair twisted into a knot at the top of her head.

'Well, what is it?'

'I came about putting a child out to nurse. You are Mrs. Spires, ain't yer?'

'Yes, that 's my name. May I ask who sent you?'

Esther told her, and then Mrs. Spires asked her to step down into the kitchen.

'Them there children you saw in the area I looks after while their mothers are out washing or charing. They takes them 'ome in the evening. I only charges them fourpence a day, and it is a loss at that, for they takes a lot of minding. What age is yours?'

'Mine is only a month old. I 've a chance to go out as wet-nurse if I can find a place to put him out to nurse. Will you look after my baby?'

'How much do you think of paying for him?'

'Five shillings a week.'

'And you a-going out as wet-nurse at a pound a week; you can afford more than that.'

'I 'm only getting fifteen shillings a week.'

'Well, you can afford to pay six. I tell you the respon-

sibility of looking after a hinfant is that awful nowadays
that I don't care to undertake it for less.'

Esther hesitated, for she didn't like this woman.

'I suppose,' said the woman, altering her tone to one of
mild interrogation, 'you would like your baby to have the
best of everything, and not the drainings of any bottle
that's handy?'

'I should like my child to be well looked after, and I
must see him every three weeks.'

'Do you expect me to bring up the child to wherever the
lady lives, and pay my bus fare, all out of five shillings a
week? It can't be done!' Esther didn't answer. 'You
ain't married, of course?' Mrs. Spires said suddenly.

'No, I ain't; what about that?'

'Oh, nothing; there is so many of you, that's all. You
can't lay yer 'and on the father and get a bit out of 'im?'

They stopped speaking. Esther looked round suspiciously, and noticing the look the woman said:

'Your baby will be well looked after 'ere; a nice warm
kitchen, and I've no other babies for the moment; them
children don't give no trouble, they plays in the area. You
had better let me have the child; you won't do better
than 'ere.'

Esther promised to think it over and let her know to-
morrow. It took her many omnibuses to get home, and
it was quite dark when she pushed the door to. The first
thing that caught her ear was her child crying. 'What is
the matter?' she cried, hurrying down the passage.

'Oh, is that you? You have been away a time. The
poor child is that hungry he has been crying this hour or
more. If I'd 'ad a bottle I'd 'ave given him a little milk.'

'Hungry, is he? Then he shall have plenty soon. It is
nearly the last time I shall give the poor darling my breast.'
She told Mrs. Jones about Mrs. Spires, and both women
tried to arrive at a decision.

'Since you 'ave to put the child out to nurse, you might
as well put him there as elsewhere; the woman will look
after him as well as she can—she'll do that, if it is for the
sake of the six shillings a week.'

'Yes, yes, I know; but I've always heard that children
die that are put out to nurse. If mine died I never should
forgive myself.'

She could not sleep; she lay with her arms about her baby, distracted at the thought of parting from him, and wondering what had she done that her baby should be separated from her? And of all what had the poor little darling done? He at least was innocent; yet he was to be deprived of his mother. And at midnight she threw her legs out of bed, lighted a candle, looked at him, took him in her arms, squeezed him to her bosom till he cried, and the thought came that it would be sweeter to kill him with her own hands than to be parted from him.

But the thought of murder went with the night, and she almost enjoyed the journey to Wandsworth. Her baby laughed and cooed, and was much admired in the omnibus, and the little street where Mrs. Spires lived seemed different. A cart of hay was being unloaded, and this gave the place a pleasant rural air. Mrs. Spires, too, was cleaner, tidier; Esther no longer disliked her; she had a nice little cot ready for the baby, and he seemed so comfortable in it that Esther did not feel the pain at parting which she had expected to feel. She would see him in a few weeks, and in those weeks she would be richer. It seemed quite wonderful to earn so much money in so short a time, and she returned thinking that her luck seemed to have turned at last; and so engrossed was she in thoughts and dreams of her good fortune that she nearly forgot to get out of her bus at Charing Cross, and had it not been for the attention of the conductor might have gone on, she did not know where— perhaps to Clerkenwell, or maybe to Islington. And when the second bus turned into Oxford Street she jumped out, not wishing to spend more money than she could help. Mrs. Jones approved of all she had done, aided her to pack up her box, and sent her away full of the adventure and the prospect. She went wondering if the house she was going to was as grand as Woodview, and was much struck by the appearance of the maidservant who opened the door to her.

'Oh, here you are,' Mrs. Rivers said. 'I have been anxiously expecting you; my baby is not at all well. Come up to the nursery at once. I don't know your name,' she said, turning to Esther.

'Waters, ma'am.'

'Emily, you 'll see that Waters's box is taken to her room.'

'I 'll see to it, ma'am.'

'Then come up at once, Waters. I hope you 'll succeed better than the others.'

A tall, handsome gentleman stood at the door of a room full of beautiful things, and as they went past him Mrs. Rivers said, 'This is the new nurse, dear.' Higher up, Esther saw a bedroom of soft hangings and bright porcelain. Then another staircase, and the little wail of a child caught on the ear, and Mrs. Rivers said, 'The poor little thing; it never ceases crying. Take it, Waters, take it.'

Esther sat down, and soon the little thing ceased crying.

'It seems to take to you,' said the anxious mother.

'So it seems,' said Esther; 'it is a wee thing, not half the size of my boy.'

'I hope the milk will suit her, and that she won't bring it up. This is our last chance.'

'I dare say she will come round, ma'am. I suppose you weren't strong enough to suckle her yourself, and yet you looks 'ealthy.'

'I? No, I could not undertake to nurse it.' Then, glancing suspiciously at Esther, whose breast was like a little cup, Mrs. Rivers said, 'I hope you have plenty of milk?'

'Oh, yes, ma'am; they said at the hospital I could bring up twins.'

'Your supper will be ready at nine. But that will be a long time for you to wait. I told them to cut you some sandwiches, and you 'll have a glass of porter. Or perhaps you 'd prefer to wait till supper? You can have your supper, you know, at eight, if you like.'

Esther took a sandwich and Mrs. Rivers poured out a glass of porter. And later in the evening Mrs. Rivers came down from her drawing-room to see that Esther's supper was all right, and, not satisfied with the handsome fare that had been laid before her child's nurse, she went into the kitchen and gave strict orders that the meat for the future was not to be quite so much cooked.

Something jarred, however; such constant mealing did not seem natural, and her self-respect was wounded; she hated her position in this house, and sought and found consolation in the thought that she was earning good money for her baby. She noticed, too, that she never was allowed out alone, and that her walks were limited to just enough exercise to keep her in health.

A fortnight passed, and one afternoon, after having put baby to sleep, she said to Mrs. Rivers, 'I hope, ma'am, you 'll be able to spare me for a couple of hours; baby won't want me before then. I 'm very anxious about my little one.'

'Oh, nurse, I couldn't possibly hear of it; such a thing is never allowed. You can write to the woman, if you like.'

'I do not know how to write, ma'am.'

'Then you can get someone to write for you. But your baby is no doubt all right.'

'But, ma'am, you are uneasy about your baby; you are up in the nursery twenty times a day; it is only natural I should be uneasy about mine.'

'But, nurse, I 've no one to send with you.'

'There is no reason why anybody should go with me, ma'am; I can take care of myself.'

'What! let you go off all the way to—where did you say you had left it—Wandsworth?—by yourself! I really couldn't think of it. I don't want to be unnecessarily hard—but I really couldn't—no mother could. But I don't want you to agitate yourself, and if you like I 'll write myself to the woman who has charge of your baby. I cannot do more, and I hope you 'll be satisfied.'

By what right, by what law, was she separated from her child? She was tired of hearing Mrs. Rivers speak of 'my child, my child, my child,' and of seeing this fine lady turn up her nose when she spoke of her own beautiful boy. And when Mrs. Rivers came to engage her she said that it would be better for the baby to be brought to see her every three or four weeks, for two had died already. At the time she had not understood. She supposed vaguely, in a passing way, that Mrs. Rivers had already lost two children. But yesterday the housemaid told her that that little thing in the cradle had had two wet-nurses before Esther, and that both their babies had died. It was then a life for a life. It was more. For the children of two poor girls had been sacrificed so that this rich woman's child might be saved. Even that was not enough: the life of her beautiful boy was called for. And then other memories swept by. She remembered vague hints,

allusions that Mrs. Spires had thrown out; and, as in a
dream darkly, it seemed to this ignorant girl that she was
the victim of a far-reaching conspiracy; she experienced
the sensation of the captured animal, and scanned the
doors and windows, thinking of some means of escape.

At that moment a knock was heard and the housemaid
came in.

'The woman who has charge of your baby has come to
see you.'

Esther started up from her chair, and fat little Mrs.
Spires waddled into the room, the ends of her shawl touching the ground.

'Where is my baby?' said Esther. 'Why haven't you
brought him?'

'Why, you see, my dear, the sweet little thing didn't
seem as well as usual this afternoon, and I didn't like to
bring 'im out, it being a long way and a trifle cold. But it
is nice and warm in here. May I sit down?'

'Yes, there 's a chair; but tell me what is the matter
with him?'

'A little cold, dear—nothing to speak of. You must not
worry yourself, it isn't worth while; besides, it 's bad for
you and the little darling in the cradle. May I have a
look? A little girl, isn't it?'

'Yes, it is a girl.'

'And a beautiful little girl too. 'Ow 'ealthy she do
look! I 'll be bound you have made a difference in her.
I suppose you are beginning to like her just as if she was
your own?'

Esther did not answer.

'Yer know, all you girls are dreadful taken with your
babies at first. But they is a awful drag on a girl who gets
her living in service. For my part I do think it a provi-
dence that rich folk don't suckle their own. If they did,
I dunno what would become of all you poor girls. The
situation of wet-nurse is just what you wants at the time,
and it is good money. I hope yer did what I told you and
stuck out for a pound a week. Rich folks like these 'ere
would think nothing of a pound a week, nor yet two,
when they sees their child is suited.'

'Never mind about my money, that 's my affair. Tell
me what 's the matter with my baby?'

''Ow yer do 'arp on it! I 've told yer that 'e 's all right; nothing to worry about, only a little poorly, but knowing you was anxious I thought it better to come up. I didn't know but what you might like to 'ave in the doctor.'

'Does he require the doctor? I thought you said it was nothing to worry about.'

'That depends on 'ow yer looks at it. Some likes to 'ave in the doctor, however little the ailing; then others won't 'ave anything to do with doctors—don't believe in them. So I thought I 'd come up and see what you thought about it. I would 'ave sent for the doctor this morning—I 'm one of those who 'as faith in doctors—but being a bit short of money I thought I 'd come up and ask you for a trifle.'

At that moment Mrs. Rivers came into the nursery and her first look went in the direction of the cradle, then she turned to consider curtsying Mrs. Spires.

'This is Mrs. Spires, the lady who is looking after my baby, ma'am,' said Esther; 'she has come with bad news—my baby is ill.'

'Oh, I 'm sorry. But I dare say it is nothing.'

'But Mrs. Spires says, ma'am——'

'Yes, ma'am, the little thing seemed a bit poorly, and I being short of money, ma'am, I had to come and see nurse. I knows right well that they must not be disturbed, and of course your child's 'ealth is everything; but if I may make so bold I 'd like to say that the little dear do look beautiful. Nurse is bringing her up that well that yer must have every satisfaction in 'er.'

'Yes, she seems to suit the child; that 's the reason I don't want her upset.'

'It won't occur again, ma'am, I promise you.'

Esther did not answer, and her white, sullen face remained unchanged. She had a great deal on her mind, and would have spoken if the words did not seem to betray her when she attempted to speak.

'When the baby is well, and the doctor is satisfied there is no danger of infection, you can bring it here—once a month will be sufficient. Is there anything more?'

'Mrs. Spires thinks my baby ought to see the doctor.'

'Well, let her send for the doctor.'

'Being a bit short of money——'

'How much is it?' said Esther.

'Well, what we pays is five shillings to the doctor, but then there's the medicine he will order, and I was going to speak to you about a piece of flannel: if yer could let me have ten shillings to go on with.'

'But I haven't so much left. I must see my baby,' and Esther moved towards the door.

'No, no, nurse, I cannot hear of it; I'd sooner pay the money myself. Now, how much do you want, Mrs. Spires?'

'Ten shillings will do for the present, ma'am.'

'Here they are; let the child have every attendance, and remember you are not to come troubling my nurse. Above all, you are not to come up to the nursery. I don't know how it happened, it was a mistake on the part of the new housemaid. You must have my permission before you see my nurse.' And while talking rapidly and imperatively Mrs. Rivers, as it were, drove Mrs. Spires out of the nursery. Esther could hear them talking on the staircase, and she listened, all the while striving to collect her thoughts. Mrs. Rivers said when she returned, 'I really cannot allow her to come here upsetting you.' Then, as if impressed by the sombre look on Esther's face, she added: 'Upsetting you about nothing. I assure you it will be all right; only a little indisposition.'

'I must see my baby,' Esther replied.

'Come, nurse, you shall see your baby the moment the doctor says it is fit to come here. You can't expect me to do more than that.' Esther did not move, and thinking that it would not be well to argue with her, Mrs. Rivers went over to the cradle. 'See, nurse, the little darling has just woke up; come and take her, I'm sure she wants you.'

Esther did not answer her. She stood looking into space, and it seemed to Mrs. Rivers that it would be better not to provoke a scene. She went towards the door slowly, but a little cry from the cradle stopped her, and she said:

'Come, nurse, what is it? Come, the baby is waiting for you.'

Then, like one waking from a dream, Esther said: 'If my baby is all right, ma'am, I'll come back, but if he wants me, I'll have to look after him first.'

'You forget that I'm paying you fifteen shillings a week.

I pay you for nursing my baby; you take my money, that's sufficient.'

'Yes, I do take your money, ma'am. But the house-maid has told me that you had two wet-nurses before me, and that both their babies died, so I cannot stop here now that mine's ill. Every one for her own; you can't blame me. I'm sorry for yours—poor little thing, she was getting on nicely, too.'

'But, Waters, you won't leave my baby. It's cruel of you. If I could nurse it myself——'

'Why couldn't you, ma'am? You look fairly strong and healthy.'

Esther spoke in her quiet, stolid way, finding her words unconsciously.

'You don't know what you're saying, nurse; you can't. You've forgotten yourself. Next time I engage a nurse I'll try to get one who has lost her baby, and then there'll be no bother.'

'It is a life for a life—more than that, ma'am—two lives for a life; and now the life of my boy is asked for.'

A strange look passed over Mrs. Rivers's face. She knew, of course, that she stood well within the law, that she was doing no more than a hundred other fashionable women were doing at the same moment; but this plain girl had a plain way of putting things, and she did not care for it to be publicly known that the life of her child had been bought with the lives of two poor children. But her temper was getting the better of her.

'He'll only be a drag on you. You'll never be able to bring him up, poor little bastard child.'

'It is wicked of you to speak like that, ma'am, though it is I who am saying it. It is none of the child's fault if he hasn't got a father, nor is it right that he should be deserted for that, and it is not for you to tell me to do such a thing. If you had made sacrifice of yourself in the beginning and nursed your own child such thoughts wouldn't have come to you. But when you hire a poor girl such as me to give the milk that belongs to another to your child, you think nothing of the poor deserted one. He is only a love-child, you say, and had better be dead and done with. I see it all now; I have been thinking it out. It is all so hidden up that the meaning is not clear at first, but what it comes to is this, that fine folks like you pays the money, and Mrs. Spires and her like gets rid of the poor little things. Change the milk a few times, a little neglect, and the poor servant-girl is spared the trouble of bringing up her baby and can make a handsome child of the rich woman's little starveling.'

At that moment the baby began to cry; both women looked in the direction of the cradle.

'Nurse, you have forgotten yourself, you have talked a great deal of nonsense, you have said a great deal that is untrue. You accused me of wishing your baby were dead; indeed, I hardly know what wild remarks you did not indulge in. Of course, I cannot put up with such conduct —to-morrow you will come to me and apologize. In the meantime the baby wants you; are you not going to her?'

'I'm going to my own child.'

'That means that you refuse to nurse my baby?'

'Yes; I'm going straight to look after my own.'

'If you leave my house you shall never enter it again.'

'I don't want to enter it again.'

'I shall not pay you one shilling if you leave my baby. You have no money.'

'I shall try to manage without. I shall go with my baby to the workhouse. However bad the living may be there, he'll be with his mother.'

'If you go to-night my baby will die. She cannot be brought up on the bottle.'

'Oh, I hope not, ma'am. I should be sorry, indeed I should.'

'Then stay, nurse.'

'I must go to my baby, ma'am.'

'Then you shall go at once—this very instant.'

'I'm going this very instant, as soon as I've put on my hat and jacket.'

'You had better take your box with you. If you don't, I shall have it thrown into the street.'

'I dare say you're cruel enough to do that if the law allows you, only be careful that it do.'

## CHAPTER XIX

THE moment Esther got out of the house in Curzon Street she felt in her pocket for her money. She had only a few pence—enough for her bus fare, however, and her thoughts did not go further. She was absorbed by one desire, how to save her child—how to save him from Mrs. Spires, whom she vaguely suspected; from the world, which called him a bastard, and denied to him the right to live. And she sat as if petrified in the corner of the bus, seeing nothing but a little street of four houses facing some hay-lofts, the low-pitched kitchen, the fat woman, the cradle in the corner. The intensity and the oneness of her desire seemed to annihilate time, and when she got out of the omnibus she walked with a sort of animal-like instinct straight for the house. There was a light in the kitchen just as she expected, and as she descended the four wooden steps into the area she looked to see if Mrs. Spires was there. She was there, and Esther pushed open the door.

'Where's my baby?'

'Lord, 'ow yer did frighten me!' said Mrs. Spires, turning from the range and leaning against the table, which was laid for supper. 'Coming like that into other folk's places without a word of warning—without as much as knocking at the door.'

'I beg your pardon, but I was anxious about my baby.'

'Was you indeed? It is easy to see it is the first one. There it is in the cradle there.'

'Have you sent for the doctor?'

'Sent for the doctor! I've to get my husband's supper.'

Esther took her baby out of the cradle. It woke up crying, and Esther said: 'You don't mind my sitting down a moment. The poor little thing wants its mother.'

'If Mrs. Rivers saw you now a-nursing of yer baby?'

'I shouldn't care if she did. He's thinner than when I left him; ten days 'ave made a difference in him.'

'Well, you don't expect a child to do as well without its mother as with her. But tell me, how did yer get out? You must have come away shortly after me.'

'I wasn't going to stop there and my child ill.'

'Yer don't mean to tell me that yer 'ave gone and thrown hup the situation?'

'She told me, if I went out, I should never enter her door again.'

'And what did you say?'

'Told her I didn't want to.'

'And what, may I ask, are yer thinking of doing? I 'eard yer say yer 'ad no money.'

'I don't know.'

'Take my advice, and go straight back and ask 'er to overlook it, this once.'

'Oh, no, she 'd never take me back.'

'Yes, she will. You suits the child, and that 's all they thinks of.'

'I don't know what will become of me and my baby.'

'No more don't I. Yer can't stop always in the work'us, and a baby 'll be a 'eavy drag on you. Can't you lay 'ands on 'is father some'ow?'

Esther shook her head, and Mrs. Spires noticed that she was crying.

'I 'm all alone,' she said; 'I don't know 'ow I 'm ever to pull through.'

'Not with that child, yer won't—it ain't possible. You girls is all alike; yer thinks of nothing but yer babies for the first few weeks, then yer tires of them, the drag on yer is that 'eavy—I knows yer—and then yer begins to wish they 'ad never been born, or yer wishes they had died afore they knew they was alive. I don't say I 'm not often sorry for them, poor little dears, but they takes less notice than you 'd think for, and they 're better out of the way, and that 's a fact; it saves a lot of trouble hereafter. I often do think that to neglect them, to let them go off quiet, that I be their best friend; not wilful neglect, yer know, but what is a woman to do with ten or a dozen, and I often 'as as many? I am sure they 'd thank me for it.'

Esther did not answer, but judging by her face that she had lost all hope, Mrs. Spires was tempted to continue.

'There 's that other baby in the far corner that was brought 'ere since you was 'ere by a servant-girl like yerself. She 's out a-nursing of a lady's child, getting a pound a week, just as you was. Well, now, I asks 'ow she can 'ope to bring up that 'ere child—a weakly little thing that wants the doctor and all sorts of looking after. If that child was to live, it would be the ruin of that girl's life. Don't yer 'ear what I 'm saying?'

'Yes, I hear,' said Esther, speaking like one in a dream; 'don't she care for her baby, then?'

'She used to care for them, but if they had all lived I should like to know where she 'd be. There 'as been three of them—that 's the third—so, instead of them a-costing 'er money, they brings 'er money. She 'as never failed yet to suit 'erself in a situation as wet-nurse.'

'And they all died?'

'Yes, they all died; and this little one don't look as if it was long for the world, do it?' said Mrs. Spires, who had taken the infant from the cradle; and Esther looked at the poor wizened features, twitched with pain.

'It goes to my 'eart,' said Mrs. Spires, 'it do indeed, but, Lord, it is the best that could 'appen to 'em; who 's to care for 'em? and there is 'undreds and 'undreds of them—ay, thousands and thousands every year—and they all dies like the early flies. It is 'ard, very 'ard, poor little dears, but they 're best out of the way—they 're only an expense and a disgrace.'

Mrs. Spires talked on in a rapid, soothing, soporific voice. She had just finished pouring some milk in the baby's bottle and had taken down a jug of water from the dresser.

'But that 's cold water,' said Esther, waking from the stupor of her despair; 'it will give the baby gripes for certain.'

'I 've no 'ot water ready; I 'll let the bottle stand afore the fire, that 'll do as well.' Watching Esther all the while, Mrs. Spires held the bottle a few moments before the fire, and then gave it to the child to suck. Very soon after a cry of pain came from the cradle.

'The little dear never was well; it wouldn't surprise me a bit if it died—went off before morning. It do look that poorly. One can't 'elp being sorry for them, though one knows there is no 'ouse for them 'ere. Poor little angels, and not even baptized. There 's them that thinks a lot of getting that over. But who 's to baptize the little angels?'

'Baptize them?' Esther repeated. 'That 's not the way

with the Lord's people;' and to escape from a too over-powering reality she continued to repeat the half-forgotten patter of the Brethren, 'You must wait until it is a symbol of living faith in the Lord!' And taking the baby in her hands for a moment, the wonder crossed her mind whether he would ever grow up and find salvation and testify to the Lord as an adult in voluntary baptism.

All the while Mrs. Spires was getting on with her cooking. Several times she looked as if she were going to speak, and several times she checked herself. In truth, she didn't know what to make of Esther. Was her love of her child such love as would enable her to put up with all hardships for its sake; or was it the fleeting affection of the ordinary young mother, which, though ardent at first, gives way under difficulties? Mrs. Spires had heard many mothers talk as Esther talked, but when the real strain of life was put upon them they had yielded to the temptation of rid-ding themselves of their burdens. So Mrs. Spires could not believe that Esther was really different from the others, and if carefully handled she would do what the others had done. Still, there was something in Esther which kept Mrs. Spires from making any distinct proposal. But it were a pity to let the girl slip through her fingers—five pounds were not picked up every day. There were three five-pound notes in the cradles; if Esther would listen to reason there would be twenty pounds. And once more greed set Mrs. Spires's tongue flowing, and, representing herself as a sort of guardian angel, she spoke again about the mother of the dying child, pressing Esther to think what the girl's circumstances would have been if all her babies had lived.

'And they all died?' said Esther.

'Yes, and a good job, too,' said Mrs. Spires, whose temper for the moment outsped her discretion. Was this penniless drab doing it on purpose to annoy her? A nice one indeed to high-and-mighty it over her. She would show her in mighty quick time she had come to the wrong shop. Just as Mrs. Spires was about to speak out she noticed that Esther was in tears. Mrs. Spires always looked upon tears as a good sign, so she resolved to give her one more chance. 'What are you crying about?' she said.

'Oh,' said Esther, 'I don't even know where I shall

sleep to-night. I have only threepence, and not a friend in the world.'

'Now look 'ere, if you 'll listen to reason I 'll talk to you. Yer mustn't look upon me as a henemy. I 've been a good friend to many a poor girl like you afore now, and I 'll be one to you if you 're sensible like. I 'll do for you what I 'm doing for the other girl. Give me five pounds——'

'Five pounds! I 've only a few pence.'

''Ear me out. Go back to yer situation—she 'll take you back: yer suits the child, that 's all she cares about. Ask 'er for an advance of five pounds; she 'll give it when she 'ears it is to get rid of yer child. They 'ates their nurses to be a-'ankering after their own; they likes them to be forgotten like; they asks if the child is dead very often, and won't engage them if it isn't. So believe me she 'll give yer the money when yer tells 'er that it is to give the child to someone who wants to adopt it. That 's what you 'as to say.'

'And you 'll take the child off my hands for ever for five pounds?'

'Yes; and if you likes to go out again as wet-nurse, I 'll take the second off yer 'ands too, and at the same price.'

'You wicked woman! Oh, this is awful!'

'Come, come. What do you mean by talking to me like that? And because I offered to find someone who would adopt your child.'

'You did nothing of the kind; ever since I 've been in your house you have been trying to get me to give you up my child to murder as you are murdering those poor innocents in the cradles.'

'It is a lie, but I don't want no hargument with yer; pay me what you owe me and take yerself hoff. I want no more of yer, do you 'ear?'

Esther did not shrink before her as Mrs. Spires expected. Clasping her baby more tightly, she said: 'I 've paid you what I owe you; you 've had more than your due. Mrs. Rivers gave you ten shillings for a doctor which you didn't send for. Let me go.'

'Yes, when yer pays me.'

'What 's all this row about?' said a tall, red-bearded man who had just come in; 'no one takes their babies out of this 'ere 'ouse before they pays. Come now, come now, who are yer getting at? If yer thinks yer can come here insulting of my wife, yer mistaken; yer 've come to the wrong shop.'

'I 've paid all I owe,' said Esther. 'You 're no better than murderers, but yer shan't have my poor babe to murder for a five-pound note.'

'Take back them words, or else I 'll do for yer; take them back,' he said, raising his fist.

'Help, help, murder!' Esther screamed. Before the brute could seize her she slipped past, but before she could scream again he laid hand on her at the door. Esther thought her last moment had come.

'Let 'er go, let 'er go!' cried Mrs. Spires, clinging to her husband's arm. 'We don't want the perlice in 'ere.'

'Perlice! What do I care about the perlice? Let 'er pay what she owes.'

'Never mind, Tom; it is only a trifle. Let her go. Now then, take yer hook,' she said, turning to Esther; 'we don't want nothing to do with such as you.'

With a growl the man loosed his hold, and feeling herself free Esther rushed into the area and up the wooden steps. Some men drinking in a public-house frightened her and she ran on again, and to avoid the cabmen and the loafers in the next street she hastily crossed to the other side. Her heart beat violently, her thoughts were in disorder, and she walked on and on, stopping to ask the way, and then remembered there was no whither she might go unless the workhouse; no matter, any whither. All sorts of thoughts came upon her unsought till she came to the river, and saw vast water rolling. Was she to die, she and her child? Why she more than the next one? Why not go to the workhouse for the night? She didn't mind for herself, only she did not wish her boy to go there. But if God willed it . . .

She drew her shawl about her baby and tried once more to persuade herself into accepting the shelter of the workhouse. It seemed strange even to her that a pale, glassy moon should float high up in the sky, and that she should suffer, and then she looked at the lights that fell into the river from the Surrey shore, and wondered what had she done to deserve the workhouse? and of all, what had the poor, innocent child done to deserve it? If she once entered the workhouse she would remain there. She and her child paupers for ever. 'But what can I do?' she asked herself crazily, and sat down on one of the seats.

A young man coming home from an evening party looked at her as he passed, and she asked herself if she should run after him and tell him her story. Why should he not assist her? He could so easily spare it. Would he? But before she could decide to appeal to him he had called a passing hansom and was soon far away. Then looking at the windows of the great hotels, she thought of the folk there who could so easily save her from the workhouse if they knew. There must be many a kind heart behind those windows who would help her if she could only make known her trouble. But that was the hardship. She could not make known her trouble; she could not tell the misery. She couldn't understand it herself; why it had all come about she didn't know, for, after all—— Her thoughts melted away and when she returned to herself she was thinking that she would be mistaken for a common beggar. Nowhere would she find any one to listen to her, and in the delirium of her misery she asked herself would it not have been better, perhaps, if she had left him with Mrs. Spires. What indeed had the poor little fellow to live for? A young man in evening dress came towards her, looking so happy and easy in life, walking with long, swinging strides. He stopped and asked her if she was out for a walk.

'No, sir; I'm out because I've no place to go.'

'How's that?'

She told him the story of the baby-farmer and he listened kindly, and she thought the needful miracle was about to happen. But he only complimented her on her pluck and got up to go. Then she understood that he did not care to listen to sad stories, and a vagrant came and sat down.

'The "copper,"' he said, 'will be moving us on presently. It don't much matter; it's too cold to get to sleep, and I think it will rain. My cough is that bad.'

She might beg a night's lodging of Mrs. Jones. But it was so far away that she didn't think she could walk so far. Mrs. Jones might have left, then what would she do? The workhouse up there was much the same as the work-house down here. Mrs. Jones couldn't keep her for nothing, and there was no use trying for another situation as wet-nurse; the hospital would not recommend her again. So there was nothing for it but the workhouse. Her thoughts melted away, and she had been so near to sleep that it was almost a surprise to her to find herself on the Embankment. Her father, brothers, and sisters were on their way to Australia. But there was no use thinking of them, she and her baby were on their way to the workhouse, going to become paupers. . . . The vagrant had fallen asleep. He knew all about the workhouse—should she ask him what it was like? He, too, was friendless. If he had a friend he would not be sleeping on the Embankment. Should she ask him? Poor chap, he was asleep. People were happy when they were asleep.

A full moon floated high up in the sky, and the city was no more than a faint shadow on the glassy stillness of the night; and she longed to float away with the moon out of sight of this world. Her baby grew heavy in her arms, and the vagrant, a bundle of rags thrown forward in a heap, slept at the other end of the bench. But she could not sleep, and the moon whirled on her miserable way. At last the glassy stillness was broken by the measured tramp of the policeman going his rounds, and in reply to her inquiry he directed her to Lambeth Workhouse. As she walked away she heard him rousing the vagrant and bidding him move onward.

## CHAPTER XX

THOSE who came to the workhouse for servants never
offered more than fourteen pounds a year, and these wages
would not pay for her baby's keep out at nurse.   Her friend
the matron did all she could, but it was always fourteen
pounds, till at last an offer of sixteen pounds a year came
from a tradesman in Chelsea; and the matron introduced
Esther to Mrs. Lewis, a lonely widowed woman, who for
five shillings a week would undertake to look after the
child.

What luck!

The shop was placed at a street corner, and twelve feet
of fronting on the King's Road, and more than half that
amount on the side street, exposed to every view wallpapers
and stained-glass designs.   The dwelling-house was over the
shop; and the Bingleys were Dissenters who exacted the
uttermost farthing from their customers and their work-
people.  Mrs. Bingley spoke in a sour, resolute voice,
when she came down in a wrapper to superintend the
cooking, but on Sundays she wore a black satin, fastened
with a cameo brooch, and then her manners were lofty.
When her husband called 'Mother,' she answered testily,
'Don't keep on mothering me,' overlooking Mr. Bingley's
ill-fitting frock-coat.   On weekdays he wore a short jacket,
and every day a ring of discoloured hair, neither brown
nor red, but the neutral tint that hair which does not turn
grey acquires, under his chin.   When he spoke he opened
his mouth wide, and seemed quite unashamed of the
empty spaces and the three or four yellow fangs that
remained.

John, the elder of the two brothers, a silent youth, whose
one passion seemed to be eavesdropping, hung round doors
in the hopes of overhearing his sister's conversation, and if
he heard Esther and the little girl who helped Esther in her
work talking in the kitchen, he would steal cautiously
half-way down the stairs.   Esther often thought that his
young woman must be sadly in want of a sweetheart to

take on with one such as he. 'Come along, Amy,' he would
cry, passing out before her; never thinking even at the
end of a long walk to offer her his arm; and they came
strolling home just like boy and girl.

Hubert, John's younger brother, was quite different,
having escaped the family temperament, as he had escaped
the family upper lip, and Esther liked to hear him call
back to his mother, 'All right, mother, I've got the key;
no one need wait up for me. I'll make the door fast.'

'Oh, Hubert, don't be later than eleven. You're not
going out dancing again, are you? Your father will have
the electric bell put on the door, so that he may know when
you come in.'

The four girls were all ruddy-complexioned and the
eldest, the plainest, kept her father's books, and made the
pastry. The second and third did not look upon themselves as unmarriageable: but the youngest was subject to
hysterics, fits of some kind.

The house the Bingleys lived in reproduced the taste
they had imposed upon the neighbourhood—a staircase
covered with white drugget, with white-enamelled walls
kept scrupulously clean, a drawing-room furnished with
substantial tables, cabinets and chairs, and antimacassars,
long and wide, china ornaments and glass vases. The
drawing-room was used only on Sundays. The family
retired thither and hymns were played by one of the young
ladies, the entire family joining in the chorus.

And it was into this house that Esther entered as general
servant, with wages fixed at sixteen pounds a year; and
for seventeen long hours every day, for two hundred and
thirty hours every fortnight, she washed, she scrubbed,
she cooked, she ran errands, with never a moment that she
might call her own. She was allowed every second Sunday
out for four, perhaps for four and a half hours; the time
fixed was from three to nine, but she was expected to be
back in time to get the supper ready, and if it were many
minutes later than nine there were complaints. On entering this service she had no money and few clothes. Her
quarter's wages would not be due for another fortnight,
and, as they did not coincide with her Sunday out, she
would not see her baby for another three weeks, and a great
longing was in her heart to clasp him in her arms again,

to feel his soft cheek against hers, to take his warm, chubby legs and fat feet in her hands. The four lovely hours of liberty would slip by too quickly. But to get them she must pawn her dress—the only decent dress she had left. No matter, she must see the child. She would be able to get the dress out of pawn when she was paid her wages. Then she would have to buy herself a pair of boots; and she owed Mrs. Lewis a lot of money. For five shillings a week came to thirteen pounds a year, which left her three a year for boots and clothes, journeys back and forward, and everything the baby might want. It was not to be done—she never would be able to pull through. As for the dress, on second thoughts she didn't dare to pawn it, for if she did she'd never be able to get it out again. At that moment something bright lying on the floor, under the basin-stand, caught her eye. It was a half-crown, and as the temptation came into her heart to steal, she raised her eyes and looked round the room.

She was in John's room—in the sneak's room. No one was about. She would have cut off one of her fingers for the coin. That half-crown meant pleasure and a happiness so tender and seductive that she closed her eyes for a moment. The half-crown she held between forefinger and thumb presented a ready solution of the besetting hardship of her wages. She threw out the insidious temptation, but it came quickly upon her again. If she didn't take the half-crown she wouldn't be able to go to Peckham on Sunday. She could replace the money where she found it when she was paid her wages. No one knew it was there; it had evidently rolled there, and, having tumbled between the carpet and the wall, had not been discovered. It had probably lain there for months, perhaps it was utterly forgotten. Besides, she need not take it now. It would be quite safe if she put it back in its place; on Sunday afternoon she would take it, and if she changed it at once—— It was not marked. She examined it all over. No, it was not marked. Then the desire paused, and she wondered how she, an honest girl, who had never harboured a dishonest thought in her life before, could desire to steal, and a loathly shame fell upon her.

It was a case of flying from temptation, and she left the room so hurriedly that John, who was spying in the passage, had not time either to slip downstairs or to hide in his brother's room.

'Oh, I beg pardon, sir, but I found this half-crown in your room.'

'Well, there's nothing wonderful in that. What are you so agitated about? I suppose you intended to return it to me?'

'Intended to return it! Of course.'

An expression of hate and contempt leaped into her handsome grey eyes, and, like a dog's, the red lip turned down, for she suddenly understood that this pasty-faced, despicable chap had placed the coin where it might have rolled accidentally. He had complained that morning that she did not keep his room sufficiently clean! It was a carefully laid plan, he was watching her all the while, and no doubt thought that it was his own indiscretion that had prevented her from falling into the trap. She dropped the half-crown at his feet without a word; and all the time she remained in her present situation she persistently refused to speak to him; she brought him what he asked for, but never answered him, even with a Yes or No.

It was during the few minutes' rest after dinner that the burden of the day pressed heaviest upon her; then a painful weariness grew into her limbs, and it seemed impossible to summon strength and will to beat carpets or sweep down the stairs. But if she were not moving about before the clock struck, Mrs. Bingley came down to the kitchen.

'Now, Esther, is there nothing for you to do?'

And again, about eight o'clock, she felt too tired to bear the weight of her own flesh. She had been through fourteen hours of toil, with no breaks but hasty meals, and it seemed to her that she would never be able to summon enough courage to get through the last three hours. It was this last climb that taxed all her strength and all her will. Even the rest that awaited her at eleven o'clock was blighted by the knowledge of the day that was coming; and she was often too tired to rest, and rolled over and over in her garret bed, her whole body aching, all that was human crushed out of her; even her baby was growing indifferent to her. Ah, if he was to die! She didn't desire her boy's death, but she couldn't forget what the baby-farmer had told her, that the burden wouldn't become lighter, but heavier and heavier. Was there no hope? She buried her face in her pillow.

One morning she was startled out of her sleep by a loud knocking at the door. It was Mrs. Bingley, who had come to ask her if she knew what time it was. It was nearly seven o'clock. But Mrs. Bingley could not blame her much, having herself forgotten to put on the electric bell, and Esther hurried through her dressing. But in hurrying she trod on her dress, tearing it right across, a most unfortunate thing to happen, and just when her mistress was calling her. There was nothing for it but to run down and tell her what had happened.

'Haven't you got another dress that you can put on?'

'No, ma'am.'

'Really, I can't have you going to the door in that thing. You don't do credit to my house; you must get yourself a new dress at once.'

Esther muttered that she had no money to buy one.

'Then I don't know what you do with your money.'

'What I do with my wages is my affair; I 've plenty of use for my money.'

'I cannot allow any servant of mine to speak to me like that.'

Esther did not answer, and Mrs. Bingley continued:

'It is my duty to know what you do with your money, and to see that you do not spend it in any wrong way. I am responsible for your moral welfare.'

'Then, ma'am, I think I had better leave you.'

'Leave me, because I don't wish you to spend your money wrongfully, because I know the temptations that a young girl's life is beset with?'

'There ain't much chance of temptation for them who work seventeen hours a day.'

'Esther, you seem to forget——'

'No, ma'am; but there 's no use talking about what I do with my money—there are other reasons; the place is too hard a one. I 've felt it so for some time, ma'am. My 'ealth ain't equal to it.'

Once she had spoken, Esther showed no disposition to retract, and she resisted all Mrs. Bingley's solicitations to remain with her, knowing well the risk she was running in leaving her situation, but compelled like the hunted animal to leave the cover and seek safety in the open country. Her whole body cried out for rest, she must have rest; that was the thing that must be. Mrs. Lewis would keep her and her baby for twelve shillings a week; the present was the Christmas quarter, and she was richer by five-and-twenty shillings than she had been before. Mrs. Bingley had given her ten shillings, Mr. Hubert five, and the other ten had been contributed by the four young ladies. Out of this money she hoped to be able to buy a dress and a pair of boots, as well as a fortnight's rest with Mrs. Lewis, and her plans had been settled some three weeks before her month's warning would expire.

Henceforth the days of her servitude drew out, seeming more than ever exhausting, and the longing in her heart to be free, at times rose to her head, and her brain turned as if in delirium, for every time she sat down she remembered she was so many hours nearer to rest—a fortnight's rest—she could not afford more; but in her present slavery that fortnight seemed at once as a paradise and an eternity. Her fear was that her health might break down, and that she would be laid up during the time she intended for rest. Her baby was lost sight of in her desire of rest, for even a mother demands something in return for her love, and in the last year Jackie had taken much and given nothing. But when she opened Mrs. Lewis's door he came running to her, calling her 'mummie'; and the immediate preference he showed for her, climbing on her knees instead of on Mrs. Lewis's, was a fresh sowing of love in the mother's heart.

They were in the midst of those few days of sunny weather which come in January, deluding us so with their brightness and warmth that we look round for roses and are astonished to see the earth bare of flowers. And these bright afternoons Esther spent entirely with Jackie. At the top of the hill their way led through a narrow passage between a brick wall and a high paling. She had always to carry him through this passage, for the ground there was sloppy and dirty, and the child wanted to stop to watch the pigs through the chinks in the boards. But when they came to the smooth, wide, high roads over looking the valley, she put him down, and he would run on ahead, crying, 'Tum for a walk, mummie, tum along,' and his little feet went so quickly beneath his frock that it

seemed as it he were on wheels. She followed, often forced
to break into a run, tremulous lest he should fall, and
together they descended the hill into the ornamental park,
and spent happy hours amid geometrically designed flower-
beds and curving walks. She ventured with him as far
as the old Dulwich village, and they strolled through the
long street; and, when Jackie called to his mother to carry
him, she rejoiced in the labour of his weight; and when he
grew too heavy, she rested on the farm-gate, and looked
into the low-lying, shiftless fields, intersected with broken
hedges. And when the chill of night awoke her from
dreams already forgotten she clasped Jackie to her bosom
and turned towards home, very soon to lose herself again
in another tide of happiness.

The evenings, too, were charming. When the candles
were lighted, and tea was on the table, Esther sat with the
dozing child on her knee, looking into the flickering fire,
her mind a reverie, occasionally broken by the homely
talk of her companion; and when the child was laid in his
cot she took up her sewing—she was making herself a new
dress; or else the great kettle was steaming on the hob, and
the women stood over the washing-tubs. On the following
evening they worked on either side of the ironing-table,
the candle burning brightly and their vague woman's
chatter sounding pleasant in the hush of the cottage. A
little after nine they were in bed, and so the days went by
softly, like happy, trivial dreams, and it was not till the
end of the third week that Mrs. Lewis would hear of Esther
looking out for another place. And then Esther was surprised at her good fortune. A friend of Mrs. Lewis's knew
a servant who was leaving her situation in the West End of
London. Esther got the address, and went next day after
the place. She was fortunate enough to obtain it, and her
mistress seemed well satisfied with her. But one day in
the beginning of her second year of service she was told
that her mistress wished to speak to her in the dining-room.

'I fancy,' said the cook, 'that it is about that baby of
yours; they're very strict here.'

Mrs. Trubner was sitting on a low wicker chair by the
fire. She was a large woman with eagle features. Her
eyesight had been failing for some years, and her maid was
reading to her. The maid closed the book and left the room.

'It has come to my knowledge, Waters, that you have a child. You're not a married woman, I believe?'

'I've been unfortunate; I've a child, but that don't make no difference so long as I gives satisfaction in my work. I don't think that the cook has complained, ma'am.'

'No, the cook hasn't complained, but had I known this I don't think I should have engaged you. In the character which you showed me, Mrs. Barfield said that she believed you to be a thoroughly religious girl at heart.'

'And I hope I am that, ma'am. I am truly sorry for my fault. I've suffered a great deal.'

'So you all say; but supposing it were to happen again, and in my house? Supposing——'

'Then don't you think, ma'am, there is repentance and forgiveness? Our Lord said——'

'You ought to have told me; and as for Mrs. Barfield, her conduct is most reprehensible.'

'Then, ma'am, would you prevent every poor girl who has had a misfortune from earning her bread? If they was all like you there would be more girls who'd do away with themselves and their babies. You don't know how hard pressed we are. The baby-farmer says, "Give me five pounds and I'll find a good woman who wants a little one, and you shall hear no more about it." Them very words were said to me. I took him away and hoped to be able to rear him, but if I'm to lose my situations——'

'I should be sorry to prevent any one from earning their bread——'

'You're a mother yourself, ma'am, and you know what it is.'

'Really, it's quite different. . . . I don't know what you mean, Waters.'

'I mean that if I am to lose my situations on account of my baby, I don't know what will become of me. If I give satisfaction——'

At that moment Mr. Trubner arrived, his glasses perched on his high aquiline nose, his mother's feature as it was his: a large, stout man slightly out of breath.

'Oh, oh, I didn't know, mother,' he blurted out, and was about to withdraw when Mrs. Trubner said:

'This is the new servant whom that lady in Sussex recommended.'

Esther saw a look of instinctive repulsion come over his face.

'I 'll leave you to settle with her, mother.'

'I must speak to you, Harold—I must.'

'I really can't; I know nothing of this matter.'

He tried to leave the room, and when his mother stopped him he said testily, 'Well, what is it? I am very busy just now, and——' Mrs. Trubner told Esther to wait in the passage.

'Well,' said Mr. Trubner, 'have you discharged her? I leave all these things to you.'

'She has told me her story, and truthfully I think, saying that if she is kept from earning her bread she doesn't know what would become of her. Her position is a very hard one.'

'I know that. But we can't have loose women about the place. They all can tell a fine story; the world is full of impostors.'

'I don't think the girl is an impostor.'

'Very likely not, but every one has a right to protect themselves.'

'Don't speak so loud, Harold,' said Mrs. Trubner, lowering her voice. 'Remember her child is dependent upon her; if we send her away we don't know what may happen. I 'll pay her a month's wages if you like, but you must take the responsibility.'

'I won't take any responsibility in the matter. If she had been here two years—she has only been here a year, not so much more—and had proved a satisfactory servant, I don't say that we 'd be justified in sending her away. But there are plenty of good girls who want a situation as much as she. I don't see why we should harbour loose women when there are so many deserving cases.'

'Then you want me to send her away?'

'I don't want to interfere; you ought to know how to act. Supposing the same thing were to occur again? My cousins, young men, coming to the house——'

'But she won't see them.'

'Do as you like; it is your business, not mine. It doesn't matter to me, so long as I 'm not interfered with; keep her if you like. You ought to have looked into her character more closely before you engaged her. I think that the lady who recommended her ought to be written to very sharply.'

They had forgotten to close the door, and Esther stood in the passage burning and choking with shame.

'It is a strange thing that religion should make some people so unfeeling,' she thought as she left Onslow Square.

It was thus she learnt her lesson that she must keep her child secret, and in her next situation she shunned intimacy with her fellow-servants, thereby exposing herself to their sneers. She feared the remark that she always went out, but once she was out of the house her daily life fell behind her, and she arrived breathless with expectation at a cottage where a little boy stood by a stout middle-aged woman, turning over the pages of the illustrated papers that his mother had brought him. She had no money to buy him toys, and dropping the *Illustrated London News*, he cried, 'Here is mummie,' running to her with outstretched arms while Mrs. Lewis continued her sewing. And for an hour or more Esther talked about her fellow-servants, about the people she lived with, the conversation interrupted by the child calling his mother's attention to the pictures, or by the trustful intrusion of his little hand into hers.

Her clothes were her great hardship, and she often thought that she would rather go back to the slavery of the house in Chelsea than bear the humiliation of going out any longer on Sunday in the old things that the servants had seen her in for eight or nine months or more. She was made to feel that she was the lowest of the low—the servant of servants. She had to accept everybody's sneer and everybody's bad language, and oftentimes gross familiarity, in order to avoid arguments and disputes which might endanger her situation. She had to shut her eyes to the thefts of cooks; she had to fetch them drink, and to do their work when they were unable to do it themselves. But there was no help for it. She could not pick and choose where she would live, and any wages above sixteen pounds a year she must always accept, and put up with whatever inconvenience she might meet.

Hers is a heroic adventure if one considers it—a mother's fight for the life of her child against all the forces that civilization arrays against the lowly and the illegitimate.

She is in a situation to-day, but on what security does she hold it? She is strangely dependent on her own health, and still more upon the fortunes and the personal caprice of her employers; and she realized the perils of her life when an outcast mother at the corner of the street, stretching out of her rags a brown hand and arm, asked alms for the sake of the little children. For three months out of a situation and she, too, would be on the street as a flower-seller, match-seller, or——

It did not seem, however, that any of these fears were to be realized. Her luck had mended. For nearly two years she had been living with some rich people in the West End; she liked her mistress and was on good terms with her fellow-servants, and had it not been for an accident she could have kept this situation. The young gentlemen had come home for their summer holidays, and one day as she stepped aside to let Master Harry pass her on the stairs, he did not go by, but stood looking at her with a strange smile on his face.

'Look here, Esther, I'm awfully fond of you. You are the prettiest girl I've ever seen. Come out for a walk with me next Sunday.'

'Master Harry, I'm surprised at you; will you let me go by at once?'

There was no one near, the house was silent, and the boy stood on the step above her. He tried to throw his arm round her waist, but she shook him off and went up to her room calm with indignation. A few days afterwards she suddenly became aware that he was following her in the street. She turned sharply upon him.

'Master Harry, I know that this is only a little foolishness on your part, but if you don't leave off I shall lose my situation, and I'm sure you don't want to do me an injury.'

Master Harry seemed sorry, and he promised not to follow her in the street again. And never thinking that it was he who had written the letter she received a few days after, she asked Annie, the upper housemaid, to read it. It contained reference to meetings and unalterable affection, and it concluded with a promise to marry her if she lost her situation through his fault. Esther listened like one stunned. A schoolboy's folly, the first silly sentimentality of a boy, a thing lighter than the lightest leaf that falls, had brought disaster upon her.

If Annie had not seen the letter she might have been able to get the boy to listen to reason; but Annie had seen the letter, and Annie could not be trusted. The story would be sure to come out, and then she would lose her character as well as her situation. It was a great pity, for her mistress had promised to have her taught cooking at South Kensington, and a cook's wages would secure her and her child against all usual run of accidents. She would never get such a chance again, and would remain a kitchenmaid to the end of her days. But there was no help for it, and acting on the impulse of the moment she went straight to the drawing-room. Her mistress was alone, and Esther handed her the letter. 'I thought you had better see this at once, ma'am. I did not want you to think it was my fault. Of course the young gentleman means no harm.'

'Has any one seen this letter?'

'I showed it to Annie. I'm no scholar myself, and the writing was hard.'

'You have no reason for supposing—— How often did Master Harry speak to you in this way?'

'Only twice, ma'am.'

'Of course it is only a little foolishness. I needn't say that he doesn't mean what he says.'

'I told him, ma'am, that if he continued I should lose my situation.'

'I'm sorry to part with you, Esther, but I really think that the best way will be for you to leave. I am much obliged to you for showing me this letter. Master Harry, you see, says that he is going away to the country for a week. He left this morning. So I really think that a month's wages will settle matters nicely. You are an excellent servant, and I shall be glad to recommend you.'

Then Esther heard her mistress mutter something about the danger of good-looking servants. She was paid a month's wages, and left that afternoon.

## CHAPTER XXI

IT was the beginning of August, and London yawned in
every street; the dust blew unslaked, and a little cloud
curled and disappeared over the crest of the hill at Hyde
Park Corner; the streets and St. George's Place looked out
with blind, white eyes; and in the deserted Park the trees
tossed their foliage restlessly, as if they wearied and
missed the fashion of their season. And all through Park
Lane and Mayfair, caretakers and gaunt cats were the
traces that the caste on which Esther depended had left of
its departed presence. She was coming from the Alexandra
Hotel, where she had heard a kitchenmaid was wanted.
Another disappointment! Good situations were seldom
found in the summer months, and it would be bad policy to
take a bad one, even if it were only for a while. Besides,
she had saved a little money, and, feeling that she required
a rest, she took Mrs. Lewis's advice to wait. But as luck
would have it Jackie fell ill before she had been at Dulwich
a week; his illness made a big hole in her savings, and it
became plain that she 'd have to go to work at once.

She was going north, to a registry office near Oxford
Street, which Mrs. Lewis had recommended. Holborn
Row was difficult to find, and she had to ask the way very
often, but she suddenly knew that she was in the right
street by the number of servant-girls going and coming
from the office, and in company with five others she
ascended a gloomy little staircase and passed into an odour
of poverty.

The benches were occupied by fifteen or twenty poorly
dressed women, and a little old woman, very white and
pale, stood near the window recounting her misfortunes to
no one in particular.

'I lived with her more than thirty years; I brought up
all the children. I entered her service as nurse, and when
the children grew up I was given the management of
everything  For the last fifteen years my mistress was
a confirmed invalid. She entrusted everything to me.

Oftentimes she took my hand and said, "You are a good creature, Holmes, you mustn't think of leaving me; how should I get on without you?" But when she died they had to part with me; they said they were very sorry, and wouldn't have thought of doing so, only they were afraid I was getting too old for the work. I dare say I was wrong to stop so long in one situation. I shouldn't have done so but she always used to say, "You mustn't leave us; we never shall be able to get on without you."'

At that moment the secretary, an alert young woman with a decisive voice, came through the folding doors.

'I will not have all this talking,' she said. Her quick eyes fell on the little old woman, and she came forward a few steps. 'What, you here again, Miss Holmes? I told you that when I hear of anything that will suit you I'll write.'

'So you said, miss, but my little savings are running short. I'm being pressed for my rent.'

'I can't help that; when I hear of anything I'll write. But I can't have you coming here every third day wasting my time; now run along.' And having made casual remarks about the absurdity of people of that age coming after situations, she called to her desk three or four women, of whom Esther was one, and—after examining them critically, she seemed especially satisfied with Esther's appearance.

'It will be difficult,' she said, 'to find you the situation you want before people begin to return to town. Now if you were only an inch or two taller I could get you a dozen places as housemaid; tall servants are all the fashion, and you are the right age—about five-and-twenty.'

Esther left a dozen stamps with her, and soon after she began to receive letters containing the addresses of ladies who required servants. They were of all sorts, and Esther set out on long journeys from Brixton to Notting Hill to visit poor people who could hardly afford a maid-of-all-work. Sometimes she was asked to call at a house in Bayswater, and thence she had to go to High Street, Kensington, or Earl's Court; a third address might be in Chelsea. She could only guess which was the best chance, and while she was hesitating the situation might be given away. Very often the ladies were out, and she was asked to call later in the day. These casual hours she spent in the parks, mending Jackie's socks or hemming pocket-handkerchiefs, so she was frequently delayed till evening; and in the mildness of the summer twilight, with some fresh disappointment lying heavy on her heart, she made her way from the Marble Arch round the barren Serpentine into Piccadilly, with its stream of lights beginning in the sunset.

And standing at the kerb of Piccadilly Circus, waiting for a bus to take her to Ludgate Hill Station, the girl grew conscious of the moving multitude that filled the streets. The great restaurants rose up calm and violet in the evening sky, the Café Monico, with its air of French newspapers and Italian wines; and before the grey façade of the fashionable Criterion hansoms stopped and dinner parties walked across the pavement. The fine weather brought the wenches up earlier than usual from the suburbs, and they came up the long road from Fulham, with white dresses floating from their hips, and feather boas waving a few inches from the pavement. But through this elegant disguise Esther could pick out the servant-girls. Their stories were her story. Each and all had been deserted; and perhaps each had a child to support. But they hadn't been as lucky as she had been in finding situations, that was all.

But her luck seemed to have left her for good. They were now in the middle of September and she was not able to find the situation she wanted, and it became more and more distressing to her to refuse sixteen pounds a year, but nothing less than eighteen pounds was of any use to her. With eighteen pounds and a kind mistress who would give her an old dress occasionally she could do very well. But if she didn't find these two pounds she did not know what she should do. She might drag on for a time on sixteen pounds, but such wages would drive her in the end into the workhouse. Jackie cost her more than he used to. A sudden imagination let her see him playing in the little street, waiting for her to come home, and her love for him went to her head like madness, and she wondered at herself; for it seemed almost unnatural to love anything as she did this child.

And then, in a shiver of fear, determined to save her

bus fare, she made her way through Leicester Square, hastening her steps when addressed by a passer-by, which was hard to do, for she had been walking all day and had not tasted food since the morning, and the weakness of the flesh brought a sudden weakness of the spirit. She felt that she could struggle no more, that the whole world was against her—she felt that she must have food and drink and rest. All this London tempted her; the cup was at her lips, for a young man in evening clothes was speaking to her. His voice was soft, the look in his eyes seemed kindly.

Thinking of the circumstances ten minutes later, it seemed to her that she had intended to answer him. But she was now at Charing Cross. There was a lightness, an emptiness in her head which she could not overcome, and the crowd appeared to her like a blurred, noisy dream. And then the dizziness left her, and she realized the temptation she had escaped. Here, as in Piccadilly, she could pick out the servant-girls; but here their service was yesterday's lodging - house — poor and dissipated girls, dressed in vague clothes fixed with hazardous pins. Two young women came out of an eating-house, hanging on each other's arms, talking lazily. The skirt on the outside was a soiled mauve, and the bodice that went with it was a soiled chocolate. A broken yellow plume hung out of a battered hat. The skirt on the inside was a dim green, and little was left of the cotton-velvet jacket but the cotton. A girl of sixteen walking sturdily, like a little man, crossed the road, her left hand thrust deep into the pocket of her red cashmere dress. She wore on her shoulders a strip of beaded mantle; her hair was plaited and tied with a red ribbon. Elderly women passed, their eyes liquid with invitation; and the huge bar-loafer, the man of fifty, the hooked nose and the waxed moustache, stood at the door of a restaurant, passing the women in review.

A true London of the water's edge—a London of theatres, music-halls, wine-shops, public-houses—the walls painted various colours, nailed over with huge gold lettering; the pale air woven with delicate wire, a gossamer web underneath which the crowd moved like lazy flies, one half watching the perforated spire of St. Mary's, and all the City spires behind it now growing cold in the east; the other half seeing the spire of St. Martin's above the chimney-pots aloft in a sky of cream-pink. Stalwart policemen urged along groups of slattern boys and girls; and after vulgar remonstrance these took the hint and disappeared down strange passages. Suddenly Esther came face to face with a woman whom she recognized as Margaret Gale.

'What, is it you, Margaret?'

'Yes, it is me all right. What are you doing up here? Got tired of service? Come and have a drink, old gal.'

'No, thank you; I'm glad to have seen you, Margaret, but I've a train to catch.'

'That won't do,' said Margaret, catching her by the arm; 'we must have a drink and talk over old times.'

Esther felt that if she didn't have something she would faint before she reached Ludgate Hill, and Margaret led the way through the public-house, opening all the varnished doors, seeking a quiet corner. 'What's the matter?' she said, startled at the pallor of Esther's face.

'Only a little faintness; I've not had anything to eat all day.'

'Quick, quick, four of brandy and some water,' Margaret cried to the barman, and a moment after she was holding the glass to her friend's lips. 'Not had anything to eat all day, dear? Then we'll have a bite and a sup together. I feel a bit peckish myself. Two sausages and two rolls and butter,' she cried. Then the women had a long talk. Margaret told Esther the story of her misfortune. The Barfields were all gone broke. They had been very unlucky racing, and when the servants got the sack Margaret had come up to London. She had been in several situations, and finally, one of her masters had got her into trouble, his wife had turned her out neck and crop, and what was she to do? Esther told how Master Harry had lost her her situation.

'And you left like that? Well I never! The better one behaves the worse one gets treated, and them that goes on with service find themselves in the end without as much as will buy them a Sunday dinner.'

Margaret insisted on accompanying Esther, and they walked together as far as Wellington Street. 'I can't go any farther,' and pointing to where London seemed to end in a piece of desolate sky, she said; 'I live on the other side of the water, in Stamford Street. You might come and see me. If ever you get tired of service you 'll get decent rooms there.'

Bad weather followed fine, and under a streaming umbrella Esther went from one address to another, her damp skirts clinging about her and her boots clogged with mud. She looked upon the change as unfortunate, for in getting a situation so much depended on personal appearance and cheerfulness of manner; and it is hard to seem a right and tidy girl after two miles' walk through the rain.

One lady told Esther that she liked tall servants, another said she never engaged good-looking girls, and another place that would have suited her was lost through answering that she was chapel. The lady would have nothing in her house but church. Then there were the disappointments occasioned by the letters which she received from people who she thought would have engaged her, saying they were sorry, but that they had seen someone whom they liked better.

Another week passed; Esther had to pawn her clothes to get money for her train fare to London and keep the registry office supplied with stamps; and she lay awake thinking that she and Jackie must go back to the workhouse. Mrs. Lewis had been very good to them, but Esther owed her two weeks' money. She had heard of charitable institutions, but she was an ignorant girl and didn't know how to make the necessary inquiries. Money, money! oh, the want of a little money—of a very little money! The thought beat into her brain. For just enough to hold on till the people came back to town.

One day Mrs. Lewis, who read the newspapers for her, came to her with an advertisement which she said seemed to read like a very likely chance. Esther looked at the pence which remained out of the last dress that she had pawned.

'I 'm afraid,' she said, 'it will turn out like the others; I 'm out of my luck.'

'Don't say that,' said Mrs. Lewis. 'Keep your pecker up; I 'll stick to you as long as I can.'

The women had a good cry in each other's arms, and then Mrs. Lewis advised Esther to take the situation, even if it were no more than sixteen. 'A lot can be done by constant saving, and if she gives yer 'er dresses and ten shillings for a Christmas-box, I don't see why you shouldn't pull through. And the child shan't cost you more than five shillings a week till you get a situation as plain cook, I 'll see to that. Here is the address—Miss Rice, Avondale Road, West Kensington.'

## CHAPTER XXII

AVONDALE ROAD was an obscure corner of the suburb—obscure, for it had just sprung into existence. The scaffolding that had built it now littered an adjoining field, where in a few months it would rise about Horsley Gardens, whose red gables and tiled upper walls will correspond with Avondale Road. 'Nothing much like eighteen pounds a year,' she said, 'in this neighbourhood. Hot joint to-day, cold the next,' and raising her eyes she saw the tiny gable windows of the cupboard-like rooms where the single servant kept in these houses slept.

A few steps more brought her to 41, the corner house, and the thin passage and the meagre staircase confirmed Esther in the poor opinion she had formed from the aspect of the street; and she felt that the place was more suitable to the gaunt woman with iron-grey hair whom she found waiting in the passage. The woman looked apprehensively at Esther, and when Esther said that she had come after the place a painful change of expression passed over her face, and she answered:

'You 'll get it; I 'm too old for anything but charing. How much are you going to ask?'

'I can't take less than sixteen.'

'Sixteen! I used to get that once; I 'd be glad enough to get twelve now. You can't think of sixteen once you 've turned forty, and I 've lost my teeth, and they means a couple of pound off.'

Then the door opened, and a woman's voice called to the gaunt woman to come in. She went in, and Esther breathed a prayer that she might not be engaged. A minute intervened, and the gaunt woman came out; there were tears in her eyes, and she whispered to Esther as she passed, 'No good; I told you so. I 'm too old for anything but charing.' The abruptness of the interview suggested a hard mistress, and Esther was surprised to find herself in the presence of a slim lady, about seven-and-thirty, whose small grey eyes seemed to express a kind and gentle nature.

The room almost said that the occupant was a spinster and a writer, and Esther remembered that she had noticed even at the time Miss Rice's writing; it was such a beautiful clear round hand, and it lay on the table, ready to be continued the moment she should have settled with her.

'I saw your advertisement in the paper, miss; I 've come after the situation.'

'You are used to service?'

'Yes, miss, I 've had several situations in gentlemen's families, and have excellent characters from them all.' Miss Rice put up her glasses and her grey eyes smiled, and she seemed pleased with the somewhat rugged but pleasant-featured girl before her.

'I live alone,' she said; 'the place is an easy one and, if the wages satisfy you, I think you will suit me very well. My servant, who has been with me some years, is leaving me to be married.'

'What are the wages, miss?'

'Fourteen pounds a year.'

'I 'm afraid, miss, there would be no use my taking the place; I 've so many calls on my money that I could not manage on fourteen pounds. I 'm very sorry, for I feel sure I should like to live with you, miss.'

'I think we should suit each other,' Miss Rice said reflectively. 'I should like to have you for my servant if I could afford it. How much would you take?'

'Placed as I am, miss, I could not take less than sixteen. I 've been used to eighteen.'

'Sixteen pounds is more than I can afford, but I 'll think it over. Give me your name and address.'

'Esther Waters, 13 Poplar Road, Dulwich.'

As Esther turned to go she became aware of the kindness of the eyes that looked at her. Miss Rice said:

'I 'm afraid you 're in trouble. Sit down; tell me about it.'

'No, miss, what 's the use?' But Miss Rice looked at her so kindly that Esther could not restrain herself. 'There 's nothing for it,' she said, 'but to go back to the work-house.'

'But why should you go to the workhouse? I offer you fourteen pounds a year and everything found.'

'You see, miss, I 've a baby. We 've been in the work-house already; I had to go there the night I left my situation to get him away from Mrs. Spires. She wanted to kill him; she 'd have done it for five pounds—that 's the price. But, miss, my story is not one that can be told to a lady such as you.'

'I think I 'm old enough to listen to your story; sit down, and tell it to me.'

And all the while Miss Rice's eyes were filled with tenderness and pity.

'A very sad story—just such a story as happens every day. But you have been punished, you have indeed.'

'Yes, miss, I think I have; and after all these years of striving it is hard to have to take him back to the work-house. Not that I want to give out that I was badly treated there, but it is the child I 'm thinking of. He was then a little baby and it didn't matter; we was only there a few months. There 's no one that knows of it but me. But he 's a growing boy now, he 'll remember the work-house, and it will be always a disgrace.'

'How old is he?'

'He was six last May, Miss. It has been a hard job to bring him up. I now pay six shillings a week for him, that 's more than fourteen pounds a year, and you can't do much in the way of clothes on two pounds a year. And now that he 's growing up he 's costing more than ever; but Mrs. Lewis—that 's the woman what has brought him up—is as fond of him as I am myself. She don't want to make nothing out of his keep, and that 's how I 've managed up to the present. But I see well enough that it can't be done; his expense mounts up, and the wages stay the same. It was my pride to bring him up on my earnings, and my hope to see him an honest man earning good money. But it wasn't to be, miss, it wasn't to be. We must be humble and go back to the workhouse.'

'I can see that it has been a hard fight.'

'It has indeed, miss; no one will ever know how hard. I shouldn't mind if it wasn't going to end by going back to where it started. They 'll take him from me; I shall never see him while he is there. I wish I was dead, miss, I can't bear my trouble no longer.'

'You shan't go back to the workhouse so long as I can help you, Esther: I'll give you the wages you ask for. It is more than I can afford.  Eighteen pounds a year! But your child shall not be taken from you.  You shall not go to the workhouse.  There aren't many such good women in the world as you, Esther.'

## CHAPTER XXIII

THEY were not unlike—quiet, instinctive Englishwomen, strong, warm natures, under an appearance of formality and reserve, and it took some time before either was able to put aside her natural reserve. But the instincts of the dog soon began to develop in Esther, and she watched the household expenses, likewise her mistress's health.

'Now, miss, I must 'ave you take your soup while it is 'ot. You 'd better put away your writing; you 've been at it all the morning. You 'll make yourself ill, and then I shall have the nursing of you.' If Miss Rice was going out in the evening she would find herself stopped in the passage: 'Now, miss, I really can't see you go out like that; you 'll catch your death of cold. You must put on your warm cloak.'

Miss Rice's friends were principally middle-aged ladies. Her sisters, large, stout women, came to see her, and there was a fashionably dressed young man whom her mistress seemed to like very much, Mr. Alden, who was often at the house; Miss Rice told Esther that he wrote novels; they used to talk for hours, and Esther bethought herself that Miss Rice was giving her heart to one who did not care for her. But mayhap it was only about books they were talking; if so, Esther didn't think she 'd care, if she had a young man, to see him come and go like a shadow. But she hadn't a young man, and did not want one. All she now wanted was to awake in the morning and know that her child was safe. And for more than a year she followed her plan of life, laughing the casual suitor into silence, and rarely persuaded into a promise to walk out with any of them.

One of these swains was a stationer's foreman, and almost every day Esther went to the stationer's for the sermon-paper on which her mistress wrote her novels, for blotting-paper, for stamps, or to post letters. Fred Parsons was his name—a meagre little man about thirty-five, whose high prominent forehead rose above a small pointed face, a scanty growth of blond beard and moustache failing to hide the receding chin and the red-sealing-wax lips; his faded yellow hair was beginning to grow thin on the crown; and his threadbare frock-coat hung limp from his sloping shoulders. But his voice was bell-like; into it no trace of doubt ever seemed to come, and his mind was neatly packed with a few religious and political ideas. These were the man, and he had already begun to wonder what were Esther's religious beliefs. He had been in business in the West End, but an unrestrained desire to ask every customer if he were sure he believed in the second coming of Christ had been the cause of his dismissal, and so it was that he kept himself from questioning Esther. But at the end of a certain week they were alone in the shop; Esther had come for a packet of note-paper. Fred was sorry she had not come for sermon-paper; if she had it would have been easier to inquire her opinions regarding the second coming. But the opportunity, such as it was, was not to be resisted.

'Your mistress seems to use a great deal of paper; it was only a day or two ago that I served you with four quires.'

'That was for her books; what she now wants is note-paper.'

'So your mistress writes books!'

'Yes.'

'I hope they're good books — books that are helpful.' He paused to see that no one was within earshot. 'Books that bring sinners back to the Lord.'

'I don't know what she writes; I only know she writes books; I think I've heard she writes novels.'

Fred did not approve of novels—Esther could see that—and she was sorry; for he seemed a nice, well-spoken young man, and she would have liked to tell him that her mistress was not one who would write anything that could do harm to anybody. But her mistress was waiting for her paper, and she took leave of him hastily. The next time they met was in the evening. She was going to see if she could get some fresh eggs for her mistress's breakfast before the shops closed, and coming towards her, walking at a great pace, she saw one whom she thought she recognized, a meagre little man with long reddish hair curling under the brim of a large soft black hat. He nodded, smiling pleasantly as he passed her.

'Lor',' she thought, 'I didn't know him; it's the stationer's foreman.' And the very next evening they met in the same street; she being out for a little walk, and he hurrying to catch his train. And three days after they met at the same time, and as nearly as possible at the same place.

'We're always meeting,' he said.

'Yes, isn't it strange? You come this way from business?' she answered.

'Yes; about eight o'clock is my time.'

It was at the end of August; the stars were catching fire slowly in the murky London sunset; and, vaguely conscious of a feeling of surprise at the pleasure they took in each other's company, they wandered round a little bleak square in which a few shrubs had just been planted. 'I'm sorry the paper isn't going to be put to better use,' Fred said, taking up the conversation exactly at the point where it had broken off.

'You don't know my mistress, or you wouldn't say that.'

'Perhaps you haven't considered that novels are very often stories about the loves of men for other men's wives. Such books can serve no good purpose.'

'I'm sure my mistress don't write about such things. How could she, poor dear innocent lamb? It is easy to see you don't know her.' In the course of their argument it transpired that Miss Rice went to neither church nor chapel. Fred was much shocked. 'I hope,' he said, 'you do not follow your mistress's example.' Esther admitted she had for some time past neglected her religion, and Fred went so far as to put it forward as her duty to leave her present situation and enter a truly religious family.

'I owe her too much ever to think of leaving her. And it has nothing to do with her if I haven't thought as much about the Lord as I ought to have. It's the first place I've been in where there was time for religion.'

This answer seemed to satisfy Fred.

'Where did you used to go?'

'My people — father and mother — belonged to the Brethren.'

'To the Close or the Open?'

'I don't remember; I was only a little child at the time.'

'I'm a Plymouth Brother.'

'Well, that is strange.'

'Do not forget that it is only through belief in our Lord, in the sacrifice of the Cross, that we can be saved.'

'Yes, I believe that.'

The avowal seemed to have brought them strangely near to each other, and on the following Sunday Fred took Esther to meeting, and introduced her as one who had strayed, but who had never ceased to be one of them.

She had not been to meeting since she was a little child; and the bare room and bare dogma, in such immediate sympathy with her own nature—were they not associated with memories of home, of father and mother, of all that had gone?—touched her with a delight that went to the roots of her nature. Fred was the preacher on this occasion, and he spoke of the second coming of Christ, when the faithful would be carried away in clouds of glory, of the rapine and carnage to which the world would be delivered up before final absorption in everlasting hell. A sense of awe and dread passed over the listening faces, and a young girl who sat with closed eyes put out her hand to assure herself that Esther was still there. And as they walked home, Esther told Fred that she hadn't been happy for a long time, not so happy. He pressed her hand, and thanked her with a look in which appeared all his soul; she was his for ever and ever; nothing could wholly disassociate them, for he had saved her. His exaltation moved her to wonder. But her own innate faith had supported her during many a troublous year, and though she did not share Fred's exaltations she understood them. But Fred would want her to come to meeting with him next Sunday, and she was going to Dulwich. Sooner or later he would find out that she had had a child, then she would see him no more. That child came between her and every chance of settling herself. It were better to break with Fred. But what excuse could she give? Everything went wrong with her. He might ask her to marry him, and then she would have to tell him.

Towards the end of the week she heard someone tap at the window; it was Fred. He asked her why he had not seen her, and she answered that she hadn't had the time.

'Can you come out this evening?'

'Yes, if you like.'

She put on her hat, and they went out, their feet taking the pavement instinctively that led to the little square where they had walked the first time they went out together.

'I 've been thinking of you a good deal, Esther, in the last few days. I want to ask you to marry me.'

Esther did not answer.

'Will you?' he said.

'I can't; I 'm very sorry; don't ask me.'

'Why can't you?'

'If I told you I don't think you 'd want to marry me. But I suppose I 'd better tell you. I 'm not the good woman you think me. I 've got a child. There, you have it now, and you can take your hook when you like.'

It was her blunt, sullen nature that had spoken, she didn't care if he left her on the spot—now he knew all and could do as he liked. At last he said:

'But you 've repented, Esther?'

'I should think I had, and been punished too, enough for a dozen children.'

'Ah, then it wasn't lately?'

'Lately! It 's nearly eight year ago.'

'And all that time you 've been a good woman?'

'Yes, I think I 've been that.'

'Then if——'

'I don't want no ifs. If I am not good enough for you, you can go elsewhere and get better; I 've had enough of reproaches.'

'I did not mean to reproach you; I know that a woman's path is more difficult to walk in than ours. It may not be a woman's fault if she falls, but it is always a man's. He can always fly from temptation.'

'Yet there isn't a man that can say he hasn't gone wrong.'

'No, not all, Esther.'

Esther looked him full in the face.

'I understand what you mean, Esther, but I can honestly say that I never have.'

Esther did not like him any better for his purity, and was irritated by the clear tones of his icy voice.

'But that is no reason why I should be 'ard on those who have not been so fortunate. I didn't mean to reproach you just now, Esther; I only meant to say that I wish you 'ad told me this before I took you to meeting.'

'So you 're ashamed of me, is that it? Well, you can keep your shame to yourself.'

'No, not that, Esther——'

'Then you 'd like to see me took down before the others, as if I haven't 'ad enough of that already.'

'No, Esther, listen to me. Those who transgress the moral law may not kneel at the table for a time, until they have repented; but those who believe in the sacrifice of the Cross are acquitted, and I believe you do that.'

'Yes.'

'A sinner that reproach—— I will speak about this at our next meeting; you will come with me?'

'Next Sunday I 'm going to Dulwich to see the child.'

'Can't you go after meeting?'

'No, I can't be out morning and afternoon both.'

'May I go with you?'

'To Dulwich!'

'You won't go until after meeting; I can meet you at the railway station.'

'If you like.'

As they walked home Esther told Fred the story of her betrayal and he was interested in the story, and sorry for her.

'I love you, Esther, and it is easy to forgive those we love.'

'You 're very good; I never thought to find a man so good.' She looked up in his face; her hand was on the gate, and in that moment she felt that she almost loved him.

## CHAPTER XXIV

AN elderly person who looked after a bachelor's establishment two doors up, Mrs. Humphries, who often ran in about tea-time, soon began to speak of Fred as a very nice young man who would be likely to make a woman happy. But Esther moved about the kitchen in her taciturn way, hardly answering. Suddenly she told Mrs. Humphries that she had been to Dulwich with him, and that it was wonderful how he and Jackie had taken to one another.

'You don't say so! Well, it is nice to find them religious folks less 'ard-'earted than they gets the name of.'

Mrs. Humphries was of the opinion that henceforth Esther should give herself out as Jackie's aunt. 'None believe them stories, but they make you seem more respectable like, and I am sure Mr. Parsons will think so too.' Esther did not answer, but she thought of what Mrs. Humphries had said, and that it might be better if Jackie were to leave off calling her mummie. Auntie! But no, she could not bear it. Fred must take her as she was or not at all. Why shouldn't he? They seemed to understand each other, and he was earning good money, thirty shillings a week; she was now going on for eight-and-twenty, and if she was ever going to be married it was time to think about it.

'I don't know how that dear soul will get on without me,' she said one October morning as they jogged out of London by a slow train from St. Paul's, for Fred was taking her into Kent to see his people.

'How do you expect me to get on without you?'

Esther laughed.

'Trust you to manage somehow. There ain't much fear of a man not looking after his little self.'

'But the old folk will want to know when. What shall I tell them?'

'This time next year; that 'll be soon enough. Perhaps you 'll get tired of me before then.'

'Say next spring, Esther.'

The train stopped.

'There's father waiting for us in the spring cart. Father! He don't hear us. He's gone a bit deaf of late years. Father!'

'Ah, so here you are. Train late.'

'This is Esther, father.'

'And we be right glad to see you. Now if you'll jump into the cart, we'll be at the farm in ten minutes' time.'

'The old pony is going as well as ever, father?' Fred asked.

'Much the same, but none of us be younger than we were,' Esther heard the old man say, and the words stirred her to remember her own age and that she was going to be introduced to Fred's sisters and to his brother. But these did not concern her much: her thoughts were set on Mrs. Parsons, Fred having spoken a great deal about his mother, telling her that when she was told about Jackie she was of course very sorry; but that when she heard the whole of Esther's story she had said, 'We are all born into temptation, and if your Esther has really repented and prayed to be forgiven, we must not say nay to her.' All the same, Esther was not quite easy in her mind, and half regretted she had consented to see Fred's people until he had made her his wife. But it was too late to think of such things. Fred had just pointed to the farmhouse, over yonder, and, scenting his stable, the old grey pony ascended the hill at a trot. 'We had a fine show of flowers all the summer, but there's no more than a few Michaelmas daisies left,' the old man said, and Esther admired the Virginia creeper that covered one side of the house with a crimson mantle, while Parsons answered Fred that he would take the trap round to the stable, and this being settled Fred led the way up the red-bricked pavement and lifting the latch they passed through the kitchen, Fred introducing Esther to his two sisters, Mary and Lily, who were busy cooking.

'Mother is in the parlour,' said Mary; 'she is waiting for you.'

And by the window they found her sitting in a wide wooden arm-chair, a large woman about sixty, dressed in black, wearing on either side of her long white face two corkscrew curls, which gave her a somewhat ridiculous appearance. But when she rose from her chair to greet her son she ceased to be ridiculous or grotesque, for her face beamed, and she held out her hands in a beautiful gesture of welcome.

'Oh, how do you do, dear Fred? I am that glad to see you! How good of you to come all this way! Come and sit ye down by me.'

'Mother, this is Esther.'

'How do you do, Esther? It was good of you to come. I am glad to see you. Let me get you a chair. Take off your things, dear; come and sit by me.'

She insisted on relieving Esther of her hat and jacket, and, having laid them on the sofa, she waddled across the room, drawing over two chairs.

'Come and sit ye down; you 'll tell me everything. I can't get about much now, but I like to have my children round me. Take this chair, Esther.' Then turning to Fred, 'Tell me, Fred, how you 've been getting on. Are you still living at 'Ackney?'

'Yes, mother; but when we 're married we 're going to have a cottage at Mortlake. Esther will like it better than 'Ackney. It is nearer the country.'

'Then you 'aven't forgotten the country. Mortlake is on the river, I think. I 'ope you won't find it too damp.'

'No, mother, there are some nice cottages there. I think we shall find that Mortlake suits us. There are many friends there; more than fifty meet together every Sunday. And there 's a lot of political work to be done there. I know that you 're against politics, but men can't stand aside nowadays. Times change, mother.'

'So long as we have God in our hearts, my dear boy, all that we do is well. But you must want something after your journey. Fred, dear, knock at that door. Your sister Clara 's dressing there. Tell her to make haste.'

'All right, mother,' cried a voice from behind the partition which separated the rooms, and a moment after the door opened and a young woman about thirty entered. She was better-looking than the other sisters, and the fashion of her skirt, and the worldly manner with which she kissed her brother and gave her hand to Esther, marked her off at once from the rest of her family. She was forewoman in a large millinery establishment, but spent Saturday afternoon and Sunday at the farm. To-day she had got away earlier, and, with the view to impressing Esther, she explained how this had come about.

Mrs. Parsons suggested a glass of currant wine, and Lily came in with a tray and glasses. Clara said she was starving. Mary said she would have to wait, and Lily whispered, 'In about half an hour.'

After dinner the old man said that they must be getting on with their work in the orchard, and Esther answered that she would be glad to help, but as she was about to follow the others Mrs. Parsons detained her.

'You don't mind staying with me a few minutes, do you, dear? I shan't keep you long.' She drew over a chair for Esther. 'I shan't perhaps see you again for some time. I am getting an old woman, and the Lord may be pleased to take me at any moment. But I wanted to tell you, dear, that I put my trust in you. You'll make a good wife to Fred, I feel sure, and he will make a good father to your child, and if God blesses you with other children he'll treat your first no different than the others. He's told me so, and my Fred is a man of his word. You were led into sin, but you've repented We was all born into temptation, and we must trust to the Lord to lead us out lest we should dash our foot against a stone.'

'I was to blame; I don't say I wasn't, but——'

'We won't say no more about that. We're all sinners, the best of us. You're going to be my son's wife; you're therefore my daughter, and this house is your home whenever you please to come to see us. And I hope that that will be often. I like to have my children about me. I can't get about much now, so they must come to me. It is very sad not to be able to go to meeting. I've not been to meeting since Christmas, but I can see them going there from the kitchen window, and how 'appy they look coming back from prayer. It is easy to see that they have been with God. The Salvationists come this way sometimes. They stopped in the lane to sing. I could not hear the words, but I could see by their faces that they was with God. Now, I've told all that was on my mind. I must not keep you; Fred is waiting for you.'

Esther kissed the old woman, and went into the orchard, where she found Fred on a ladder shaking the branches. He came down when he saw Esther, and Harry, his brother, took his place. Esther and Fred filled one basket, and then, yielding to a mutual inclination, they wandered about the orchard, stopping on the little plank bridge, speaking hardly at all, words seeming unnecessary; each felt happiness to be a mutual possession. Apart they would be blind and deaf, but together they heard the water trickling through the weeds, and the sound of apples falling in the dusk, and a breeze shivered among the tops of the apple trees and sered leaves were blown from the branches. As the gatherers crossed the plank bridge they put jokes on the lovers, who stood aside to let them pass.

And when all and sundry entered the house they saw the old farmer, who had slipped in before them, sitting by his wife holding her hand, patting it in a curious old-time way, and the attitude of the old couple was so pregnant with significance that it fixed itself on Esther's mind. It seemed to her that she had never seen anything so beautiful. 'So they have lived for forty years,' she said to herself, 'faithful to each other,' and she wondered if Fred forty years hence would be sitting by her side holding her hand.

'Of what are you thinking, Esther?' Fred asked. And not knowing what answer to make him she said: 'It must be near time to be getting home.'

'Are you tired of us already?' Mrs. Parsons asked. Fred interposed, and the old man lighted a lantern, went round to the stable to get a trap out, and drove them through the dark country. A peasant came like a ghost out of the darkness: he stepped aside and called, 'Good night!' which the old farmer echoed somewhat gruffly, while Fred answered in a ringing, cheery tone.

The train rattled on through suburbs beginning far away in the country; rattled on through suburbs that thickened at every mile; rattled on through a brick entanglement; rattled over iron bridges, rattled on over deep streets, over endless lines of lights.

He bade her good-bye at the area gate on a promise that they should be married in the spring. She ran upstairs to tell her dear mistress of the happy day which her kindness had allowed her to spend in the country, and Miss Rice laid the book she was reading on her knees to listen to Esther's pleasures as if they were her own.

## CHAPTER XXV

BUT when the spring came Esther put Fred off till the autumn, pleading as an excuse that Miss Rice had not been very well lately, and that she did not like to leave her.

It was one of those long and pallid evenings at the end of July, when the sky seems as if it could not darken. The roadway was very still in its dust and heat, and Esther, her print dress trailing, watched a poor horse striving to pull a four-wheeler through the loose heavy gravel that had just been laid down. And so absorbed was she in her pity for the poor animal that she did not see the gaunt, broad-shouldered man coming towards her, looking very long-legged in a pair of light-grey trousers and a black jacket a little too short for him. He walked with long, even strides, a small cane in one hand, the other in his trousers pocket; a heavy gold chain showed across his waistcoat. He wore a round bowler hat and she caught sight of a red necktie. The side whiskers and the shaven upper lip gave him the appearance of a gentleman's valet. She took him for such as he went by without noticing Esther, but a sudden step taken sideways as she lingered, her eyes fixed on the cab-horse, brought her into collision with him.

'Look where you are going to,' he exclaimed, jumping back to avoid the beer-jug, which fell to the ground. 'What, Esther, is it you?'

'There, you have made me drop the beer.'

'Plenty more in the public; I 'll get another jug.'

'It is very kind of you, but I can get what I want myself.'

They looked at each other, and at the end of a long silence William said: 'Just fancy meeting you, and in this way. Well I never! I am glad to see you again.'

'Are you really! Well, so much for that—your way and mine aren't the same. I wish you good evening.'

'Stop a moment, Esther.'

'And my mistress waiting for her dinner. I 've to go and get some more beer.'

'Shall I wait for you?

'Wait for me! I should think not, indeed.'

Esther ran down the area steps. Her hand pàused as it was about to lift the jug down from the dresser, and a number of thoughts fled across her mind. That man would be waiting for her outside. What was she to do? How unfortunate! If he continued to come after her he and Fred would be sure to meet.

'What are you waiting for, I should like to know?' she cried, as she came up the steps.

'That's 'ardly civil, Esther, and after so many years too; any one would think——'

'I want none of your thinking; get out of my sight. Do you 'ear? I want no truck with you whatever. Haven't you done me enough mischief already?'

'Be quiet; listen to me. I'll explain.'

'I don't want none of your explanation. Go away.'

Her whole nature was now in full revolt, and quick with passionate remembrance of the injustice that had been done her, she drew back from him, her eyes flashing, and it may have been some passing remembrance of the breakage of the first beer-jug that prevented her from striking him with the second. The spasm passed, and then her rage, instead of venting itself in violent action, assumed the form of dogged silence. She handed the jug across the counter, and while the barman filled it she searched her pocket for the money. She had brought none with her. William produced sixpence. Esther answered him with a quick angry glance, and addressing the barman, she said, 'I'll pay you to-morrow; that'll do, I suppose? 41 Avondale Road.'

'That will be all right, but what am I to do with this sixpence?'

'I know nothing about that,' Esther said, picking up her skirt; 'I'll pay you for what I have had.'

Holding the sixpence in his short, thick, and wet fingers, the barman looked at William. William smiled, and said, 'Well, they do run sulky sometimes.'

He caught at the leather strap and pulled the door open for her, and as she passed out she became aware that William still admired her. Having ruined her life, this man passed out of sight and knowledge, but only to re-appear when a new road leading to a new life seemed open before her. Her temper flamed in her face.

'It was that temper of yours that did it; you wouldn't speak to me for a fortnight. You haven't changed, I can see that,' he said, watching Esther's face, which did not alter until he spoke of how unhappy he had been in his marriage. 'A regular brute she was—we're no longer together, you know; haven't been for the last three years; couldn't put up with 'er. She was that—but that's a long story.' Esther did not answer him. He looked at her, and seeing that she would not be won over easily, he spoke of his money.

'Look 'ere, Esther,' he said, laying his hand on the area gate. 'You won't refuse to come out with me some Sunday. I've a half a share in a public-house, the "King's Head," and have been backing winners all this year. I've plenty of money to treat you. I should like to make it up to you for you've 'ad rather a 'ard time. Now tell me, what 'ave yer been doing all these years? I want to 'ear.'

'What 'ave I been doing? Trying to bring up your child! That's what I've been doing.'

'There's a child, then?' said William, taken aback, and before he could recover himself Esther dodged past him down the area into the house. For a moment he looked as if he were going to follow her; his mind changed, he lingered a moment, and then walked slowly away in the direction of the Metropolitan Railway.

'I'm sorry to 'ave kept you waiting, miss, but I met with an accident and had to come back for another jug.'

'And what was the accident you met with, Esther?'

'I wasn't paying no attention, miss; but was looking at a cab that could 'ardly get through the stones they've been laying down in the Pembroke Road; the poor little 'orse was pulling that 'ard that I thought he'd drop down dead, and while I was looking I ran up against a passer-by, and being a bit taken aback I dropped the jug.'

'How was that? Did you know the passer-by?'

Esther busied herself with the dishes on the sideboard and, Miss Rice divining that something serious had happened to her servant, refrained and allowed the dinner to pass in silence. Half an hour later Esther came into the study with her mistress's tea, and as she set the wicker table by her mistress's knees the shadows about the book-case and the light of the lamp upon the book and the pensive content on Miss Rice's face impelled her to think of her own troubles, the hardship, the passion, the despair of her life compared with this tranquil existence. Never had she felt more certain that misfortune was inherent in her life, and remembering all the trouble she had had, she wondered how she had come out of it all alive; and now, just as things seemed like settling, everything was going to be upset again. Fred was away for a fortnight's holiday —she was safe for eleven or twelve days. After that she did not know what might happen. Her instinct told her that although he had passed over her fault very lightly, so long as he knew nothing of the father of her child, he might not care to marry her if William continued to come after her. Ah! if she hadn't happened to go out at that particular time she might never have met William. He didn't live in the neighbourhood; if he did they would have met before. Perhaps he had just settled in the neighbourhood. That would be worst of all. No, no, no; it was a mere accident; if the cask of beer had held out a day or two longer, or if it had run out a day or two sooner, she might never have met William! But now she couldn't keep out of his way and she knew he'd come after her.

She was right. He spent the whole of the next day in the street waiting for her. If she went out on an errand he followed her there and back. If she'd only listen. She was prettier than ever. He had never cared for any one else. He would marry her when he got his divorce, and then the child would be theirs. She didn't answer him, and her blood boiled at the word 'theirs.' How could Jackie become their child? Was it not she who had worked for him, brought him up? and she thought as little of his paternity as if he had fallen from heaven into her arms.

One evening as she was laying the table her grief took her unawares, and she was obliged to dash aside the tears that had risen to her eyes. The action was so apparent that Miss Rice thought it would be an affectation to ignore it. So she said in her kind, musical, intimate manner: 'Esther, I'm afraid you have some trouble on your mind; can I do anything for you?'

'No, miss, no, it's nothing; I shall get over it presently.'

But the effort of speaking was too much for her, and a bitter sob caught her in the throat.

'You had better tell me your trouble, Esther; even if I
cannot help you it will ease your heart to tell me about it.
I hope nothing is the matter with Jackie?'

'No, miss, no; thank God, he's well enough. It's
nothing to do with him; leastways——' Then with a
violent effort she put back her tears. 'Oh, it is silly of me,'
she said, 'and your dinner getting cold.'

'I don't want to pry into your affairs, Esther, but you
know that——'

'Yes, miss, I know you to be kindness itself; but there's
nothing to be done but to bear it. You asked me just now
if it had anything to do with Jackie. Well, it is no more
than that his father has come back.'

'But surely, Esther, that's hardly a reason for sorrow; I
should have thought that you would have been glad.'

'It is only natural that you should think so, miss; them
what hasn't been through the trouble never thinks the same
as them that 'as. You see, miss, it's nearly nine years
since I've seen him, and during them nine years I 'ave
been through so much. I 'ave worked and slaved, and
been through all the 'ardship, and now, when the worst is
over, he comes and wants me to marry him when he gets
his divorce.'

'Then you like someone else better?'

'Yes, miss, I do, and what makes it so 'ard to bear is that
for the last two months or more I 've been keeping company
with Fred Parsons—that's the stationer's assistant; you 've
seen him in the shop, miss—and he and me is engaged to
be married. He's earning good money, thirty shillings a
week; he's as good a young man as ever stepped—religious,
kind-hearted, everything as would make a woman 'appy in
'er 'ome. It is 'ard for a girl to keep up with 'er religion in
some of the situations we have to put up with, and I 'd
mostly got out of the habit of chapel-going till I met him;
it was 'e who led me back again to Christ. But for all that,
understanding very well, not to say allowing for the failings
of others, like yourself, miss. He knew all about Jackie
from the first, and never said nothing about it, but that I
must have suffered cruel, which I have. He's been with
me to see Jackie, and they both took to each other wonderful like; it couldn't 'ave been more so if 'e 'd been 'is own
father. But now all that's broke up, for when Fred

meets William it is as likely as not as he 'll think quite different.'

The evening died behind the red-brick suburb, and Miss Rice's strip of garden grew greener. She had finished her dinner, and she leaned back thinking of the story she had heard. She was one of those secluded maiden ladies so common in England, whose experience of life is limited to a tea-party, and whose further knowledge of life is derived from the yellow-backed French novels which fill their bookcases.

'How was it that you happened to meet William—I think you said his name was William?'

'It was the day, miss, that I went to fetch the beer from the public-house. It was he that made me drop the jug; you remember, miss, I had to come back for another. I told you about it at the time. When I went out again with a fresh jug he was waiting for me, he followed me to the "Greyhound" and wanted to pay for the beer—not likely that I 'd let him. So I told them to put it on the slate, saying I 'd pay for it to-morrow, and didn't speak to him on leaving the bar, but he followed me to the gate. He wanted to know what I 'd been doing all the time. My temper got the better of me, and I says, "Looking after your child." "My child!" says he. "So there 's a child, is there?"'

'I think you told me that he married one of the young ladies at the place you were then in situation?'

'Young lady! No fear, she wasn't no young lady. Anyway, she was too good or too bad for him; for they didn't get on, and are now living separate.'

'Does he speak about the child? Does he ask to see him?'

'Lor', yes, miss; he 'd the cheek to say the other day that we 'd make him our child—our child, indeed! and after all these years I 've been working and he doing nothing.'

'Perhaps he might like to do something for him! perhaps that 's what he 's thinking of.'

'No, miss, I know him better than that. For that 's his cunning; he thinks he 'll get me through the child.'

'In any case I don't see what you 'll gain by refusing to speak to him; if you want to do something for the child, you can.'

'I don't want his money; please God, we'll be able to do without it to the end.'

'If I were to die to-morrow, Esther, remember that you would be in exactly the same position as you were when you entered my service. You remember what that was? You have often told me there was only eighteenpence between you and the workhouse; you owed Mrs. Lewis two weeks' money for the support of the child. I dare say you've saved a little money since you've been with me, but it cannot be more than a few pounds. I don't think that you ought to let this chance slip through your fingers: if not for your own, for Jackie's sake. William, according to his own account, is making money. He may become a rich man; he has no children by his wife; he might like to leave some of his money—in any case, he'd like to leave something—to Jackie.'

'He was always given to boasting about money. I don't believe all he says about money or anything else.'

'That may be, but he may have money, and you have no right to refuse to allow him to provide for Jackie. Supposing later on Jackie were to reproach you?'

'Jackie'd never do that, miss; he'd know I acted for the best.'

'If you again found yourself out of a situation, and saw Jackie crying for his dinner, you'd reproach yourself.'

'I don't think I should, miss.'

'I know you are very obstinate, Esther. When does Parsons return?'

'In about a week, miss.'

'Without telling William anything about Parsons, you'll be able to find out whether it is his intention to interfere in your life. I quite agree with you that it is important that the two men should not meet; but it seems to me, by refusing to speak to William, and by refusing to let him see Jackie, you're doing all you can to bring about the meeting that you wish to avoid. Is he much about here?'

'Yes, miss, he seems hardly ever out of the street, and it do look so bad for the 'ouse. I feel that ashamed. Since I've been with you, miss, I don't think you've 'ad to complain of followers.'

'Well, don't you see, you foolish girl, that he'll remain

hanging about, and the moment Parsons comes back he 'll hear of it? You 'd better see to this at once.'

'Whatever you says, miss, always do seem right, some'ow. What you says seems reasonable, and yet I don't know how to bring myself to go to 'im. I told 'im that I didn't want no truck with 'im.'

'Yes, I think you said so. It is a delicate matter to advise any one in, but I feel sure I am right when I say that you have no right to refuse to allow him to do something for the child. Jackie is now eight years old, you 've not the means of giving him a proper education, and you know the disadvantage it has been to you not to know how to read and write.'

'Jackie can read beautifully — Mrs. Lewis 'as taught him.'

'Yes, Esther; but there 's much besides reading and writing. Think over what I 've said; you 're a sensible girl; think it out when you go to bed to-night.'

Next day, seeing William in the street, she went up-stairs to ask Miss Rice's permission to go out. 'Could you spare me, miss, for an hour or so?' was all she said, and Miss Rice, who had noticed a man loitering, replied, 'Certainly, Esther.'

'You aren't afraid to be left in the house alone, miss? I shan't be far away.'

'No. I am expecting Mr. Alden. I 'll let him in, and can make the tea myself.'

Esther ran up the area steps and walked quickly down the street, as if she were going on an errand. William crossed the road and was soon alongside of her.

'Don't be so 'ard on a chap,' he said. 'Just listen to reason.'

'I don't want to listen to you; you can't have much to say that I care for.'

Her tone was still stubborn, but he perceived that it contained a change of humour.

'Come for a little walk, and then, if you don't agree with what I says, I 'll never come after you again.'

'You must take me for a fool if you think I 'd listen to your promises.'

'Esther, 'ear me out; you 're very unforgiving, but if you 'd 'ear me out——'

'You can speak; no one's stopping you that I can see.'

'I can't say it off like that; it is a long story. I know that I've behaved badly to you, but it wasn't as much my fault as you think for; I could explain a good lot of it.'

'I 'aven't time to 'ear all your rubbish. Now what 'ave you to say? Come, get it out.'

'There's the boy.'

'Oh, it is the boy you 're thinking of?'

'Yes, and you too, Esther. The mother can't be parted from the child.'

'Very likely; the father can, though.'

'If you talk so snappish I shall never get out what I've to say. I 've treated you badly, and it is to make up for the past as far as I can——'

'And how do you know that you aren't doing harm by coming after me?'

'You mean you 're keeping company with a chap and don't want me?'

'You don't know I 'm not a married woman; you don't know what kind of situation I 'm in. You comes after me just because it pleases your fancy, and don't give it a thought that you mightn't get me the sack as you got it me before.'

'There's no use nagging; just let's go where we can have a talk, and then if you aren't satisfied you can go your way and I can go mine. You said I didn't know that you wasn't married. I don't, but if you aren't, so much the better. If you are, you 've only to say so and I 'll take my hook. I 've done quite enough harm, without coming between you and your husband.'

William spoke earnestly, and his words came so evidently from his heart that Esther was touched against her will.

'No, I ain't married yet,' she replied.

'I 'm glad of that.'

'I don't see what odds it can make to you whether I 'm married or not. If I ain't married, you are.'

William and Esther walked on in silence, listening to the day as it hushed in quiet suburban murmurs under an almost colourless sky—a faded grey, that passed into an insignificant blue; and upon this almost neutral tint the red suburb appeared in rigid outline, the wind raising a cloud of dust in the roadway at intervals.

'Let's go in there,' he said, stopping before a piece of waste ground, 'we'll be able to talk easier'; and they went in and looked for a place where they could sit down.

'This is just like old times,' said William, moving a little closer.

'If you are going to begin any of that nonsense I'll get up and go. I only came out with you because you said you had something particular to say about the child.'

'Well, it is only natural that I should like to see my son.'

'How do you know it's a son?'

'I thought you said so. I should like it to be a boy— is it?'

'Yes, it is a boy, and a lovely boy too; very different to his father. I've always told him that his father is dead.'

'And is he sorry?'

'Not a bit. I've told him his father wasn't good to me; and he don't care for those who haven't been good to his mother.'

'I see, you've brought him up to hate me?'

'He don't know nothing about you—how should 'e?'

'Very likely; but there's no need to be nasty. As I've said before, what's done can't be undone. I treated you badly, I know that; and I've been badly treated myself— damned badly treated. You've 'ad a 'ard time; so have I, if that's any comfort to ye.'

'I suppose it is wrong of me, but seeing you has brought up a deal of bitterness, more than I thought there was in me.'

William lay at length, his body resting on one arm, with a long grass stalk between his small, discoloured teeth. Esther sat straight up, her stiff cotton dress spread over the rough grass; her cloth jacket unbuttoned. He thought her a nice-looking woman, one who'd do well behind the bar of the 'King's Head.' His marriage had proved childless, in every way a failure; and he now desired a wife such as he felt sure she would be. And, his heart hankering after his son sorely, he tried to read Esther's quiet, subdued face, which was now graver than usual, betraying none of the passion that choked in her as she sat thinking that she must manage somehow. But how? She noticed that he was looking at her, and to lead his thoughts away from herself she asked him where he had gone with his wife when they left Woodview.

'Peggy knew all the time I was gone on you.'

'It don't matter about that. Tell me where you went—they said you went foreign.'

'We first went to Boulogne, that 's in France; but every one speaks English there, and there was a nice billiard-room handy, where all the big betting men came in of an evening. We went to the races. I backed three winners on the first day—the second I didn't do so well. Then we went on to Paris. The race-meetings is very 'andy—I will say that for Paris—half an hour's drive and there you are.'

'Did your wife like Paris?'

'Yes, she liked it pretty well—it is all the place for fashion, and the shops is grand; but she got tired of it too, and we went to Italy.'

'Where 's that?'

'That 's down south. A beast of a place—nothing but sour wine, and all the cookery done in oil, and nothing to do but seeing picture-galleries. I got that sick of it I could stand it no longer, and I said, 'I 've 'ad enough of this. I want to go home, where I can get a glass of Burton and a cut from the joint, and where there 's a 'orse worth looking at.''

'But she was very fond of you. She must have been.'

'She was, in her way. But she always liked talking to the singers and the painters that we met out yonder. Nothing wrong, you know. That was after we had been married about three years.'

'What was that?'

'That I caught her out.'

'How do you know there was anything wrong? Men always think bad of women.'

'No, it was right enough; she had got dead sick of me, and I had got dead sick of her. It never did seem natural like. There was no 'omeliness in it, and a marriage that ain't 'omely is no marriage for me. Her friends weren't my friends; and as for my friends, she never left off insulting me about them. If I was to ask a chap in she wouldn't sit in the same room with him. That 's what it got to at last. And I was always thinking of you, and your name used to come up when we was talking. One day she said, "I suppose you are sorry you didn't marry a servant?" and I said, "I suppose you are sorry you did?"'

'That was a good one for her. Did she say she was?'

'She put her arms round my neck and said she loved none but her big Bill. But all her flummery didn't take me in. And I says to myself, "Keep an eye on her." For there was a young fellow hanging about in a manner I didn't particularly like. He was too anxious to be polite to me, he talked to me about 'orses, and I could see he knew nothing about them. He even went so far as go down to Kempton with me.'

'And how did it all end?'

'I said I'll keep my eye on this young whipper-snapper, and coming up from Ascot by an earlier train than they expected me, I let myself in and ran up to the drawing-room, and there I found them sitting side by side on the sofa. The young fellow turned red, and he got up, stammering, and speaking a lot of rot.

'"What! you back already? How did you get on at Ascot? Had a good day?"

'"Rippin'; but I'm going to have a better one now," I said, keeping my eye all the while on my wife. I could see by her face that there was no doubt about it. Then I took him by the throat. "I just give you two minutes to confess the truth; I know it, but I want to hear it from you. Now, out with it, or I'll strangle you." I gave him a squeeze just to show him that I meant it. He turned up his eyes, and my wife cried "Murder!" I threw him back from me and got between her and the door, locked it, and put the key in my pocket. "Now," I said, "I'll drag the truth out of you both." He did look white, he shrivelled up by the chimney-piece, and she—well, she looked as if she could have killed me, only there was nothing to kill me with. I saw her look at the fire-irons. Then, in her nasty sarcastic way, she said, "There's no reason, Percy, why he shouldn't know. Yes," she said, "he is my lover; you can get your divorce when you like."

'I was a bit taken aback; my idea was to squeeze it all out of the fellow and shame him before her. But she spoilt my little game there, and I could see by her eyes that she knew that she had. "Now, Percy," she said, "we'd better go." That put my blood up. I said, "Go you shall, but not till I give you leave," and without another word I took him by the collar and led him to the door; he came like a lamb, and I sent him off with as fine a kick as he ever got in his life.  He went rolling down, and didn't stop till he got to the bottom.  You should have seen her look at me; there was murder in her eyes.  If she could she 'd have killed me, but she couldn't and calmed down a bit.  "Let me go; what do you want me for?  You can get a divorce.  I 'll pay the costs."

'"I don't think I 'd gratify you so much.  So you 'd like to marry him, would you, my beauty?"

'"He 's a gentleman, and I 've had enough of you; if you want money you shall have it."

'I laughed at her, and so it went on for an hour or more. Then she suddenly calmed down.  I knew something was up, only I didn't know what.  I don't know if I told you we was in lodgings—the usual sort, drawing-room with folding doors, the bedroom at the back.  She went into the bedroom, and I followed, just to make sure she couldn't get out that way.  There was a chest of drawers before the door; I thought she couldn't move it, and went back into the sitting-room.  But somehow she managed to move it without my hearing her, and before I could stop her she was down the stairs like lightning.  I went after her, but she had too long a start of me, and the last I heard was the street door go bang.'

The conversation paused.  William took the stalk he was chewing from his teeth, and threw it aside.  Esther had picked one, and with it she beat impatiently among the grass.

'But what has all this to do with me?' she said.  'If this is all you have brought me out to listen to——'

'That 's a nice way to round on me.  Wasn't it you what asked me to tell you the story?'

'So you 've deserted two women instead of one, that 's about the long and short of it.'

'Well, if that 's what you think I 'd better be off,' said William, and he rose to his feet and stood looking at her. She sat quite still, not daring to raise her eyes; her heart was throbbing violently.  Would he go away and never come back?  Should she answer him indifferently or say nothing?  She chose the latter course.  Perhaps it was the wrong one, for her dogged silence irritated him, and he sat down and begged of her to forgive him. He would wait for her. Then her heart ceased throbbing, and a cold numbness came over her hands.

'My wife thought that I had no money, and could do what she liked with me. But I had been backing winners all the season, and had a couple of thousand in the bank. I put aside a thousand for working expenses, for I intended to give up backing horses and go in for bookmaking instead. I have been at it ever since. A few ups and downs, but I can't complain. I am worth to-day close on three thousand pounds.'

At the mention of so much money Esther raised her eyes. She looked at William steadfastly. Her object was to rid herself of him, so that she might marry another man; but at that moment a sensation of the love she had once felt for him sprang upon her suddenly.

'I must be getting back, my mistress will be waiting for me.'

'You needn't be in such a hurry. It is quite early. Besides, we haven't settled nothing yet.'

'You've been telling me about your wife. I don't see much what it's got to do with me.'

'I thought you was interested, that you wanted to see that I wasn't as much to blame as you thought.'

'I must be getting back,' she said; 'anything else you have to say to me you can tell me on the way home.'

'Well, it all amounts to this, Esther; if I get a divorce we might come together again. What do you think?'

'I think you'd much better make it up with her. I dare say she's very sorry for what she's done.'

'That's all rot, Esther. She ain't sorry, and wouldn't live with me no more than I with her. We could not get on; what's the use? You'd better let bygones be bygones. You know what I mean—marry me.'

'I don't think I could do that.'

'You like some other chap. You like some chap, and don't want me interfering in your life. That's why you wants me to go back and live with my wife. You don't think of what I've gone through with her already.'

'You've not been through half of what I have. I'll be bound that you never wanted a dinner. I have.'

'Esther, think of the child.'

'You 're a nice one to tell me to think of the child, I who worked and slaved for him all these years.'

'Then I 'm to take no for an answer?'

'I don't want to have nothing to do with you.'

'And you won't let me see the child?'

A moment later Esther answered, 'You can see the child, if you like.'

'Where is he?'

'You can come with me to see him next Sunday, if you like. Now let me go in.'

'What time shall I come for you?'

'About three—a little after.'

## CHAPTER XXVI

WILLIAM was waiting for her by the area railings; and while pinning on her hat she thought of what she should say, and how she should act. But she didn't know her mind, and it was not till the long black pin that held her hat to her hair went through the straw with a little sharp sound, that she decided that when the time came she would know what to say.

As he stepped aside to let her go up the area steps, she noticed how beautiful were his grey trousers, and that he wore a bunch of carnations in his spick-and-span morning coat. 'Quite a toff,' she said to herself, and they walked some half-dozen yards up the street in silence.

'But why do you want to see the boy? You never thought of him all these years.'

'I'll tell you, Esther. But it is nice to be walking out with you again. If you'd only let bygones be bygones we might settle down together yet. What do you think?'

She did not answer, and he continued: 'It do seem strange to be walking out with you again, meeting you after all these years, and I'm never in your neighbourhood. I just happened to have a bit of business with a friend who lives your way, and was coming along from his 'ouse, turning over in my mind what he had told me about Rising Sun for the Stewards' Cup, when I saw you coming along with the jug in your 'and. I said, "That's the prettiest girl I've seen this many a day; that's the sort of girl I'd like to see behind the bar of the 'King's Head.'" You always keeps your figure—you know you ain't a bit changed; and when I caught sight of those white teeth I said, "Lor', why, it's Esther."'

'I thought it was about the child you was going to speak to me.'

'So I am, but you came first in my estimation. The moment I looked into your eyes I felt it had been a mistake all along, and that you was the only one I had cared about.'

'Then all about wanting to see the child was a pack of lies?'

'No, they weren't lies. I wanted both mother and child —if I could get 'em. I'm telling you the plain truth, Esther. I thought of the child as a way of getting you back; but little by little I began to take an interest in him, to wonder what he was like, and with thoughts of the boy came different thoughts of you, Esther, who is the mother of my boy. Then I wanted you both back; I've thought of nothing else ever since.'

At that moment they reached the Metropolitan Railway, and William pressed forward to get the tickets. A subterraneous rumbling was heard, and they ran down the steps as fast as they could; seeing them so near, the ticket-collector held the door open for them, and just as the train was moving from the platform William pushed Esther into a second-class compartment.

'We're in the wrong class,' she cried.

'No, we ain't; get in, get in,' he shouted. And with the guard crying to him to desist, he hopped in after her, saying, 'You very nearly made me miss the train. What 'ud you've done if the train had taken you away and left me behind?'

'Then you travel second-class?' Esther said.

'Yes, I always travel second-class now; Peggy never would, but second seems to me quite good enough. I don't care about third, unless I'm with a lot of pals, and can keep the carriage to ourselves. That's the way we manage it when we go down to Newmarket or Doncaster.'

And they being alone in the compartment William leaned forward and took her hand.

'Try to forgive me, Esther.'

She drew her hand away; he got up and sat down beside her, and put his arm around her waist.

'No, no. I'll have none of that. All that sort of thing is over between us.'

He looked at her inquisitively, not knowing how to act. 'I know you've had a hard time, Esther. Tell me about it. What did you do when you left Woodview? Did you ever meet any one since that you cared for?'

The question irritated her, and she said, 'It don't matter to you who I met or what I went through.'

William spoke about the Barfields, and Esther could not but listen to the tale of what had happened at Woodview during the last eight years.

Woodview had been all her unhappiness and all her misfortune. She had gone there when the sap of life was flowing fastest in her, and Woodview had become the most precise and distinct vision she had gathered from life. She remembered that wholesome and ample country house, with its park and its down lands, and the valley farm, sheltered by the long lines of elms. She remembered the racehorses, their slight shapes showing under the grey clothing, the round black eyes looking out through the eyelet holes in the hanging hoods, the odd little boys astride—a string of six or seven passing always before the kitchen windows, going through the paddock gate under the bunched ilex trees. She remembered the rejoicings when the horse won at Goodwood, and the ball at the Shoreham Gardens. Woodview had meant too much in her life to be forgotten; its hill-side and its people, and something in William's voice recalled her from her reverie, and she heard him say:

'The poor Gaffer, 'e never got over it; it regular broke 'im up; for I was nearly forgetting to tell you it was Ginger who was riding, and that he did all he knew; he lost start, he tried to get shut in, but it warn't no go, luck was against them; the 'orse was full of running, and, of course, he couldn't sit down and saw his blooming 'ead off, right in th' middle of the course, with Sir Thomas's (that's the 'andicapper) field-glasses on him. He 'd have been warned off the blooming 'eath, and he couldn't afford that, even to save his own father. The 'orse won in a canter: they clapped eight stun on him for the Cambridgeshire, and it broke the Gaffer's 'eart. He had to sell off his 'orses, and he died soon after the sale, of consumption. It generally takes them off earlier; but they say it is in the family. Miss Mary——'

'Oh, tell me about her,' said Esther, who had been thinking all the while of Mrs. Barfield and of Miss Mary. 'Tell me, there 's nothing the matter with Miss Mary?'

'Yes, there is: she can't live no more in England; she has to go to winter, I think it is, in Algeria.'

At that moment the train screeched along the rails, and,

vibrating under the force of the brakes, it passed out of the tunnel into Blackfriars.

'We shall just be able to catch the ten minutes past four to Peckham,' she said, and they ran up the high steps. William strode along so fast that Esther was obliged to cry out, 'There's no use, William; train or no train, I can't walk at that rate.'

There was just time for them to get their tickets at Ludgate Hill. They were in a carriage by themselves, and he proposed to draw up the windows so that they might be able to talk more easily.

'Never mind about the 'orses, tell me about the Saint.'

'You seem to be very fond of her; what did she do for you?'

'Everything—that was after you went away. She was kind.'

'I'm glad to hear that,' said William.

'So they spends the summer at Woodview and goes to foreign parts for the winter?'

'Yes, that's it. Most of the estate was sold; but the Saint has her fortune, about five hundred a year, and they just manage to live there in a sort of hole-and-corner sort of way, not able to afford to keep a trap, and towards the end of October they go off and don't return till the beginning of May. You remember the stables they were putting up when Silver Braid won the two cups? Well, they are just as when you last saw them—rafters and walls.'

'Racing don't seem to bring no luck to any one. It ain't my affair, but if I was you I'd give it up and get to some honest work.'

'Racing has been a good friend to me. I don't know where I should be without it to-day.'

'So all the servants have left Woodview? I wonder what has become of them.'

'You remember my mother, the cook? She died a couple of years ago.'

'Mrs. Latch! Oh, I'm so sorry.'

'She was an old woman. You remember John Randal, the butler? He's in a situation in Cumberland Place, near the Marble Arch. He sometimes comes round and has a glass in the "King's Head." Sarah Tucker—she's in a situation somewhere in town. I don't know what has become of Margaret Gale.'

'I met her one day in the Strand. I'd had nothing to eat all day. I was almost fainting, and she took me into a public-house and gave me a sausage.'

The train began to slacken speed; William said, 'This is Peckham,' and they passed into the air of an irregular little street—low disjointed shops and houses, where the tram-cars tinkled through a slacker tide of humanity than the Londoners were accustomed to.

'This way,' said Esther. 'This is the way to the Rye.'

'Then Jackie lives at the Rye?'

'Not far from the Rye. Do you know East Dulwich?'

'No, I never was here before.'

'Mrs. Lewis (that's the woman who looks after him) lives at East Dulwich, but it ain't very far. I always gets out here. I suppose you don't mind a quarter of an hour's walk.'

'Not when I'm with you,' William replied gallantly, and he followed her through the passers-by, the Rye opening up before them like a large park, with slender trees and a Japanese pavilion quaintly placed on a little mound. At the Peckham end there were a dozen handsome trees, and under them a piece of artificial water where boys were sailing toy boats and a spaniel was swimming; and as Esther and William passed on they saw two old ladies in black come out of a garden full of hollyhocks, and walk towards a seat and sit down in the autumn landscape to enjoy the vast expanse full of the last days of cricket. An upland background in gradations, interspaced with villas, terraces, and gardens, and steep hill-side, showing fields and hayricks, brought the Rye to a picturesque and abrupt end. And turning to the right, leaving the Rye behind them, the twain ascended a long, monotonous, and very ugly road composed of artificial little houses, each set in a portion of very metallic garden. These continued all the way to the top of a long hill, straggling into a piece of waste ground where there were some trees and a few rough cottages. A little boy came running towards them, stumbling over the cinder heaps and the tin canisters with which the place was strewn, and William felt that that child was his.

'That child will break 'is blooming little neck if 'e don't take care,' he remarked tentatively.

She hated him to see the child, and to assert her complete ownership she clasped Jackie to her bosom without a word of explanation, and questioned him on matters about which William knew nothing, William standing by all the while like a stranger looking tenderly on his son, waiting for Esther to introduce them. The boy looked suddenly towards his father, and Esther repented a little of her cruelty.

'Jackie,' she said, 'do you know who this gentleman is who has come to see you?'

'No, I don't.'

She didn't care that Jackie should love his father, and yet she could not help feeling sorry for William.

'I'm your father,' said William.

'No, you ain't. I ain't got no father.'

'How do you know, Jackie?'

'Father died before I was born; mother told me.'

'But mother may be mistaken.'

'If my father hadn't died before I was born he'd 've been to see us before this. Come, mother, come to tea. Mrs. Lewis 'as got hot cakes, and they'll be burnt if we stand talking.'

'Yes, dear, but what the gentleman says is quite true; he is your father.'

Jackie made no answer, and Esther said: 'I told you your father was dead, but I was mistaken.'

'Won't you come and walk with me?' said William.

'No, thank you; I like to walk with mother.'

'He's always like that with strangers,' said Esther; 'it is shyness; but he'll come and talk to you presently, if you leave him alone.'

Each cottage had a rough piece of garden, and Mrs. Lewis's large face showed over the broken paling among the yellow crowns of the sunflowers. A moment later she was at the gate welcoming her visitors. The affection of her welcome was checked on seeing that William was with Esther, and she drew aside respectfully to let this fine gentleman pass.

'This is Jackie's father.'

'What, never! I thought—but I'm sure we're very glad to see you.' Then noticing the fine gold chain that hung across his waistcoat, the cut of his clothes, and the air of money which his whole bearing seemed to represent, she became a little obsequious in her welcome.

'I'm sure, sir, we're very glad to see you. Won't you sit down?' and, dusting a chair with her apron, she handed it to him. Then turning to Esther, she said:

'Sit yourself down, dear; tea 'll be ready in a moment.' She was one of those women who, although their apron-strings are a good yard in length, preserve a strange agility of movement and a pleasant vivacity of speech. 'I 'ope, sir, we 've brought 'im up to your satisfaction; we 've done the best we could. He 's a dear boy. There 's been a bit of jealousy between us on 'is account, but for all that we 'aven't spoilt him. I don't want to praise him, but he 's as well-behaved a boy as I knows of. Maybe a bit wilful, but there ain't much fault to find with him, and I ought to know, for it is I that 'ad the bringing up of him since he was a baby of two months old. Jackie dear, why don't you go to your father?'

He stood by his mother's chair, twisting his slight legs in a manner that was peculiar to him. His dark hair fell in thick, heavy locks over his small face, and from under the shadow of his locks his great luminous eyes glanced at his father furtively. Mrs. Lewis told him to take his finger out of his mouth, and thus encouraged he went towards William, still twisting his legs and looking curiously dejected. He did not speak for some time, but he allowed William to put his arm round him and draw him against his knees. And then fixing his eyes on the toes of his shoes he said abruptly, but confidentially:

'Are you really my father? No humbug, you know,' he added, raising his eyes, and for a moment looking William searchingly in the face.

'I 'm not humbugging, Jack. I 'm your father right enough. Don't you like me? But I think you said you didn't want to have a father?'

Jackie did not answer this question at once. After a moment's reflection, he said, 'If you be father, why didn't you come to see us before?'

William glanced at Esther, who, in her turn, glanced at Mrs. Lewis.

'I 'm afraid that 's rather a long story, Jackie. I was away in foreign parts.'

Jackie looked as if he would like to hear about 'foreign parts,' and William awaited the question that seemed to tremble on the child's lips. But, instead, he turned suddenly to Mrs. Lewis:

'The cakes aren't burnt, are they? I ran as fast as I could the moment I saw them coming.'

The childish abruptness of the transition made them laugh. Mrs. Lewis took the plate of cakes from the fender and poured out the tea; and, the door and window being open, the dying light lent a tenderness to the tea-table, to the quiet solicitude of the mother watching her son, knowing him in all his intimate habits; to the eager curiosity of the father on the other side, leaning forward delighted at every look and word, thinking it all astonishing, wonderful, and to the child sitting between the women, who seemed to understand that his chance of eating as many tea-cakes as he pleased had come at last. He ate with his eyes fixed on the plate, considering which piece he would have when he had finished the piece he had in his hand. Little was said —a few remarks about the fine weather, and offers to pour out another cup of tea. By their silence Mrs. Lewis began to understand that they had differences to settle, and she took her shawl from the peg, and pleaded that she had an appointment with a neighbour. But she wouldn't be more than half an hour away; would they look after the house till her return? And William watched her, thinking of what he would say when she was out of hearing.

'That boy of ours is a dear little fellow; you've been a good mother, I can see that. If I had only known.'

'There's no use talking no more about it; what's done is done.'

The cottage door was open, and in the still evening they could see their child swinging on the gate. The moment brimmed with responsibility, and yet the words as they fell from their lips seemed accidental.

At last he said:

'Esther, I can get a divorce.'

'You'd much better go back to your wife. Once married, always married, that's my way of thinking.'

'I'm sorry to hear you say it, Esther. Do you think a man should stop with his wife who's been treated as I have been?'

Esther avoided a direct reply, asking him instead, why he should care about a child for whom he had never done anything? To which William answered that if he had known there was a child he would have left his wife long ago, for that he loved Jackie just as much as she did.

'That would have been very wrong.'

'We ain't getting no for'arder by discussing them things,' he said, interrupting her. 'We can't say good-bye after this evening and never see one another again.'

'Why not? I 'm nothing to you now; you 've got a wife of your own; you 've no claim upon me; you can go your way and I can keep to mine.'

'There 's that child. I must do something for him.'

'Well, you can do something for him without ruining me.'

'Ruining you, Esther?'

'Yes, ruining me. I ain't going to lose my character by keeping company with a married man. You 've done me harm enough already, and should be ashamed to think of doing me any more. You can pay for the boy's schooling if you like, you can pay for his keep too, but you mustn't think that in doing so you 'll get hold of me again.'

'Do you mean it, Esther?'

'Followers ain't allowed where I am. You 're a married man. I won't have it.'

'But when I get my divorce?'

'When you get your divorce! I don't know how it 'll be then. But here 's Mrs. Lewis; she 's a-scolding of Jackie for swinging on that 'ere gate. Naughty boy; he 's been told twenty times not to swing on the gate.'

Esther complained that they had stayed too long, that he had made her late, saying he might write if he had anything important to say, but she wouldn't keep company with a married man. Whereupon William seemed very downcast. Esther, too, was unhappy, and without knowing why, for she had succeeded as well as she had expected, her idea being to keep William out of the way and hurry on her marriage with Fred. But this marriage, once desired, no longer gave her pleasure, filled her rather with misgiving. She had told Fred about the child. He had forgiven her. But men were all for forgiving before marriage, but afterwards how would it be? Would he reproach her with her fault the first time they came to disagree about anything? She had no luck, and didn't want to marry any one.

The visit to Dulwich had upset her. She ought to have kept out of William's way, but that man seemed to have a power over her, and she hated him for it. Now what did he want to see the child for? The child was nothing to him. She had been a fool! and through this fever of trouble there raged up and down her mind the thought of what Jackie thought of his father, and what Mrs. Lewis thought of William.

And the desire to know what was happening becoming great, she went to her mistress to ask for leave to go out, without her agitation betraying itself in her demeanour, yet Miss Rice's sharp eyes guessed that her servant's life was at a crisis. Her book dropped on her knee, she asked a few kind, discreet questions, and after dinner Esther hurried towards the Underground.

The door of the cottage was open, and as she crossed the little garden she heard Mrs. Lewis say:

'Now you must be a good boy, and not go out in the garden and spoil your new clothes.' And when Esther entered Mrs. Lewis was giving the finishing touches to the necktie which she had just tied. 'Now you'll go and sit on that chair, like a good boy, and wait there till your father comes.'

'Oh, here's mummie,' cried the boy, and he escaped out of Mrs. Lewis's hand. 'Look at my new clothes, mummie; look at them!' And Esther saw her boy dressed in a suit of velveteen knickerbockers with brass buttons, and a sky-blue necktie.

'His father—I mean Mr. Latch—came here on Thursday morning, and took him to——'

'Took me up to London——'

'And brought him back in those clothes.'

'We went to such a big shop in Oxford Street for them, and they took down many suits before they could get one to fit. Father is that difficult to please, and I thought we should go away without any clothes, and I couldn't walk about London with father in these old things. Aren't they shabby?' he added, kicking them contemptuously. It was a little grey suit that Esther had made for him with her own hands.

'Father had me measured for another suit, but it won't be ready for a few days. Father took me to the Zoological Gardens, and we saw the lions and tigers, and there are such a lot of monkeys. There is one—— But what makes you look so cross, mummie dear? Don't you ever go out with father in London? London is such a beautiful place. And then we walked through the park and saw a lot of boys sailing boats. Father asked me if I had a boat. I said you were too poor to buy me toys. He said that was hard lines on me, and on the way back to the station we stopped at a toyshop and he bought me a boat. May I show you my boat?'

Jackie was so primed with thoughts of his boat that he did not notice the gloom that was gathering on his mother's face; and before Mrs. Lewis could make up her mind what to do, he was forcing his toy into his mother's hands, saying: 'This is a cutter-rigged boat, because it has three sails and only one mast. Father told me so, and he'll be here in half an hour, for we're going to sail the boat in the pond on the Rye, and if it gets across all right he'll take me to the park where there's a big piece of water, twice, three times as big as the water on the Rye. Do you think, mummie, that I shall ever be able to get my boat across such a piece of water as the—I've forgotten the name. What do they call it, mummie?'

'Oh, I don't know; don't bother me with your boat.'

'Oh, mummie, what have I done that you won't look at my boat? Aren't you coming with father to the Rye to see me sail it?'

'I don't want to go with you. Come, don't plague me any more with your boat,' she said, pushing it away, and then in a moment of passion she threw it across the room. Jackie ran to his toy, he picked it up, and his face showed his grief. 'I shan't be able to sail my boat now; it won't sail, its mast and the sails is broke. Mummie, what did you break my boat for?' and the child burst into tears. At that moment William entered.

'What is the child crying for?' he asked, stopping abruptly on the threshold. There was a slight tone of authority in his voice which angered Esther still more.

'What is it to you what he is crying for?' she said, turning quickly round. 'What has the child got to do with you that you should come down ordering people about for? A nice sort of mean trick, and one that is just like you. You beg and pray of me to let you see the child, and when I do you come down here on the sly, and with the present of a suit of clothes and a toy boat you try to win his love away from his mother.'

'Esther, Esther, I never thought of getting his love from you. I meant no harm. Mrs. Lewis said that he was looking a trifle moped; we thought that a change would do him good, and so——'

'Ah! it was Mrs. Lewis that asked you to take him up to London. It is a strange thing what a little money will do. Ever since you set foot in this cottage she has been curtsying and handing you chairs. I didn't much like it, but I didn't think that she would round on me in this way.' And then turning suddenly on her old friend, she said: 'Who told you to let him have the child? Is it he or I who pays you for his keep? Answer me that. How much did he give you—a new dress?'

'Oh, Esther, I am surprised at you! I didn't think it would come to accusing me of being bribed, and after all these years.' Mrs. Lewis put her apron to her eyes, and Jackie stole over to his father.

'It wasn't I who smashed the boat, it was mummie; she's in a temper. I don't know why she smashed it. I didn't do nothing.'

William took the child on his knee.

'She didn't mean to smash it. There's a good boy, don't cry no more.'

Jackie looked at his father. 'Will you buy me another? The shops aren't open to-day.' Then getting off his father's knee he picked up the toy, and coming back he said, 'Could we mend the boat somehow? Do you think we could?'

'Jackie dear, go away; leave your father alone. Go into the next room,' said Mrs. Lewis.

'No, he can stop here; let him be,' said Esther. 'I want to have no more to say to him; he can look to his father for the future.' Esther turned on her heel and walked straight for the door. But dropping his boat with a cry, the little fellow ran after her and clung to her skirt despairingly. 'No, mummie dear, you mustn't go; never mind the boat; I love you better than the boat—I'll do without a boat.'

'Esther, Esther, this is all nonsense. Just listen.'

'No, I won't listen to you. But you shall listen to me. When I brought you here last week you asked me in the train what I had been doing all these years. I didn't answer you, but I will now. I've been in the workhouse.'

'In the workhouse!'

'Yes, do that surprise you?'

Then jerking out her words, throwing them at him as if they were half-bricks, she told him the story of the last eight years—Queen Charlotte's Hospital, Mrs. Rivers, Mrs. Spires, the night on the Embankment, and the workhouse. 'And when I came out of the workhouse I travelled London in search of sixteen pounds a year wages, which was the least I could do with, and when I didn't find them I sat here and ate dry bread. She'll tell you—she saw it all. I haven't said nothing about the shame and sneers I had to put up with—you'd understand nothing about that—and there was more than one situation I was thrown out of when they found I had a child. For they didn't like loose women in their houses; I had them very words said about me. And while I was going through all that you was living in riches with a lady in foreign parts; and now when she could put up with you no longer, and you're kicked out, you come to me and ask for your share of the child. Share of the child! What share is yours, I'd like to know?'

'Esther!'

'In your mean, underhand way you come here on the sly to see if you can't steal the love of the child from me.'

She could speak no more; her strength was giving way before the tumult of her passion, and the silence that had come suddenly into the room was more terrible than her words. William stood quaking, horrified, wishing the earth would swallow him; Mrs. Lewis watched Esther's pale face, fearing that she would faint; Jackie, his grey eyes open round, held his broken boat still in his hand. The sense of the scene had hardly caught on his childish brain; he was very frightened, and Mrs. Lewis took him in her arms and tried to soothe him. William tried to speak; his lips moved, but no words came.

Mrs. Lewis whispered, 'You'll get no good out of her

now, her temper's up; you'd better go. She don't know
what she's a-saying of.'

'If one of us has to go,' said William, taking the hint,
'there can't be much doubt which of us.' He stood at
the door holding his hat, just as if he were going to put it
on. Esther stood with her back turned to him. At last
he said:

'Good-bye, Jackie. I suppose you don't want to see
me again?'

For reply Jackie threw his boat away and clung to Mrs.
Lewis for protection. William's face showed that he was
pained by Jackie's refusal.

'Try to get your mother to forgive me; but you are right
to love her best. She's been a good mother to you.' He
put on his hat and went without another word. No one
spoke, and every moment the silence grew more paralysing.
Jackie examined his broken boat for a moment, and then he
put it away, as if it had ceased to have any interest for him.
There was no chance of going to the Rye that day; he might
as well take off his velvet suit; his mother liked him better
in his old clothes.

'You shall have another boat, my darling,' she said,
leaning across the table, 'and quite as good as the one I
broke.'

'Will you, mummie? One with three sails, cutter-
rigged, like that?'

'Yes, dear, you shall have a boat with three sails.'

'And when will you buy me the boat, mummie—to-
morrow?'

'As soon as I can, Jackie.'

This promise appeared to satisfy him. Suddenly he
looked:

'Is father coming back no more?'

'Do you want him back?'

Jackie hesitated; his mother pressed him for an answer.
'Not if you don't, mummie.'

'But if he was to give you another boat, one with four
sails?'

'They don't have four sails, not them with one mast.'

'If he was to give you a boat with two masts, would you
take it?'

'I should try not to, I should try ever so hard.'

There were tears in Jackie's voice, and then, as if doubt-ful of his power to resist temptation, he buried his face in his mother's bosom and sobbed.

'You shall have another boat, my darling.'

'I don't want no boat at all! I love you better than a boat, mummie, I do.'

'And what about those clothes? You'd sooner stop with me and wear those shabby clothes than go to him and wear a pretty velvet suit?'

'You can send back the velvet suit.'

'Can I? My darling, mummie will give you another velvet suit,' and she embraced the child with all her strength, and covered him with kisses.

'But why can't I wear that velvet suit, and why can't father come back? Why don't you like father? You shouldn't be cross with father because he gave me the boat. He didn't mean no harm.'

'I think you like your father. You like him better than me.'

'Not better than you, mummie.'

'You wouldn't like to have any other father except your own real father?'

'How could I have a father that wasn't my own real father?'

Esther did not press the point, and soon after Jackie began to talk about the possibility of mending his boat; and feeling that something irrevocable had happened, Esther put on her hat and jacket, and Mrs. Lewis and Jackie accompanied her to the station. The women kissed each other on the platform and were reconciled, but there was a vague sensation of sadness in the leave-taking which neither understood. And a moment after Esther sat alone in a third-class carriage absorbed in consideration of the problem of her life. The life she had dreamed would never be hers—somehow she seemed to know that she would never be Fred's wife.

She had made up her mind to see William no more, but he wrote asking how she would like him to contribute towards the maintenance of the child, and this could not be settled without personal interviews. Miss Rice and Mrs. Lewis seemed to take it for granted that she would marry William when he obtained his divorce. He had been to a lawyer about it, and the lawyer said there would be no difficulty, the adultery being admitted; and whenever she saw Jackie he inquired after his father; he hoped, too, that she had forgiven poor father, who had 'never meant no harm at all.' So everything was working to get her away from Fred, and she could see that she had done wrong in allowing her feelings to be overruled by Miss Rice, who had, of course, advised her for the best. Jackie would never take kindly to Fred as a stepfather, and would grow to dislike him more and more; and when he grew older he would keep away from the house on account of the presence of his stepfather; it would end by his going to live with William, and his being led into a life of betting and drinking.

## CHAPTER XXVII

IT was one evening as she was putting things away in the kitchen before going up to bed that she heard someone rap at the window. Could this be Fred? Her heart was beating; she must let him in. The area was in darkness; she could see no one.

'Who is there?' she cried.

'It's only me. I had to see you to-night on——'

She drew an easier breath, and asked him to come in.

William had expected a rougher reception. The tone in which Esther invited him in was almost one of welcome, and there was no need of so many excuses; but he had come prepared with excuses, and a few ran off his tongue before he was aware.

'Well,' said Esther, 'it is rather late. I was just going up to bed; but you can tell me what you've come about, if it won't take long.'

'It won't take long. I've seen my solicitor this afternoon, and he says that I shall find it very difficult to get a divorce.'

'So you can't get your divorce?'

'Are you glad?'

'I don't know.'

'What do you mean? You must be either glad or sorry.'

'I said what I mean. I am not given to telling lies.' Esther set the large tin candlestick, on which a wick was spluttering, on the kitchen table, and William looked at her inquiringly. She was always a bit of a mystery to him. And then he told her, speaking very quickly, how he had neglected to secure proofs of his wife's infidelity at the time; and, as she had lived a circumspect although a guilty life ever since, the solicitor thought that it would be difficult to establish a case against her.

'Perhaps she never was guilty,' said Esther, unable to restrain the temptation to irritate.

'Not guilty! what do you mean? Haven't I told you

how I found them the day I came up from Ascot? And didn't she own up to it? What more proof do you want?'

'Anyway, it appears you haven't enough; what are you going to do? Wait until you catch her out?'

'There is nothing else to do, unless——' William paused, and his eyes wandered from Esther's.

'Unless what?'

'Well, you see, my solicitors have been in communication with her solicitors, and her solicitors say that if it were the other way round, that if I gave her reason to go against me for a divorce, she would be glad of the chance. That's all they said at first, but since then I've seen my wife, and she says that if I'll give her cause to get a divorce she'll not only go for it, but will pay all the legal expenses; it won't cost us a penny. What do you think, Esther?'

'I don't know that I understand. You don't mean——'

'You see, Esther, that to get a divorce—there is no one who can hear us, is there?'

'No, there's no one in the 'ouse except me and the missus, and she's in the study reading. Go on.'

'It seems that one of the parties must go and live with another party before either can get a divorce. Do you understand?'

'You don't mean that you want me to go and live with you, and perhaps get left a second time?'

'That's all rot, Esther, and you know it.'

'If that's all you've got to say to me you'd better take your hook.'

'Do you see, there's the child to consider? And you know well enough, Esther, that you've nothing to fear; you knows as well as can be that I mean to run straight this time. So I did before. But let bygones be bygones, and I know you'd like the child to have a father; so if only for his sake——'

'For his sake! I like that; as if I hadn't done enough for him. Haven't I worked and slaved myself to death and gone about in rags? That's what that child has cost me. Tell me what he's cost you. Not a penny piece—a toy boat and a suit of velveteen knickerbockers—and yet you come telling me—I'd like to know what's expected of me. Is a woman never to think of herself? Do I count for nothing? For the child's sake, indeed! Now, if it was

any one else but you! Just tell me where do I come in?
That's what I want to know. I've played the game long
enough. Where do I come in? That's what I want to
know.'

'There's no use flying in a temper, Esther. I know
you've had a hard time. I know it was all very unlucky
from the very first. But there's no use saying that you
might get left a second time, for you know well enough
that that ain't true. Say you won't do it; you're a free
woman, you can act as you please. It would be unjust to
ask you to give up anything more for the child; I agree
with you in all that. But don't fly in a rage with me
because I came to tell you there was no other way out of
the difficulty,'

'You can go and live with another woman, and get a
divorce that way.'

'Yes, I can do that; but I first thought I'd speak to you
on the subject. For if I did go and live with another
woman I couldn't very well desert her after getting a
divorce.'

'You deserted me.'

'Why go back on that old story?'

'It ain't an old story, it's the story of my life, and I
haven't come to the end of it yet.'

'But you'll have got to the end of it if you'll do what I
say.'

A moment later Esther said:

'I don't know what you want to get a divorce for at all.
I dare say your wife would take you back if you were to
ask her.'

'She's no children, and never will have none, and
marriage is a poor lookout without children—all the worry
and anxiety for nothing. What do we marry for but
children? There's no other happiness. I've tried everything else——'

'But I haven't.'

'I know all that. I know you've had a damned hard
time, Esther. I've had a good week at Doncaster, and
have enough money to buy my partner out; we shall 'ave
the 'ouse to ourselves, and, working together, I don't think
we'll 'ave much difficulty in building it up into a very nice
property, all of which will in time go to the boy. I'm

doing pretty well, I told you, in the betting line, but if you like I 'll give it up. I 'll never lay or take the odds again. I can't say more, Esther, can I? Come, say yes,' he said, reaching his arm towards her.

'Don't touch me,' she said surlily, and drew back a step with an air of resolution that made him doubt if he would be able to persuade her.

'Now, Esther——' William didn't finish. It seemed useless to argue with her, and he looked at the great red ash of the tallow candle.

'You are the mother of my boy, so it is different; but to advise me to go and live with another woman! I shouldn't have thought it of a religious girl like you.'

'Religion! There 's very little time for religion in the places I 've had to work in.' Then, thinking of Fred, she added that she had returned to Christ, and hoped he would forgive her. William encouraged her to speak of herself, remarking that, chapel or no chapel, she seemed just as severe as ever. 'If you won't, I can only say I am sorry; but that shan't stop me from paying you as much a week as you think necessary for Jack's keep and his schooling. I don't want the boy to cost you anything. I 'd like to do a great deal more for the boy, but I can't do more unless you make him my child.'

'And I can only do that by going away to live with you?' The words brought an instinctive look of desire into her eyes.

'In six months we shall be man and wife. . . . Say yes.'

'I can't. I can't, don't ask me.'

'You 're afraid to trust me, is that it?'

Esther did not answer.

'I can make that all right: I 'll settle £500 on you and the child.'

She looked up: the same look was in her eyes, only modified, softened by some feeling of tenderness which had come into her heart.

He put his arm round her; she was leaning against the table; he was sitting on the edge.

'You know that I mean to act rightly by you.'

'Yes, I think you do.'

'Then say yes.'

'I can't—it is too late.'

'There's another chap?'

She nodded.

'I thought as much. Do you care for him?'

She didn't answer.

He drew her closer to him; he could see that she was weeping, and he kissed her on her neck first, and then on her face; and he continued to ask her if she loved the other chap. At last she signified that she did not.

'Then say yes.' She murmured that she couldn't.

'You can, you can, you can.' He kissed her, all the while reiterating, 'You can, you can, you can,' until it became a sort of parrot cry. Several minutes elapsed, and the candle began to splutter in its socket. She said:

'Let me go; let me light the gas.'

As she sought for the matches she caught sight of the clock.

'I didn't know it was so late.'

'Say yes before I go.'

'I can't.'

And it was impossible to extort a promise from her. 'I'm too tired,' she said, 'let me go.'

He took her in his arms and kissed her, and said, 'My own little wife.'

As he went up the area steps she remembered that he had used the same words before, and tried to think of Fred, but William's great square shoulders had come between her and this meagre little man. She sighed, and felt once again that her will was overborne by a force which she could not control or understand.

## CHAPTER XXVIII

SHE went round the house bolting and locking the doors, seeing that everything was made fast for the night, and it was not till she came to the foot of the stairs that sad thoughts came upon her, and she drew her hand across her eyes, for she was whelmed in a sense of sorrow, which she could not understand, which she had not strength to grapple with, and she was aware that life was proving too strong for her, that she could make nothing of it, and it seemed to her that she did not care much what happened to her. She hadn't even strength for blame, and merely wondered why she had let William kiss her. She oughtn't to have spoken to him; above all, she ought not to have taken him to see the child.

She slept on the same landing as Miss Rice, and was moved by a sudden impulse to go in and tell her the story of her trouble. But what good? No one could help her. She liked Fred: they seemed to suit each other, and she could have made him a good wife if she hadn't met William. She thought of the cottage at Mortlake, and their lives in it; and she sought to encourage her liking for him with thoughts of the meeting-house; she thought even of the simple black dress she would wear, and how they'd stand side by side among the Lord's people. But if she were to marry William she'd go to the 'King's Head,' to stand behind the bar and serve the customers. She had never seen much life, and felt somehow that she would like to see a little life; there would not be much life in the cottage at Mortlake; nothing but the prayer-meeting. She stopped thinking, for she had never thought like that before, and it seemed as if some other woman whom she hardly knew was thinking for her. She seemed like one standing at cross-roads, unable to decide which road she would take. If she took the road leading to the cottage and the prayer-meeting her life would henceforth be secure. She could see her life from end to end, even to the time when Fred would come and sit by her, and hold her hand as she had seen his father and mother sitting side by side. If she took the road to the public-house and the racecourse she did not know what might not happen. But William had promised to settle £500 on her and Jackie. Her life would be secure either way.

All the same, she must marry Fred, for she had promised to marry him; she wished to be a good woman, and he would give her the life she was most fitted for, the life she had always desired; the life of her father and mother, the life of her childhood. Yes, she would marry Fred in spite of all, only—something at that moment seemed to take her by the throat—William had come between her and that life. If she had not met him at Woodview long ago; if she had not met him in the Pembroke Road that night she went to fetch the beer for her mistress's dinner, how different everything would have been! If she had met him only a few months later, when she was Fred's wife!

Wishing she might go to sleep, and awake the wife of one or the other, she fell asleep to dream of a husband possessed of the qualities of both, and a life that was neither all chapel nor all public-house. But soon the one became two, and Esther awoke in terror, believing she had married them both.

## CHAPTER XXIX

IF Fred had said, 'Come away with me,' Esther would have
followed him. But when she called at the shop he only
spoke of his holiday, of the long walks he had taken, and
the religious and political meetings he had attended. To
this talk Esther listened vaguely; and there was in her mind
unconscious regret that he was not a little different. Little
irrelevant thoughts came upon her. She would like him
better if he wore coloured neckties and a short jacket; she
wished half of him away—his dowdiness, his sandy-coloured
hair, the vague eyes, the black neckties, the long loose
frock-coat. But his voice was keen and ringing, and when
listening her heart always went out to him, and she felt
that she might entrust her life to him. But he didn't seem
to understand her, and day by day, against her will, the
thought gripped her more and more closely that she could
not separate Jackie from his father. She would have to
tell Fred the whole truth, and he would not understand it;
that she knew. But it would have to be done, and she
sent round to say she'd like to see him when he left
business. Would he step round about eight o'clock?

The clock had hardly struck eight when she heard a tap
at the window. She opened the door and he came in,
surprised by the silence with which she received him.

'I hope nothing has happened. Is anything the
matter?'

'Yes, a great deal's the matter. I'm afraid we shall
never be married, Fred, that's what's the matter.'

'How's that, Esther? What can prevent us getting
married?' She didn't answer, and then he said, 'You've
not ceased to care for me?'

'No, that's not it.'

'Jackie's father has come back?'

'You've hit it, that's what's happened.'

'I'm sorry that man has come across you again. I
thought you told me he was married. But, Esther, don't
keep me in suspense; what has he done?'

'Sit down; don't stand staring at me in that way, and I'll tell you the story.'

Then in a strained voice, in which there was genuine suffering, Esther told her story, laying special stress on the fact that she had done her best to prevent him from seeing the child.

'I don't see how you could have forbidden him access to the child.'

He often used words that Esther did not understand, but, guessing his meaning, she answered:

'That's just what the missus said; she argued me into taking him to see the child. I knew once he'd seen Jackie there'd be no getting rid of him. I shall never get rid of him again.'

'He has no claim upon you. It is just like him, low blackguard fellow that he is, to come after you, persecuting you. But don't you fear; you leave him to me. I'll find a way of stopping his little game.'

Esther looked at his frail figure.

'You can do nothing; nobody can do nothing,' she said, and the tears trembled in her handsome eyes. 'He wants me to go away and live with him, so that his wife may be able to divorce him.'

'Wants you to go away and live with him! But surely, Esther, you do not——'

'Yes, he wants me to go and live with him, so that his wife can get a divorce,' Esther answered, for the suspense irritated her; 'and how can I refuse to go with him?'

'Esther, are you serious? You cannot—— You told me that you did not love him, and after all——' He waited for Esther to speak.

'Yes,' she said, very quickly, 'there is no way out of it that I can see.'

'Esther, that man has tempted you, and you haven't prayed.'

She did not answer.

'I don't want to hear more of this,' he said, catching up his hat. 'I shouldn't have believed it if I had not heard it from your lips: no, not if the whole world had told me. You are in love with this man, though you may not know it, and you've invented this story as a pretext to throw me over. Good-bye, Esther.'

'Fred, dear, listen, hear me out. You'll not go away in that hasty way. You're the only friend I have. Let me explain.'

'Explain! how can such things be explained?'

'That's what I thought until all this happened to me. I have suffered dreadful in the last few days. I've wept bitter tears, and I thought of all you said about the 'ome you was going to give me.' Her sincerity was unmistakable, and Fred doubted her no longer. 'I'm very fond of you, Fred, and if things had been different I think I might have made you a good wife. But it wasn't to be.'

'Esther, I don't understand. You need never see this man again if you don't wish it.'

'Nay, nay, things ain't so easily changed as all that. He's the father of my child, he's got money, and he'll leave his money to his child if he's made Jackie's father in the eyes of the law.'

'That can be done without your going to live with him.'

'Not as he wants. I know what he wants; he wants a 'ome, and he won't be put off with less.'

'How men can be so wicked as——'

'No, you do him wrong. He ain't no more wicked than another; he's just one of the ordinary sort—not much better nor worse. If he'd been a real bad lot it would have been better for us, for then he'd never have come between us. You're beginning to understand, Fred, ain't you? If I don't go with him my boy'll lose everything. He wants a 'ome—a real 'ome with children, and if he can't get me he'll go after another woman.'

'And are you jealous?'

'No, Fred. But think if we was to marry. As like as not I should have children, and they'd be more in your sight than my boy.'

'Esther, I promise that——'

'Just so, Fred; even if you loved him like your own, you can't make sure that he'd love you.'

'Jackie and I——'

'Ah, yes; he'd have liked you well enough if he'd never seen his father. But he's so taken to his father, and it would be worse later on. He'd never be contented in our 'ome. He'd be always after him, and then I should never see him, and he would be led away into betting and drink.'

'If his father is that sort of man, the best chance for Jackie would be to keep him out of his way. If he gets divorced and marries another woman he will forget all about Jackie.'

'Yes, that might be,' said Esther, and Fred pursued his advantage. But, interrupting him, Esther said:

'Anyway, Jackie would lose all his father's money; the public-house would——'

'So you 're going to live in a public-house, Esther?'

'A woman must be with her husband.'

'But he 's not your husband; he 's another woman's husband.'

'He 's to marry me when he gets his divorce.'

'He may desert you and leave you with another child.'

'You can't say nothing I ain't thought of already. I must put up with the risk. I suppose it is a part of the punishment for the first sin. We can't do wrong without being punished—at least women can't. But I thought I 'd been punished enough.'

'The second sin is worse than the first. A married man, Esther—you who I thought so religious.'

'Ah, religion is easy enough at times, but there is other times when it don't seem to fit in with a body's duty. I may be wrong, but it seems natural like—he 's the father of my child.'

'I 'm afraid your mind is made up, Esther. Think twice before it 's too late.'

'Fred, I can't help myself—can't you see that? Don't make it harder for me by talking like that.'

'When are you going to him?'

'To-night; he 's waiting for me.'

'Then good-bye, Esther, good——'

'But you 'll come and see us.'

'I hope you 'll be happy, Esther, but I don't think we shall see much more of each other. You know that I do not frequent public-houses.'

'Yes, I know; but you might come and see me in the morning when we 're doing no business.'

Fred smiled sadly.

'Then you won't come?' she said.

'Good-bye, Esther.'

They shook hands, and he rushed away. She dashed a

tear from her eyes, and went upstairs to her mistress, who had rung for her.

Miss Rice was in her easy-chair, reading. A long slanting ray entered the room; the bead curtain glittered, and so peaceful was the impression that Esther could not but perceive the contrast between her own troublous life and the contented privacy of this slender little spinster's.

'Well, miss,' she said, 'it's all over. I've told him.'

'Have you, Esther?' said Miss Rice. Her white, delicate hands fell over the closed volume. She wore two little colourless rings and a ruby ring which caught the light.

'Yes, miss, I've told him all. He seemed a good deal cut up. I couldn't help crying myself, for I could have made him a good wife—I'm sure I could; but it wasn't to be.'

'You've told him you were going off to live with William?'

'Yes, miss; there's nothing like telling the whole truth while you're about it. I told him I was going off to-night.'

'He's a very religious young man?'

'Yes, miss; he spoke to me about religion, but I told him I didn't want Jackie to be a fatherless boy, and to lose any money he might have a right to. It don't look right to go and live with a married man; but you knows, miss, how I'm situated, and you knows that I'm only doing it because it seems for the best.'

'What did he say to that?'

'Nothing much, miss, except that I might get left a second time—and, he wasn't slow to add, with another child.'

'Have you thought of that danger, Esther?'

'Yes, miss, I've thought of everything; but thinking don't change nothing. Things remain just the same, and you've to chance it in the end—leastways a woman has. Not the likes of you, miss, but the likes of us.'

'Yes,' said Miss Rice reflectively, 'it is always the woman who is sacrificed.' And her thoughts went back for a moment to the novel she was writing, so pale and conventional did it seem compared with this rough page torn out of life.

'So you're going to live in a public-house, Esther? You're going to-night? I've paid you everything I owe you?'

'Yes, miss, you 'ave; you 've been very kind to me, indeed you 'ave, miss—I shall never forget you, miss. I 've been very happy in your service, and should like nothing better than to stay on with you.'

'All I can say, Esther, is that you have been a very good servant, and I 'm very sorry to part with you. And I hope you 'll remember if things do not turn out as well as you expect them to, that I shall always be glad to do anything in my power to help you. You 'll always find a friend in me. When are you going?'

'As soon as my box is packed, miss, and I shall have about finished by the time the new servant comes in. She 's expected at nine; there she is, miss—that 's the area bell. Good-bye, miss.'

Miss Rice held out her hand. Esther took it, and thus encouraged she said:

'There never was any one that clear-headed and warm-hearted as yerself, miss. I may have a lot of trouble, miss. If I wasn't yer servant I 'd like to kiss you.'

Miss Rice did not answer, and before she was aware, Esther had taken her in her arms and kissed her. 'You 're not angry with me, miss; I couldn't help myself.'

'No, Esther, I 'm not angry.'

'I must go now and let her in.'

Miss Rice walked towards her writing-table, and a sense of the solitude of her life coming upon her caused her to burst into tears—one of those moments of sudden effusion which take women unawares. But her new servant was coming upstairs. And soon after she heard the cabman's feet on the staircase as he went up for Esther's box, and Esther begging him to be careful of the paint.

The girl had been a good and faithful servant to her; she was sorry to lose her. Esther was sorry that any one but herself should have the looking after of that dear, kind soul. But what could the girl do? She was going to be married. There would be a parlour behind the bar, in which she would sit. She would be mistress of the house. There would be a servant, a potboy, and perhaps a bar-maid. This sudden change of feeling surprised her, and she found excuses in the recollection that she had striven hard for Fred, but as she had failed to get him, it was only right that she should think of her husband, and she thought of his stalwart figure as he walked down the street.

When the cab swerved round the Circus, she was putting it to herself: 'Was she up to conducting a business like the "King's Head"?'

The black, crooked perspectives of Soho were roofed with the sunset's gold. She had never been in this part of London before; the adventure stimulated her imagination, and she wondered where she was going and which of the many public-houses was hers. But the cabman jingled past every one. It seemed as if he were never going to pull up. At last he stopped at the corner of Dean Street and Old Compton Street, nearly opposite a cab rank. The cabmen were inside, having a glass; the usual vagrant was outside, looking after the horses, and when she asked him if he had seen Mr. Latch he directed her round to the private bar, where she saw William leaning over the counter deep in talk and the sporting paper spread out before him.

'Oh, so here you are at last,' said William, coming towards her. 'I expected you an hour ago.'

'The new servant was late, and I couldn't leave before she came.'

'Never mind; glad you 've come. You know John Randal, or Mr. Leopold, as we used to call him at Woodview.'

Mr. Leopold shook hands with Esther, and he muttered a 'Glad to see you again.' But it was the welcome of a man who regards a woman's presence as an intrusion, and Esther understood the quiet contempt with which he looked at William. 'Can't keep away from them,' his face said for one brief moment. But William didn't notice these things. He asked Esther what she 'd take to drink, and Mr. Leopold looked at his watch and said he must be getting home.

'Try to come round to-morrow night if you 've an hour to spare.'

'Then you don't think you 'll go to Newmarket?'

'No, I don't think I shall do much in the betting way this year. But come round to-morrow night if you can; you 'll find me here. I must be here to-morrow night,' he said, turning to Esther; 'I 'll tell you presently.' The men had a few more words; William bade John good night, and coming back to Esther he said:

'What do you think of the place? Cosy, ain't it?' But before she had time to reply, he said: 'You 've brought me good luck. I won two 'undred and fifty pounds to-day, and the money will come in very 'andy, for Jim Stevens, that 's my partner, has agreed to take half the money on account and a bill of sale for the rest. There he is; I 'll introduce you to him. Jim, come this way, will you?'

'In a moment, when I 've finished drawing this 'ere glass of beer,' answered a thick-set, short-limbed man. He was in his shirt-sleeves, and he crossed the bar wiping the beer from his hands.

'Let me introduce you to a very particular friend of mine, Jim, Miss Waters.'

'Very 'appy, I 'm sure, to make your acquaintance,' said Jim, and he extended his fat hand across the counter. 'You and my partner are, I 'ear, going to take this 'ere 'ouse off my hands. Well, you ought to make a good thing of it. There 's always room for a 'ouse that supplies good liquor. What can I hoffer you, madam? Some of our whisky 'as been fourteen years in bottle; or, being a lady, perhaps you 'd like to try some of our best unsweetened.'

Esther declined, but William said they could not leave without drinking the health of the house.

'Irish or Scotch, ma'am? Mr. Latch drinks Scotch.'

Seeing that she could not avoid taking something, Esther decided that she would try the unsweetened. The glasses were clinked across the counter, and William whispered, 'This isn't what we sell to the public; this is our own special tipple. You didn't notice, perhaps, but he took the bottle from the third row on the left.'

At that moment Esther's cabman came in and wanted to know if he was to have the box taken down. William said it had better remain where it was.

'I don't think I told you I 'm not living here; my partner has the upper part of the house, but he says he 'll be ready to turn out at the end of the week. I 'm living in lodgings near Shaftesbury Avenue, so we 'd better keep the cab on.'

## CHAPTER XXX

THE 'King's Head' was a humble place in the old-fashioned
style, the floor some inches lower than the street and the
ceiling hardly more than a couple of feet above the head of a
tall man. There were three bars. The private was in
Dean Street; a few swells came over from the theatre to
call for brandies and sodas, and Esther served them between the little shelves of the little mahogany what-not on
the counter. Special customers were asked into the parlour,
and the public bar was inconveniently crowded by a dozen
people. It is true there was a jug-and-bottle entrance, but
the 'King's Head' was not an up-to-date public-house,
quite the reverse. It had, however, one thing in its favour
—it was a free house, and William said they had only to go
on supplying good stuff, and trade would be sure to come
back to them. The last lease-holder had done them much
harm by systematic adulteration, and Esther was more
anxious than William to know what loss the books showed.
'You're never here in the daytime; you do not have these
empty bars staring you in the face morning and afternoon,'
and then she would tell him; a dozen pots of beer about
dinner-time and a few glasses of bitter, for there had been
a rehearsal over the way—that was about all.

She envied the painted tiles and brass lamps in the other
public-houses as she returned home after marketing, for
she couldn't help having a peep as she went by, and she was
weary of sitting behind the bar sewing, waiting for Jackie to
come home from school. At last the clock struck five, and
Jackie peeped through the doors, dived under the counter,
and ran into his mother's arms.

'Well, did you get full marks to-day?'

'Yes, mummie, I got full marks.'

'That's a good boy—and you want your tea?'

'Yes, mummie; I'm that hungry I could hardly walk
home.'

'Hardly walk home! What, as bad as that?'

'Yes, mummie. There's a new shop open in Oxford

Street. The window is all full of boats. Do you think that if all the favourites were to be beaten for a month, father would buy me one?'

'I thought you was so hungry you couldn't walk home, dear?

'Well, mummie, so I was, but——'

Esther laughed. 'Well, come this way and have your tea.' She went into the parlour and rang the bell.

'Mummie, may I have buttered toast?'

'Yes, dear, you may.'

'And may I go downstairs and help Jane to make it?'

'Yes, you can do that too; it will save her the trouble of coming up. Let me take off your coat—give me your hat; now run along, and help Jane to make the toast.'

Esther opened a glass door, curtained with red silk; it led from the bar to the parlour, a tiny room, hardly larger than the private bar, holding with difficulty a small round table, three chairs, and an arm-chair. She took a cloth from the cupboard and laid the table for Jackie's tea, who came up at her call, telling how many marbles he had won, and at that moment voices were heard in the bar.

It was William, tall and gaunt, buttoned up in a grey frock-coat, a pair of field-glasses slung over his shoulders, returned from Newmarket with his clerk, Fred Blamey, a feeble, wizen little man, dressed in a shabby tweed suit, covered with white dust.

'Put that bag down, Teddy, and come and have a drink.'

Esther saw at once that things had not gone well with him.

'Have the favourites been winning?'

'Yes, every bloody one. Five first favourites straight off the reel—three yesterday, and two second favourites the day before. By God, no man can stand up against it. Come, what'll you have to drink, Teddy?'

'A little whisky, please, guv'nor.'

The men had their drink. Then William told Teddy to take his bag upstairs, and he followed Esther into the parlour. She could see that he had been losing heavily, but she refrained from asking questions.

'Now, Jackie, you keep your father company; tell him how you got on at school. I'm going downstairs to look after his dinner.'

'Don't you mind about my dinner, Esther, don't you trouble; I was thinking of dining at a restaurant. I 'll be back at nine.'

'Then I 'll see nothing of you. We 've hardly spoken to one another this week; all the day you 're away racing, and in the evening you 're talking to your friends over the bar. We never have a moment alone.'

'Yes, Esther, I know; but the truth is, I 'm a bit down in the mouth. I 've had a very bad week. The favourites has been winning, and I overlaid my book against Wheatear; I 'd heard that she was as safe as 'ouses. I 'll meet some pals down at the "Cri"; it will cheer me up.'

Seeing how disappointed she was, he hesitated, and asked what there was for dinner. 'A sole and a nice piece of steak; I 'm sure you 'll like it. I 've a lot to talk to you about. Do stop, Bill, to please me.' She was very winning in her quiet, grave way, so he took her in his arms, kissed her, and said he would stop, that no one could cook a sole as she could, that it gave him an appetite to think of it.

'And may I stop with father while you are cooking his dinner?' said Jackie.

'Yes, you can do that; but you must go to bed when I bring it upstairs. I want to talk with father then.'

Jackie seemed quite satisfied with this arrangement, but when Esther came upstairs with the sole, and was about to hand him over to Jane, he begged lustily to be allowed to remain until father had finished his fish. 'It won't matter to you,' he said; 'you 've to go downstairs to fry the steak.'

But when she came up with the steak he was unwilling as ever to leave. She said he must go to bed, and he knew from her tone that argument was useless. As a last consolation, she promised him that she would come upstairs and kiss him before he went to sleep.

'You will come, won't you, mummie? I shan't go to sleep till you do.' Esther and William both laughed, and Esther was pleased, for she was still a little jealous of his love for his father.

'Come along,' Jackie cried to Jane, and he ran upstairs, chattering to her about the toys he had seen in Oxford Street. Charles was lighting the gas. Esther had to go into the bar to serve some customers, and, when she

returned, William was smoking his pipe, her dinner having
had its effect—he had forgotten his losses, and was willing
to tell her the news. And he had a bit of news for her.
He had seen Ginger; Ginger had come up as cordial as you
like to ask him what price he was laying.

'Did he bet with you?'

'Yes, I laid him ten pounds to five.'

Once more William began to lament his luck. 'You'll
have better luck to-morrow,' she said. 'The favourites
can't go on winning. Tell me about Ginger.'

'There isn't much to tell. We'd a little chat. He
knew all about the little arrangement, the five hundred,
you know, and laughed heartily. Peggy's married. I've
forgotten the chap's name.'

'The one that you kicked downstairs?'

'No, not him. I can't think of it. No matter, Ginger
remembered you; he wished us luck, took the address, and
said he'd come in to-night to see you if he possibly could.
I don't think he's been doing too well lately, if he had he'd
have been more stand-offish. I saw Jimmy White—you remember Jim, the little fellow we used to call the Demon, 'e
that won the Stewards' Cup on Silver Braid? Didn't you
and 'e 'ave a tussle together at the end of dinner—the first
day you come down from town?'

'The second day it was.'

'You're right, it was the second day. The first day I
met you in the avenue I was leaning over the railings having
a smoke, and you come along with a heavy bundle and
asked me the way. I wasn't in service at that time. Good
Lord, how times does slip by! It seems like yesterday.
And after all those years to meet you as you was going to
the public for a jug of beer, and 'ere we are man and wife
sitting side by side in our own 'ouse.'

She was now in the 'King's Head' nearly a year, and had
begun to realize that she had got a good husband long
before they stepped round to the nearest registry office to
be married.

Charles opened the door. 'Mr. Randal is in the bar, sir,
and would like to have a word with you.'

'All right,' said William. 'Tell him I'm coming into
the bar presently.' Charles withdrew. 'I'm afraid,' said
William, lowering his voice, 'that the old chap is in a bad

way. He 's been out of a place a long while, and will find it
'ard to get back again. Once yer begin to age a bit, they
won't look at you. We 're both well out of that business.'

Mr. Randal sat in his favourite corner by the wall,
smoking his clay. He wore a large frock-coat, vague
in shape, pathetically respectable. The round hat was
greasy round the edges, brown and dusty on top. The
shirt was clean but unstarched, and the thin throat was
tied with an old black silk cravat. He looked himself, the
old servant out of situation—the old servant who would
never be in situation again.

'Been 'aving an 'ell of a time at Newmarket,' said
William: 'favourites romping in one after the other.'

'I saw that the favourites had been winning. But I
know of something, a rank outsider, for the Leger. I got
the letter this morning. I thought I 'd come round and
tell yer.'

'Much obliged, old mate, but it don't do for me to listen
to such tales; we bookmakers must pay no attention to
information, no matter how correct it may be. Much
obliged all the same. What are you drinking?'

'I 've not finished my glass yet.' He tossed off the last
mouthful.

'The same?' said William.

'Yes, thank you.'

William drew two glasses of porter. 'Here 's luck.' The
men nodded, drank, and then William turned to speak to a
group at the other end of the bar. 'One moment,' John
said, touching William on the shoulder. 'It is the best tip
I ever had in my life. I 'aven't forgotten what I owe you,
and if this comes off I 'll be able to pay you all back. Lay
the odds, twenty sovereigns to one against——' Old John
looked round to see that no one was within earshot, then he
leant forward and whispered the horse's name in William's
ear. William laughed. 'If you 're so sure about it as all
that,' he said, 'I 'd sooner lend you the quid to back the
horse elsewhere.'

'Will you lend me a quid?'

'Lend you a quid and five first favourites romping in one
after another!—you must take me for Baron Rothschild.
You think because I 've a public-house I 'm coining money;
well, I ain't. It 's cruel the business we do here. You

wouldn't believe it, and you know that better liquor can't be got in the neighbourhood.' Old John listened with the indifference of a man whose life is absorbed in one passion and who can interest himself with nothing else. Esther asked him after Mrs. Randal and his children, but conversation on the subject was always distasteful to him, and he passed it over with few words. As soon as Esther moved away he leant forward and whispered: 'Lay me twelve pounds to ten shillings. I'll be sure to pay you; there's a new restaurant going to open in Oxford Street and I'm going to apply for the place of head waiter.'

'Yes, but will you get it?' William answered brutally. He didn't mean to be unkind, but his nature was as hard and as plain as a kitchen table. The chin dropped into the unstarched collar and the old-fashioned necktie, and old John continued smoking unnoticed by any one. Esther looked at him. She saw he was down on his luck, and she remembered the tall, melancholy, pale-faced woman whom she had met weeping by the seashore the day that Silver Braid had won the cup. She wondered what had happened to her, in what corner she lived, and where was the son that John Randal had not allowed to enter the Barfield establishment as page-boy, thinking he would be able to make something better of him than a servant?

The regular customers had begun to come in. Esther greeted them with nods and smiles of recognition. She drew the beer two glasses at once in her hand, and picked up little zinc measures, two and four of whisky, and filled them from a small tap. She usually knew the taste of her customers. When she made a mistake she muttered 'stupid,' and Mr. Ketley was much amused at her forgetting that he always drank out of the bottle; he was one of the few who came to the 'King's Head' who could afford sixpenny whisky. 'I ought to have known by this time,' she said. 'Well, mistakes will occur in the best-regulated families,' the little butterman replied. He was meagre and meek, with a sallow complexion and blond beard. His pale eyes were anxious, and his thin, bony hands restless. His general manner was oppressed, and he frequently raised his hat to wipe his forehead, which was high and bald. At his elbow stood Journeyman, Ketley's very opposite. A tall, harsh, angular man, long features, a dingy complexion, and the air of a dismissed soldier. He held a glass of whisky and water in a hairy hand, and bit at the corner of a brown moustache. He wore a threadbare black frock-coat, and carried a newspaper under his arm. Ketley and Journeyman held widely different views regarding the best means of backing horses. Ketley was preoccupied with dreams and omens; Journeyman, a clerk in the parish registry office, studied public form: he was guided by it in all his speculations, and paid little heed to the various rumours always afloat regarding private trials. Public form he admitted did not always come out right, but if a man had a headpiece and could remember all the running, public form was good enough to follow. Racing with Journeyman was a question of calculation, and great therefore was his contempt for the weak and smiling Ketley, whom he went for on all occasions. But Ketley was pluckier than his appearance indicated, and the duels between the two were a constant source of amusement in the bar of the 'King's Head.'

'Well, Herbert, the omen wasn't altogether up to the mark this time,' said Journeyman, with a malicious twinkle in his small brown eyes.

'No, it was one of them unfortunate accidents.'

'One of them unfortunate accidents,' repeated Journeyman derisively; 'what 's accidents to do with them that 'as to do with the reading of omens? I thought they rose above such trifles as weights, distances, bad riding. A stone or two should make no difference if the omen is right.'

Ketley was no way put out by the slight titter that Journeyman's retort had produced in the group about the bar. He drank his whisky and water deliberately, like one, to use a racing expression, who had been over the course before.

'I 've 'eard that argument. I know all about it, but it don't alter me. Too many strange things occur for me to think that everything can be calculated with a bit of lead-pencil in a greasy pocket-book.'

'What has the grease of my pocket-book to do with it?' replied Journeyman, looking round. The company smiled and nodded. 'You says that signs and omens is above any calculation of weights. Never mind the pocket-book, greasy or not greasy; you says that these omens is more to be depended on than the best stable information.'

'I thought that you placed no reliance on stable information, and that you was guided by the weights that you calculated in that 'ere pocket-book.'

'What 's my pocket-book to do with it? You want to see my pocket-book; well, here it is, and I 'll bet two glasses of beer that it ain't greasier than any other pocket-book in this bar.'

'I don't see meself what pocket-books, greasy or not greasy, has to do with it,' said William. 'Walter put a fair question to Herbert. The omen didn't come out right, and Walter wanted to know why it didn't come out right.'

'That was it,' said Journeyman.

All eyes were now fixed on Ketley. 'You want to know why the omen wasn't right? I 'll tell you—because it was no omen at all, that 's why. The omens always comes right; it is we who aren't always in the particular state of mind that allows us to read the omens right.' Journeyman shrugged his shoulders contemptuously. Ketley looked at him with the same expression of placid amusement. 'You 'd like me to explain; well, I will. The omen is always right, but we aren't always in the state of mind for the reading of the omen. You think that ridiculous, Walter: but why should omens differ from other things? Some days we can get through our accounts in 'alf the time we can at other times, the mind being clearer. I asks all present if that isn't so.'

Ketley had got hold of his audience, and Journeyman's remark about closing time only provoked a momentary titter. Ketley looked long and steadily at Journeyman and then said: 'Perhaps closing time won't do no more for your calculation of weights than for my omens. I know them jokes, we 've heard them afore; but I 'm not making jokes; I 'm talking serious.' The company nodded approval. 'I was saying there was times when the mind is fresh like the morning. That 's the time for them what 'as got the gift of reading the omens. It is a sudden light that comes into the mind, and it points straight as a dart, if there be nothing to stop it. Now do you understand?' No one had understood, but all felt that they were on the point of understanding. 'The whole thing is in there being nothing to interrupt the light.'

'But you says yourself that yer can't always read them,' said Journeyman; 'an accident will send you off on the wrong tack, so it all comes to the same thing, omens or no omens.'

'A man will trip over a piece of wire laid across the street, but that don't prove he can't walk, do it, Walter?'

Walter was unable to say that it did not, and so Ketley scored another point over his opponent. 'I made a mistake, I know I did, and if it will help you to understand I'll tell you how it was made. Three weeks ago I was in this 'ere bar 'aving what I usually takes. It was a bit early; none of you fellows had come in. I don't think it was much after eight. The governor was away in the north racin'— hadn't been home for three or four days; the missus was beginning to look a bit lonely.' Ketley smiled and glanced at Esther, who had told Charles to serve some customers, and was listening as intently as the rest. 'I'd 'ad a nice bit of supper, and was just feeling that fresh and clear-'eaded as I was explaining to you just now is required for reading, thinking of nothing in perticler, when suddenly the light came. I remembered a conversation I 'ad with a chap about American corn. He wouldn't 'ear of the Government taxing corn to 'elp the British farmer. Well, that conversation came back to me as clear as if the dawn had begun to break. I could see the bloody corn; I could pretty well 'ave counted it. I felt there was an omen about somewhere, and all of a tremble I took up the paper; it was lying on the bar just where your hand is, Walter. But at that moment, just as I was about to cast my eye down the list of 'orses, a cab comes down the street as 'ard as it could tear. There was but two or three of us in the bar, and we rushed out—the shafts was broke, 'orse galloping and kicking, and the cabby 'olding on as 'ard as he could. But it was no good, it was bound to go, and over it went against the kerb. The cabby, poor chap, was pretty well shook to pieces; his leg was broke, and we 'd to 'elp to take him to the hosspital. Now I asks if it was no more than might be expected that I should have gone wrong about the omen. Next day, as luck would have it, I rolled up 'alf a pound of butter in a piece of paper on which "Cross Roads" was written.'

'But if there had been no accident and you 'ad looked down the list of 'orses, 'ow do yer know that yer would 'ave spotted the winner?'

'What, not Wheatear, and with all that American corn in my 'ead? Is it likely I 'd have missed it?'

No one answered, and Ketley drank his whisky in the midst of a most thoughtful silence. At last one of the group said, and he seemed to express the general mind of the company:

'I don't know if omens be worth a-following of, but I 'm blowed if 'orses be worth backing if the omens is again them.'

His neighbour answered: 'And they do come wonderful true occasional. They 'as 'appened to me, and I dare say to all 'ere present.' The company nodded. 'You 've noticed how them that knows nothing at all about 'orses—the less they knows the better their luck—will look down the lot and spot the winner from pure fancy—the name that catches their eye as likely.'

'There 's something in it,' said a corpulent butcher with huge, pursy, prominent eyes and a portentous stomach. 'I always held with going to church, and I hold still more with going to church since I backed Vanity for the Chester Cup. I was a-falling asleep over the sermon, when suddenly I wakes up hearing, "Vanity of vanities, and all is vanity."'

Several similar stories were told, and then various systems for backing horses were discussed. 'You don't believe that no 'orses is pulled?' said Mr. Stack, the porter at Sutherland Mansions, Oxford Street, a large, bluff man, wearing a dark blue square-cut frock-coat with brass buttons. A curious-looking man, with red-stained skin, dark beady eyes, a scanty growth of beard, and a loud, assuming voice. 'You don't believe that no 'orses is pulled?' he reiterated.

'I didn't say that no 'orse was never pulled,' said Journeyman. He stood with his back leaning against the partition, his long legs stretched out. 'If one was really in the know, then I don't say nothing about it; but who of us is ever really in the know?'

'I 'm not so sure about that,' said Mr. Stack. 'There 's a young man in my mansions that 'as a servant; this servant's cousin, a girl in the country, keeps company with

one of the lads in the White House stable. If that ain't
good enough, I don't know what is; good enough for my
half-crown and another pint of beer too, Mrs. Latch, if
you 'll be that kind.'

Esther drew the beer, and old John, who had said nothing
till now, suddenly joined in the conversation. He, too, had
heard of something; he didn't know if it was the same as
Stack had heard of; he didn't expect it was. It couldn't
very well be, 'cause no one knew of this particular horse,
not a soul—not 'alf a dozen people in the world. No, he
would tell no one until his money and the stable money
was all right. And he didn't care for no half-crowns or
dollars this time, if he couldn't get a sovereign or two on
the horse he 'd let it alone. This time he 'd be a man or a
mouse. Every one was listening intently, but old John
suddenly assumed an air of mystery and refused to
say another word. The talk worked back whence it
had started, and again the best method of backing horses
was passionately discussed. Interrupting someone whose
theories seemed silly, Journeyman said:

'Let 's 'ear what 's the governor's opinion; he ought to
know what kind of backer gets the most out of him.'

Even the vagrant who had taken his tankard of porter
to the bench where he could drink and eat what fragments
of food he had collected, came forward, interested to know
what kind of backer got most out of the bookmaker.

'Well,' said William, 'I haven't been making a book as
long as some of them, but since you ask me what I think I
tell you straight. I don't care a damn whether they backs
according to their judgment, or their dreams, or their fancy.
The cove that follows favourites, or the cove that backs a
jockey's mount, the cove that makes an occasional bet
when he hears of a good thing, the cove that bets regular,
'cording to a system—the cove, yer know, what doubles
every time—or the cove that bets as the mood takes him—
them and all the other coves, too numerous to be mentioned,
I 'm glad to do business with. I cries out to one as 'eartily
as to another: "The old firm, the old firm, don't forget the
old firm. . . . What can I do for you to-day, sir?" There 's
but one sort of cove I can't abide.'

'And he is——' said Journeyman.

'He is Mr. George Buff.'

'Who's he? who's he?' asked several; and the vagrant caused some amusement by the question, 'Do 'e bet on the course?'

'Yes, he do,' said William, 'an' nowhere else. He's at every meeting as reg'lar as if he was a bookie himself. I 'ates to see his face. I'd be a rich man if I'd all the money that man 'as 'ad out of me in the last three years.'

'What should you say was his system?' asked Mr. Stack.

'I don't know no more than yerselves.'

This admission seemed a little chilling; for every one had thought himself many steps nearer El Dorado.

'But did you ever notice,' said Mr. Ketley, 'that there was certain days on which he bet?'

'No, I never noticed that.'

'Are they outsiders that he backs?' asked Stack.

'No, only favourites. But what I can't make out is that there are times when he won't touch them; and when he don't, nine times out of ten they're beaten.'

'Are the 'orses he backs what you'd call well in?' said Journeyman.

'Not always.'

'Then it must be on information from the stable authorities?' said Stack.

'I don't care,' said William; 'have it that way if you like, but I'm glad there ain't many about like him. I wish he'd take his custom elsewhere. He gives me the solid hump, he do.'

'What sort of man should you say he was? 'as he been a servant, should you say?' asked old John.

'I can't tell you what he is. Always new suit of clothes and a heye-glass. Whenever I see that 'ere heye-glass and that brown beard my heart goes down in my boots. When he don't bet he takes no notice, walks past with a far-away look on his face, as if he didn't see the people, and he don't care that for the 'orses. Knowing he don't mean no business, I cries to him, "The best price, Mr. Buff; two to one on the field, ten to one bar two or three." He just screws up his heye-glass tighter in his eye and looks at me, smiles, shakes his head, and goes on. He is a warm 'un; he is just about as 'ot as they make 'em.'

'What I can't make out,' said Journeyman, 'is why

he bets on the course. You say he don't know nothing about horses. Why don't he remain at 'ome and save the exes?'

'I 've thought of all that,' said William, 'and can't make no more out of it than you can yerselves. All we know is that, divided up between five or six of us, Buff costs not far short of six 'undred a year.'

At that moment a small blond man came into the bar. Esther knew him at once. It was Ginger. He had hardly changed at all—a little sallower, a little dryer, a trifle less like a gentleman.

'Won't you step round, sir, to the private bar?' said William. 'You 'll be more comfortable.'

'Hardly worth while. I was at the theatre, and I thought I 'd come in and have a look round. I see that you haven't forgotten the old horses,' he said, catching sight of the prints of Silver Braid and Summer's Dean which William had hung on the wall. 'That was a great day, wasn't it? Fifty to one chance, started at thirty; and you remember the Gaffer tried him to win with twenty pound more than he had to carry. Hallo, John! very glad to see you again; growing strong and well, I hope?'

Esther wondered if he would remember her, and as the thought passed through her mind he extended his hand across the bar.

'I 'ope I may have the honour of drinking a glass of wine with you, sir,' said William. Ginger raised no objection, and William told Esther to go downstairs and fetch up a bottle of champagne.

To meet the celebrated gentleman-rider was a great event in the lives of Ketley, Journeyman, and Stack. But the talk was of the Barfield horses, carried on by the merest allusion, so that Journeyman wearied of it, and said he must be getting home; the others nodded, finished their glasses, and bade William good night. As they left a couple of flower-girls with loose hair, shawls, and trays of flowers, suggestive of street-faring, came in and ordered four ale, and the same moment Charles, who had gone through with the ladder to turn out the street lamp, returned with a light overcoat on his arm which he said a cove outside wanted to sell him for two and six.

'Do you know him?' said William.

'Yes, I knowed him. I had to put him out the other night—Bill Evans, the cove that wears the blue Melton.'

As he spoke a man between thirty and forty came in. A dark olive skin, black curly hair, picturesque and disreputable, like a bird of prey in his blue Melton jacket and billycock hat.

'You 'd better 'ave the coat,' he said; 'you won't better it'; and coming into the bar he planked down a penny as if it were a sovereign. 'Glass of porter; nice warm weather, good for the 'arvest. Just come up from the country—a bit dusty, ain't I?'

'Ain't you the chap,' said William, 'what laid Mr. Ketley six 'alf-crowns to one against Cross Roads?'

Charles nodded, and William continued:

'I like your cheek coming into my bar.'

'No harm done, guv'nor; no one was about; wouldn't 'ave done it if they had.'

'That 'll do,' said William. 'No, he don't want the coat. We likes to know where our things comes from.'

Bill Evans finished his glass. 'Good night, guv'nor; no ill feeling.'

The flower-girls laughed; one offered him a flower. 'Take it for love,' she said, and the three went out together.

'I don't like the looks of that chap,' said William, and he let go the champagne cork. 'Yer health, sir.' They raised their glasses, and the conversation turned on next week's racing.

'I dunno about next week's events,' said old John, 'but I 've heard of something for the Leger—an outsider will win.'

'Have you backed it?'

'I would if I had the money, but things have been going very unlucky with me lately. But I 'd advise you, sir, to have a trifle on. It 's the best tip I 'ave had in my life.'

'Really!' said Ginger, beginning to feel interested, 'so I will, and so shall you. I 'm damned if you shan't have your bit on. Come, what is it? William will lay the odds. What is it?'

'Briar Rose, the White House stable, sir.'

'Why, I thought that——'

'No such thing, sir; Briar Rose 's the one.'

Ginger took up the paper.  'Twenty-five to one Briar Rose taken.'

'You see, sir, it was taken.'

'Will you lay the price, William—twenty-five half-sovereigns to one?'

'Yes, I'll lay it.'

Ginger took a half-sovereign from his pocket and handed it to the bookmaker.

'I never take money over this bar.  You're good for a thin 'un, sir,' William said, with a smile, as he handed back the money.

'But I don't know when I shall see you again,' said Ginger.  'It will be very inconvenient.  There's no one in the bar.'

'None but the match-seller and them two flower-girls.  I suppose they don't matter?'

Henceforth something to live for.  Each morning bringing news of the horse, and the hours of the afternoon passing pleasantly, full of thoughts of the evening paper and the gossip of the bar.  A bet on a race brings hope into lives which otherwise would be hopeless.

## CHAPTER XXXI

NEVER had a Derby excited greater interest. Four hot favourites, between which the public seemed unable to choose. Two to one taken and offered against Fly-leaf, winner of the Two Thousand; four to one taken and offered against Signet-ring, who, half trained, had run Fly-leaf to a head. Four to one against Necklace, the winner of the Middle Park Plate and the One Thousand. Seven to one against Dewberry, the brilliant winner of the Newmarket stakes. The chances of these horses were argued every night at the 'King's Head.' Ketley's wife used to wear a string of yellow beads when she was a girl, but she wasn't certain what had become of them. Ketley did not wear a signet-ring, and had never known any one who did. Dewberries grew on the river banks, but they were not ripe yet. Fly-leaf, he could not make much of that—not being a reader of books. So what with one thing and another Ketley didn't believe in this 'ere Derby. Journeyman caustically remarked that, omens or no omens, one horse was bound to win. Why didn't Herbert look for an omen among the outsiders? Old John's experiences led him to think that the race lay between Fly-leaf and Signet-ring. He had a great faith in blood, and Signet-ring came of a more staying stock than did Fly-leaf. 'When they begin to climb out of the dip Fly-leaf will have had about enough of it.' Stack nodded approval. He had five bob on Dewberry. He didn't know much about his staying powers, but all the stable is on him; 'and when I know the stable money is right I says, "That's good enough for me!"'

Ginger, who came in occasionally, was very sweet on Necklace, whom he declared to be the finest mare of the century. He was listened to with hushed attention, and there was a deathlike silence in the bar when he described how she had won the One Thousand. He wouldn't have ridden her quite that way himself; but then what was a steeplechase-rider's opinion worth regarding a flat race?

The company demurred, and old John alluded to Ginger's magnificent riding when he won the Liverpool on Foxcover, steadying the horse about sixty yards from home, and bringing him up with a rush in the last dozen strides, nailing Jim Sutton, who had persevered all the way, on the very post by a head. Bill Evans, who happened to look in that evening, said he wouldn't be surprised to see all the four favourites bowled out by an outsider. He didn't suppose the guv'nor would take him on the nod, but he had a nice watch which ought to be good for three ten.

'Turn it up, old mate,' said William.

'All right, guv'nor, I never presses my goods on them that don't want 'em. If there's any other gentleman who would like to look at this 'ere timepiece, or a pair of sleeve-links, they're in for fifteen shillings. I'm a bit short of money, and having a fancy for a certain outsider, I'll dispose of the ticket for—what do you say to a thin 'un, Mr. Ketley?'

'Did you 'ear me speak just now?' William answered angrily, 'or shall I have to get over the counter?'

'I suppose, Mrs. Latch, you have seen a great deal of racing?' said Ginger.

'No, sir. I've heard a great deal about racing, but I never saw a race run.'

'How's that, shouldn't you care?'

'You see, my husband has his betting to attend to, and there's the house to look after.'

'I never thought of it before,' said William. 'You've never seen a race run, no more you haven't. Would you care to come and see the Derby run next week, Esther?'

'I think I should.'

At that moment the policeman stopped and looked in. All eyes went up to the clock, and Esther said: 'We shall lose our licence if——'

'If we don't get out,' said Ginger.

William apologized.

'The law is the law, sir, for rich and poor alike; should be sorry to hurry you, sir, but in these days very little will lose a man his house. Now, Herbert, finish your drink. No, Walter, can't serve any more liquor to-night. Charles, close the private bar, let no one else in. Now, gentlemen, gentlemen.'

Old John lit his pipe and led the way. William held the door for them. A few minutes after the house was closed.

A locking of drawers, fastening of doors, putting away glasses, making things generally tidy, an hour's work before bedtime, and then they lighted their candle in the little parlour and went upstairs.

William flung off his coat. 'I 'm dead beat,' he said, 'and all this to lose——' He didn't finish the sentence. Esther said:

'You 've a heavy book on the Derby. Perhaps an outsider 'll win.'

'I 'ope so. But if you 'd care to see the race, I think it can be managed. I shall be busy, but Journeyman or Ketley will look after you.'

'I don't know that I should care to walk about all day with Journeyman, nor Ketley neither.'

They were both tired, and with an occasional remark they undressed and got into bed. Esther laid her head on the pillow and closed her eyes.

'I wonder if there 's any one going who you 'd care for?'

'I don't care a bit about it, Bill.' At the end of a long silence William said:

'It do seem strange that you who has been mixed up in it so much should never have seen a race.' Esther didn't answer. She was falling asleep, and William's voice was beginning to sound vague in her ears. Suddenly she felt him give her a great shove. 'Wake up, old girl, I 've got it. Why not ask your old pal, Sarah Tucker, to go with us? I heard John say she 's out of situation. It 'll be a nice treat for her.'

'Ah. I should like to see Sarah again.'

'You 're half asleep.'

'No, I 'm not; you said we might ask Sarah to come to the Derby with us.'

William regretted that he hadn't a nice trap to drive them down. But to hire one would run into a deal of money, and he was afraid it might make him late on the course. Besides, the road wasn't what it used to be; every one goes by train now; and they dropped off to sleep talking of how they should get Sarah's address.

Three or four days passed, and one morning William jumped out of bed and said:

'I think it will be a fine day, Esther.' He took out his best suit of clothes, and selected a handsome silk scarf for the occasion. Esther was a heavy sleeper, and she lay close to the wall, curled up. Taking no notice of her, William went on dressing; then he said: 'Now then, Esther, get up. Teddy will be here presently to pack up my clothes.'

'Is it time to get up?'

'Yes, I should think it was. For God's sake, get up.'

She had a new dress for the Derby, one that had been bought in Tottenham Court Road. A real summer dress! A lilac pattern on a white ground, the sleeves and throat and the white hat tastefully trimmed with lilac and white lace, and a nice sunshade to match. At that moment a knock came at the door.

'All right, Teddy, wait a moment, my wife's not dressed yet. Do make haste, Esther.'

Esther stepped into the skirt so as not to ruffle her hair, and she was buttoning the bodice when little Mr. Blamey entered.

'Sorry to disturb you, ma'am, but there isn't no time to lose if the governor don't want to lose his place on the 'ill.'

'Now then, Teddy, make haste, get the toggery out; don't stand talking.'

The little man spread the Gladstone bag upon the floor and took a suit of checks from the chest of drawers, each square of black and white nearly as large as a sixpence.

'You'll wear the green tie, sir?' William nodded. The green tie was a yard of flowing sea-green silk. 'I've got you a bunch of yellow flowers, sir; will you wear them now, or shall I put them in the bag?'

William glanced at the posy. 'They look a bit loud,' he said; 'I'll wait till we get on the course; put them in the bag.'

The card to be worn in the white hat—'William Latch, London,' in gold letters on a green ground—was laid on top. The boots with soles three inches high went into the box on which William stood while he halloaed his prices to the crowd. Then there were the two poles which supported a strip of white linen, on which was written in gold letters, 'William Latch, "The King's Head," London. Fair prices, prompt payment.'

It was a grey day, with shafts of sunlight coming through, and as the cab passed over Waterloo Bridge, London, various embankments and St. Paul's on one side, wharves and warehouses on the other, appeared in grey curves and straight silhouettes. The pavements were lined with young men—here and there a girl's dress was a spot of colour in the grey morning. At the station they met Journeyman and old John, but Sarah was nowhere to be found. William said:

'We shall be late; we shall have to go without her.'

Esther's face clouded. 'We can't go without her; don't be so impatient.' At that moment a white muslin was seen in the distance, and Esther said, 'I think that that 's Sarah.'

'You can chatter in the train—you 'll have a whole hour to talk about each other's dress; get in, get in.' William pressed them into a third-class carriage, and there was so much to say that they didn't know where to begin.

'It was kind of you to think of me,' said Sarah. 'So you 've married, and to him after all!' she added, lowering her voice.

Esther laughed. 'It do seem strange, don't it?'

'You 'll tell me all about it,' she said. 'I wonder we didn't run across one another before.'

Out of the grey station they rolled into the light, the plate glass drawing the rays together till they burnt the face and hands. Now they were speeding alongside of the upper windows nearly on a level with the red and yellow chimney-pots. A moment after they were passing by open spaces filled with cranes, old iron, stacks of railway sleepers, pictorial advertisements, sky signs, and great gasometers rising round and black in their iron cages, overtopping, or nearly, the distant church spires. A train steamed along a hundred-arched viaduct; and along a black embankment the other trains rushed by in a whirl of wheels, bringing thousands of clerks up from the suburbs to their city toil.

The excursion jogged on, stopping for long intervals before strips of sordid garden where shirts and pink petti-coats were blowing. Little streets ascended the hill-sides; no more trains; buses, too, had disappeared, and afoot the folk hurried along the lonely pavements of their suburbs.

At Clapham Junction betting men had crowded the platform; they all wore grey overcoats with race-glasses slung over their shoulders. And the train still rolled through the brick wilderness which old John said was all country forty years ago.

The men puffed at their pipes; old John's anecdotes about the days when he and the Gaffer, in company with all the great racing men of the day, used to drive down by road, were listened to with admiration, and just as Esther finished telling Sarah the circumstances in which she had met Margaret, the train stopped outside of a little station, and the blue sky, with its light wispy clouds, became the topic of conversation, old John not liking the look of those clouds, and the women glancing at the waterproofs which they carried on their arms.

They passed bits of common with cows and a stray horse, also a little rural cemetery; but London suddenly began again parish after parish, the same blue roofs, the same tenement houses. The train had passed the first cedar and the first tennis lawn, and knowing it to be a Derby excursion the players paused in their play and looked up. Again the line was blocked; the train stopped, but it had left London behind, and the next stoppage was in front of a thick meadow with a square weather-beaten church showing between the spreading trees, and all around green corn, with birds flying in the bright air, and lazy clouds going out, making way for the endless blue of a long summer's day.

## CHAPTER XXXII

IT had been arranged that William should don his betting toggery at the 'Spread Eagle Inn.' It stood at the cross-roads, only a little way from the station—a square house with a pillared porch. Even at this early hour the London pilgrimage was filing by. Horses were drinking in the trough, their drivers in the bar; girls in light dresses shared glasses of beer with young men; but the greater number of vehicles passed without stopping, anxious to get on the course. And they went round the turn in long procession, a policeman on a strong horse occupying the middle of the road. The wagonettes and coaches had red-coated guards, and the ear wearied of the tooting of long brass horns. Every kind of dingy trap went by, sometimes drawn by two, sometimes by only one horse—shays half a century old jingled along; there were even donkey-carts. Esther and Sarah were astonished at the number of costers, but old John told them that that was nothing to what it was fifty years ago. The year that Andover won, the block began seven or eight miles from Epsom. They were often half an hour without moving. Such chaffing and laughing, the coster cracked his joke with the duke: but all that was done away with now.

'Gracious!' said Esther, when William appeared in his betting toggery. 'I shouldn't have known you.'

He did seem very wonderful in his checks, green neck-tie, yellow flowers, and white hat with its gold inscription, 'William Latch, London.'

'It's all right,' he said; 'you never saw me before in these togs—fine, ain't they? But we're very late. Mr. North has offered to run me up to the course, but he's only two places. Teddy and me must be getting along—but you needn't hurry. The races won't begin for hours yet. It's only about a mile—a nice walk. These gentlemen will look after you. You know where to find me,' he said, turning to John and Walter. 'You'll look after my wife and Miss Tucker, won't you?' and he and

Teddy jumped forthright into a wagonette and drove away.

'Well, that's what I calls cheek,' said Sarah. 'Going off by himself in a wagonette and leaving us to foot it.'

'He must look after his place on the 'ill or else he 'll do no betting,' said Journeyman. 'We've plenty of time; racing don't begin till after one.'

Recollections of what the road had once been had loosened John's tongue, and he continued his reminiscences of the great days when Sir Thomas Hayward had laid fifteen thousand to ten thousand three times over against the favourite. The third bet had been laid at this very spot, but the duke wouldn't accept the third bet, saying that the horse was then being backed on the course at evens. So Sir Thomas had only lost thirty thousand pounds on the race. Journeyman was deeply interested in the anecdote; but Sarah looked at the old man with a look that said, 'Well, if I'm to pass the day with you two I never want to go to the Derby again. Come on in front,' she whispered to Esther, 'and let them talk about their racing by themselves.' The way led through a field ablaze with buttercups; it passed by a fish-pond into which three drunkards were gazing. 'Do you hear what they're saying about the fish?' said Sarah.

'Don't pay no attention to them,' said Esther. 'If you knew as much about drunkards as I do, you'd want no telling to give them a wide berth. Isn't the country lovely? Isn't the air soft and warm?'

'Oh, I don't want no more country. I'm glad to get back to town. I wouldn't take another situation out of London if I was offered twenty a year.'

'But look,' said Esther, 'at the trees. I've hardly been in the country since I left Woodview, unless you call Dulwich the country—that's where Jackie was at nurse.'

The Cockney pilgrimage passed into a pleasant lane over-hung with chestnut and laburnum trees. The spring had been late, and the white blossoms stood up like candles—the yellow dropped like tassels, and the streaming sunlight filled the leaves with tints of pale gold, and their light shadows patterned the red earth of the pathway. But very soon this pleasant pathway debouched on a thirsting roadway where tired horses harnessed to heavy vehicles

toiled up a long hill leading to the downs. The trees inter-
cepted the view, and the blown dust whitened the foliage
and the wayside grass, now in possession of hawker and
vagrant. The crowd made way for the vehicles; and the
young men in blue and grey trousers, and their girls in
white dresses, turned and watched the four horses bringing
along the tall drag crowned with London fashion, and the
unwieldy omnibus, and the brake filled with fat girls in
pink dresses and yellow hats, and the spring cart drawn
up under a hedge. The cottage gates were crowded with
folk come to see London going to the Derby. Outhouses
had been converted into refreshment bars, and from these
came a smell of beer and oranges; farther on there was
a lamentable harmonium — a blind man singing hymns
to its accompaniment, and a one-legged man holding his
hat for alms; and not far away there stood an earnest-eyed
woman offering tracts, warning folk of their danger, beseeching them to retrace their steps.

At last the trees ceased and they found themselves on
the hill-top in a glare of sunlight, on a space of worn ground
where donkeys were tethered.

'Is this the Derby?' said Sarah.

'I hope you 're not disappointed?'

'No, dear; but where 's all the people—the drags, the
carriages?'

'We 'll see them presently,' said old John, and he volun-
teered some explanations. The white building was the
Grand Stand. The winning-post was a little farther this
way.

'Where do they start?' said Sarah.

'Over yonder, where you see that clump. They run
through the furze right up to Tattenham Corner.'

A vast crowd swarmed over the opposite hill, and beyond
the crowd the women saw a piece of open downland dotted
with bushes, and rising in gentle incline to a belt of trees
which closed the horizon. 'Where them trees are, that 's
*Tattenham Corner*.' The words seemed to fill old John with
enthusiasm, and he described how the horses came round
this side of the trees. 'They comes right down that 'ere
'ill—there 's the dip—and they finishes opposite to where
we is standing. Yonder, by Barnard's Ring.'

'What, all among the people?' said Sarah.

'The police will get the people right back up the hill.'

'That's where we shall find William,' said Esther.

'I'm getting a bit peckish; ain't you, dear? He's got the luncheon-basket. But, lor', what a lot of people! Look at that.'

What had attracted Sarah's attention was a boy walking through the crowd on a pair of stilts fully eight feet high. He uttered short warning cries from time to time, held out his wide trousers and caught pennies in his conical cap. Drags and carriages continued to arrive. The sweating horses were unyoked, and grooms and helpers rolled the vehicles into position along the rails. Lackeys drew forth cases of wine and provisions, and the flutter of table-cloths had begun to attract vagrants, itinerant musicians, fortune-tellers, begging children. All these plied their trades round the fashion of grey frock-coats and silk sunshades. All along the rails rough fellows lay asleep with their hats over their faces, clay pipes sticking from under the brims, their brown-red hands upon the grey grass.

Suddenly old John pleaded an appointment; he was to meet a friend who would give him the very latest news respecting a certain horse; and Esther, Sarah, and Journeyman wandered along the course in search of William. Along the rails strangely dressed men stood on stools, satchels and race-glasses slung over their shoulders, great bouquets in their button-holes. Each stood between two poles on which was stretched a piece of white-coloured linen, on which was inscribed their name in large gold letters. Sarah read some of these names out: 'Jack Hooper, Marylebone. All bets paid.' 'Tom Wood's famous boxing-rooms, Epsom.' 'James Webster, Commission Agent, London.' And these betting men bawled the prices from the top of their high stools, shaking their money-filled satchels to attract custom. 'What can I do for you to-day, sir?' they shouted when they caught the eye of any respectably dressed man. 'On the Der-by, on the Der-by, I'll bet the Der-by. To win or a place, to win or a place, to win or a place—seven to one bar two or three, seven to one bar two or three. The old firm, the old firm'—like so many challenging cocks, each trying to outshrill the other.

Under the hill-side in a quiet hollow had been pitched a large and commodious tent. Journeyman mentioned that it was the West London Gospel-tent. He thought the parson would have it pretty well all to himself, and they stopped before a van filled with barrels of Watford ales. A barrel had been taken from the van and placed on a small table; glasses of beer were being served to a thirsty crowd; and all around were little canvas shelters, whence men shouted, ''Commodation, 'commodation.'

The sun had risen high, and what clouds remained floated away like filaments of white cotton. The Grand Stand, dotted like a ceiling with flies, stood out distinct and harsh upon a burning plain of blue. The light beat fiercely upon the booths, the carriages, the vehicles, the 'rings,' the various stands. The country around was lost in the haze and dazzle of the sunlight; but a square mile of downland fluttered with flags and canvas, and the great mob swelled, and smoked, and drank, shied sticks at Aunt Sally, and rode wooden horses. And through this crash of perspiring, shrieking humanity Journeyman, Esther, and Sarah sought vainly for William. The form of the ground was lost in the multitude and they could only tell by the strain in their limbs whether they were walking up or down hill. Sarah declared herself to be done up, and it was with difficulty that she was persuaded to persevere a little longer. At last Journeyman caught sight of the bookmaker's square shoulders.

'Well, so here you are. What can I do for you, ladies? Ten to one bar three or four. Will that suit you?'

'The luncheon-basket will suit us a deal better,' said Sarah.

At that moment a chap came up jingling two half-crowns in his hand. 'What price the favourite?' 'Two to one,' cried William. The two half-crowns were dropped into the satchel, and, thus encouraged, William called out louder than ever, 'The old firm, the old firm; don't forget the old firm.' There was a smile on his lips while he halloaed— a cheery, good-natured smile, which made him popular and brought him many a customer.

'On the Der-by, on the Der-by, on the Der-by!' All kinds and conditions of men came to make bets with him; custom was brisk; he could not join the women, who were busy with the lunch-basket, but he and Teddy would be thankful for the biggest drink they could get them.

'Ginger beer with a drop of whisky in it, that's about it, Teddy?'

'Yes, guv'nor, that'll do for me. We're getting pretty full on Dewberry; might come down a point, I think.'

'All right, Teddy. And if you'd cut us a couple each of strong sandwiches—you can manage a couple, Teddy?'

'I think I can, guv'nor.'

There was a nice piece of beef in the basket, and Esther cut several large sandwiches, buttering the bread thickly and adding plenty of mustard. When she brought them over William bent down and whispered:

'My own duck of a wife, there's no one like her.'

Esther blushed and laughed with pleasure, and every trace of the resentment for the suffering he had occasioned her dropped out of her heart. For the first time he was really her husband; for the first time she felt that sense of unity in life which is marriage, and knew henceforth he was the one thing that she had to live for.

After luncheon Journeyman, who was making no way with Sarah, took his leave, pleading that he had some friends to meet in Barnard's Ring. They were glad to be rid of him. Sarah had many a tale to tell; and, while listening to the matrimonial engagements that had been broken off, Esther shifted her parasol from time to time to watch her tall, gaunt husband. He shouted the odds, willing to bet against every horse, distributed tickets to the various folk that crowded round him, each with his preference, his prejudice, his belief in omens, in tips, or in the talent and luck of a favourite jockey. Sarah continued her cursive chatter regarding the places she had served in. She felt inclined for a snooze, but was afraid it would not look well. While hesitating she ceased speaking, and both women fell asleep under the shade of their parasols. It was the shallow, glassy sleep of the open air, through which they divined easily the great blur that was the racecourse.

They could hear William's voice, and they heard a bell ring and shouts of 'Here they come!' Then a lull came, and their perceptions grew a little denser, and when they awoke the sky was the same burning blue, and the multitude moved to and fro like puppets.

Sarah was in no better temper after than before her

sleep. 'It's all very well for you,' she said. 'You have your husband to look after. I'll never come to the Derby again without a young man. . . . I'm tired of sitting here, the grass is roasting. Come for a walk.'

They were two nice-looking English women of the lower classes, prettily dressed in light gowns with cheap sunshades in their cotton-gloved hands. Sarah looked at every young man with regretful eyes. In such moods acquaintanceships are made; and she did not allow Esther to shake off Bill Evans, who, just as if he had never been turned out of the bar of the 'King's Head,' came up with his familiar, 'Good morning, ma'am—lovely weather for the races.' Sarah's sidelong glances at the blue Melton jacket and the billycock hat defined her feelings; Esther held her tongue; her warning would not have been heeded; and soon Bill and Sarah were engaged in animated talk, and Esther was left to follow them if she liked.

She walked by Sarah's side, almost forgotten, till they passed the mission tent, where Fred was calling upon the folk to leave the ways of Satan for those of Christ. Bill Evans was about to answer some brutal insult; but seeing that 'the Christian' knew Esther he checked himself in time, and seized the opportunity to slip away with Sarah.

'I didn't expect to meet you here, Esther.'

'I'm here with my husband. He said a little pleasure——'

'This is not innocent pleasure, Esther; this is drunkenness and debauchery. I hope you'll never come again, unless you come with us,' he said, pointing to some girls dressed as bookmakers, with Salvation and Perdition written on the satchels hung round their shoulders. They sought to persuade the passers-by to come into the tent. 'We shall be very glad to see you,' they said, and they distributed mock racing cards on which was inscribed news regarding certain imaginary racing. 'The Paradise Plate, for all comers,' 'The Salvation Stakes, an Eternity of Happiness added.'

Fred repeated his request. 'I hope the next time you come here it will be with us; you'll strive to collect some of Christ's lost sheep.'

'And my husband making a book yonder?'

An awkward silence intervened, and then he said:

'Won't you come in? service is going on.'

In the tent there were some benches, and on a platform a grey-bearded man with an anxious face spoke of sinners and redemption. A harmonium began to play a hymn, and, standing by Fred, Esther sang, joining in the psalm, prayer being so inherent in her that she felt no sense of incongruity, and had she been questioned she would have answered that it did not matter where we are, or what we are doing, we can always have God in our hearts.

Fred followed her out.

'You haven't forgotten your religion, I hope?'

'No, I never could forget that.'

'Then why do I find you in such company?  You don't come here like us to find sinners.'

'I haven't forgotten God, but I must do my duty to my husband.  It would be like setting myself up against my husband's business, and you don't think I ought to do that?  A wife that brings discord into the family is not a good wife, so I've often heard.'

'You always thought more of your husband than of Christ, Esther.'

'Each one must follow Christ as best he can!  It would be wrong of me to set myself against my husband.'

'So he married you?' Fred answered bitterly.

'Yes.  You thought he'd desert me a second time; but he's been the best of husbands.'

'I place little reliance on those who are not with Christ. His love for you is not of the Spirit.  Let us not speak of him.  I loved you very deeply, Esther.  I would have brought you to Christ. . . . But perhaps you'll come to see us sometimes.'

'I do not forget Christ.  He's always with me, and I believe you did care for me.  I was sorry to break it off; you know I was.  It was not my fault.'

'Esther, it was I who loved you.'

'You mustn't talk like that.  I'm a married woman.'

'I mean no harm, Esther.  I was only thinking of the past.'

'You must forget all that. . . . Good-bye; I'm glad to have seen you, and that we said a prayer together.'

Fred didn't answer, and Esther moved away, wondering where she should find Sarah.

## CHAPTER XXXIII

THE crowd shouted. She looked where the others looked, but saw only the burning blue with the white stand marked upon it. It was crowded like the deck of a sinking vessel, and Esther wondered at the excitement, the cause of which was hidden from her. She wandered to the edge of the crowd until she came to a chalk road where horses and mules were tethered. A little higher up she entered the crowd again, and came suddenly upon a switchback railway. Full of laughing and screaming girls, it bumped over a middle hill, and then rose slowly till it reached the last summit. It was shot back again into the midst of its fictitious perils, and this mock voyaging was accomplished to the sound of music from a puppet orchestra. Bells and drums, a fife and a triangle, cymbals clashed mechanically, and a little soldier beat the time. Farther on, under a striped awning, were the wooden horses. They were arranged so well that they rocked to and fro, imitating as nearly as possible the action of real horses. Esther watched the riders. A blue skirt looked like a riding habit, and a girl in salmon pink leaned back in her saddle just as if she had been taught how to ride. A girl in a grey jacket encouraged a girl in white who rode a grey horse. But before Esther could make out for certain that the man in the blue Melton jacket was Bill Evans he had passed out of sight, and she had to wait until his horse came round the second time. At that moment she caught sight of the red poppies in Sarah's hat.

The horses began to slacken speed. They went slower and slower, then stopped altogether. The riders began to dismount, and Esther pressed through the bystanders, afraid that she would not be able to overtake her friends.

'Oh, here you are,' said Sarah. 'I thought I never should find you again. How hot it is!'

'Were you on in that ride? Let's have another, all three of us. These three horses.'

Round and round they went, their steeds bobbing nobly up and down to the sound of fifes, drums, and cymbals. They passed the winning-post many times; they had to pass it five times, and the horse that stopped nearest it won the prize. A long-drawn-out murmur, continuous as the sea, swelled up from the course—a murmur which at last passed into words: 'Here they come; blue wins, the favourite's beat.' Esther paid little attention to these cries; she did not understand them; they reached her indistinctly and soon died away, absorbed in the strident music that accompanied the circling horses. These had now begun to slacken speed. . . . They went slower and slower. Sarah and Bill, who rode side by side, seemed like winning, but at the last moment they glided by the winning-post. Esther's steed stopped in time, and she was told to choose a china mug from a great heap.

'You've all the luck to-day,' said Bill. 'Hayfield, who was backed all the winter, broke down a month ago. . . . 2 to 1 against Fly-leaf, 4 to 1 against Signet-ring, 4 to 1 against Dewberry, 10 to 1 against Vanguard, the winner at 50 to 1 offered. Your husband must have won a little fortune. Never was there such a day for the bookies.'

Esther said she was very glad, and was undecided which mug she should choose. At last she saw one on which 'Jack' was written in gold letters. . . . They visited the peep-shows, and especially liked St. James's Park with Horse Guards out on parade; the Spanish bull-fight did not stir them, and Sarah couldn't find a single young man to her taste in the House of Commons. Among the performing birds they liked best a canary that climbed a ladder. Bill was attracted by the American strength-testers, and he gave an exhibition of his muscle, to Sarah's very great admiration. They all had some shies at coco-nuts, and passed by J. Bilton's great bowling saloon without visiting it. Once more the air was filled with the cries of 'Here they come! Here they come!' Even the 'commodation men left their canvas shelters and pressed forward inquiring which had won. A moment after a score of pigeons floated and flew through the blue air and then departed in different directions, some making straight for London, others for the blue mysterious evening that had risen about the downs—the sun-baked downs strewn with waste paper and covered by tipsy men and women, a screaming and disordered animality.

'Well, so you 've come back at last,' said William. 'The favourite was beaten. I suppose you know that a rank outsider won. But what about this gentleman?'

'Met these 'ere ladies on the 'ill an' been showing them over the course. No offence, I hope, guv'nor?'

William did not answer, and Bill took leave of Sarah in a manner that told Esther that they had arranged to meet again.

'Where did you pick up that bloke?'

'He came up and spoke to us, and Esther stopped to speak to the parson.'

'To the parson. What do you mean?'

The circumstance was explained, and William asked them what they thought of the racing.

'We didn't see no racing,' said Sarah; 'we was on the 'ill on the wooden 'orses. Esther's 'orse won. She got a mug; show the mug, Esther.'

'So you saw no Derby after all?' said William.

'Saw no racin'!' said his neighbour; 'ain't she won the cup?'

The joke was lost on the women, who only perceived that they were being laughed at.

'Come up here, Esther,' said William; 'stand on my box. The 'orses are just going up the course for the preliminary canter. And you, Sarah, take Teddy's place. Teddy, get down and let the lady up.'

'Yes, guv'nor. Come up 'ere, ma'am.'

'And is those the 'orses?' said Sarah. 'They do seem small.'

The ringmen roared. 'Not up to those on the 'ill, ma'am,' said one. 'Not such beautiful goers,' said another.

There were two or three false starts, and then, looking through a multitude of hats, Esther saw five or six thin greyhound-looking horses. They passed like shadows, flitted by; and she was sorry for the poor chestnut that trotted in among the crowd.

This was the last race. Once more the favourite had been beaten; there were no bets to pay, and the bookmakers began to prepare for departure, leaving their clerks to look after the luggage. Teddy didn't seem as if he would ever reach the top of the hill. With Esther and Sarah on either arm, William struggled with the crowd. It was hard to get through the block of carriages. Everywhere horses waited with their harness on, and Sarah was afraid of being bitten or kicked. A young aristocrat cursed them from the box-seat and the groom blew a blast as the drag rolled away. It was like the instinct of departure which takes a vast herd at a certain moment. The great landscape, half country, half suburb, glinted beneath the rays of a setting sun; and through the white dust, and the drought of the warm roads, the brakes and carriages and every crazy vehicle rolled towards London; orange sellers, tract sellers, thieves, vagrants, gipsies, made for their various quarters—roadside inns, outhouses, hayricks, hedges, or the railway station. Down the long hill the vast crowd made its way, humble pedestrians and carriage folk, all together, as far as the cross-roads. At the 'Spread Eagle' there would be stoppage for a parting drink, there the bookmakers would change their clothes, and their division would happen in the crowd—half for the railway station, half for the London road. It was there that the traditional sports of the road began. A drag, with a band of exquisites armed with pea-shooters, peppering on costers who were getting angry, and threatening to drive over the leaders. A brake with two poles erected, and hanging on a string quite a line of miniature chamber - pots. A horse, with his forelegs clothed in a pair of lady's drawers—the horse stepping along so absurdly that Esther and Sarah thought they'd choke with laughter.

At the station William halloaed to old John, whom he caught sight of on the platform. He had backed the winner—forty to one about Sultan. It was Ketley who had persuaded him to risk half a sovereign on the horse. Ketley was at the Derby; he had met him on the course, and Ketley had told him a wonderful story about a packet of Turkish delight. The omen had come right this time, and Journeyman took a back seat.

'Say what you like,' said William, 'it is damned strange; and if any one did find the way of reading them omens there would be an end of us bookmakers.' He was only half in earnest, but he regretted he had not met Ketley. If he had only had a fiver on the horse—200 to 5!

At Waterloo they met Ketley, and every one wanted to hear from his own lips the story of the packet of Turkish delight. So William proposed they should all come up to the 'King's Head' for a drink. The omnibus took them as far as Piccadilly Circus; and there the weight of his satchel tempted William to invite them to dinner regardless of expense.

'Which is the best dinner here?' he asked the commissionaire.

'The East Room is reckoned the best, sir.'

The fashion of the shaded candles and the little tables, and the beauty of an open evening bodice and the black-and-white elegance of the young men at dinner, took the servants by surprise, and made them feel that they were out of place in such surroundings. Old John looked like picking up a napkin and asking at the nearest table if anything was wanted. Ketley proposed the grill-room, but William, who had had a glass more than was good for him, declared that he didn't care a damn—that he could buy up the whole blooming show. The head waiter suggested a private room; it was abruptly declined, and William took up the bill of fare. 'Bisque soup, what's that? You ought to know, John.' John shook his head. 'Ris de veau! That reminds me of when——' William stopped and looked round to see if his former wife was in the room. Finally, the head waiter was cautioned to send them up the best dinner in the place, and allusion being made to the dust and heat, they inquired their way to the lavatories for a sluice. Esther and Sarah were away longer than the men, and stood dismayed at the top of the room till William called to them at the top of his voice, whereupon the other guests seemed a little terrified, and the head waiter, to reassure them, mentioned that it was Derby Day.

William had ordered champagne, but it had not proved to the taste of any one, except perhaps of Sarah, whom it rendered unduly hilarious; nor did the delicate food afford much satisfaction; the servants played with it, and left it on their plates; and it was not until William ordered up the saddle of mutton and carved it himself that the dinner began to take hold of the company. Esther and Sarah enjoyed the ices, and the men stuck to the cheese, a fine Stilton, which was much appreciated. Coffee no one cared for, and the little glasses of brandy only served to augment the general tipsiness. William hiccuped out an order for a bottle of Jameson eight-year-old; but pipes were not allowed, and cigars were voted tedious, so they adjourned to the bar, where they were free to get as drunk as they pleased. William said, 'Now let's 'ear the blo—the bloody omen that put ye on to Sultan—that blood—packet of Turkish delight.'

'Most extra—most extraordinary thing I ever heard in my life. So yer 'ere?' said Ketley, staring at William and trying to see him distinctly.

William nodded. 'How was it? We want to 'ear all about it. Do hold yer tongue, Sarah. I beg pardon, Ketley is go—going to tell us about the bloody omen. Thought you'd like to he—ar, old girl.'

Something was said about a little girl coming home from school, and a piece of paper on the pavement, but Ketley could not concentrate his thoughts on the main lines of the story, and it was lost in various dissertations. But the company was none the less pleased with it, and willingly declared that bookmaking was only a game for mugs. Get on a winner at forty to one, and you could make as much in one bet as a poor devil of a bookie could in six months, fagging from racecourse to racecourse. And over the long bar they drank, argued, and quarrelled, until Esther noticed that Sarah was looking very pale. Old John was quite helpless; Journeyman, who seemed to know what he was doing, very kindly promised to look after him.

Ketley hung on to the commissionaire, intent on persuading him that he was not drunk. 'You shee, commissionaire, thish ish how it ish: when I look drunk I am shober, and when I look shober I am very drunk. Sho you mushn't judge by appearanshes, commissionaire.' Sarah felt obliged to step aside; and hearing her saying that she felt a little better when she returned, they stood on the pavement's edge, a little puzzled by the brilliancy of the moonlight. Now the three men who followed out of the bar-room were agreed regarding the worthlessness of life. 'All I live for is beer and women.' The phrase caught on William's ear, and he said, 'Quite right, old mate,' and held out his hand to Bill Evans. 'Beer and women, it always comes round to that in the end, but we mustn't let them hear us say it.' Bill promised to see Sarah safely home. Esther tried to interpose, but William could not be made to understand, and Sarah and Bill drove away together in a hansom, Sarah dozing off on his shoulder, and it was difficult to awaken her when the cab stopped before a house whose respectability took Bill by surprise.

## CHAPTER XXXIV

'Is that you, Sarah?'

'Yes, it is me.'

'Then come in. How is it that we 've not seen you all this time? What 's the matter?'

'I 've been out all night. Bill put me out of doors this morning, and I 've been walking about ever since.'

'Bill put you out of doors? I don't understand.'

'You know Bill Evans, the man we met on the racecourse, the day we went to the Derby. It began there. He took me home after your dinner at the "Criterion," and it has been going on ever since.'

'Good Lord! Tell me about it.'

And leaning against the partition that separated the bars, Sarah told how she had left her home and gone to live with him.

'We got on pretty well at first, but the police was after him, and we made off to Belgium. There we was very hard up, and I had to go out on the streets.'

'He made you do that?'

'He couldn't starve, could he?'

The women looked at each other, and then Sarah continued her story, telling how they had come to London, penniless. 'I think he wants to turn honest,' she said, 'but luck 's been dead against him. He 's been in work, but he can't stick to it; and now I don't know what he 's doing—no good, I fancy. Last night I got anxious and couldn't sleep, so I sat up. It was about two when he came in. We had a row and he dragged me downstairs and he put me out. He said he never wanted to see my ugly face again. I don't think I 'm as bad as that; I 've led a hard life, and am not what I used to be, but it was he who made me what I am. Oh, it don't matter now, it can't be helped, it is all over with me. I don't care what becomes of me, only I thought I 'd like to come and tell you. We was always friends.'

'You mustn't give way like that, old girl. You must

keep your pecker up. You 're dead beat. You 've been walking about all night, no wonder. You must come and have some breakfast with us.'

'I should like a cup of tea, Esther. I never touches spirits now. I got over that.'

'Come into the parlour. You 'll be better when you 've had breakfast. We 'll see what we can do for you.'

'Oh, Esther, not a word of what I 've been telling you to your husband. I don't want to get Bill into trouble. He 'd kill me. Promise me not to say a word of it. I oughtn't to have told you. I was so tired that I didn't know what I was saying.'

Esther called to her servant to bring up the breakfast.

'You seem to live pretty well,' said Sarah. 'Fried fish, a nice piece of steak, tea, and coffee. It must be nice to have a servant of one's own. I suppose you 're doing pretty well here.'

'Yes, pretty well, if it wasn't for William's health.'

'What 's the matter? Ain't he well?'

'He 's been very poorly lately. It 's very trying work going about from racecourse to racecourse, standing in the mud and wet all day long. He caught a bad cold last winter and was laid up with inflammation of the lungs; and I don't think he ever quite got over it.'

'Don't he go no more to race meetings?'

'He hasn't been to a race meeting since the beginning of the winter. It was one of them nasty steeplechase meetings that laid him up.'

'Do 'e drink?'

'He 's never drunk, but he takes too much. Spirits don't suit him. He thought he could do what he liked, great strong-built fellow that he is, but he 's found out his mistake.'

'His betting is all done in London now, I suppose?'

'Yes,' said Esther, hesitating—'when he has any to do. I want him to give it up; but trade is bad in this neighbourhood, leastways, with us, and he don't think we could do without it.'

'It 's very hard to keep it dark; someone 's sure to crab it and bring the police down on you.'

Esther asked Sarah if she 'd have some more coffee. 'Holloa! is that you, Sarah?' It was William. 'We didn't know what had become of you all this time.' William noticed that she looked like one in trouble, and poorly dressed; and she that his cheeks were thinner. The women told him the story, interrupting each other and arguing over certain bets. But the story was riddled out somehow in the end.

'I knew he was a bad lot,' William said. 'I never liked to see him inside my bar.'

'I thought,' said Esther, 'that Sarah might remain here for a time.'

'I can't have that fellow coming round my place.'

'There's no fear of his coming after me. He don't want to see my ugly face again. Well, let him try to find some-one who will do for him all I have done.'

'The best for you will be to stop here till you get a situation.'

'And what about a character?'

'You needn't say much about what you've been doing this last three months; and if questions are asked, you can say you've been stopping with us. But you mustn't see that brute again. If he ever comes into this 'ere bar, I'll give him a piece of my mind.'

'I'd give him more than a piece of my mind if I was the man I was a twelvemonth ago,' William said, and Esther looked at him anxiously.

Sarah threw her eyes over the parlour.

'You seem pretty comfortable here,' she said.

'Well, some must be down for others to be up.'

And approving this philosophy, or accepting it tacitly, they told her that what the 'King's Head' lacked was a parlour on the ground floor for the use of special customers; so William had arranged a room upstairs, where there were tables in front of the windows and chairs against the walls, and in the middle of the room a bagatelle board. Would she like to come up? And Sarah, while admiring the pictures of celebrated racehorses that William had hung up, heard from Esther, principally, that when William forswore racecourses he had intended to refuse money across the bar and to do all his betting business in this room. But as his customers multiplied he found that he could not ask them all upstairs; it attracted more attention than to take the money quietly across the bar. All the same, the room upstairs had proved a success. A man spent more money if he had a room where he could sit quietly among his friends than he would seated on a high stool in a public bar, jostled and pushed about; so it had come to be considered a sort of club-room; and a large part of the neighbourhood trooped up there to read the papers, to hear and discuss the news. And specially needful it had proved to Journeyman and Stack, who were now professional backers, wandering from daylight to dark from public-house to public-house, from tobacconist to barber's shop, in the search of tips, on the quest of stable information regarding the health of the horses and their trials, the room at the 'King's Head' always the centre of their operations. Stack was the inspired tipster, Journeyman the scientific student of public form, whose prodigious memory enabled him to note an advantage in the weights which would escape a casual reader; he often picked out horses which, if they did not actually win, nearly always stood at a short price in the betting before the race.

The 'King's Head' was crowded during the dinner-hour. Barbers and their assistants, cabmen, scene-shifters, if there was an afternoon performance at the theatre, servants out of situation and servants escaped from their service for an hour, petty shopkeepers, the many who grow weary of the scant livelihood that work brings them, came there. Eleven o'clock! In another hour the bar and the room upstairs would be crowded. At present the room was empty, and Journeyman had taken advantage of the quiet time to do a bit of work at his handicap. All the racing of the last three years lay within his mind's range; he recalled at will every trifling selling race; hardly ever was he obliged to refer to the Racing Calendar. Chimney Sweep had beaten Brick at ten pounds. Snow Queen had beaten Shoemaker at four pounds, and Shoemaker had beaten Wanderer at seven pounds. The problem was further complicated by the suspicion that Brick was better than Snow Queen over a distance of ground. Journeyman was undecided. He stroked his short brown moustache with his thin, hairy hand, and gnawed the end of his pen. In this moment of barren reflection Stack came into the room.

'Still at yer 'andicap, I see,' said Stack. 'How does it work out?'

'Pretty well,' said Journeyman. 'But I don't think it will be one of my best; there is some pretty hard nuts to crack.'

'Which are they?' said Stack. Journeyman brightened up, and he proceeded to lay before Stack's intelligence what he termed a 'knotty point in collateral running.'

Stack listened with attention, and, thus encouraged, Journeyman proceeded to point out certain distributions of weight which he said seemed to him difficult to beat.

'Any one what knows the running would say there wasn't a pin to choose between them at the weights. If this was the real 'andicap, I'd bet drinks all round that fifteen of these twenty would accept. And that's more than any one will be able to say for Courtney's 'andicap. The weights will be out to-morrow; we shall see what we shall see.'

'Now, give it a name; 'alf a pint,' said Stack, 'and we'll go steadily through your 'andicap? You've nothing to do for the next 'alf-hour,' and when the potboy appeared in answer to the bell he was told to bring up two half-pints. Journeyman read out the weights, every now and then stopping to explain his reasons for what might seem to be superficial, an unmerited severity, or an undue leniency. It was not usual for Journeyman to meet with so sympathetic a listener; he had often been made to feel that his handicapping was unnecessary, and he now noticed, and with much pleasure, that Stack's attention seemed to increase rather than to diminish as he approached the end. When he had finished, Stack said, 'I see you've given six-seven to Ben Jonson. Tell me why you did that?'

'He was a good 'orse once; he's broken down and aged; he can't be trained, so six-seven seems just the kind of weight to throw him in at. You couldn't give him less, however old and broken down he may be. He was a good horse when he won the Great Ebor Grand Cup.'

'Do you think if they brought him to the post as fit and well as he was the day he won the Ebor that he'd win?'

'What, fit and well as he was when he won the Great Ebor, and with six-seven on his back? He'd walk away with it.'

'You don't think any of the three-year-olds would have
a chance with him? A Derby winner with seven stone on
his back might beat him.'

'Yes, but nothing short of that. Even then old Ben
would make a race of it. A nailing good horse once. A
little brown horse about fifteen-two, as compact as a leg of
Welsh mutton. But there's no use in thinking of him.
They've been trying for years to train him. Didn't they
used to get the flesh off him in a Turkish bath? That was
Fulton's notion. He used to say that it didn't matter
'ow you got the flesh off so long as you got it off. Every
pound of flesh off the lungs is so much wind, he used to say.
But the Turkish-bath trained horses came to the post limp
as old rags. If a 'orse 'asn't the legs you can't train him.
Every pound of flesh yer take off must put a pound o'
'ealth on. They'll do no good with old Ben, unless they've
found out a way of growing on him a pair of new forelegs.
The old ones won't do for my money.'

'But do you think that Courtney will take the same view
of his chances as you do—do you think he'll let him off
as easily as you have?'

'He can't give him much more. The 'orse is bound to
get in at seven stone, rather under than over.'

'I'm glad to 'ear yer say so, for I know you've a headpiece, and 'as all the running in there.' Stack tapped his
forehead. 'Now, I'd like to ask you if there's any three-
year-olds that would be likely to interfere with him?'

'Derby and Leger winners will get from eight stone to
eight stone ten, and three-year-olds ain't no good over the
Cesarewitch course with more than eight on their backs.'

Surprised at Stack's silence, Journeyman said:

'Is there anything up? Have you heard anything
particular about old Ben?'

Stack bent forward. 'Yes, I've heard something, and
I'm making inquiries.'

'How did you hear it?'

Stack drew his chair a little closer. 'I've been up at
Chalk Farm, the "Yarborough Arms"; you know, where
the buses stop. Bob Barrett does a deal of business up
there. He pays the landlord's rent for the use of the bar—
Wednesdays, Fridays, and Saturdays is his days. Charley
Grove bets there on Mondays, Tuesdays, and Thursdays,

but it is Bob that does the biggest part of the business. They say he 's taken as much as twenty pounds in a morning. You know Bob, a great big man, eighteen stun if he 's an ounce. He 's a warm 'un, can put it on thick.'

'I know him; he do tell fine stories about the girls; he 'as the pick of the neighbourhood, wears a low hat, no higher than that, with a big brim. I know him. I 've heard that he 'as moved up that way. Used at one time to keep a tobacconist's shop in Great Portland Street.'

'That 's 'im,' said Stack. 'I thought you 'd heard of 'im.'

'There ain't many about that I 've not heard of. Not that I likes the man much. There was a girl I knew—she wouldn't hear his name mentioned. But he lays fair prices, and I believe he does a big trade.'

''As a nice 'ome at Brixton, keeps a trap; his wife as pretty a woman as you could wish to lay eyes on. I 've seen her with him at Kempton.'

'You was up there this morning?'

'Yes.'

'It wasn't Bob Barrett that gave you the tip?'

'Not likely.' The men laughed, and then Stack said:

'You know Bill Evans? You 've seen him here, always wore a blue Melton jacket and billycock hat; a dark, stout, good-looking fellow; generally had something to sell, or pawn-tickets that he would part with for a trifle.'

'Yes, I know the fellow. We met him down at Epsom one Derby Day. Sarah Tucker, a friend of the missus, was dead gone on him.'

'Yes, she went to live with him. There was a row, and now, I believe, they 're together again; they was seen out walking. They 're friends, anyhow. Bill has been away all the summer, tramping. A bad lot, but one of them sort often hears of a good thing.'

'So it was from Bill Evans that you heard it.'

'Yes, it was from Bill. He has just come up from Eastbourne, where he 'as been about on the Downs a great deal. I don't know if it was the 'orses he was after, but in the course of his proceedings he 'eard from a shepherd that Ben Jonson was doing seven hours' walking exercise a day. This seemed to have fetched Bill a bit. Seven hours' a day walking exercise did seem a bit odd, and being at the same time after one of the servants in the training stable—as

pretty a bit of goods as he had ever set eyes on, so Bill says
—he thought he 'd make an inquiry or two about all this
walking exercise. One of the lads in the stable is after the
girl, too, so Bill found out very soon all he wanted to know.
As you says, the 'orse is dicky on 'is forelegs, that is the
reason of all the walking exercise.'

'And they thinks they can bring him fit to the post and
win the Cesarewitch with him by walking him all day?'

'I don't say they don't gallop him at all; they do gallop
him, but not as much as if his legs was all right.'

'That won't do. I don't believe in a 'orse winning the
Cesarewitch that ain't got four sound legs, and old Ben
ain't got more than two.'

'He 's had a long rest, and they say he is sounder than
ever he was since he won the Great Ebor. They don't say
he 'd stand no galloping, but they don't want to gallop him
more than 's absolutely necessary on account of the sus-
pensory ligament; it ain't the back sinew, but the sus-
pensory ligament. Their theory is this, that it don't so
much matter about bringing him quite fit to the post, for
he 's sure to stay the course; he 'd do that three times over.
What they say is this, that if he gets in with seven stone,
and we brings him well and three parts trained, there ain't
no 'orse in England that can stand up before him. They 've
got another in the race, Laurel Leaf, to make the running
for him; it can't be too strong for old Ben. You say to
yourself that he may get let off with six-seven. If he do
there 'll be tons of money on him. He 'll be backed at the
post at five to one. Before the weights come out they 'll
lay a hundred to one on the field in any of the big clubs. I
wouldn't mind putting a quid on him if you 'll join me.'

'Better wait until the weights come out,' said Journeyman, 'for if it happened to come to Courtney's ears that old
Ben could be trained he 'd clap seven-ten on him without a
moment's hesitation.'

'You think so?' said Stack.

'I do,' said Journeyman.

'But you agree with me that if he got let off with anything less than seven stone, and be brought fit, or there-
abouts, to the post, that the race is a moral certainty
for him?'

'A thousand to a brass farthing.'

'Mind, not a word.'

'Is it likely!'

The conversation paused a moment, and then Journeyman said: 'You've not seen my 'andicap for the Cambridgeshire. I wonder what you'd think of that?' Stack said he would be glad to see it another time, and proposed that they went downstairs.

'I'm afraid the police is in,' said Stack, when he opened the door.

'Then we'd better stop where we are; I don't want to be took to the station.'

They listened for some moments, holding the door ajar.

'It ain't the police,' said Stack, 'but a row about some bet. Latch had better be careful.'

The cause of the scrimmage was a tall young English workman, whom his comrades were striving to quieten.

'Leave me alone,' he exclaimed; 'the bet was ten half-crowns to one. I won't stand being welshed.'

William's face flushed up. 'Welshed!' he said. 'No one speaks in this bar of welshing.' And he would have sprung over the counter if Esther hadn't held him back.

'I know what I'm talking about; you let me alone,' said the young workman, and he struggled out of the hands of his friends. 'The bet was ten half-crowns to one.'

'Don't mind what he says, guv'nor.'

'Don't mind what I says!' For a moment it seemed as if the friends were about to come to blows, but the young man's perceptions suddenly clouded, and he said: 'In this blo-ody bar last Monday. Horse backed in Tattersall's at twelve to one taken and offered.'

'He don't know what he's talking about; but no one must accuse me of welshing in this 'ere bar.'

'No offence, guv'nor; mistakes will occur.'

William sent Teddy upstairs for Monday's paper, and he pointed out that eight to one was being asked for the horse on Monday afternoon at Tattersall's. Esther and Charles had been selling beer and spirits as fast as they could draw it, but the disputed bet caused the company to forget their glasses.

'Just one more drink,' said the young man. 'Take the

ten half-crowns out in drinks, guv'nor, that's good enough.
What do you say, guv'nor?'

'What ten half-crowns?' William answered angrily.
'Haven't I shown you that the 'orse was backed at Tattersall's the day you made the bet at eight to one?'

'Ten to one, guv'nor.'

'I've not time to go on talking. You're interfering
with my business. You must get out of my bar.'

'Who'll put me out?'

'Charles, go and fetch a policeman.'

At the word 'policeman' the young man seemed to
recover his wits somewhat, and he answered: 'You'll bring
in no bloody policeman. Fetch a policeman! and what
about your blooming betting—what will become of that?'
William looked round to see if there was any in the bar
whom he could not trust. He knew every one present, and
believed he could trust them all. There was but one thing
to do, and that was to put on a bold face and trust to luck.
'Now out you go,' he said, springing over the counter, 'and
never you set your face inside my bar again.' Charles
followed the guv'nor over the counter like lightning, and
the drunkard was forced into the street. 'He don't mean
no 'arm,' said one of the friends; 'he'll come round to-
morrow and apologize for what he's said.'

'I don't want his apology,' said William. 'No one shall
call me a welsher in my bar. Take your friend away, and
never let me see him in my bar again.'

All of a sudden William was seized with a fit of coughing,
and Esther led him into the parlour, leaving Charles to
attend to the customers. His hand trembled like a leaf,
and she sat by his side holding it. At that moment Mr.
Blamey came in to ask if he should lay one of the young
gentlemen from the tutor's thirty shillings to ten against
the favourite. Esther said that William could attend to
no more customers that day; but Mr. Blamey returned
ten minutes after to say that there was quite a number of
people in the bar; should he refuse to take their money?

'Do you know them all?' said William.

'I think so, guv'nor.'

'Be careful to bet with no one you don't know; but I'm
so bad I can hardly speak.'

'Much better send them away,' said Esther.

'Then they 'll go somewhere else.'

'It won't matter; they 'll come back to where they 're sure of their money.'

'I 'm not so certain of that,' William answered feebly. 'I think it will be all right, Teddy; you 'll be very careful.'

'Yes, guv'nor, I 'll keep down the price.'

## CHAPTER XXXV

ONE afternoon Fred Parsons came into the bar of the 'King's Head.' He wore the cap and jersey of the Salvation Army; he was now Captain Parsons. The bars were empty. It was a time when business was slackest. The morning's betting was over, the crowd had dispersed, and would not collect again until the *Evening Standard* came in. Fred looked round and rapped with his stick, but nobody answered. William had gone for a walk, the potman was at work in the backyard, and Esther was sewing in the parlour; but she had just left the room. And, unable to make anybody hear, Parsons began to ask himself if the house was empty and anybody could come in and drink as much as he pleased without paying for it.

'Oh, it is you, Fred,' and she stood looking at him, surprised by his uniform. 'So you are in the Army?'

'Yes, I 've joined up,' he answered; 'but I was always in it in spirit from the beginning, as I think you know.'

She wondered what he had come about.

'Is your husband in?' he asked. 'If he is, I should like to speak to him.'

'No, my husband is out, and I don't expect him back for an hour or so. Can I give him any message?'

She was on the point of asking him how he was. But there was something so harsh and formal in his tone and manner that she refrained. But the idea in her mind must have expressed itself in her face, for suddenly his manner softened. He drew a deep breath, and passed his hand across his forehead. Then, putting aside the involuntary thought, he said:

'Perhaps it will come through you as well as any other way. I intended to speak to him myself, but I can explain the matter better to you. It is about the betting that is being carried on here. We mean to put a stop to it. That 's what I came to tell him. It must be put a stop to. No right-minded person—it cannot be allowed to go on.'

Esther said nothing; not a change of expression came

upon her grave face. But Fred was agitated. His words stuck in his throat, and his hands were restless. Esther raised her calm eyes, and looked at him. His eyes were pale, restless eyes.

'I've come to warn you,' he said, 'that the law will be set in motion. It is very painful for me, but something must be done.' Esther did not answer, and he said, 'Why don't you answer, Esther?'

'What is there for me to answer? You tell me that you are going to get up a prosecution against us. I can't stop you. I'll tell my husband what you say.'

'This is a very serious matter, Esther.' He had come into command of his voice, and he spoke with earnest determination. 'If we get a conviction against you for keeping a betting house, you will not only be heavily fined, but you will also lose your licence. All we ask is that the betting shall cease. No,' he said, interrupting, 'don't deny anything; it is quite useless, we know everything. The whole neighbourhood is demoralized by this betting; nothing is thought of but tips; the day's racing—that is all they think about—the evening papers, and the latest information. You don't know what harm you're doing. Every day we hear of some new misfortune—a home broken up, the mother in the workhouse, the daughter on the streets, the father in prison, and all on account of this betting. Oh, Esther, it is horrible; think of the harm you're doing.'

Fred Parsons's high, round forehead, his weak eyes, his whole face, was expressive of fear and hatred of the evil that a falsetto voice denounced.

Suddenly he seemed to grow nervous and perplexed again. Esther was looking at him, and he said: 'You don't answer, Esther?'

'What would you have me answer?'

'You used to be a good, religious woman. Do you remember how we used to speak when we used to go for walks together, when you were in service in the Avondale Road? I remember you agreeing with me that much good could be done by those who were determined to do it. You seem to have changed very much since those days.'

For a moment Esther seemed affected by these remembrances. Then she said in a low musical voice:

'No, I 've not changed, Fred, but things has turned out different. A woman can't do the good that she would like to in the world; she has to do the good that comes to her to do. I 've my husband and my boy to look to. Them 's my good. At least, that 's how I sees things.'

Fred looked at Esther, and his eyes expressed all the admiration and love that he felt for her character. 'One owes a great deal,' he said, 'to those who are near to one, but not everything; even for their sakes one should not do wrong to others, and you must see that you are doing a great wrong to your fellow-creatures by keeping on this betting. Public-houses are bad enough, but when it comes to gambling as well as drink, there 's nothing for us to do but to put the law in motion. Look you, Esther, there isn't a shopboy earning eighteen shillings a week that hasn't been round here to put his half-crown on some horse. This house is the immoral centre of the neighbourhood. No one's money is refused. The boy that pawned his father's watch to back a horse went to the "King's Head" to put his money on. His father forgave him again and again. Then the boy stole from the lodgers. There was an old woman of seventy-five who got nine shillings a week for looking after some offices; he had half a crown off her. Then the father told the magistrate that he could do nothing with him since he had taken to betting on horse-races. The boy is fourteen. Is it not shocking? It cannot be allowed to go on. We have determined to put a stop to it. That 's what I came to tell your husband.'

'Are you sure,' said Esther, and she bit her lips while she spoke, 'that it is only on account of the neighbourhood that you want to get up the prosecution?'

'You don't think there 's any other reason, Esther? You surely don't think that I 'm doing this because—because he took you away from me?'

Esther didn't answer. And then Fred said, and there was pain and pathos in his voice, 'I am sorry you think this of me; I 'm not getting up the prosecution. I couldn't prevent the law being put in motion against you even if I wanted to. . . . I only know that it is going to be put in motion, so for the sake of old times I would save you from harm if I could. I came round to tell you if you did not put a stop to the betting you 'd get into trouble. I have no right to do what I have done, but I 'd do anything to save you and yours from harm.'

'I am sorry for what I said. It was very good of you.'

'We have not any proofs as yet; we know, of course, all about the betting, but we must have sworn testimony before the law can be set in motion, so you 'll be quite safe if you can persuade your husband to give it up.' Esther did not answer. 'It is entirely on account of the friendship I feel for you that made me come to warn you of the danger. You don't bear me any ill will, Esther, I hope?'

'No, Fred, I don't. I think I understand.' The conversation paused again. 'I suppose we have said everything.' Esther turned her face from him. Fred looked at her, and though her eyes were averted from him she could see that he loved her. In another moment he was gone. In her plain and ignorant way she thought on the romance of destiny. For if she had married Fred her life would have been quite different. She would have led the life that she wished to lead, but she had married William and—well, she must do the best she could. If Fred, or Fred's friends, got the police to prosecute them for betting, they would, as he said, not only have to pay a heavy fine, but would probably lose their licence. Then what would they do? William had not health to go about from racecourse to racecourse as he used to. He had lost a lot of money in the last six months; Jack was at school—they must think of Jack. The thought of their danger lay on her heart all that evening. But she had had no opportunity of speaking to William alone, she had to wait until they were in their room. Then, as she untied the strings of her petticoats, she said:

'I had a visit from Fred Parsons this afternoon.'

'That 's the fellow you were engaged to marry. Is he after you still?'

'No, he came to speak to me about the betting.'

'About the betting—what is it to do with him?'

'He says that if it isn't stopped that we shall be prosecuted.'

'So he came here to tell you that, did he? I wish I had been in the bar.'

'I 'm glad you wasn't. What good could you have done? To have a row and make things worse!'

William lit his pipe and unlaced his boots. Esther slipped on her night-dress and got into a large brass bedstead without curtains. On the chest of drawers Esther had placed the books her mother had given her, and William had hung some sporting prints on the walls. He took his night-shirt from the pillow and put it on without removing his pipe from his mouth. He always finished his pipe in bed.

'It is revenge,' he said, pulling the bedclothes up to his chin, 'because I got you away from him.'

'I don't think it is that; I did think so at first, and I said so.'

'What did he say?'

'He said he was sorry I thought so badly of him; that he came to warn us of our danger. If he had wanted to do us an injury he wouldn't have said nothing about it. Don't you think so?'

'It seems reasonable. Then what do you think they 're doing it for?'

'He says that keeping a betting house is corruption in the neighbourhood.'

'You think he thinks that?'

'I know he do; and there is many like him. I come of them that thinks like that, so I know. Betting and drink is what my folk, the Brethren, holds as most evil.'

'But you 've forgot all about them Brethren?'

'No, one never forgets what one 's brought up in.'

'But what do you think now?'

'I 've never said nothing about it. I don't believe in a wife interfering with her husband; and business was that bad, and your 'ealth 'asn't been the same since them colds you caught standing about in them betting rings, so I don't see how you could help it. But now that business is beginning to come back to us, it might be as well to give up the betting.'

'It is the betting that brings the business; we shouldn't take five pounds a week was it not for the betting. What 's the difference between betting on the course and betting in the bar? No one says nothing against it on the course; the police is there, and they goes after the welshers and persecutes them. Then the betting that 's done at Tattersall's and the Albert Club, what is the difference? The

Stock Exchange, too, where thousands and thousands is betted every day. It is the old story—one law for the rich and another for the poor. Why shouldn't the poor man 'ave his 'alf-crown's worth of excitement? The rich man can have his thousand pounds' worth whenever he pleases. The same with the public-'ouses—there's a lot of hypocritical folk that is for docking the poor man of his beer, but there's no one that's for interfering with them that drink champagne in the clubs. It's all bloody rot, and it makes me sick when I think of it. Them hypocritical folk. Betting! Isn't everything betting? How can they put down betting? Hasn't it been going on since the world began? Rot, says I! They can just ruin a poor devil like me, and that's about all. We are ruined, and the rich goes scot-free. Hypocritical, mealy-mouthed lot. "Let's say our prayers and sand the sugar"; that's about it. I hate them that is always prating about religion. When I hears too much religion going about I says now's the time to look into their accounts.'

William leaned out of bed to light his pipe from the candle on the night-table.

'There's good people in the world, people that never thinks but of doing good, and do not live for pleasure.'

'"All work and no play makes Jack a dull boy," Esther. Their only pleasure is a bet. When they've one on they've something to look forward to; whether they win or lose they 'as their money's worth. You know what I say is true; you've seen them, how they look forward to the evening paper to see how the 'oss is going on in betting. Man can't live without hope. It is their only hope, and I says no one has a right to take it from them.'

'What about their poor wives? Very little good their betting is to them. It's all very well to talk like that, William, but you know that a great deal of mischief comes of betting; you know that once they think of it and nothing else, they neglect their work. Stack 'as lost his place as porter; and there's Journeyman, too, he's out of work.'

'And a good thing for them; they've done a great deal better since they chucked it.'

'For the time, maybe; but who says it will go on? Look at old John; he's going about in rags; and his poor wife, she was in here the other night, a terrible life she's 'ad of it.

You says that no 'arm comes of it. What about that boy that was 'ad up the other day, and said that it was all through betting? He began by pawning his father's watch. It was here that he made the first bet. You won't tell me that it is right to bet with bits of boys like that.'

'The horse he backed with me won.'

'So much the worse. The boy 'll never do another honest day's work as long as he lives. When they win, they 'as a drink for luck; when they loses, they 'as a drink to cheer them up.'

'I 'm afraid, Esther, you ought to have married the other chap. He 'd have given you the life that you 'd have been happy in. This public-'ouse ain't suited to you.'

Esther turned round and her eyes met her husband's. There was a strange remoteness in his look, and they seemed very far from each other.

'I was brought up to think so differently,' she said, her thoughts going back to her early years in the little southern seaside home. 'I suppose this betting and drinking will always seem to me sinful and wicked. I should 'ave liked quite a different kind of life, but we don't choose our lives, we just makes the best of them. You was the father of my child, and it all dates from that.'

'I suppose it do.'

William lay on his back, and blew the smoke swiftly from his mouth.

'If you smoke much more we shan't be able to breathe in this room.'

'I won't smoke no more. Shall I blow the candle out?'

'Yes, if you like.'

When the room was in darkness, just before they settled their faces on the pillow for sleep, William said:

'It was good of that fellow to come and warn us. I must be very careful for the future with whom I bet.'

## CHAPTER XXXVI

On Sunday, as soon as dinner was over, Esther had intended to go to East Dulwich to see Mrs. Lewis. But, as she closed the door behind her, she saw Sarah coming up the street.

'Ah, I see you 're going out.'

'It don't matter; won't you come in, if it 's only for a minute?'

'No, thank you, I won't keep you. But which way are you going? We might go a little way together.'

They walked down Waterloo Place and along Pall Mall. In Trafalgar Square there was a demonstration, and Sarah lingered in the crowd so long that when they arrived at Charing Cross, Esther found that she could not get to Ludgate Hill in time to catch her train, so they went into the Embankment Gardens. It had been raining, and the women wiped the seats with their handkerchiefs before sitting down. There was no fashion to interest them, and the band sounded foolish in the void of the grey London Sunday. Sarah's chatter was equally irrelevant, and Esther wondered how Sarah could talk so much about nothing, and regretted her visit to East Dulwich more and more. Suddenly Bill's name came into the conversation.

'But I thought you didn't see him any more; you promised us you wouldn't.'

'I couldn't help it. It was quite an accident. One day, coming back from church with Annie—that 's the new housemaid—he came up and spoke to us.'

'What did he say?'

'He said, "How are ye? Who 'd thought of meeting you!"'

'And what did you say?'

'I said I didn't want to have nothing to do with him. Annie walked on, and then he said he was very sorry, that it was bad luck that drove him to it.'

'And you believed him?'

'I dare say it is very foolish of me. But a woman can't help herself. Did you ever really care for a man?'

And without waiting for an answer, Sarah continued her babbling chatter, mentioning incidentally that he had been away in the country and had come back with very particular information regarding a certain horse for the Cesarewitch. If the horse won he'd be all right.

At last Esther's patience was tired out.

'It must be getting late,' she said, looking towards where the sun was setting. A faint haze rose, softening the edges of the warehouses; a wind, too, had come up with the tide, and the women shivered as they passed under the arch of Waterloo Bridge. They ascended the flight of high steps and walked through a passage into the Strand.

'I was miserable enough with him; we used to have hardly anything to eat; but I'm more miserable away from him. Esther, I know you'll laugh at me, but I'm that heart-broken. I can't live without him. I'd do anything for him.'

'He isn't worth it.'

'That don't make no difference. You don't know what love is; no woman does who hasn't loved a man who don't love her. We used to live near here. Do you mind coming up Drury Lane? I should like to show you the house.'

'I'm afraid it will be out of our way.'

'No, it won't. Round by the church and up Newcastle Street. . . . Look, there's a shop we used to go to sometimes. I've eaten many a good sausage and onions in there, and that's a pub where we often used to go for a drink.'

The courts and alleys had vomited their population into the lane. Fat girls clad in shawls sat round the slum opening nursing their babies. Old women crouched in decrepit doorways, fumbling their aprons; skipping-ropes whirled in the roadway. A little higher up a vendor of cheap ices had set up his store and was rapidly absorbing all the pennies of the neighbourhood. Esther and Sarah turned into a dilapidated court, where a hag argued the price of trotters with a family leaning one over the other out of a second-floor window.

'That's where we used to live,' said Sarah, pointing up to the third floor. 'I fancy our house will soon come down. When I see the old place it all comes back to me. I remember pawning a dress over the way in the lane; they would only lend me a shilling on it. And you see that shop—the shutters is up, it being Sunday; it is a sort of butcher's, cheap meat, livers and lights, trotters, and such-like. I bought a bullock's heart there, and stewed it down with some potatoes; we did enjoy it, I can tell you.'

They made their way out into Catherine Street, and then to Endell Street, and then, going round to St. Giles's Church, they plunged into the labyrinth of Soho.

'I 'm afraid I 'm tiring you. I don't see what interest all this can be to you.'

'We 've known each other a long time.'

Sarah looked at her, and then, unable to resist the temptation, she continued her narrative—Bill had said this, she had said that, and she rattled on, until they came to the corner of Old Compton Street, where Esther, who was a little tired of her, held out her hand. 'I suppose you must be getting back; would you like a drop of something?'

'It is going on for seven o'clock; but since you 're that kind I think I 'd like a glass of beer.'

'Do you listen much to the betting talk here of an evening?' Sarah asked, as she was leaving.

'I don't pay much attention, but I can't help hearing a good deal.'

'Do they talk much about Ben Jonson for the Cesare-witch?'

'They do, indeed; he 's all the go.'

Sarah's face brightened perceptibly, and Esther said:

'Have you backed him?'

'Only a trifle; half a crown that a friend put me on. Do they say he 'll win?'

'They say that if he don't break down he 'll win by 'alf a mile; it all depends on his leg.'

'Is he coming on in the betting?'

'Yes, I believe they 're now taking 12 to 1 about him. But I 'll ask William, if you like.'

'No, no; I only wanted to know if you 'd heard anything new.'

## CHAPTER XXXVII

DURING the next fortnight Sarah came several times to the 'King's Head.' She came in about nine in the evening, and stayed for half an hour or more. The object of her visit was to see Esther, but she declined to come into the private bar, where they would have chatted comfortably, and remained in the public bar listening to the men's conversation, listening and nodding while old John explained the horse's staying power to her. On the following evening all her interest was in Ketley. She wanted to know if anything had happened that might be considered as an omen. She said she had dreamed about the race, but her dream was only a lot of foolish rubbish without head or tail. Ketley argued earnestly against this view of a serious subject, and in the hope of convincing her of her error offered to walk as far as Oxford Street with her and put her into her bus. But on the following evening all her interest was centred in Mr. Journeyman, who declared that he could prove that according to the weight it seemed to him to look more and more like a certainty. He had let the horse in at six stone ten pounds; the official handicapper had only given him six stone seven pounds.

'They is a-sending of him along this week, and if the leg don't go it is a hundred pound to a brass farthing on the old horse.'

'How many times will they gallop him?' Sarah asked.

'He goes a mile and a 'arf every day now. The day after to-morrow they 'll try him, just to see that he hasn't lost his turn of speed, and if he don't break down in the trial you can take it from me that it will be all right.'

'When will you know the result of the trial?'

'I expect a letter on Friday morning,' said Stack. 'If you come in in the evening I 'll let you know about it.'

'Thank you very much, Mr. Stack. I must be getting home now.'

'I'm going your way, Miss Tucker. If you like we'll go together, and I'll tell you,' he whispered, 'all about the 'orse.'

When they had left the bar the conversation turned on racing as an occupation for women.

'Fancy my wife making a book on the course. I bet she'd overlay it and then turn round and back the favourite at a shorter price than she'd been laying.'

'I don't know that we should be any foolisher than you,' said Esther; 'don't you never go and overlay your book? What about Syntax and the 'orse you told me about last week?'

William had been heavily hit last week through overlaying his book against a horse he didn't believe in, and the whole bar joined in the laugh against him.

'I don't say nothing about bookmaking,' said Journeyman; 'but there's a great many women nowadays who is mighty sharp at spotting a 'orse that the handicapper had let in pretty easy.'

'This one,' said Ketley, jerking his thumb in the direction that Stack and Sarah had gone, 'seems to 'ave got hold of something.'

'We must ask Stack when he comes back,' and Journeyman winked at William.

'Women do get that excited over trifles,' old John remarked sarcastically. 'She ain't got above 'alf a crown on the 'orse, if that. She don't care about the 'orse or the race—no woman ever did; it's all about some sweetheart that's been piling it on.'

'I wonder if you're right,' said Esther reflectively. 'I never knew her before to take such an interest in a horse-race.'

On the day of the race Sarah came into the private bar about three o'clock. The news was not yet in.

'Wouldn't you like to step into the parlour; you'll be more comfortable?' said Esther.

'No thank you, dear; it is not worth while. I thought I'd like to know which won, that's all.'

'Have you much on?'

'No, five shillings altogether. But a friend of mine stands to win a good bit. I see you've got a new dress, dear. When did you get it?'

'I've had the stuff by me some time. I only had it made up last month. Do you like it?'

Sarah answered that she thought it very pretty. But Esther could see that she was thinking of something quite different.

'The race is over now. It's run at half-past two.'

'Yes, but they're never quite punctual; there may be a delay at the post.'

'I see you know all about it.'

'You never hears of anything else.'

Esther asked Sarah when her people came back to town, and was surprised at the change of expression that the question brought to her friend's face.

'They're expected back to-morrow,' she said. 'Why do you ask?'

'Oh, nothing; something to say, that's all.' And the two women looked at each other. At that moment a voice coming rapidly towards them was heard calling, 'Win-ner, win-ner!'

'I'll send out for the paper,' said Esther.

'No, no. Suppose he shouldn't have won?'

'Well, it won't make any difference.'

'Oh, Esther, no; someone will come in and tell us. The race can't be over yet; it is a long race, and takes some time to run.'

By this time the boy was far away, and fainter and fainter the terrible word, 'Win-ner, win-ner, win-ner.'

'It's too late now,' said Sarah; 'someone 'll come in presently and tell us about it. I dare say it ain't the paper at all. Them boys cries out anything that will sell.'

'Win-ner, win-ner.' The voice was coming towards them.

'If he has won, Bill and I is to marry. Somehow I feel as if he hasn't.'

'Win-ner.'

'We shall soon know.' Esther took a halfpenny from the till.

'Don't you think we'd better wait? It can't be printed in the papers, not the true account, and if it was wrong——' Esther didn't answer; she gave Charles the halfpenny; he went out, and in a few minutes came back with the paper in his hand. 'Tornado first, Ben Jonson second,

Woodcraft third,' he read out. 'That's a good thing for
the guv'nor. There was very few what backed Tornado.
He's only lost some place-money.'

'So he was only second,' said Sarah, turning deadly
pale. 'They said he was certain to win.'

'I hope you've not lost much,' said Esther. 'It wasn't
with William that you backed him.'

'No, it wasn't with William. I only had a few shillings
on. It don't matter. Let me have a drink.'

'What will you have?'

'Some whisky.'

Sarah drank it neat. Esther looked at her doubtfully.
The bars would be empty for the next two hours; Esther
wished to utilize this time; she had some shopping to do,
and asked Sarah to come with her. But Sarah complained
of being tired, and said she would see her when she came
back.

Esther went out perplexed, and was detained longer
than she expected. When she returned Sarah was staggering about in the bar-room, asking Charles for one more
drink.

'All bloody rot; who says I'm drunk? I ain't. Look
at me. The 'orse didn't win, did he? I say he did;
papers all so much bloody rot.'

'Oh, Sarah, what is this?'

'Who's this? Leave go, I say.'

'Mr. Stack, won't you ask her to come upstairs? . . .
Don't encourage her.'

'Upstairs? I'm a free woman. I don't want to go
upstairs. I'm a free woman; tell me,' she said, balancing
herself with difficulty and staring at Esther with dull,
fishy eyes, 'tell me if I'm not a free woman? What do
I want upstairs for?'

'Oh, Sarah, come upstairs and lie down. Don't go
out.'

'I'm going home. Hands off, hands off!' she said,
slapping Esther's hands from her arm.

> 'For every one was drunk last night,
>    And drunk the night before;
> And if we don't get drunk to-night,
>    We won't get drunk no more.

*(Chorus)*

'Now you will have a drink with me,
     And I will drink with you;
For we 're the very rowdiest lot
     Of the rowdy Irish crew.

'That 's what we used to sing in the lane, yer know; should 'ave seen the coster gals with their feathers, dancing and clinking their pewters. Rippin' day, Bank 'oliday, Epping, under the trees—'ow they did romp, them gals!

'We all was roaring drunk last night,
     And drunk the night before;
And if we don't get drunk to-night,
     We won't get drunk no more.

Girls and boys, you know, all together.'

'Sarah, listen to me.'

'Listen! Come and have a drink, old gal, just another drink.' She staggered up to the counter. 'One more, just for luck; do you 'ear?' Before Charles could stop her she had seized the whisky that had just been served. 'That 's my whisky,' exclaimed Journeyman. He made a rapid movement, but was too late. Sarah had drained the glass and stood looking into space. Journeyman seemed so disconcerted at the loss of his whisky that every one laughed.

A few minutes after Sarah staggered forward and fell insensible into his arms, and was carried upstairs and laid on the bed in the spare room.

'She 'll be precious bad to-morrow,' said Journeyman.

'I don't know how you could have gone on helping her,' Esther said to Charles when she got inside the bar; and she seemed so pained that out of deference to her feelings the subject was dropped out of the conversation. She felt that something shocking had happened for Sarah to have got drunk deliberately. She would not have done that unless she had some great trouble on her mind. William, too, was of this opinion. Something serious must have happened. As they went up to their room Esther said:

'It is all the fault of this betting. The neighbourhood is completely ruined. They 're losing their 'omes and their furniture, and you 'll bear the blame of it.'

'It do make me so wild to hear you talkin' that way, Esther. People will bet, you can't stop them. I lays fair prices, and they're sure of their money. Yet you says they're losin' their furniture, and that I shall have to bear the blame.'

When they got to the top of the stairs she said:

'I must go and see how Sarah is.'

'Where am I? What's happened? . . . Take that candle out of my eyes. Oh, my head is that painful.' She fell back on the pillow, and Esther thought she had gone to sleep again. But she opened her eyes. 'Where am I? . . . That's you, Esther?'

'Yes, can't you remember?'

'No, I can't. I remember that the 'orse didn't win, but don't remember nothing after. I got drunk, didn't I? It feels like it.'

'The 'orse didn't win, and then you took too much. It's very foolish of you to give way.'

'Give way! Drunk, what matter? I'm done for.'

'Did you lose much?'

'It wasn't what I lost, it was what I took. I gave Bill the plate to pledge; it's all gone, and master and missis coming back to-morrow. And I got drunk so that I shouldn't think of it.'

'Oh, Sarah, I didn't think it was as bad as that. You must tell me all about it.'

'I don't want to think about it. They'll come soon enough to take me away. Besides, I can remember nothing now. My mouth's that awful—— Give me a drink. Never mind the glass, give me the water-bottle.'

She drank ravenously, seemed to recover a little, and Esther pressed her to tell her about the pledged plate. 'You know that I am your friend. You'd better tell me. I want to help you out of this scrape.'

'No one can help me now, I'm done for. Let them come and take me. I'll go with them. I shan't say nothing.'

'How much is it in for? Don't cry like that,' Esther said, and she took out her handkerchief and wiped Sarah's eyes. 'How much is it in for? Perhaps I can get my husband to lend me the money to get it out.'

'It's no use trying to help me, Esther, I can't talk about it now; I shall go mad if I do.'

'Tell me how much you got on it.'

'Thirty pounds.'

It took a long time to undress her. Every now and then she made an effort, and another article of clothing was dragged off her. She was asleep when Esther returned to her room. William was asleep, and Esther took him by the shoulder.

'It is more serious than I thought for,' she shouted. 'I want to tell you about it.'

'What about it?' he said, opening his eyes.

'She has pledged the plate for thirty pounds to back that 'orse.'

'What 'orse?'

'Ben Jonson.'

'He broke down at the bushes. If he hadn't I should have been broke up. The whole neighbourhood was on him. So she pledged the plate to back him. She didn't do that to back him herself. Someone must have put her up to it.'

'Yes, it was Bill Evans.'

'Ah, that blackguard put her up to it. I thought she'd left him for good. She promised us that she'd never speak to him again.'

'You see, she was that fond of him that she couldn't help herself. There's many that can't.'

'How much did they get on the plate?'

'Thirty pounds.'

William blew a long whistle. Then, starting up in bed, he said, 'She can't stop here. If it comes out that it was through betting, it won't do this house any good. We're already suspected. There's that old sweetheart of yours, the Salvation cove, on the lookout for evidence of betting being carried on.'

'She'll go away in the morning. But I thought that you might lend her the money to get the plate out.'

'What! thirty pounds?'

'It's a deal of money, I know; but I thought that you might be able to manage it. You've been lucky over this race.'

'Yes, but think of all I've lost this summer. This is the first bit of luck I've had for a long while.'

'I thought you might be able to manage it.'

Esther stood by the bedside, her knee leaned against the edge. She seemed to him at that moment as the best woman in the world, and he said:

'Thirty pounds is no more to me than twopence half-penny if you wish it, Esther.'

'I haven't been an extravagant wife, have I?' she said, getting into bed and taking him in her arms. 'I never asked you for money before. She's my friend—she's yours too—we've known her all our lives. We can't see her go to prison, can we, Bill, without raising a finger to save her?'

She had never called him Bill before, and the familiar abbreviation touched him, and he said:

'I owe everything to you, Esther; everything that's mine is yours. But,' he said, drawing away so that he might see her better, 'what do you say if I ask something of you?'

'What are you going to ask me?'

'I want you to say that you won't bother me no more about the betting. You was brought up to think it wicked; I know all that, but you see we can't do without it.'

'Do you think not?'

'Don't the thirty pounds you're asking for Sarah come out of betting?'

'I suppose it do.'

'Most certainly it do.'

'I can't help feeling, Bill, that we shan't always be so lucky as we have been.'

'You mean that you think that one of these days we shall have the police down upon us?'

'Don't you sometimes think that we can't always go on without being caught? Every day I hear of the police being down on some betting club or other.'

'They've been down on a great number lately, but what can I do? We always come back to that. I haven't the health to work round from racecourse to racecourse as I used to. But I've got an idea, Esther. I've been thinking over things a great deal lately, and—give me my pipe—there, it's just by you. Now, hold the candle, like a good girl.'

William pulled at his pipe until it was fully lighted. He threw himself on his back, and then he said:

'I've been thinking things over. The betting 'as brought us a nice bit of trade here. If we can work up the business a bit more we might, let's say in a year from now, be able to get as much for the 'ouse as we gave for it. What do you think of buying a business in the country, a 'ouse doing a steady trade? I've had enough of London, the climate don't suit me as it used to. I fancy I should be much better in the country, somewhere on the south coast. Bournemouth way, what do you think?'

Before Esther could reply William was taken with a fit of coughing, and his great broad frame was shaken as if it were so much paper.

'I'm sure,' said Esther, when he had recovered himself a little, 'that a good deal of your trouble comes from that pipe. It's never out of your mouth. I feel like choking myself.'

'I dare say I smoke too much. I'm not the man I was. I can feel it plain enough. Put my pipe down and blow out the candle. I didn't ask you how Sarah was.'

'Very bad. She was half dazed and didn't tell me much.'

'She didn't tell you where she had pledged the plate?'

'No, I will ask her about that to-morrow morning,' and leaning forward she blew out the candle. The wick smouldered red for a moment, and they fell asleep happy in each other's love, seeming to find new bonds of union in pity for their friend's misfortune.

## CHAPTER XXXVIII

'SARAH, you must make an effort and try to dress yourself.'

'Oh, I do feel that bad, I wish I was dead!'

'You mustn't give way like that; let me help you put on your stockings.'

Sarah looked at Esther. 'You 're very good to me, but I can manage.' When she had drawn on her stockings her strength was exhausted, and she fell back on the pillow.

'Here 's your petticoats. Tie them round you; and I 'll lend you a dressing-gown and a pair of slippers.'

William, who was having breakfast in the parlour, asked Sarah what she 'd have. 'There 's a nice bit of fried fish,' he said. 'Not feeling up to it?'

'Oh, no! I couldn't touch anything.' She let herself drop on the sofa.

'A cup of tea 'll do you good,' said Esther. 'You must have a cup of tea, and a bit of toast just to nibble. William, pour her out a cup of tea.'

When she had drunk the tea she said she felt a little better.

'Now,' said William, 'let 's 'ear all about it. Esther has told you, no doubt, that we intend to do all we can to help you.'

'You can't help me. I 'm done for,' she replied dolefully.

'I don't know about that,' said William. 'You gave that brute Bill Evans the plate to pawn, so far as I know.'

'There isn't much more to tell. He said the horse was sure to win. He was at thirty to one at that time. A thousand to thirty. Bill said with that money we could buy a public-house in the country. He wanted to settle down, he wanted to get out of—— I don't want to say nothing against him. He said if I would only give him this chance of leading a respectable life, we was to be married immediately after.'

'He told you all that, did he? He said he 'd give you a 'ome of your own. I know. A regular rotter; that man is about as bad as they make 'em. And you believed it all?'

'It wasn't so much what I believed as that I couldn't help myself. He has got that hold over me that my will isn't my own. I don't know how it is—I suppose men have stronger natures than women. I 'ardly knew what I was doing; it was like sleep-walking. He looked at me and said, "You 'd better do it." I did it, and I suppose I 'll have to go to prison for it. What I says is just the truth, but no one believes tales like that. How long do you think they 'll give me?'

'I hope we shall be able to get you out of this scrape. You got thirty pounds on the plate. Esther has told you that I 'm ready to lend you the money to get it out.'

'Will you do this? You 're good friends, you are. But I shall never be able to pay you back such a lot of money.'

'We won't say nothing about paying back; all we want you to do is to say that you 'll never see that fellow again.'

A change of expression came over Sarah's face, and William said, 'You 're surely not still hankering after him?'

'No, that I 'm not. But whenever I meets him he somehow gets his way with me. It 's terrible to love a man as I love him. I know he don't really care for me— I know he is all you say, and yet I can't help myself. It is better to be honest with you.'

William looked puzzled. At the end of a long silence he said, 'If it 's like that I don't see that we can do anything.'

'Have patience, William. Sarah don't know what she 's saying. She 'll promise not to see him again.'

'You 're very kind to me. I know I 'm very foolish. I promised before not to see him, and I couldn't keep my promise.'

'You can stop with us until you get a situation in the country,' said Esther, 'where you 'll be out of his way.'

'I might do that.'

'I don't like to part with my money,' said William, 'if it is to do no one any good.' Esther looked at him, and he added, 'It is just as Esther wishes, of course; I 'm not giving you the money, it is she.'

'It is both of us,' said Esther; 'you 'll do what I said, Sarah?'

'Oh, yes, anything you say, Esther,' and she flung herself into her friend's arms and wept bitterly.

'Now we want to know where you pawned the plate,' said William.

'A long way from here. Bill said he knew a place where it would be quite safe. I was to say that my mistress left it to me; he said that would be sufficient. It was in the Mile End Road.'

'You 'd know the shop again?' said William.

'But she 's got the ticket,' said Esther.

'No, I ain't got the ticket; Bill has it.'

'Then I 'm afraid the game 's up.'

'Do be quiet,' said Esther angrily. 'If you want to get out of lending the money say so and have done with it.'

'That 's not true, Esther. If you want another thirty to pay him to give up the ticket, you can have it.'

Esther thanked her husband with one quick look. 'I 'm sorry,' she said, 'my temper is hasty. But you know where he lives,' she said, turning to the wretched woman who sat on the sofa, pale and trembling.

'Yes, I know where he lives—13 Milward Square, Mile End Road.'

'Then we 've no time to lose; we must go after him at once.'

'No, William dear, you must not; you 'd only lose your temper, and he might do you an injury.'

'An injury! I 'd soon show him which was the best man of the two.'

'I 'll not hear of it, Sarah. He mustn't go with you.'

'Come, Esther, don't be foolish. Let me go.'

He had taken his hat from the peg. Esther got between him and the door.

'I forbid it,' she said; 'I will not let you go—perhaps to have a fight, and with that cough.'

William was coughing. He had turned pale, and he said, leaning against the table, 'Give me something to drink, a little milk.'

Esther poured some into a cup. He sipped it slowly. 'I 'll go upstairs,' she said, 'for my hat and jacket. You 've got your betting to attend to.' William smiled. 'Sarah, mind, he 's not to go with you.'

'You forget what you said last night about the betting.'

'Never mind what I said last night about the betting;
what I say now is that you're not to leave the bar. Come
upstairs, Sarah, and dress yourself, and let's be off.'

Stack and Journeyman were waiting to speak to him.
They had lost heavily over old Ben and didn't know how
they'd pull through; and the whole neighbourhood was in
the same plight; the bar was filled with gloomy faces.

And as William scanned their disconcerted faces—clerks,
hairdressers, waiters from the innumerable eating-houses—
he could not help thinking that perhaps more than one of
them had taken money that did not belong to them to back
Ben Jonson. The unexpected disaster had upset all their
plans, and even the wary ones who had a little reserve fund
could not help backing outsiders, hoping by the longer odds
to retrieve yesterday's losses. At two the bar was empty,
and William waited for Esther and Sarah to return from
Mile End. It seemed to him that they were a long time
away. But Mile End is not close to Soho; and when they
returned, between four and five, he saw at once that they
had been unsuccessful. He lifted up the flap in the counter
and all three went into the parlour.

'He left Milward Square yesterday,' Esther said, 'and
we went to another address, and then to another; we went
to all the places Sarah had been to with him, but no tidings
anywhere.'

Sarah burst into tears. 'There's no more hope,' she said.
'I'm done for; they'll come and take me away. How
much do you think I'll get? They won't give me ten
years, will they?'

'I can see nothing else for you to do,' said Esther, 'but to
go straight back to your people and tell them the whole
story, and throw yourself on their mercy.'

'Do you mean that she should say that she pawned the
plate to get money to back a horse?'

'Of course I do.'

'It will make the police more keen than ever on the
betting houses.'

'That can't be helped.'

'She'd better not be took here,' said William; 'it will do
a great deal of harm. It don't make no difference to her
where she's took, do it?'

Esther did not answer.

'I 'll go away. I don't want to get no one into trouble,' Sarah said, and she got up from the sofa.

At that moment Charles opened the door, and said, 'You 're wanted in the bar, sir.'

William went out quickly. He returned a moment after. There was a scared look on his face. 'They 're here,' he said. He was followed by two policemen. Sarah uttered a little cry.

'Your name is Sarah Tucker?' said the first policeman.

'Yes.'

'You 're charged with robbery by Mr. Sheldon, 34 Cumberland Place.'

'Shall I be taken through the streets?'

'If you like to pay for it, you can go in a cab,' the police-officer replied.

'I 'll go with you, dear,' Esther said. William plucked her by the sleeve. 'It will do no good. Why should you go?'

## CHAPTER XXXIX

THE magistrate, of course, sent the case for trial, and the thirty pounds which William had promised to give to Esther went to pay for the defence. There seemed at first some hope that the prosecution would not be able to prove its case, but fresh evidence connecting Sarah with the abstraction of the plate was forthcoming, and in the end it was thought advisable that the plea of not guilty should be withdrawn. The efforts of counsel were therefore directed towards a mitigation of sentence. Counsel called Esther and William for the purpose of proving the excellent character that the prisoner had hitherto borne; counsel spoke of the evil influence into which the prisoner had fallen, and urged that she had no intention of actually stealing the plate. Tempted by promises, she had been persuaded to pledge the plate in order to back a horse which she had been told was certain to win. If that horse had won, the plate would have been redeemed and returned to its proper place in the owner's house, and the prisoner would have been able to marry. Possibly the marriage on which the prisoner had set her heart would have turned out more unfortunate for the prisoner than the present proceedings. Counsel had not words strong enough to stigmatize the character of a man who, having induced a girl to imperil her liberty for his own vile ends, was cowardly enough to abandon her in the hour of her deepest distress. Counsel drew attention to the trusting nature of the prisoner, who had not only pledged her employer's plate at his base instigation, but had likewise been foolish enough to confide the pawn-ticket to his keeping. Such was the prisoner's story, and he submitted that it bore on the face of it the stamp of truth. A very sad story, but one full of simple, foolish, trusting humanity; and, having regard to the excellent character the prisoner had borne, counsel hoped that his lordship would see his way to dealing leniently with her.

His lordship, whose gallantries had been prolonged over half a century, and whose betting transactions were matters

of public comment, pursed up his ancient lips and fixed his
dead glassy eyes on the prisoner.  He said he regretted that
he could not take the same view of the prisoner's character
as learned counsel had done.  The police had made every
effort to apprehend the man Evans who, according to
the prisoner's story, was the principal culprit.  But the
efforts of the police had been unavailing; they had, however,
found traces of the man Evans, who undoubtedly did exist,
and need not be considered to be a near relative of our
friend Mrs. Harris.  The trite joke provoked some little
merriment in the court.  Learned counsel settled their
robes becomingly and leant forward to listen, feeling that
they were in for a humorous speech, and that the prisoner
would get off with a light sentence.  But the grim smile
waxed duller, and it was clear that lordship was determined to make the law a terror to evil-doers.

Lordship drew attention to the fact that during the
course of their investigations the police had discovered that
the prisoner had been living for some considerable time
with the man Evans, during which time several robberies
had been effected.  There was no evidence, it was true, to
connect the prisoner with these robberies.  The prisoner
had left the man Evans and had obtained a situation in the
house of her present employers.  When the characters she
had received from her former employers were being examined she had accounted for the year she had spent with
the man Evans by saying that she had been staying with
the Latches, the publicans who had given evidence in her
favour.  It had also come to the knowledge of the police
that the man Evans used to frequent the 'King's Head,'
that was the house owned by the Latches; it was probable
that she had made there the acquaintance of the man
Evans.  The prisoner had referred her employers to the
Latches, who had lent their sanction to the falsehood
regarding the year she was supposed to have spent with
them, but which she had really spent in cohabitation with
a notorious thief.  Here lordship indulged in severe remarks against those who enabled not wholly irreproachable
characters to obtain situations by false pretences, a very
common habit, and one attended with great danger to
society—one which society would do well to take pre-
cautions to defend itself against.

The plate, his lordship remarked, was said to have been pawned, but there was nothing to show that it had been pawned, the prisoner's explanation being that she had given the pawn-ticket to the man Evans. She could not tell where she had pawned the plate, her tale being that she and the man Evans had gone down to Whitechapel together and pawned it in the Mile End Road. But she did not know the number of the pawnbroker's, nor could she give any indications as to its whereabouts—beyond the mere fact that it was in the Mile End Road she could say nothing. All the pawnbrokers in the Mile End Road had been searched, but no plate answering to the description furnished by the prosecution could be found.

Learned counsel had endeavoured to show that it had been in a measure unpremeditated, that it was the result of a passing but irresistible temptation. Learned counsel had endeavoured to introduce some element of romance into the case; he had described the theft as the outcome of the prisoner's desire of marriage, but lordship could not find such purity of motive in the prisoner's crime. There was nothing to show that there was any thought of marriage in the prisoner's mind; the crime was the result, not of any desire of marriage, but rather the result of vicious passion, concubinage. Regarding the plea that the crime was unpremeditated, it was only necessary to point out that it had been committed for a distinct purpose and had been carried out in conjunction with an accomplished thief.

'There is now only one more point which I wish to refer to, and that is the plea that the prisoner did not intend to steal the plate, but only to obtain money upon it to enable her and the partner in her guilt to back a horse for a race which they believed to be—' his lordship was about to say a certainty for him; he stopped himself, however, in time—'to be, to be, which they believed him to be capable of winning. The race in question is, I think, called the Cesarewitch, and the name of the horse [lordship had lost three hundred on Ben Jonson], if my memory serves me right [here lordship fumbled amid papers], yes, the name is, as I thought, Ben Jonson. Now, the learned counsel for the defence suggested that, if the horse had won, the plate would have been redeemed and restored to its proper place in the pantry cupboards. This, I venture to point out, is a mere hypothesis. The money might have been again used for the purpose of gambling. I confess that I do not see why we should condone the prisoner's offence because it was committed for the sake of obtaining money for gambling purposes. Indeed, it seems to me a reason for dealing heavily with the offence. The vice among the poorer classes is largely on the increase, and it seems to me that it is the duty of all in authority to condemn rather than to condone the evil, and to use every effort to stamp it out. For my part I fail to perceive any romantic element in the vice of gambling. It springs from the desire to obtain wealth without work, in other words, without payment; work, whether in the past or the present, is the natural payment for wealth, and any wealth that is obtained without work is in a measure a fraud committed upon the community. Poverty, despair, idleness, and every other vice spring from gambling as naturally, and in the same profusion, as weeds from barren land. Drink, too, is gambling's firmest ally.'

At this moment a certain dryness in his lordship's throat reminded him of the pint of excellent claret that lordship always drank with his lunch, and the thought enabled lordship to roll out some excellent invective against the evils of beer and spirits. And lordship's losses on the horse whose name he could hardly recall helped to a forcible illustration of the theory that drink and gambling mutually uphold and enforce each other. When the news came in that Ben Jonson had broken down at the bushes, lordship had drunk a magnum of champagne, and memory of this champagne inspired a telling description of the sinking feeling consequent on the loss of a wager, and the natural inclination of a man to turn to drink to counteract it. Drink and gambling are growing social evils; in a great measure they are consequential, and only require absolute legislation to stamp them out almost entirely. This was not the first case of the kind that had come before him; it was one of many, but it was a typical case, presenting all the familiar features of the vice of which he had therefore spoken at unusual length. Such cases were on the increase, and, if they continued to increase, the powers of the law would have to be strengthened. But even as the law stood at present, betting houses, public-houses in which betting was carried on, were illegal, and it was the duty of the police to leave no means untried to unearth the offenders and bring them to justice. He condemned her to eighteen months' hard labour and, gathering up the papers on the desk, dismissed her for ever from his mind, and the court adjourned for lunch, and William and Esther edged their way out of the crowd of lawyers and their clerks. Neither spoke for some time. William was much exercised by his lordship's remarks on betting public-houses, and his advice that the police should increase their vigilance and leave no means untried to uproot that which was the curse and the ruin of the lower classes. It was the old story—one law for the rich, another for the poor. William did not seek to probe the question any further, this examination seemed to him to have exhausted it; and he remembered that when he was caught he would be fined a hundred pounds, and probably lose his licence. And what would he do then? He did not confide his fears to Esther. She had promised to say no more about the betting; but she had not changed her opinion. She was one of those stubborn ones who would rather die than admit they were wrong. And then he wondered what she thought of his lordship's speech. Esther was thinking of the thin gruel Sarah would have to eat, the plank bed on which she would have to sleep, and the miserable future that awaited her when she should be released from jail.

It was a bright winter's day; the City folk were walking rapidly, tightly buttoned up in top-coats, and in a windy sky a flock of pigeons floated on straightened wings above the telegraph wires. Fleet Street was full of journalists going to luncheon bars and various eating-houses, and Esther noticed how laggard was William's walk by comparison, how his clothes hung loose about him, and that the sharp air was at work on his lungs, making him cough. She asked him to button himself up more closely.

'Isn't that old John's wife?' Esther said.

'Yes, that's her,' said William. 'She'd have seen us if that cove hadn't given her the shilling. Lord, I didn't think they was as badly off as that. Did you ever see such rags? and that thick leg wrapped up in that awful stocking.'

The morning had been full of sadness, and Mrs. Randal's wandering rags had seemed to Esther like a sign. She grew frightened, as the cattle do in the fields when the sky darkens and the storm draws near. She suddenly remembered Mrs. Barfield, and she heard her telling her of the unhappiness that she had seen come from betting. Where was Mrs. Barfield? Should she ever see her again? Mr. Barfield was dead, Miss Mary was forced to live abroad for the sake of her health; all that time of long ago was over and done with. Some words that Mrs. Barfield had said came back to her; she had never quite understood them, but she had never quite forgotten them; they seemed to chime through her life. 'My girl,' Mrs. Barfield had said, 'I am more than twenty years older than you, and I assure you that time has passed like a little dream; life is nothing. We must think of what comes after.'

'Cheer up, old girl; eighteen months is a long while, but it ain't a lifetime. She'll get through it all right; and when she comes out we'll try to see what we can do for her.'

William's voice startled Esther from the depth of her dream; she looked at him vaguely, and he saw that she had been thinking of something different from what he had suspected. 'I thought it was on account of Sarah that you was looking so sad.'

'No,' she said, 'I was not thinking of Sarah.'

Then, taking it for granted that she was thinking of the wickedness of betting, his face darkened. It was aggravating to have a wife who was always troubling about things that couldn't be helped.

The first person they saw on entering the bar was old John; and he sat in the corner of the bar on a high stool, his grey, deathlike face sunk in the old unstarched shirt-collar. The thin, wrinkled throat was hidden with the remains of a cravat; it was passed twice round, and tied according to the fashion of fifty years ago. His boots were broken; the trousers, a grey, dirty brown, were torn as high up as the ankle; they had been mended and the patches hardly held together; the frock-coat, green with age, with huge flaps over the pockets, frayed and torn, and many sizes too large, hung upon his starveling body. He seemed very feeble, and there was neither light nor expression in his glassy, watery eyes.

'Eighteen months; a devil of a stiff sentence for a first offence,' said William.

'I just dropped in. Charles said you 'd sure to be back. You 're later than I expected.'

'We stopped to have a bit of lunch. But you heard what I said. She got eighteen months.'

'Who got eighteen months?'

'Sarah.'

'Ah, Sarah. She was tried to-day. So she got eighteen months.'

'What 's the matter? Wake up; you 're half asleep. What will you have to drink?'

'A glass of milk, if you 've got such a thing.'

'Glass of milk! What is it, old man—not feeling well?'

'Not very well. The fact is, I 'm starving.'

'Starving! Then come into the parlour and have something to eat. Why didn't you say so before?'

'I didn't like to.'

He led the old chap into the parlour and gave him a chair. 'Didn't like to tell me that you was as hard up as all that? What do you mean? You didn't use to mind coming round for half a quid.'

'That was to back a horse; but I didn't like coming to ask for food—excuse me, I 'm too weak to speak much.'

When old John had eaten, William asked how it was that things had gone so badly with him.

'I 've had terrible bad luck lately, can't get on a winner nohow. I have backed 'orses that 'as been tried to win with two stone more on their backs than they had to carry, but just because I was on them they didn't win. I don't know how many half-crowns I 've had on first favourites. Then I tried the second favourites, but they gave way to outsiders or the first favourites when I took to backing them. Stack's tips and Ketley's omens was all the same as far as I was concerned. It 's a poor business when you 're out of luck.'

'It is giving way to fancy that does for the backers. The bookmaker's advantage is that he bets on principle and not on fancy.'

Old John told how unlucky he had been in business. He had been dismissed from his employment in the restaurant, not from any fault of his own—he had done his work

well. 'But they don't like old waiters; there's always a
lot of young Germans about, and customers said I smelt
bad. I suppose it was my clothes and want of convenience
at home for keeping meself tidy. We've been so hard up
to pay the three and sixpence rent which we've owed,
that the black coat and weskit had to go to the pawnshop,
so even if I did meet with a job in the Exhibition places,
where they ain't so particular about yer age, I shouldn't
be able to take it. It's terrible to think that I should have
to come to this and after having worked round the table
this forty years, fifty pounds a year and all found, and
accustomed always to a big footman and page-boy under
me. But there's plenty more like me. It's a poor game.
You're well out of it. I suppose the end of it will be the
work'us. I'm pretty well wore out, and——'

The old man's voice died away. He made no allusion to
his wife. His dislike to speak of her was part and parcel
of his dislike to speak of his private affairs. The conversation then turned on Sarah, and William spoke of how the
judge's remarks would put the police on the watch, and
how difficult it would be to continue his betting business
without being found out.

'There's no doubt that it is most unfortunate,' said old
John. 'The only thing for you to do is to be very particular
about yer introductions, and to refuse to bet with all who
haven't been properly introduced.'

'Or to give up betting altogether,' said Esther.

'Give up betting altogether!' William answered, his
face flushed; and he gradually worked himself into a passion.
'I give you a good 'ome, don't I? You want for nothing,
do yer? Well, that being so, I think you might keep your
nose out of your husband's business. There's plenty of
prayer-meetings where you can go preaching if you like.'

William would have said a good deal more, but his anger
brought on a fit of coughing. Esther looked at him contemptuously, and without answering she walked into the
bar.

'That's a bad cough of yours,' said old John.

'Yes,' said William, and he drank a little water to pass
it off. 'I must see the doctor about it. It makes a chap
so irritable. The missis is in a pretty temper, ain't she?'

Old John did not reply; it was not his habit to notice

domestic differences of opinion, especially those in which women had a share—queer cattle that he knew nothing about. The men talked for a long time regarding the danger the judge's remarks had brought the house into; they considered all the circumstances of the case, and when old John rose to go William summed up the situation in these few words:

'Bet I must, if I 'm to get my living. The only thing I can do is to be careful not to bet with strangers.'

'I don't see how they can do nothing to you if yer makes that yer principle and sticks to it,' said old John; and he put on the huge-rimmed, greasy hat, three sizes too large for him.

'A pathetic old story,' William said to himself. 'But I dare say he 's right'; and for several months William refused over and over again to make bets with comparative strangers, but the day came when his principle relaxed, and he took the money of a man who he thought was all right. It was done on the impulse of the moment, but the two half-crowns wrapped up in paper, with the name of the horse written on the paper, had hardly gone into the drawer than he felt that he had done wrong. He couldn't tell why, but the feeling came across him that he had done wrong in taking the man's money—a tall, clean-shaven man dressed in broadcloth. It was too late to draw back. The man had finished his beer and had left the bar, which in itself was suspicious.

Three days afterwards, between twelve and one, just the busiest time, when the bar was full of people, there came a cry of 'Police!' An effort was made to hide the betting plant; a rush was made for the doors. It was all too late; the sergeant and a constable ordered that no one was to leave the house; other police were outside. The names and addresses of all present were taken down; search was made, and the packets of money and the betting books were discovered. Then they all had to go to Marlborough Street.

## CHAPTER XL

NEXT day the following account was given in most of the daily papers: 'Raid on a betting man in the West End. William Latch, 35, landlord of the "King's Head," Dean Street, Soho, was charged that he, being a licensed person, did keep and use his public-house for the purpose of betting with persons resorting thereto. Thomas William, 35, billiard marker, Gaulden Street, Battersea; Arthur Henry Parsons, 25, waiter, Northumberland Street, Marylebone; Joseph Stack, 52, gentleman; Harold Journeyman, 45, gentleman, High Street, Norwood; Philip Hutchinson, grocer, Bisey Road, Fulham; William Tann, piano-tuner, Standard Street, Soho; Charles Ketley, butterman, Green Street, Soho; John Randal, Frith Street, Soho; Charles Muller, 44, tailor, Marylebone Lane; Arthur Bartram, stationer, East Street Buildings; William Burton, harness-maker, Blue Lion Street, Bond Street, were charged with using the "King's Head" for the purpose of betting. Evidence was given by the police regarding the room upstairs, where a good deal of drinking went on after hours. There had been cases of disorder, and the magistrate unfortunately remembered that a servant girl, who had pledged her master's plate to obtain money to back a horse, had been arrested in the "King's Head." Taking these facts into consideration, it seemed to him that he could not do less than inflict a fine of £100. The men who were found in Latch's house he ordered to be bound over.'

Who had first given information? That was the question. Old John sat smoking in his corner. Journeyman leaned against the yellow-painted partition, his legs thrust out. Stack stood square, his dark, crimson-tinted skin contrasting with sallow-faced little Ketley.

'Don't the omens throw no light on this 'ere matter?' said Journeyman.

Ketley started from his reverie.

'Ah,' said William, 'if I only knew who the b—— was.'

'Ain't you got no idea of any sort?' said Stack.

'There was a Salvation chap who came in some months ago and told my wife that the betting was corrupting the neighbourhood—that it would have to be put a stop to. It may 'ave been 'e.'

'You don't ask no one to bet with you. They does as they like.'

'Does as they like! No one does that nowadays. There's a temperance party, a purity party, and a hanti-gambling party, and what they're all working for is just to stop folk from doing as they like.'

'That's it,' said Journeyman.

Stack raised his glass to his lips and said, 'Here's luck.'

'There's not much of that about,' said William. 'We seem to be losing all round. I'd like to know where the money goes. I think it is the 'ouse; it's gone unlucky, and I'm thinking of clearing out.'

'We may live in a 'ouse a long while before we find what its luck really is,' said Ketley. 'I've been in my old 'ouse these twenty years, and it ain't nothing like what I thought it.'

'You're so superstitious,' said Journeyman. 'If there was anything the matter with the 'ouse you'd 've know'd it before now.'

'Ain't you doing the trade you was?' said Stack.

'No, my butter-and-egg trade have fallen dreadful lately.'

The conversation paused. It was Stack who broke the silence.

'Do you intend to do no more betting 'ere?' he asked.

'What after being fined £100? You 'eard the way he went on about Sarah, and all on account of her being took here. I think he might have left Sarah out.'

'It warn't for betting she took the plate,' said Journeyman; 'it was 'cause her chap said if she did he'd marry her.'

'I wonder you ever left the course,' said Stack.

'It was on account of my 'ealth. I caught a dreadful cold at Kempton, standing about in the mud. I've never quite got over that cold.'

'I remember,' said Ketley; 'you couldn't speak above a whisper for two months.'

'Two months! more like three.'

'Fourteen weeks,' said Esther.

She was in favour of disposing of the house and going to live in the country. But it was soon found that the conviction for keeping a betting house had spoiled their chance of an advantageous sale. If, however, the licence were renewed next year, and the business did not in the meantime decline, they would be in a position to obtain better terms. So all their energies should be devoted to the improvement of their business. Esther engaged another servant, and she provided the best meat and vegetables that money could buy; William ordered beer and spirits of a quality that could be procured nowhere else in the neighbourhood; but all to no purpose. As soon as it became known that it was no longer possible to pass half a crown or a shilling wrapped up in a piece of paper across the bar, their custom began to decline.

At last William could stand it no longer, and he obtained his wife's permission to begin bookmaking once more on the course. His health had begun to improve with the spring weather, and there was no use keeping him at home eating his heart out with vexation because they were doing no business. So did Esther reason, and it reminded her of old times when he came back with his race-glasses slung round his shoulder. 'Favourites all beaten to-day; what have you got for me to eat, old girl?' Esther forgot her dislike of racing in the joy of seeing her husband happy. If he'd only pick up a bit of flesh! but he seemed to get thinner and thinner, and his food didn't seem to do him any good.

One day he came home complaining that the ring was six inches of soft mud; he was wet to the skin, and he sat shivering the whole evening, with the sensation of a long illness upon him. His voice seemed as if it would never return to him again, and there was little or no occupation for him in the bar. Instead of laying he began to take the odds. He backed a few winners, it is true; but they could not rely on that. Most of their trade had slipped from them, so it did not much matter to them if they were found out. He might as well be hung for an old sheep as a lamb, and surreptitiously at first, and then more openly, he began to take money across the bar, and with every shilling he took for a bet another shilling was spent in drink. Custom came back in ripples, and then in stronger waves, until once again the bar of the 'King's Head' was full to over-flowing. Another conviction meant ruin, but they must risk it, so said William; and Esther, like a good wife, acquiesced in her husband's decision. But he took money only from those whom he was quite sure of. He required an introduction, and was careful to make inquiries concerning every new backer. 'In this way,' he said to Ketley, 'so long as you keep the book on a small scale, I think it can be kept dark; but if you try to extend your connection you're bound to come across a wrong 'un sooner or later. It was that room upstairs that did for me.'

'I never did think much of that room upstairs,' said Ketley. 'There was a something about it that I didn't like. Be sure you never bet in that jug-and-bottle bar, whatever you do. There's just the same luck in that 'ere bar there as in the room upstairs. Haven't you noticed it?'

'Can't say I 'ave, nor am I sure that I know exactly what you mean.'

'If you don't see it, you don't see it; but it's plain enough to me, and don't you bet with nobody standing in that bar. I wouldn't go in there for a sovereign.'

William laughed. He thought at first that Ketley was joking, but he soon saw that Ketley regarded the jug-and-bottle entrance with real suspicion. When pressed to speak his mind, he told Journeyman that it wasn't that he was afraid of the place, he merely didn't like it. 'There's some places that you likes better than others, ain't they?' Journeyman was obliged to confess that there were.

'Well, then, that's one of the places I don't like. Don't you hear a voice talking there, a soft, low voice, with a bit of a jeer in it?'

On another occasion he shaded his eyes and peered curiously into the left-hand corner.

'What are you looking at?' asked Journeyman.

'At nothing that you can see,' Ketley answered; and he drank his whisky as if lost in consideration of grave and difficult things. A few weeks later they noticed that he always got as far from the jug-and-bottle entrance as possible, and he was afflicted with a long story concerning a danger that awaited him. 'He's waiting; but nothing will happen if I don't go in there. He can't follow me; he is waiting for me to go to him.'

'Then keep out of his way,' said Journeyman. 'You might ask your bloody friend if he can tell us anything about the Leger.'

'I'm trying to keep out of his way, but he's always watching and a-beckoning of me.'

'Can you see him now?' asked Stack.

'Yes,' said Ketley; 'he's a-sitting there, and he seems to say that if I don't come to him worse will happen.'

'Don't say nothing to him,' William whispered to Journeyman. 'I don't think he's quite right in 'is 'ead; he's been losing a lot lately.'

One day Journeyman was surprised to see Ketley sitting quite composedly in the jug-and-bottle bar.

'He got me at last; I had to go, the whispering got so loud in my head as I was a-coming down the street. I tried to get out into the middle of the street, but a drunken chap pushed me across the pavement, and he was at the door waiting, and he said, "Now, you'd better come in; you know what will happen if you don't."'

'Don't talk rot, old pal; come round and have a drink with us.'

'I can't just at present—I may later on.'

'What do he mean?' said Stack.

'Lord, I don't know,' said Journeyman. 'It's only his barmy talk.'

They tried to discuss the chances of the various horses they were interested in, but they could not detach their thoughts from Ketley, and their eyes went back to the queer little sallow-faced man who sat on a high stool in the adjoining bar paring his nails.

They felt something was going to happen, and before they could say the word he had plunged the knife deep into his neck, and had fallen heavily on the floor. William vaulted over the counter. As he did so he felt something break in his throat, and when Stack and Journeyman came to his assistance he was almost as white as the corpse at his feet. Blood flowed from his mouth and from Ketley's neck in a deep stream that swelled into a great pool and thickened on the sawdust.

'It was jumping over that bar,' William replied, faintly.

'I 'll see to my husband,' said Esther.

A rush of blood cut short his words, and, leaning on his wife, he walked feebly round into the back parlour. Esther rang the bell violently.

'Go round at once to Doctor Green,' she said; 'and if he isn't in inquire which is the nearest. Don't come back without a doctor.'

William had broken a small blood-vessel, and the doctor said he would have to be very careful for a long time. It was likely to prove a long case. But Ketley had severed the jugular at one swift, keen stroke, and had died almost instantly. Of course there was an inquest, and the coroner asked many questions regarding the habits of the deceased. Mrs. Ketley was one of the witnesses called, and she deposed that he had lost a great deal of money lately in betting, and that he went to the 'King's Head' for the purpose of betting. The police deposed that the landlord of the 'King's Head' had been fined a hundred pounds for keeping a betting house, and the foreman of the jury remarked that betting houses were the ruin of the poorer classes, and that they ought to be put a stop to. The coroner added that such places as the 'King's Head' should not be licensed. That was the simplest and most effectual way of dealing with the nuisance.

'There never was no luck about this house,' said William, 'and what there was has left us; in three months' time we shall be turned out of it neck and crop. Another conviction would mean a fine of a couple of hundred, or most like three months, and that would just about be the end of me.'

'They 'll never license us again,' said Esther, 'and the boy 's at school and doing so well.'

'I 'm sorry, Esther, to have brought this trouble on you. We must get the best price we can for the 'ouse. I may be lucky enough to back a few winners. That 's all there is to be said—the 'ouse was always an unlucky one. I hate the place, and shall be glad to get out of it.'

Esther sighed. She didn't like to hear the house spoken ill of, and after so many years it did seem a shame.

## CHAPTER XLI

ESTHER kept William within doors during the winter months. If his health did not improve it got no worse, and she had begun to hope that the breakage of the blood-vessel did not mean lung disease. But the harsh winds of spring did not suit him, and there was business with his lawyer to which he was obliged to attend. A determined set was going to be made against the renewal of his licence, and he was determined to defeat his opponents. Counsel was instructed, and a great deal of money was spent on the case. But the licence was nevertheless refused, and the north-east wind seemed resolved on William's death, and with a sick husband on her hands, and all the money they had invested in the house lost, Esther began to make preparations for moving.

William had proved a kind husband, and in the seven years she had spent in the 'King's Head' there had been some enjoyment of life. She couldn't say that she had been unhappy. She had always disapproved of the betting. They had tried to do without it. There was a great deal in life which one couldn't approve of. But Ketley had never been very right in his head, and Sarah's misfortune had had very little to do with the 'King's Head.' They had all tried to keep her from that man; it was her own fault. There were worse places than the 'King's Head.' It wasn't for her to abuse it. She had lived there seven years; she had seen her boy growing up—he was almost a young man now, and had had the best education. That much good the 'King's Head' had done. But perhaps it was no longer suited to William's health. The betting, she was tired thinking about that; and that constant nipping, it was impossible for him to keep from it with every one asking him to drink with them. A look of fear and distress passed across her face.

She was rolling up a pair of curtains, and she stopped for a moment, for she did not know how they were to live, that was the worst of it. If they only had back the money they had sunk in the house she would not so much mind. Seven years of hard work—for she had worked hard—and nothing to show for it. If she had been doing the grand lady all the time it would have been no worse. Horses had won and horses had lost—a great deal of trouble and fuss and nothing to show for it. That was what stuck in her throat. Nothing to show for it. She looked round the dismantled walls, and descended the vacant staircase. She would never serve another pint of beer in that bar. What a strong, big fellow he was when she first went to live with him! He was sadly changed. Would she ever see him strong and well again? She remembered that he had told her he was worth nearly £3,000. She hadn't brought him luck. He wasn't worth anything like that to-day.

'How much have we in the bank, dear?'

'A bit over six hundred pounds. I was reckoning of it up yesterday. But what do you want to know for? To remind me that I 've been losing. Well, I have been losing. I hope you 're satisfied.'

'I wasn't thinking of such a thing.'

'Yes, you was, there 's no use saying you wasn't. It ain't my fault if the 'orses don't win; I do the best I can.'

She did not answer him. Then he said, 'It 's my 'ealth that makes me irritable, dear; you aren't angry, are you?'

'No, dear, I know you don't mean it, and I don't pay no attention to it.' She spoke so gently that he looked at her surprised, for he knew her quick temper, and he said, 'You 're the best wife a man ever had.'

'No I 'm not, Bill, but I tries to do my best.'

The spring was the harshest ever known, and his cough grew worse and the blood-spitting returned. Esther grew seriously alarmed. Their doctor spoke of Brompton Hospital, and she insisted on his going there to be examined. William would not have her come with him; and she did not press the point, fearing to irritate him, but sat at home waiting anxiously for him to return, hoping against hope, for their doctor had told her that he feared very long trouble. And she could tell from his face and manner that he had bad news for her. All her strength left her, but she conquered her weakness and said:

'Now, tell me what they said. I 've a right to know; I want to know.'

'They said it was consumption.'

'Oh, did they say that?'

'Yes, but that don't mean that I'm going to die. They said they hoped they could patch me up; people often live for years with only half a lung, and it is only the left one that's gone.'

He coughed slightly and wiped the blood from his lips. Esther was quite overcome.

'Now, don't look like that,' he said, 'or I shall fancy I'm going to die to-morrow.'

'They said they thought that they could patch you up?'

'Yes; they said I might go on a long while yet, but that I would never be the man I was.'

This was so plain that she could not check a look of pity.

'If you're going to look at me like that I'd sooner go into the hospital at once. It ain't the cheerfullest of places, but it will be better than here.'

'I'm sorry it was consumption. But if they said they could patch you up, it will be all right. It was a great deal for them to say.'

Her duty was to overcome her grief and speak as if the doctors had told him that there was nothing the matter that a little careful nursing would fail to put right. William had faith in the warm weather, and she resolved to put her trust in it. It was hard to see him wasting away before her eyes and keep cheerful looks in her face and an accent of cheerfulness in her voice. The sunshine which had come at last seemed to suck up all the life that was in him; he grew paler, and withered like a plant. Then ill luck seemed to have joined in the hunt; he could not 'touch' a winner, and their fortune drained away with his life. Favourites and outsiders—it mattered not; whatever he backed lost; and Esther dreaded the cry 'Win-ner, all the win-ners!' He sat on the little balcony in the sunny evenings looking down the back street for the boy to appear with the 'special.' Then she had to go and fetch the paper. On the rare occasions when he won, the spectacle was even more painful. He brightened up, his thin arm and hand moved nervously, and he began to make projects and indulge in hopes which she knew were vain.

She insisted, however, on his taking regularly the medicine they gave him at the hospital, and this was difficult to do. For his irritability increased in measure as he perceived the medicine was doing him no good; he found fault with the doctors, railed against them unjustly, and all the while the little cough continued, and the blood-spitting returned at the end of cruel intervals, when he had begun to hope that at least that trouble was done with. One morning he told his wife that he was going to ask the doctors to examine him again. They had spoken of patching up; but he wanted to know whether he was going to live or die. There was a certain relief in hearing him speak so plainly; she had had enough of the torture of hope, and would like to know the worst. He liked better to go to the hospital alone, but she felt that she could not sit at home counting the minutes for him to return, and begged to be allowed to go with him. To her surprise, he offered no opposition. She had expected that her request would bring about quite a little scene, but he had taken it so much as a matter of course that she should accompany him that she was doubly glad that she had proposed to go with him; if she hadn't he might have accused her of neglecting him. She put on her hat—the day was too hot for a jacket, it was the beginning of August, and the poor, dry, dusty air that remained after the season made William cough, and she hoped the doctors would order him to the seaside. At Hyde Park Corner the blown dust whirled about the hill-top; and the wide pavements of the Brompton Road, and a semi-detached public-house at the cross-roads, announced the beginning of suburban London to the Londoner.

'You see,' said William, 'where them trees are, where the road turns off to the left. That 'ouse is the "Bell and Horns." And that 's the sort of house I should like to see you in.'

'It 's a pity we didn't buy it when we had the money.'

'Buy it! That 'ouse is worth ten thousand pounds if it 's worth a penny.'

'I was once in a situation not far from here.'

Her first service was with Mrs. Dunbar, in Sydney Street, and she remembered the square church tower at the Chelsea end; a little farther on there was the Vestry Hall in the King's Road, and then Oakley Street on the left, leading down to Battersea. Mrs. Dunbar used to go to some gardens at the end of the King's Road. Cremorne Gardens, that was the name; and she often spent the evening at the back window watching the rockets go up. The neighbourhood came back to her—Palmer the butterman, Hyde the grocer. And everything was just the same; not much change. How many years ago? Fifteen or sixteen. And so enwrapped was she in memories that William had to touch her. 'Here we are,' he said.

'So we are,' she answered, startled by the familiar aspect of the great red-brick building, a centrepiece with two wings, surrounded by high iron railings and lined with gloomy shrubs. The long straight walks, the dismal trees arow, where pale-faced men walked or rested feebly, had impressed themselves on her young mind—thin patient men, pacing their sepulchre. She used to wonder who they were, if they would get well; and then, with sensation of lingering death in her mind, she hurried away on her errands. The low wooden yellow-painted gates were unchanged. She had never seen them open before, and it was new to her to see the gardens filled with bright sunshine and numerous visitors. A little yellow was creeping through the leaves, and from time to time a leaf fell exhausted from the branches.

William, who was already familiar with the custom of the place, nodded to the porter and was let pass without question. He did not turn to the principal entrance in the middle of the building, but went towards a side entrance, where the house physician was standing talking with a young man whom Esther recognized as Mr. Alden. The thought that he, too, might be dying of consumption crossed her mind, but his appearance and his healthy, hearty laugh reassured her. A stout, common girl, healthy too, came out of the building, with a child, a little thing of twelve or thirteen, with death in her face. Mr. Alden stopped her, and in his cheerful, kind manner hoped the little one was better. She answered that she was. The doctor bade him good-bye and beckoned William and Esther to follow him. Esther would have liked to have spoken to Mr. Alden. But he did not see her, and she followed her husband, who was talking with the doctor, through the doorway into a long passage. At the end of the passage there were a number of girls in print dresses.

The gaiety of the dresses led Esther to think that they must be visitors. But the little cough warned her that death was among them. As she went past she caught sight of a wasted form in a bath-chair. Thin hands were laid on the knees, on a little handkerchief, and there were spots on the whiteness deeper than the colour of the dress. They passed down another passage, meeting a sister on their way; pretty and discreet she was in her black dress and veil, and she raised her eyes, glancing affectionately at the young doctor. No doubt they loved each other. The eternal love-story among so much death!

Esther wished to be present at the examination, but a sudden whim made William say that he would prefer to be alone with the doctor, and she returned to the gardens. Mr. Alden had not yet gone, and the little girl she had seen him speaking to was sitting on a bench under the trees, holding in her hands a skein of yellow worsted which her companion was winding into a ball. Two other young women were with them, and all four were smiling and whispering and looking towards Mr. Alden, seeking to attract his attention, hoping he would come and speak to them—just the natural desire of women to please; and moved by the pathos of this poor coquetting he went to them, and Esther could see that they all wanted to talk to him. She too would have liked to have spoken to him, for he was an old friend. And she walked up the grounds, intending to pass by him as she walked back. His back was still turned to her, and they were all so interested that they gave no heed to anything else. One of the young women had an exceedingly pretty face—a small oval, perfectly snow-white—and large blue eyes shaded with long dark lashes, a little aquiline nose—and Esther heard her say, 'I should be well enough if it wasn't for the cough. It isn't no better since——' The cough interrupted the end of the sentence, and affecting to misunderstand her, Mr. Alden said:

'No better than it was a week ago.'

'A week ago!' said the poor girl. 'It is no better since Christmas.'

There was surprise in her voice; the pity of it took Mr. Alden in the throat, and it was with difficulty that he answered that he hoped that the present fine weather would enable her to get well. 'Such weather as this,' he said, 'is as good as going abroad.'

One of the women had been to Australia for her health, and the story of travel was interspersed by the little coughs, terrible in their apparent insignificance. But it was Mr. Alden that the others wished to hear speak; they knew all about their companion's trip to Australia, and in their impatience their eyes went towards Esther. So Mr. Alden became aware of a new presence, and he turned.

'What! is it you, Esther?'

'Yes, sir.'

'But there doesn't seem much the matter with you. You're all right.'

'Yes, I'm all right, sir; it's my husband.'

They walked a few yards up the path.

'Your husband! I'm very sorry.'

'He's been an outdoor patient for some time; he's being examined by the doctors now.'

'Whom did you marry, Esther?'

'William Latch, a betting man, sir.'

'You married a betting man, Esther. How strangely things work out! I remember you were engaged to a pious young man, the stationer's foreman. That was when you were with Miss Rice; you know, I suppose, that she's dead.'

'No, sir, I didn't know it. I've had so much trouble lately that I've not been to see her for nearly two years. When did she die, sir?'

'About two months ago. So you married a betting man! Miss Rice did say something about it, but I don't think I understood that he was a betting man; I thought he was a publican.'

'So he was, sir. We lost our licence through the betting.'

'You say he's being examined by the doctor. Is it a bad case?'

'I am afraid it is, sir.'

They walked on in silence until they reached the gate.

'To me this place is infinitely pathetic. That little cough never silent for long. Did you hear that poor girl say with surprise that her cough is no better than it was last Christmas?'

'Yes, sir. Poor girl, I don't think she's long for this world.'

'But tell me about your husband, Esther,' he said, and his face filled with an expression of true sympathy. 'I am a subscriber, and if your husband would like to become an indoor patient, I hope you'll let me know.'

'Thank you, sir; you was always the kindest, but there's no reason why I should trouble you. Some friends of ours have already recommended him, and it only rests with himself to remain out or go in.'

He pulled out his watch and said, 'I am sorry to have met you in such sad circumstances, but I am glad to have seen you. It must be seven years or more since you left Miss Rice. You haven't changed much; you keep your good looks.'

'Oh, sir.'

He laughed at her embarrassment and walked across the road hailing a hansom just as he used to in old times when he came to see Miss Rice. The memory of those days came back upon her, and she felt she had seen him for the last time. But it was foolish, and wicked too, to think of such things—her husband dying. But she couldn't help it; he reminded her of so much of what was past and gone. A moment after she dashed these personal tears aside and walked open-hearted to meet William. What had the doctor said? She must know the truth. If she was to lose him she would lose everything. No, not everything; her boy would still remain to her, and she felt that, after all, her boy was most what was real to her in life. These were the thoughts that passed through her mind before William had time to answer her question.

'He said the left lung was gone, that I'd never be able to stand another winter in England. He said I must go to Egypt.'

'Egypt,' she repeated. 'Is that very far from here?'

'What matter how far it is! If I can't live in England I must go where I can live.'

'Don't be cross, dear. I know it's your health that makes you that irritable, but it's hard to bear at times.'

'You won't care to go to Egypt with me.'

'How can you think that, Bill? Have I ever refused you anything?'

'Quite right, old girl, I'm sorry. I know you'd do anything for me. I've always said so, haven't I? It's this cough that makes me sharp-tempered and fretful. I shall be different when I get to Egypt.'

'When do we start?'

'If we get away by the end of October it will be all right. It will cost a lot of money; the journey is expensive, and we shall have to stop there six months. I couldn't think of coming home before the end of April.'

Esther did not answer. They walked some yards in silence. Then he said:

'I've been very unlucky lately; there isn't much over a hundred pounds in the bank.'

'How much shall we want?'

'Three or four hundred pounds at least. We won't take the boy with us, we couldn't afford that; but I should like to pay a couple of quarters in advance.'

'That won't be much.'

'Not if I have any luck. The luck must turn, and I have some splendid information about the Great Ebor and the Yorkshire Stakes. Stack knows of a horse or two that's being kept for Sandown. Unfortunately there is not much doing in August. I must try to make up the money: it's a matter of life and death.'

It was for his very life that her husband was now gambling on the racecourse, and a sensation of great wickedness came up in her mind, but she stifled it. But William noticed the look of fear that appeared in her eyes, and he said:

'It's my last chance. I can't get the money any other way; and I don't want to die yet awhile. I haven't been as good to you as I'd like, and I want to do something for the boy, you know.'

He had been told not to remain out after sundown, but he was resolved to leave no stone unturned in his search for information, and often he returned home as late as nine and ten o'clock at night coughing—Esther could hear him all up the street. He came in ready to drop with fatigue, his pockets filled with sporting papers, and these he studied, spreading them on the table under the lamp, while Esther sat striving to do some needlework. It often dropped out of her hands, and her eyes filled with tears. But she took care that he should not see these tears. Sometimes he read out the horses' names and asked her which she thought would win, which seemed to her a likely name. But she begged of him not to ask her; they had many quarrels on this subject, but in the end he understood that it was not fair to ask her. Sometimes Stack and Journeyman came in, and they argued about weights and distances, until midnight; old John came to see them and every day he had heard some new tip. It often rose to Esther's lips to tell William to back his fancy and have done with it; she could see that these discussions only fatigued him; that he was no nearer to the truth now than he was a fortnight ago. Meanwhile, the horse he had thought of backing had gone up in the betting. But he said that he must be very careful. They had only a hundred pounds left; he must be careful not to risk this money foolishly—it was his very life-blood. If he were to lose all this money, he wouldn't only sign his own death-warrant, but also hers. He might linger on a long while—there was no knowing—but he would never be able to do any work, that was certain (unless he went out to Egypt); the doctor had said so, and then it would be she who would have to support him. And if God were merciful enough to take him off at once he would leave her in a worse plight than he had found her in, and the boy growing up! Oh, it was terrible! He buried his face in his hands, and seemed quite overcome. Then the cough would take him, and for a few minutes he could only think of himself. Esther gave him a little milk to drink, and he said:

'There's a hundred pounds left, Esther. It isn't much, but it's something. I don't believe that there's much use in my going to Egypt. I shall never get well. It is better that I should pitch myself into the river. That would be the least selfish way out of it.'

'William, I will not have you talk in that way,' Esther said, laying down her work and going over to him. 'If you was to do such a thing I should never forgive you. I could never think the same of you.'

'All right, old girl, don't be frightened. I've been thinking too much about them horses, and am a bit depressed. I dare say it will come out all right. I think that Mahomet is sure to win the Great Ebor, don't you?'

'I don't think there's no better judge than yourself. They all say if he don't fall lame that he's bound to win.'

'Then Mahomet shall carry my money. I'll back him to-morrow.'

Now that he had made up his mind what horse to back his spirits revived. He was able to dismiss the subject from his mind, and they talked of other things, of their son, and they laid projects for his welfare. But on the day of the race, from early morning, William could barely contain himself. Usually he took his winnings and losings very quietly. When he had been especially unlucky he swore a bit, but Esther had never seen any great excitement before a race was run. The issues of this race were extraordinary, and it was heart-breaking to see him suffer; he could not remain still a moment. A prey to all the terrors of hope, exhausted with anticipation, he rested himself against the sideboard and wiped drops of sweat from his forehead. A broiling sunlight infested their window-panes, the room grew oven-like, and he was obliged at last to go into the back parlour and lie down. He lay there in his shirt sleeves quite exhausted, hardly able to breathe; the arm once so strong and healthy was shrunken to a little nothing. He seemed quite bloodless, and looking at him Esther could hardly hope that any climate would restore him to health. He just asked her what the time was, and said, 'The race is being run now.' A few minutes after he said, 'I think Mahomet has won. I fancied I saw him get first past the post.' He spoke as if he were sure, and said nothing about the evening paper. If he were disappointed, Esther felt that it would kill him, and she knelt down by the bedside and prayed that God would allow the horse to win. It meant her husband's life, that was all she knew. Oh, that the horse might win! Presently he said, 'There's no use praying, I feel sure it is all right. Go into the next room, stand on the balcony so that you may see the boy coming along.'

With agonized soul the woman viewed the serenity of the evening sky and heard the cry 'Win-ner, win-ner' coming up the street. It came from the north, from the east, and now from the west. Ah, if it should prove bad news! But somehow she too felt that the news was good, and ran to meet the boy. She had a halfpenny ready in her hand; he fumbled, striving to detach a single paper from the quire under his arm. Seeing her impatience, he said, 'Mahomet's won.' Then the pavement seemed to slide beneath her feet, and she hardly could see, so full was her heart, so burdened with the happiness that she was bringing to the poor sick fellow who lay in his shirt sleeves on the bed in the back room. 'It's all right,' she said. 'I thought so too; it seemed like it.' His face flushed, life seemed to come back. He sat up and took the paper from her. 'There,' he said, 'I've got my place-money, too. I hope Stack and Journeyman come in to-night. I'd like to have a chat about this. Come, give me a kiss, dear. I'm not going to die, after all. It isn't a pleasant thing to think that you must die, that there's no hope for you, that you must go under ground.'

The next thing to do was to pick the winner of the York-shire Handicap. In this he was not successful, but he backed several winners at Sandown Park, and at the close of the week had made nearly enough to take him to Egypt.

The Doncaster week, however, proved disastrous. He lost most of his winnings, and had to look forward to re-trieving his fortunes at Newmarket. 'The worst of it is, if I don't make up the money by October, it will be no use. They say the November fogs will polish me off.'

Between Doncaster and Newmarket he lost a bet, and this bet carried him back into despondency. He felt it was no use struggling against fate. Better remain in London and be taken away at the end of November or December; he couldn't last much longer than that. This would allow him to leave Esther at least fifty pounds to go on with. The boy would soon be able to earn money. It would be better so. No use wasting all this money for the sake of his health, which wasn't worth twopence three-farthings. It was like throwing sovereigns after farthings. He didn't want to do any betting; he was as hollow as a shell inside, he could feel it. Egypt could do nothing for him, and, as he had to go, better sooner than later. Esther argued with him. What should she have to live for if he was taken from her? The doctors had said that Egypt might set him right. She didn't know much about such things, but she had always heard that it was extraordinary how people got cured out there.

'That's true,' he said. 'I've heard that people who couldn't live a week in England, who haven't the length of your finger of lung left, can go on all right out there. I might get something to do out there, and the boy might come out after us.'

'That's the way I like to hear you talk. Who knows, at Newmarket we might have luck! Just one big bet, a winner at fifty to one, that's all we want.'

'That's just what has been passing in my mind. I've got particular information about the Cesarewitch and Cambridgeshire. I could get the price you speak of—fifty to one against the two, Matchbox and Chasuble—the double event, you know. I'm inclined to go it. It's my last chance.'

## CHAPTER XLII

WHEN Matchbox galloped home the winner of the Cesare-witch by five lengths, William was lying in his bed, seemingly at death's door. He had remained out late one evening, had caught cold, and his mouth was constantly filled with blood. He was much worse, and could hardly take notice of the good news. When he revived a little he said, 'It has come too late.' But when Chasuble was backed to win thousands at ten to one, and Journeyman and Stack assured him that the stable was quite confident of being able to pull it off, his spirits revived. He spoke of hedging. 'If,' he said to Esther, 'I was to get out at eight or nine to one I should be able to leave you something, you know, in case of accidents.' But he would not entrust laying off his bet to either Stack or Journeyman; he spoke of a cab and seeing to it himself. If he did this the doctor assured him that it would not much matter whether Chasuble won or lost. 'The best thing he could do,' the doctor said, 'would be to become an indoor patient at once. In the hospital he would be in an equable temperature, and he would receive an attention which he could not get at home.'

William did not like going into the hospital; it would be a bad omen. If he did, he felt sure that Chasuble would not win.

'What has going or not going to the hospital to do with Chasuble's chance of winning the Cambridgeshire?' said the doctor. 'This window is loose in its sash, a draught comes under the door and if you close out the draughts the atmosphere of the room becomes stuffy. You 're thinking of going abroad; a fortnight's nice rest is just what you want to set you up for your journey.'

So he allowed himself to be persuaded; he was taken to the hospital, and Esther remained at home waiting for the fateful afternoon. Now that the dying man was taken from her she had no work to distract her thought. The unanswerable question—would Chasuble win?—was always before her. She saw the slender greyhound creatures as she had seen them at Epsom, through a sea of heads and hats, and she asked herself if Chasuble was the brown horse that had galloped in first, or the chestnut that had trotted in last. She often thought she was going mad— her head seemed like it—a sensation of splitting like a piece of calico. She went to see her boy, a great tall fellow of fifteen, who had happily lost none of his affection for his mother, and great sweetness rose up within her as she looked at his long, straight, yellow-stockinged legs, and settled the collar of his cloak, and slipped her fingers into his leathern belt as they walked side by side. He was bare-headed, according to the fashion of his school, and she kissed the wild, dark curls with which his head was run over; they were much brighter in colour when he was a little boy—those days when she slaved seventeen hours a day for his dear life! But he paid her back tenfold for the hardship she had undergone, and she listened to the excellent report his masters gave of his progress, and walked through the quadrangles and the corridors with him, thinking of the sound of his voice as he told her the story of his classes and his studies. She must live for him; though for herself she had had enough of life. But, thank God, she had her darling boy, and whatever unhappiness there might be in store for her she would bear it for his sake. He knew that his father was ill, but she checked her tongue and told him no word of the tragedy that was hanging over them, for the noble instincts which were so intrinsically Esther's told her that it were a pity to soil at the outset a young life with a sordid story, and, though it would have been a great relief to her to have shared her trouble with her boy, she forced back her tears and bore her cross alone, without once allowing its edge to touch him.

And every day that visitors were allowed she went to the hospital with the newspaper containing the last betting. 'Chasuble, ten to one taken,' William read out. The mare had advanced three points, and William looked at Esther inquiringly, and with hope in his eyes.

'I think she 'll win,' he said, raising himself in his cane chair.

'I hope so, dear,' she murmured, and she settled his cushions.

Two days after the mare was back again at thirteen to one taken and offered; she went back even as far as eighteen to one, and then returned for a while to twelve to one. This fluctuation meant that something was wrong, and William began to lose hope. But on the following day the mare was backed to win a good deal of money at Tattersall's, and once more she stood at ten to one. Seeing her back at the old price made William look so hopeful that a patient stopped as he passed down the corridor, and, catching sight of the *Sportsman* on William's lap, he asked him if he was interested in racing. William told him that he was, and that if Chasuble won he would be able to go to Egypt.

'Them that has money can buy health as well as everything else. We'd all get well if we could get out there.'

William told him how much he stood to win.

'That'll keep you going long enough to set you straight. You say the mare's backed at ten to one—two hundred to twenty. I wonder if I could get the money. I might sell up the 'ouse.'

But before he had time to realize the necessary money the mare was driven back to eighteen to one, and he said:

'She won't win. I might as well leave the wife in the 'ouse. There's no luck for them that comes 'ere.'

On the day of the race Esther walked through the streets like one daft, stupidly interested in the passers-by and the disputes that arose between the drivers of cabs and omnibuses. Now and then her thoughts collected, and it seemed to her impossible that the mare should win. If she did they would have £2,500, and would go to Egypt. But she could not imagine such a thing; it seemed so much more natural that the mare should lose, and that her husband should die, and that she should have to face the world once more. She offered up prayers that Chasuble might win, although it did not seem right to address God on the subject, but her heart so often felt like breaking that she had to do something. God would forgive her. But now that the day had come she did not feel as if He had granted her request. Yet it did not seem that her husband was going to die.

She stopped at the 'Bell and Horns' to see what the time was, and was surprised to find it was half an hour later than she had expected. The race was being run, Chasuble's hoofs were deciding whether her husband was to live or die. It was on the wire by this time. The wires were distinct upon a blue and dove-coloured sky. Did that one go to Newmarket, or the other? Which?

The red building came in sight, and a patient walked slowly up the walk, his back turned to her; another had sat down to rest. Sixteen years ago patients were walking there, and the leaves were scattering then just as now. She began to wonder when the first boy would appear with the news. William was not in the grounds; he was upstairs behind those windows. Poor fellow, she could fancy him sitting there. Perhaps he was watching for her out of one of those windows. But there was no use her going up until she had the news; she must wait for the paper. She walked up and down listening for the cry. Every now and then expectation led her to mistake some ordinary cry for the terrible 'Win-ner, all the win-ners,' with which the whole town would echo in a few minutes. She hastened forward. No, it was not it. At last she heard the word shrieked behind her. She hastened after the boy, but failed to overtake him. Returning, she met another, gave him a halfpenny and took a paper. Then she re-membered she must ask the boy to tell her who won. But heedless of her question he had run across the road to sell papers to some men who had come out of a public-house. She must not give William the paper and wait for him to read the news to her. If the news were bad the shock might kill him. She must learn first what the news was, so that her face and manner might prepare him for the worst if need be. So she offered the paper to the porter and asked him to tell her. 'Bramble, King of Trumps, Young Hopeful,' he read out.

'Are you sure that Chasuble hasn't won?'

'Of course I 'm sure, there it is.'

'I can't read,' she said as she turned away.

The news had stunned her; the world seemed to lose reality; she was uncertain what to do, and several times repeated to herself, 'There 's nothing for it but to go up and tell him. I don't see what else I can do.' The staircase was very steep; she climbed it slowly, and stopped at the first landing and looked out of the window. A poor hollow-chested creature, the wreck of a human being, struggled up behind her. He had to rest several times, and in the hollow building his cough sounded loud and sepulchral. 'It isn't generally so loud as that,' she thought, and wondered how she could tell William the news. 'He wanted to see Jack grow up to be a man. He thought that we might all go to Egypt, and that he'd get quite well there, for there's plenty of sunshine there, but now he'll have to make up his mind to die in the November fogs.' Her thoughts came strangely clear, and she was astonished at her indifference, until a sudden revulsion of feeling took her as she was going up the last flight. She couldn't tell him the news; it was too cruel. She let the patient pass her, and when alone on the landing she looked down into the depth. She thought she'd like to fall over; anything rather than to do what she knew she must do. But her cowardice only endured for a moment, and with a firm step she walked into the corridor. It seemed to cross the entire building, and was floored and wainscoted with the same brown varnished wood as the staircase. There were benches along the walls; and emaciated and worn-out men lay on the long cane chairs in the windowed recesses by which the passage was lighted. The wards, containing sometimes three, sometimes six or seven beds, opened on to this passage. The doors of the wards were all open, and as she passed along she started at the sight of a boy sitting up in bed. His head had been shaved, and only a slight bristle covered the crown. The head and face were a large white mass with two eyes.

At the end of the passage there was a window; and William sat there reading a book. He saw her before she saw him, and when she caught sight of him she stopped, holding the paper loose before her between finger and thumb, and as she approached she saw that her manner had already broken the news to him.

'I see that she didn't win,' he said.

'No, dear, she didn't win. We wasn't lucky this time; next time——'

'There is no next time, at least for me. I shall be far away from here when flat racing begins again. The November fogs will do for me, I feel that they will. I hope there'll be no lingering, that's all. Better to know the worst and make up your mind. So I have to go, have I? So there's no hope, and I shall be under ground before the next meeting. I shall never lay or take the odds again. It do seem strange. If only that mare had won. I knew damned well she wouldn't if I came here.'

Then, catching sight of the pained look on his wife's face, he said, 'I don't suppose it made no difference; it was to be, and what has to be has to be. I've got to go under ground. I felt it was to be all along. Egypt would have done me no good; I never believed in it—only a lot of false hope. You don't think what I say is true. Look 'ere, do you know what book this is? This is the Bible; that 'll prove to you that I knew the game was up. I knew, I can't tell you how, but I knew the mare wouldn't win. You always seems to know. Even when I backed her I didn't feel about her like I did about the other one, and ever since I've been feeling more and more sure that it wasn't to be. Somehow it didn't seem likely, and to-day something told me that the game was up, so I asked for this book. . . . There's wonderful, beautiful things in it.'

'There is, indeed, Bill; and I hope you won't get tired of it, but will go on reading it.'

'It's extraordinary how consoling it is. Listen to this. Isn't it beautiful; ain't them words heavenly?'

'They is, indeed. I knew you'd come to God at last.'

'I'm afraid I've not led a good life. I wouldn't listen to you when you used to tell me of the lot of harm the betting used to bring on the poor people what used to come to our place. There's Sarah, I suppose she's out of prison by this. You've seen nothing of her, I suppose?'

'No, nothing.'

'There was Ketley.'

'No, Bill, don't let's think about it. If you're truly sorry, God will forgive.'

'Do you think He will—and the others that we know nothing about? I wouldn't listen to you; I was head-strong, but I understand it all now. My eyes 'ave been opened. Them pious folk that got up the prosecution knew what they was about. I forgive them one and all.'

William coughed a little. The conversation paused, and the cough was repeated down the corridor. Now it came from the men lying on the long cane chairs; now from the

poor emaciated creature, hollow cheeks, brown eyes and
beard, who had just come out of his ward and had sat down
on a bench by the wall. Now it came from an old man six
feet high, with snow-white hair. He sat near them, and
worked assiduously at a piece of tapestry. 'It 'll be
better when it 's cut,' he said to one of the nurses, who had
stopped to compliment him on his work; 'it 'll be better
when it 's cut.' Then the cough came from one of the
wards, and Esther thought of the fearsome boy sitting
bolt up, his huge tallow-like face staring through the
silence of the room. A moment after the cough came from
her husband's lips, and they looked at each other. Both
wanted to speak, and neither knew what to say. At last
William spoke.

'I was saying that I never had that feeling about
Chasuble that you 'as about a winner. Did she run
second? Just like my luck if she did. Let me see the
paper.'

Esther handed it to him.

'Bramble, a fifty to one chance, not one man in a hundred
backed her; King of Trumps, there was some place-money
lost on him; Young Hopeful, a rank outsider. What a day
for the bookies!'

'You mustn't think of them things no more,' said Esther.
'You 've got the Book; it 'll do you more good.'

'If I 'd only have thought of Bramble. I could have
had a hundred to one against Matchbox and Bramble
coupled.'

'What 's the use of thinking of things that 's over? We
should think of the future.'

'If I 'd only been able to hedge that bet I should have
been able to leave you something to go on with, but now,
when everything is paid for, you 'll have hardly a five-
pound note. You 've been a good wife to me, and I 've
been a bad husband to you.'

'Bill, you mustn't speak like that. You must try to
make your peace with God. Think of Him. He 'll think
of us that you leave behind. I 've always had faith in
Him. He 'll not desert me.'

Her eyes were quite dry; the instinct of life seemed to
have left her. They spoke some little while longer, until it
was time for visitors to leave the hospital. It was not until

she got into the Fulham Road that tears began to run down her cheeks; they poured faster and faster, like rain after long dry weather. The whole world disappeared in a mist of tears. And so overcome was she by her grief that she had to lean against the railings, and the passers-by turned and looked at her curiously.

## CHAPTER XLIII

WITH fair weather he might hold on till Christmas, but if much fog was about he would go off earlier, with the last leaves. One day Esther received a letter asking her to defer her visit from Friday to Sunday, for he hoped to be better on Sunday, and then they would arrange when she should come to take him away. He wanted to see his boy before he died.

Mrs. Collins, a woman who lived in the next room, read the letter to Esther.

'If you can, do as he wishes. Once they gets them fancies into their heads there 's no getting them out.'

'If he leaves the hospital on a day like this it 'll be the death of him.' The street lamps burnt low, mournful, as in a city of the dead, and the sounds that rose out of the street added to the terror of the strange darkness. 'What do he say about Jack? That I 'm to send for him. It 's natural he should like to see the boy before he goes, but it would be cheerfuller to take him to the hospital.'

'You see, he wants to die at home; he wants you to be with him at the last.'

'Yes, I want to see the last of him. But the boy, where 's he to sleep?'

'We can lay a mattress down in my room—an old woman like me, it don't matter.'

Sunday morning was harsh and cold, and when she came out of South Kensington Station a fog was thickening in the squares, and a great drift of yellow cloud settled down upon the house-tops. In the Fulham Road the tops of the houses disappeared, and the light of the third gas-lamp was not visible.

'This is the sort of weather that takes them off. I can hardly breathe it myself.'

Everything was shadow-like; those walking in front of her passed out of sight like shades, and once she thought she must have missed her way, though that was impossible, for her way was quite straight. Suddenly the silhouette of the winged building rose up enormous on the sulphur sky. The low-lying gardens were full of poisonous vapour, and the thin trees seemed like the ghosts of consumptive men. The porter coughed like a dead man as she passed, and he said, 'Bad weather for the poor sick ones upstairs.'

She was prepared for a change for the worse, but she did not expect to see a living man looking so like a dead one.

He could no longer lie back in bed and breathe, so he was propped up with pillows, and he looked even as shadow-like as those she had half seen in the fog-cloud. There was fog even in the ward, and the lights burned red in the silence. There were five beds—low iron bedsteads—and each was covered with a dark red rug. In the farthest corner lay the wreck of a great working man. He wore his hobnails and his corduroys, and his once brawny arm lay along his thigh, shrivelled and powerless as a child's. In the middle of the room a little clerk, wasted and weary, without any strength at all, lay striving for breath. The navvy was alone; the little clerk had his family round him—his wife and his two children, a baby in arms and a little boy three years old. The doctor had just come in, and the woman was prattling gaily about her confinement. She said:

'I was up the following week. Wonderful what we women can go through. No one would think it. Brought the youngsters to see their father; they is a little idol to him, poor fellow.'

'How are you to-day, dearie?' Esther said, as she took a seat by her husband's bed.

'Better than I was on Friday, but this weather 'll do for me if it continues much longer. You see them two beds? They died yesterday, and I 've 'eard that three or four that left the hospital are gone, too.'

The doctor came to William's bed. 'Well, are you still determined to go home?' he said.

'Yes; I 'd like to die at home. You can't do nothing for me. I 'd like to die at home; I want to see my boy.'

'You can see Jack here,' said Esther.

'I 'd sooner see him at 'ome. I suppose you don't want the trouble of a death in the 'ouse.'

'Oh, William, how can you speak so!' The patient coughed painfully, and leaned against the pillows, unable to speak.

Esther remained with William till the time permitted to

visitors expired.   He couldn't speak to her, but she knew
he liked her to be with him.

When she came on Thursday to take him away, he was a
little better.   The clerk's wife was chattering; the great
navvy lay in the corner, still as a block of stone.   Esther
often looked at him and wondered if he had no friend who
could spare an hour to come and see him.

'I was beginning to think that you wasn't coming,' said
William.

'He's that restless,' said the clerk's wife; 'asking the
time every three or four minutes.'

'How could you think that?' said Esther.

'I dunno.   You're a bit late, aren't you?'

'It often do make them restless,' said the clerk's wife.
'But my poor old man is quiet enough—aren't you, dear?'
The dying clerk couldn't answer, and the woman turned
again to Esther.

'And how do you find him to-day?'

'Much the same.   I think he's a bit better and stronger.
But this weather is so trying.   I don't know how it was up
your way, but down my way I never seed such a fog.   I
thought I'd have to turn back.'   At that moment the baby
began to cry, and the woman walked up and down the ward,
rocking it violently, talking loud, and making a great deal
of noise.   But she could not quiet him.   'Hungry again,'
she said.   'I never seed such a child for the breast,' and
she sat down and unbuttoned her dress.   When the young
doctor entered she hurriedly covered herself; he begged her
to continue, and spoke about her little boy.   She showed
him a scar on his throat.   He had been suffering, but it was
all right now.   The doctor glanced at the breathless father.

'A little better to-day, thank you, doctor.'

'That's all right'; and the doctor went over to William.
'Are you still bent to leave the hospital?' he said.

'Yes, I want to go home.   I want to——'

'You'll find this weather very trying; you'd better——'

'No, thank you, sir.   I should like to go home.   You've
been very kind; you've done everything that could be done
for me.   But it's God's will.   My wife is very grateful to
you, too.'

'Yes, that I am, sir.   However am I to thank you for
your kindness to my husband?'

'I'm sorry I couldn't do more. But you'll want the sister to help you to dress him. I'll send her to you.'

When they got him out of bed, Esther was shocked at the spectacle of his poor body, for there was nothing left of him. His poor chest, his wasted ribs, his legs gone to nothing, and the strange weakness, worst of all, which made it so hard for them to dress him. At last it was nearly done: Esther laced one boot, the nurse the other, and, leaning on Esther's arm, he looked round the room for the last time. The navvy turned round on his bed and said:

'Good-bye, mate.'

'Good-bye. Good-bye, all.'

The clerk's little son clung to his mother's skirt, frightened at the weakness of so big a man.

'Go and say good-bye to the gentleman.'

The little boy came forward timidly, offering his hand. William looked at the poor little white face; he nodded to the father and went out.

As he went downstairs he said he would like to go home in a hansom. The doctor and nurse expostulated, but he persisted until Esther begged of him to forgo the wish for her sake.

'They do rattle so, these four-wheelers, especially when the windows are up. You can't hear yourself speak.'

The cab jogged up Piccadilly, and as it climbed out of the hollow the dying man's eyes were fixed on the circle of lights that shone across the Green Park. They looked like a distant village, and Esther wondered if William was thinking of Shoreham—she had seen Shoreham look like that sometimes—or if he was thinking that he was looking on London for the last time. Was he saying to himself, 'I shall never, never see Piccadilly again'? They passed St. James's Street. The Circus, with its mob of prostitutes, came into view; the 'Criterion' bar, with its loafers standing outside. William leaned a little forward, and Esther was sure he was thinking that he would never go into that bar again. The cab turned to the left, and Esther said that it would cross Soho, perhaps pass down Old Compton Street, opposite their old house. It happened that it did, and Esther and William wondered who were the new people who were selling beer and whisky in the bar. All the while boys were crying, 'Win-ner, all the win-ners!'

'The —— was run to-day. Flat racing all over, all over for this year.'

Esther did not answer. The cab passed over a piece of asphalt, and he said:

'Is Jack waiting for us?'

'Yes, he came home yesterday.'

The fog was thick in Bloomsbury, and when he got out of the cab he was taken with a fit of coughing, and had to cling to the railings. She had to pay the cab. It took some time to find the money. Would no one open the door? At last, having got her change, she followed him into the house.

'I can manage. Go on first; I 'll follow.'

And stopping every three or four steps for rest, he slowly dragged himself up to the first landing. A door opened and Jack stood on the threshold of the lighted room.

'Is that you, mother?'

'Yes, dear; your father is coming up.'

The boy came forward to help, but his mother whispered, 'He 'd rather come up by himself.'

He had strength to walk into the room; they gave him a chair, and he looked round, and seemed pleased to see his home again. Esther gave him some milk, into which she had put a little brandy, and he gradually revived.

'Come this way, Jack; I want to look at you; come into the light where I can see you.'

'Yes, father.'

'I haven't long to see you, Jack. I wanted to be with you and your mother in our own home. I can talk a little now; I may not be able to to-morrow.'

'Yes, father.'

'I want you to promise me, Jack, that you 'll never have nothing to do with racing and betting. It hasn't brought me or your mother any luck.'

'Very well, father.'

'You promise me, Jack. Give me your hand. You promise me that, Jack?'

'Yes, father, I promise.'

'I see it all clearly enough now. Your mother, Jack, is the best woman in the world. She loved you better than I did. She worked for you—that is a sad story. I hope you 'll never hear it.'

M

Husband and wife looked at each other, and in that look the wife promised the husband that the son should never know the story of her desertion.

'She was always against the betting, Jack; she always knew it would bring us ill luck. I was once well off, but I lost everything. No good comes of money that you don't work for.'

'I'm sure you worked enough for what you won,' said Esther; 'travelling day and night from racecourse to racecourse. Standing on them racecourses in all weathers; it was the colds you caught standing on them racecourses that began the mischief.'

'I worked hard enough, that's true; but it was not the right kind of work. I can't argue, Esther. But I know the truth now, what you always said was the truth. No good comes of money that hasn't been properly earned.'

He sipped the brandy and milk and looked at Jack, who was crying bitterly.

'You mustn't cry like that, Jack; I want you to listen to me. I've still something on my mind. Your mother, Jack, is the best woman that ever lived. You're too young to understand how good. I didn't know how good for a long time, but I found it all out in time, as you will later, Jack, when you are a man. I'd hoped to see you grow up to be a man, Jack, and your mother and I thought that you'd have a nice bit of money. But the money I hoped to leave you is all gone. What I feel most is that I'm leaving you and your mother as badly off as she was when I married her.' He heaved a deep sigh, and Esther said:

'What is the good of talking of these things, weakening yourself for nothing?'

'I must speak, Esther. I should die happy if I knew how you and the boy was going to live. You'll have to go out and work for him as you did before. It will be like beginning it all again.'

The tears rolled down his cheeks; he buried his face in his hands and sobbed, until the sobbing brought on a fit of coughing. Suddenly his mouth filled with blood. Jack went for the doctor, and all remedies were tried without avail. 'There is one more remedy,' the doctor said, 'and if that fails you must prepare for the worst.' But this last remedy proved successful, and the haemorrhage was stopped, and William was undressed and put to bed. The doctor said, 'He mustn't get up to-morrow.'

'You lie in bed to-morrow, and try to get up your strength. You 've overdone yourself to-day.'

She had drawn his bed into the warmest corner, close by the fire, and had made up for herself a sort of bed by the window, where she might doze a bit, for she did not expect to get much sleep. She would have to be up and down many times to settle his pillows and give him milk or a little weak brandy and water.

Night wore away, the morning grew into day, and about twelve o'clock he insisted on getting up. She tried to persuade him, but he said he could not stop in bed; and there was nothing for it but to ask Mrs. Collins to help her dress him. The cough had entirely ceased, and on Saturday night he slept better than he had done for a long while, and woke up on Sunday morning refreshed to eat a nice bit of boiled rabbit for his dinner. Esther fancied that he was still thinking of them. And when the afternoon waned, about four o'clock, he called Jack; he told him to sit in the light where he could see him, and he looked at his son with such wistful eyes that Esther had to turn aside to hide her tears.

'I should have liked to have seen you a man, Jack.'

'Don't speak like that—I can't bear it,' said the poor boy, bursting into tears. 'Perhaps you won't die yet.'

'Yes, Jack; I 'm wore out. I can feel,' he said, pointing to his chest, 'that there is nothing here to live upon. It is the punishment come upon me.'

'Punishment for what, father?'

'I wasn't always good to your mother, Jack.'

'If to please me, William, you 'll say no more.'

'The boy ought to know; it will be a lesson for him, and it weighs upon my heart.'

'I don't want my boy to hear anything bad about his father, and I forbid him to listen.'

The conversation paused, and soon after William said that his strength was going from him, and that he would like to go back to bed. Esther helped him off with his clothes, and together she and Jack lifted him into bed.

'It is hard to part from you,' he said. 'If Chasuble had

won we would have all gone to Egypt. I could have lived out there.'

'You must speak of them things no more. We all must obey God's will.' Esther dropped on her knees; she drew Jack down beside her. William asked Jack to read something from the Bible, and Jack read where he first opened the book, and when he had finished William said that he liked to listen, for Jack's voice sounded to him like heaven.

About eight o'clock William bade his son good night.

'Good night, my boy; perhaps we shan't see each other again. This may be my last night.'

'I won't leave you, father.'

'No, my boy, go to your bed. I feel I'd like to be alone with mother.' The voice sank almost to a whisper.

'You'll remember what you promised me about racing. Be good to your mother—she's the best mother a son ever had.'

'I'll work for mother, father, I'll work for her.'

'You're too young, my son, but when you're older I hope you'll work for her. She worked for you. Good-bye, my boy.'

The dying man sweated profusely, and Esther wiped his face from time to time. Mrs. Collins came in. She had a large tin candlestick in her hand in which there was a fragment of candle-end. He motioned to her to put it aside. She put it on the table out of the way of his eyes.

'You'll help Esther to lay me out. I don't want any one else. I don't like the other woman.'

'Esther and me will lay you out, make your mind easy; none but we two shall touch you.'

Once more Esther wiped his forehead, and he signed to her how he wished the bedclothes to be arranged, for he could no longer speak. Mrs. Collins whispered to Esther that she did not think that the end could be far off, and, compelled by a morbid sort of curiosity, she took a chair and sat down. Esther wiped away the little drops of sweat as they came upon his forehead; his chest and throat had to be wiped also, for they too were full of sweat. All the while his eyes were fixed on the darkness and he moved his hand restlessly, and Esther always understood what he wanted. She gave him a little brandy and water, and when he could not take it from the glass she gave it to him with a spoon.

The silence seemed to grow more solemn, and as Esther turned from the bedside for the brandy, Mrs. Collins's candle spluttered and went out; a little thread of smoke evaporated, leaving only a morsel of blackened wick; the flame had disappeared for ever, gone as if it had never been, and Esther saw darkness where there had been a light.

'I think it is all over, dear.'

The profile on the pillow seemed very little.

'Hold up his head, so that if there is any breath it may come on the glass.'

'He's dead, right enough.   You see, dear, there's not a trace of breath on the glass.'

'I'd like to say a prayer.   Will you say a prayer with me?'

'Yes, I feel as if I should like to myself; it eases the heart wonderful.'

## CHAPTER XLIV

She stood on the platform watching the receding train. The white steam curled above the few bushes that hid the curve of the line, evaporating in the pale evening. A moment more and the last carriage would pass out of sight, the white gates at the crossing swinging slowly forward to let through the impatient passengers.

An oblong box painted reddish brown lay on the seat beside a woman of seven or eight and thirty, stout and strongly built, short arms and hard-worked hands, dressed in dingy black skirt and a threadbare jacket too thin for the dampness of a November day. Her face was a blunt outline, and the grey eyes reflected all the natural prose of the Saxon.

The porter told her that he would try to send her box up to Woodview to-morrow. That was the way to Woodview, right up the lane. She could not miss it. She would find the lodge gate behind that clump of trees. And thinking how she could get her box to Woodview that evening, she looked at the barren strip of country lying between the downs and the shingle beach. The little town clamped about its deserted harbour seemed more than ever like falling to pieces like a derelict vessel, and when Esther passed over the level crossing she noticed that the line of little villas had not increased; they were as she had left them eighteen years ago, laurels, iron railing, antimacassars. For it was about eighteen years ago, on a beautiful June day, that she passed up this lane for the first time. At the very spot she was now passing she stopped to wonder if she would be able to keep the place of kitchenmaid, and she remembered regretting that she hadn't a new dress. The sun was shining, and she met William leaning over the paling in the avenue smoking his pipe. Eighteen years had gone by, eighteen years of labour, suffering, disappointment. A great deal had happened, so much that she could not remember it all. The situations she had been in; her life with that dear good soul, Miss Rice; then Fred Parsons; then William again: her marriage, the life in the public-house, money lost and money won, heart-breakings, death, everything that could happen had happened to her. And now it all seemed like a dream. No, her boy remained to her. Thank God for that; she had been able to bring him up. But how had she done it? How often had she found herself within sight of the workhouse? No later than last week it had seemed that she would have to accept the workhouse once more. But she had escaped, and now here she was back at the very point from which she started, going back to Woodview, going back to Mrs. Barfield's service.

William's illness and his funeral had taken Esther's last few pounds away from her, and when she and Jack came back from the cemetery she found that she had broken into her last sovereign. She clasped him to her bosom—he was a tall boy of fifteen—and burst into tears. But she did not tell him what she was crying for. She did not say, 'God only knows how we shall find bread to eat next week'; she merely said, wiping away her tears, 'We can't afford to live here any longer. It's too expensive for us now that father's gone.' And they went to live in a slum for three and sixpence a week. If she had been alone in the world she would have gone into a situation, but she could not leave the boy, and so she had to look out for charing. It was hard to have to come down to this, particularly when she remembered that she had had a house and a servant of her own; but there was nothing for it but to look out for some charing, and get along as best she could till Jack was able to look after himself. But the various scrubbings and general cleaning that had come her way had been so badly paid that she soon found that she could not make both ends meet. She would have to leave her boy and go out as a general servant. And as her necessities were pressing, she accepted a situation in a coffee-shop in the London Road. She would give all her wages to Jack, seven shillings a week, and he would have to live on that. So long as she had her health she didn't mind.

It was a squat brick building with four windows that looked down on the pavement with a short-sighted stare. On each window was written in letters of white enamel, 'Well-aired beds.' A board nailed to a post by the side door announced that tea and coffee were always ready.

On the other side of the sign was an upholsterer's, and the vulgar brightness of the Brussels carpets seemed in keeping with the sloplike appearance of the coffee-house.

Sometimes a workman came in the morning; a couple more might come in about dinner-time. Sometimes they took rashers and bits of steak out of their pockets.

'Won't you cook this for me, missis?'

But it was not until about nine in the evening that the real business of the house began, and it continued till one, when the last straggler knocked for admittance. The house lived on its beds. The best rooms were sometimes let for eight shillings a night, and there were four beds which were let at fourpence a night in the cellar under the area where Esther stood by the great copper washing sheets, blankets, and counterpanes when she was not cleaning the rooms upstairs. There was a double-bedded room underneath the kitchen, and over the landings, wherever a space could be found, the landlord, who was clever at carpentering work, had fitted up some sort of closet place that could be let as a bedroom. The house was a honeycomb. The landlord slept under the roof, and a corner had been found for his housekeeper, a handsome young woman, at the end of the passage. Esther and the children—the landlord was a widower—slept in the coffee-room upon planks laid across the tops of the high backs of the benches where the customers mealed. Mattresses and bedding were laid on these planks, and the sleepers lay with their faces hardly two feet from the ceiling. Esther slept with the baby, a little boy of five; the two big boys slept at the other end of the room by the front door. The eldest was about fifteen, but he was only half-witted; and he helped in the housework, and could turn down the beds and see quicker than any one if the occupant had stolen sheet or blanket. Esther always remembered how he would raise himself up in bed in the early morning, rub the glass, and light a candle so that he could be seen from below. He shook his head if every bed was occupied, or signed with his fingers the prices of the beds if they had any to let.

The landlord, a tall, thin man, with long features and hair turning grey, was a quiet man, and Esther was surprised one night at the abruptness with which he stopped a couple who were going upstairs.

'Is that your wife?' he said.

'Yes, she's my wife all right.'

'She don't look very old.'

'She's older than she looks.'

Then he said, half to Esther, half to his housekeeper, that it was hard to know what to do. If you asked them for their marriage certificates they'd be sure to show you something. The housekeeper answered that they paid well, and that was the principal thing. But when an attempt was made to steal the bedclothes the landlord and his housekeeper were more severe. As Esther was about to let a most respectable woman out of the front door, the idiot boy called down the stairs, 'Stop her! There's a sheet missing.'

'Oh, what in the world is all this? I haven't got your sheet. Pray let me pass; I'm in a hurry.'

'I can't let you pass until the sheet is found.'

'You'll find it upstairs under the bed. It's got mislaid. I'm in a hurry.'

'Call in the police,' shouted the idiot boy.

'You'd better come upstairs and help me to find the sheet,' said Esther.

The woman hesitated a moment, and then walked up in front of Esther. When they were in the bedroom she shook out her petticoats, and the sheet fell on the floor.

'There, now,' said Esther, 'a nice botheration you'd 've got me into. I should 've had to pay for it.'

'Oh, I could pay for it; it was only because I'm not very well off at present.'

'Yes, you *will* pay for it if you don't take care,' said Esther.

It was very soon after that Esther had her mother's books stolen from her. They had not been doing much business, and she had been put to sleep in one of the bedrooms. The room was suddenly wanted, and she had no time to move all her things, and when she went to make up the room she found that her mother's books and a pair of jet earrings that Fred had given her were stolen. She could do nothing; the couple who occupied the room were far away by this time. There was no hope of ever recovering her books and earrings; and the loss of these things caused her a great deal of unhappiness. The only little treasure she possessed were those earrings. Everything had gone from her; she was alone in the world, and if her health were to break down to-morrow she would have to go to the workhouse. What would become of her boy? She was afraid to think; for thinking did no good. She mustn't think, but must just work on, washing the bed-clothes until she could wash no longer. Wash, wash, all the week long; and it was only by working on till one o'clock in the morning that she sometimes managed to get the Sabbath free from washing. Never, not even in the house in Chelsea, had she had such hard work, and she was not as strong now as she was then. But her courage did not give way until one Sunday Jack came to tell her that the people who employed him had sold their business.

Then a strange weakness came over her. She thought of the endless week of work that awaited her in the cellar, the great copper on the fire, the heaps of soiled linen in the corner, the steam rising from the wash-tub, and she felt she had not enough strength to get through another week of such work. She looked at her son with despair in her eyes. She had whispered to him as he lay asleep under her shawl, a tiny infant, 'There is nothing for us, my poor boy, but the workhouse,' and the same thought rose up in her mind as she looked at him, a tall lad with large grey eyes and dark curling hair. But she didn't trouble him with her despair. She merely said:

'I don't know how we shall pull through, Jack. God will help us.'

'You're washing too hard, mother. You're wasting away. Do you know no one, mother, who could help us?'

She looked at Jack fixedly, and she thought of Mrs. Barfield. Mrs. Barfield might be away in the South with her daughter. If she were at Woodview Esther felt sure that she would not refuse to help her. So Jack wrote at Esther's dictation, and before they expected an answer, a letter came from Mrs. Barfield saying that she remembered Esther perfectly well. She had just returned from the South. She was all alone at Woodview, and wanted a servant. Esther could come and take the place if she liked. She enclosed five pounds, and hoped that the money would enable Esther to leave London at once.

But this returning to former conditions filled Esther with strange trouble. Her heart beat as she recognized the spire of the church between the trees, and the undulating line of downs behind the trees awakened terrible recollections. She knew the white gate was somewhere in this plantation, but could not remember its exact position. The gate had fallen from its hinge, and the lodge where the blind gatekeeper used to play the flute was closed; the park paling was falling, and the great holly hedge worn away by wandering sheep and cattle; and an elm in falling had broken through the garden wall.

On arriving at the iron gate under the bunched ilexes her steps paused, for it was there she met William for the first time, and the memory stung her. He had taken her through the stables and pointed out to her Silver Braid's box! She remembered the horses going to the downs, horses coming from the downs—stabling and the sound of hoofs everywhere. But now silence. She could see that many a roof had fallen, and that ruins of outhouses filled the yard. She remembered the kitchen windows, bright in the setting sun, and the white-capped servants moving about the great white table. But now the shutters were up, nowhere a light; the knocker had disappeared from the door, and she asked herself how she was to get in. She even felt afraid. Supposing she should not find Mrs. Barfield! She made her way through the shrubbery, tripping over fallen branches and trunks of trees; rooks rose out of the evergreens with a great clatter, her heart stood still, and she hardly dared to tear herself through the mass of underwood. At last she gained the lawn, and, still very frightened, sought for the bell. The socket plate hung loose on the wire, and only a faint tinkle came through the solitude of the empty house.

At last footsteps and a light; the chained door was opened a little, and a voice asked: 'Who is it?' Esther explained; and then the door was opened, and she stood lace to face with her old mistress, Mrs. Barfield, who stood, holding the candle high, so that she could see Esther. She had not changed very much. She still kept her beautiful white teeth and her girlish smile; the pointed, vixen-like face had not altered in outline, but the reddish hair was so thin that it had to be parted on the side and drawn over the skull; her figure was delicate and sprightly as ever. Esther noticed all this. Mrs. Barfield noticed that Esther was stouter, and that her face kept that look of blunt, honest nature which had always been her charm in the years gone by, and was attractive in the thick-set working woman of forty, who stood holding the hem of her jacket in her rough hands.

'We'd better put the chain up, for I'm alone in the house.'

'Aren't you afraid, ma'am?'

'A little, but there's nothing to steal; and I asked the policeman to keep a lookout.'

In the library were the round table, the little green sofa, the piano, the parrot's cage, and the yellow-painted presses; and it seemed only a little while since she was summoned to this room, since she stood facing her mistress, her confession on her lips. It seemed like yesterday, yet seventeen years and more had gone by—a dream, the connecting links of which were gone.

'You've had a cold journey, Esther; you'd like some tea?'

'Oh, don't trouble, ma'am.'

'It's no trouble; I should like some myself. The fire's out in the kitchen, but we can boil the kettle here.'

They went through the baize door into the long passage. Mrs. Barfield told Esther where was the pantry, the kitchen, and the larder. Esther answered that she remembered quite well, and it seemed to her not a little strange that she should know these things. Mrs. Barfield said:

'So you haven't forgotten Woodview, Esther?'

'No, ma'am. It seems like yesterday. But I'm afraid the damp has got into the kitchen, ma'am, the range is that neglected——'

'Ah, Woodview isn't what it was.'

Mrs. Barfield told how she had buried her husband in the old village church. She had taken her daughter to Egypt; and she dwindled till there was little more than a skeleton to lay in the grave.

'Yes, ma'am, I know how it takes them, inch by inch. My husband died of consumption.'

One thing led to another, and Esther gradually told Mrs. Barfield the story of her life from the day they bade each other good-bye in the room they were now sitting in.

'It is quite a romance, Esther.'

'It was a hard fight, and it isn't over yet, ma'am. It won't be over until I see him settled in some regular work. I hope I shall live to see him settled.'

They sat over the fire a long time. At last Mrs. Barfield said:

'It must be getting on for bedtime.'

'I suppose it must, ma'am.'

She asked if she should sleep in the room she had once shared with Margaret Gale. Mrs. Barfield answered with a sigh that as all the bedrooms were empty Esther had better sleep in the room next to hers.

## CHAPTER XLV

ESTHER seemed to have quite naturally accepted Woodview as a final stage. Any further change in her life she did not seem to regard as possible or desirable. One of these days her boy would get settled; he would come down now and again to see her. She did not want any more than that. No, she did not find the place lonely. A young girl might, but she was no longer a young girl; she had her work to do, and when it was done she was glad to sit down to rest.

And, dressed in long cloaks, the women went for walks together; sometimes they went up the hill, sometimes into Southwick to make some little purchases. On Sundays they walked to Beeding to attend meeting. And they came home along the winter roads, the peace and happiness of prayer upon their faces, holding their skirts out of the mud, unashamed of their common boots. They made no acquaintances, seeming to find in each other all necessary companionship. Their heads bent a little forward, they trudged home, talking of what they were in the habit of talking, that another tree had been blown down, that Jack was now earning good money—ten shillings a week. Esther hoped it would last. Or else Esther told her mistress that she had heard that one of Mr. Arthur's horses had won a race. He lived in the north of England, where he had a small training stable, and his mother never heard of him except through the sporting papers. 'He hasn't been here for four years,' Mrs. Barfield said; 'he hates the place; he wouldn't care if I were to burn it down to-morrow. However, I do the best I can, hoping that one day he 'll marry and come and live here.'

Mr. Arthur—that was how Mrs. Barfield and Esther spoke of him—did not draw any income from the estate. The rents only sufficed to pay the charges and the widow's jointure. All the land was let; the house he had tried to let, but it had been found impossible to find a tenant, unless Mr. Arthur would expend some considerable sum in putting the house and grounds into a state of proper repair. This

he did not care to do; he said that he found racehorses a
more profitable speculation. Besides, even the park had
been let on lease; nothing remained to him but the house
and lawn and garden; he could no longer gallop a horse on
the hill without somebody's leave, so he didn't care what
became of the place. His mother might go on living there,
keeping things together as she called it; he did not mind
what she did as long as she didn't bother him. So did he
express himself regarding Woodview on the rare occasion
of his visits, and when he troubled to answer his mother's
letters. Mrs. Barfield, whose thoughts were limited to the
estate, was pained by his indifference; she gradually
ceased to consult him, and when Beeding was too far for
her to walk she had the furniture removed from the drawing-room and a long deal table placed there instead. She
had not asked herself if Arthur would object to her inviting
a few Brethren to her house for meeting, or publishing the
meetings by notices posted on the lodge gate. And one
day, while walking in the avenue, they saw Mr. Arthur open
the white gate and come through. The mother hastened
forward to meet her son, but paused, dismayed by the
anger that looked out of his eyes. He did not like the
notices, and she was sorry that he was annoyed. She didn't
think that he would mind them, and she hastened by his
side, pleading her excuses. But to her great sorrow
Arthur did not seem to be able to overcome his annoyance.
He refused to listen, and continued his reproaches, saying
the things that he knew would most pain her.

He did not care whether the trees stood or fell, whether
the cement remained upon the walls or dropped from them;
he didn't draw a penny of income from the place, and did
not care a damn what became of it. He allowed her to live
there; she got her jointure out of the property, and he didn't
want to interfere with her, but what he could not stand was
the snuffy little folk from Shoreham coming round his
house. The Barfields at least were county, and he wished
Woodview to remain county as long as the walls held
together. He wasn't a bit ashamed of all this ruin. You
could receive the Prince of Wales in a ruin, but he wouldn't
care to ask him into a dissenting chapel. Mrs. Barfield
answered that she didn't see how the mere assembling of a
few friends in prayer could disgrace a house. There was

no place nearer than Beeding where they could meet, and she could no longer walk so far, so she would have to give up meeting.

'It seems to me a strange taste to want to kneel down with a lot of little shopkeepers. Is this where you kneel?' he said, pointing to the long deal table. 'The place is a regular little Bethel.'

'Our Lord said that when two or three should gather together for prayer, He would be among them. Those are true words, and as we get old we feel more and more the want of this communion of spirit. It is only then that we feel that we're really with God. The folk that you despise are equal in His sight. And living here alone, what should I be without prayer? and Esther, after her life of trouble and strife, what would she be without prayer? It is our consolation.'

'I think one should choose one's company for prayer as for everything else. Besides, what do you get out of it? Miracles don't happen nowadays.'

'You're still young, Arthur, and you cannot feel the want of prayer as we do—two old women living in this lonely house. As age and solitude overtake us, the realities of life float away and we become more and more sensible to the mystery which surrounds us. And our Lord Jesus Christ gave us love and prayer so that we might see a little further.'

An expression of great beauty came upon her face—that unconscious resignation which, like the twilight, hallows and transforms. In such moments the humblest hearts are at one with nature, and speak out of the eternal wisdom of things. So even this common racing man was touched, and he said:

'I'm sorry if I said anything to hurt your religious feelings.'

Mrs. Barfield did not answer.

'Do you not accept my apologies, mother?'

'My dear boy, what do I care for your apologies; what are they to me? All I think of now is your conversion to Christ. Nothing else matters. I shall always pray for that.'

'You may have whom you like up here; I don't mind if it makes you happy. I'm ashamed of myself. Don't let's

say any more about it.   I 'm only down for the day.   I 'm
going home to-morrow.'

'Home, Arthur! this is your home.   I can't bear to hear
you speak of any other place as your home.'

'Well, mother, then I shall say that I 'm going back to
business to-morrow.'

Mrs. Barfield sighed.


## CHAPTER XLVI

DAYS, weeks, months passed away, and the two women
came to live more and more like friends and less like mistress and maid.   Not that Esther ever failed to use the
respectful 'ma'am' when she addressed her mistress, nor
did they ever sit down to a meal at the same table.   But
these slight social distinctions, which habit naturally
preserved, and which it would have been disagreeable to
both to forgo, were no check on the intimacy of their
companionship.   In the evening they sat in the library
sewing, or Mrs. Barfield read aloud, or they talked of their
sons.   On Sundays they had their meetings.   The folk
came from quite a distance, and sometimes as many as five-
and-twenty knelt round the deal table in the drawing-room,
and Esther felt that these days were the happiest of her
life.   She was content in the peaceful present, and she knew
that Mrs. Barfield would not leave her unprovided for.   She
was almost free from anxiety.   But Jack did not seem to
be able to obtain regular employment in London, so the
sight of his handwriting made her tremble, and she sometimes did not show the letter to Mrs. Barfield for some
hours after.

One Sunday morning, after meeting, as the two women
were going for their walk up the hill, Esther said:

'I 've a letter from my boy, ma'am.   I hope it is to tell
me that he 's got back to work.'

'I 'm afraid I shan't be able to read it, Esther.   I haven't
my glasses with me.'

'It don't matter, ma'am—it 'll keep.'

'Give it to me—his writing is large and legible.   I think

I can read it. "My dear mother, the place I told you of in my last letter was given away, so I must go on in the toy-shop till something better turns up. I only get six shillings a week and my tea, and can't quite manage on that." Then something—something—"pay three and sixpence a week"—something—"bed"—something—something.'

'I know, ma'am; he shares a bed with the eldest boy.'

'Yes, that 's it; and he wants to know if you can help him. "I don't like to trouble you, mother; but it is hard for a boy to get his living in London."'

'But I 've sent him all my money. I shan't have any till next quarter.'

'I 'll lend you some, Esther. We can't leave the boy to starve. He can't live on two and sixpence a week.'

'You 're very good, ma'am; but I don't like to take your money. We shan't be able to get the garden cleared this winter.'

'We shall manage somehow, Esther. The garden must wait. The first thing to do is to see that your boy doesn't want for food.'

The women resumed their walk up the hill. When they reached the top Mrs. Barfield said:

'I haven't heard from Mr. Arthur for months. I envy you, Esther, those letters asking for a little money. What 's the use of money to us except to give it to our children? Helping others, that is the only happiness.'

At the end of the coombe, under the shaws, stood the old red-tiled farmhouse in which Mrs. Barfield had been born. Beyond it, downlands rolled on and on, reaching half-way up the northern sky. Mrs. Barfield was thinking of the days when her husband used to jump off his cob and walk beside her through those gorse patches on his way to the farmhouse. She had come from the farmhouse beneath the shaws to go to live in an Italian house sheltered by a fringe of trees. That was her adventure. She knew it, and she turned from the view of the downs to the view of the sea. The plantations of Woodview touched the horizon, then the line dipped, and between the top branches of a row of elms appeared the roofs of the town. Over a long spider-legged bridge a train wriggled like a snake, the bleak river flowed into the harbour, and the shingle banks saved the low land from inundation. Then the train passed behind the square, dogmatic tower of the village church. Her husband lay beneath the chancel; her father, mother, all her relations, lay in the churchyard, and she would go there in a few years. Upon this downland all her life had been passed, all her life except the few months she had spent by her daughter's bedside in Egypt. She came from that coombe, from that farmhouse beneath the shaws, and only crossed the down.

And this barren landscape meant as much to Esther as to her mistress. It was on these downs that she had walked with William. He was born and bred on these downs; but he lay far away in Brompton Cemetery; it was she who had come back! and in her simple way she too wondered at the sadness of destiny.

As they descended the hill Mrs. Barfield asked Esther if she ever heard of Fred Parsons.

'No, ma'am, I don't know what's become of him.'

'And if you were to meet him again, would you care to marry him?'

'Marry and begin life over again! All the worry and bother over again! Why should I marry?—all I live for now is to see my boy settled in life.'

The women walked on in silence, passing by long ruins of stables, coach-houses, granaries, rickyards—all in ruin and decay. The women paused and went towards the garden; and removing some pieces of the broken gate they entered a miniature wilderness. The espalier apple trees had disappeared beneath climbing weeds, and long briars had shot out from the bushes, leaving few traces of the former walks —a damp, dismal place that the birds seemed to have abandoned. Of the greenhouse only some broken glass and a black broken chimney remained. A great elm had carried away a large portion of the southern wall, and under the dripping trees an aged peacock screamed for his lost mate.

'I don't suppose that Jack will be able to find any more paying employment this winter. We must send him six shillings a week; that, with what he is earning, will make twelve; he'll be able to live nicely on that.'

'I should think he would, indeed. But then, what about the wages of them who was to have cleared the gardens for us?'

'We shan't be able to get the whole garden cleared, but

Jim will be able to get a piece ready for us to sow some spring vegetables—not a large piece, but enough for us. The first thing to do will be to cut down those apple trees. I'm afraid we shall have to cut down that walnut; nothing could grow beneath it. Did any one ever see such a mass of weed and briar? Yet it is only about ten years since we left Woodview, and the garden was let run to waste. Nature does not take long—a few years, a very few years.'

## CHAPTER XLVII

ALL the winter the north wind roamed on the hills; many trees fell in the park, and at the end of February Woodview seemed barer and more desolate than ever; broken branches littered the roadway, and the tall trunks showed their wounds. The women sat over their fire in the evening listening to the blast, cogitating on the work that awaited them as soon as the weather showed signs of breaking.

Mrs. Barfield had laid by a few pounds during the winter; and the day that Jim cleared out the first piece of espalier trees she spent entirely in the garden, hardly able to take her eyes off him. But the pleasure of the day was in a measure spoilt for her by the knowledge that on that day her son was riding in the great steeplechase. She was full of fear for his safety; she did not sleep that night, and hurried down at an early hour to the garden to ask Jim for the newspaper which she had told him to bring her.

'Oh, Jim, do be quick.'

'My pocket is torn, ma'am. Here it is.'

'He isn't in the first three,' said Mrs. Barfield. 'I always know that he's safe if he's in the first three. We must turn to the account of the race to see if there were any accidents.'

She turned over the paper.

'Thank God, he's safe,' she said; 'his horse ran fourth.'

'You worry yourself without cause, ma'am. A good rider like him don't meet with accidents.'

'The best riders are often killed, Esther. I never have an easy moment when I hear he's going to ride in these races. Supposing one day I were to read that he was carried back on a shutter.'

'We mustn't let our thoughts run on such things, ma'am. If a war was to break out to-morrow, what should I do? His regiment would be ordered out. It is sad to think that he had to enlist. But, as he said, he couldn't go on living on me any longer. Poor boy! We must keep on working, doing the best we can for them. There are all sorts of chances, and we can only pray that God may spare them.'

'Yes, Esther, that 's all we can do. Work on, work on to the end. But your boy is coming to see you to-day.'

'Yes, ma'am, he 'll be here by twelve o'clock.'

'You 're luckier than I am. I wonder if I shall ever see my boy again.'

'Yes, ma'am, of course you will. He 'll come back to you right enough one of these days. There 's a good time coming; that 's what I always says. . . . And now I 've got work to do in the house. Are you going to stop here, or are you coming in with me? It 'll do you no good standing about in the wet clay.'

Mrs. Barfield smiled and nodded, and Esther paused at the broken gate to watch her mistress, who stood superintending the clearing away of ten years' growth of weeds, as much interested in the prospect of a few peas and cabbages as in former days she had been in the culture of expensive flowers. She stood on what remained of a gravel walk, the heavy clay clinging to her boots, watching Jim piling weeds upon his barrow. Would he be able to finish the plot of ground by the end of the week? What should they do with that great walnut tree? Nothing would grow underneath it. Jim was afraid that he would not be able to cut it down and remove it without help. Mrs. Barfield suggested sawing away some of the branches, but Jim was not sure that lopping would make much difference, for in his opinion the tree took all the goodness out of the soil, and while it stood they could not expect a very great show of vegetables. Mrs. Barfield asked if the sale of the tree trunk would indemnify her for the cost of cutting it down. Jim paused in his work, and, leaning on his spade, considered if there was any one in the town, who, for the sake of the timber, would cut the tree down and take it away for nothing. There ought to be some such person in town; if it came to that, Mrs. Barfield ought to receive something for the tree. Walnut was a valuable wood, was much used by cabinet-makers, and so on, until Mrs. Barfield begged him to get on with his digging.

At twelve o'clock Esther and Mrs. Barfield walked out on the lawn. A loud wind came up from the sea, and it shook the evergreens as if it were angry with them. A rook carried a stick to the tops of the tall trees, and the women drew their cloaks about them. The train passed across the vista, and the women wondered how long it would take Jack to walk from the station. Then another rook stooped to the edge of the plantation, gathered a twig, and carried it away. The wind was rough; it caught the evergreens underneath and blew them out like umbrellas; the grass had not yet begun to grow, and the grey sea harmonized with the grey-green land. The women waited on the windy lawn, their skirts blown against their legs, keeping their hats on with difficulty. It was too cold for standing still. They turned and walked a few steps towards the house, and then looked round.

A tall soldier came through the gate. He wore a long red cloak, and a small cap jauntily set on the side of his close-clipped head. Esther uttered a little exclamation, and ran to meet him. He took his mother in his arms, kissed her, and they walked towards Mrs. Barfield together. All was forgotten in the happiness of the moment—the long fight for his life, and the possibility that any moment might declare him to be mere food for powder and shot. She was only conscious that she had accomplished her woman's work—she had brought him up to man's estate; and that was her sufficient reward. What a fine fellow he was! She did not know he was so handsome, and blushing with pleasure and pride she glanced shyly at him out of the corners of her eyes as she introduced him to her mistress.

'This is my son, ma'am.'

Mrs. Barfield held out her hand to the young soldier.

'I have heard a great deal about you from your mother.'

'And I of you, ma'am. You 've been very kind to my mother. I don't know how to thank you.'

And in silence they walked towards the house.